Dark Water

CARO RAMSAY

PENGUIN BOOKS

PENGUIN BOOKS

Published by the Penguin Group
Penguin Books Ltd, 80 Strand, London WC2R ORL, England
Penguin Group (USA) Inc., 375 Hudson Street, New York, New York 10014, USA
Penguin Group (Canada), 90 Eglinton Avenue East, Suite 700, Toronto, Ontario, Canada M4P 2Y3
(a division of Pearson Penguin Canada Inc.)
Penguin Ireland, 25 St Stephen's Green, Dublin 2, Ireland (a division of Penguin Books Ltd)
Penguin Group (Australia), 250 Camberwell Road, Camberwell, Victoria 3124, Australia
(a division of Pearson Australia Group Pty Ltd)
Penguin Books India Pvt Ltd, 11 Community Centre, Panchsheel Park, New Delhi – 110 017, India
Penguin Group (NZ), 67 Apollo Drive, Rosedale, Auckland 0632, New Zealand
(a division of Pearson New Zealand Ltd)
Penguin Books (South Africa) (Pty) Ltd, Block D, Rosebank Office Park,
181 Jan Smuts Avenue, Parktown North, Gauteng 2193, South Africa

Penguin Books Ltd, Registered Offices: 80 Strand, London WC2R ORL, England

www.penguin.com

First published 2010
This edition published 2012
001

Set in 12.5/14.75 pt Garamond MT Std
Typeset by TexTech International
Printed in England by Clays Ltd, St Ives plc

ISBN: 978-0-718-19753-7

www.greenpenguin.co.uk

ALWAYS LEARNING   **PEARSON**

For Jessie Ramsay
1904–2009
Sleep tight, Snookie Pie

Author's Note

Dark Water is a work of fiction. Names, characters, places and incidents either are the product of the author's imagination or are used entirely fictitiously.

Prologue

31 December 1999

Emily Corbett flicked the headlights of the Punto on to full beam, highlighting the puffballs of soft drifting grey fog. To either side lay the braes, and high flat bleak moorland, but all she could see was dapples of mist and darkness.

She slowed down. Fifty was too fast for this road, in this weather, at this time of night. She looked at the dashboard clock: 23.20. She would make it home in time to hear the midnight bells herald in the new millennium. She yawned, fighting tiredness, and turned up Robbie Williams on the CD player. She wasn't sorry she'd walked out of the Hogmanay party, only seething with anger that she'd had to after seeing her boyfriend – her ex-boyfriend, she corrected herself – disappearing into an upstairs bedroom with a bucketful of punch and some peroxided art student with unhygienic piercings. Well, screw him.

So now she was driving back home on this dark moorland road to a houseful of drunken first-footers and a bowl of hot lentil soup, wary of bad bends, potholes and the surface water that pooled dangerously in unseen dips.

Emily concentrated on the tarmac ribbon that seemed to waver in the drifting mist. She heard her dad's words. *It's too easy to build up speed on a straight road like that, not notice until it's too late and the car's aquaplaned into a drystane dyke, and*

I'll be getting a call to fetch you from Casualty on the busiest night of the year, and me in my good suit. She'd smiled at him but she hadn't really been listening. She was eighteen now. She could look after herself.

The road in front of her side-shifted as the Punto was nudged by a gust of wind, and the full beam caught the ghostly shadows of some trees before settling back to the solidity of the tarmac and the drystane dyke. Emily looked at the speedo, watching it drop . . . thirty-five . . . thirty . . . She indicated left, breaking for the dog-leg junction that would lead her to the braes road and home to Glasgow. Ahead of her she saw lights, dull yellow squares in the gloom. The letters on the Paraffin Lamp pub sign had been rearranged and graffitoed to read 'The Puffing Lump'. Emily smiled, and steered carefully through the small flood at the bottom of the hill, feeling the car slow with the drag of the water. When clear, she squeezed her brakes dry and indicated right. She glanced in the rear-view mirror, her eyes drawn by the lights of another vehicle. Somebody had left the pub car park and pulled in behind her, somebody possibly as nervous as she was about crossing the braes on their own, wanting the guiding security of another driver's tail lights.

The digital clock on the dashboard clicked to 23.25. The headlights of the following vehicle flashed in her mirror again and disappeared as Emily turned on to the straight road that ran across the top of the moor. It was the quickest way home to Glasgow, though maybe not the safest. She checked the mirror again; no lights. The other car must have gone straight on to Dalry.

As the road gained height, the fog grew denser, blinding. She shivered and turned up the heating. As the needle started to nudge fifty again, she thought she could hear something. A drone from somewhere. *A problem with the car?*

High up on the braes, close on midnight, was not the time or place to have a puncture. She turned off Robbie Williams and listened intently. The noise was still there.

Coming from somewhere behind her. From outside.

She calmed herself, took a deep breath and pushed her foot down. The needle edged towards sixty.

She jumped violently at the sound of a horn blaring right behind her, blinded as the car filled with light from headlights on full beam inches from her rear bumper. Then back to darkness.

Back to silence.

She closed her eyes briefly to readjust her vision. She could see nothing behind her. Nothing but the fog.

Everything was quiet now, but for the pernicious return of the drone, and the pounding of her heart. She put her foot down.

Sixty-five.

She took another deep breath and glanced at the milometer, trying to figure out how far she still had to go before she saw the lights of Glasgow. She dared to ease her foot off the accelerator a little, watching the needle fall. Then she felt a jarring thud, and the car juddered and ricocheted forward. Emily cried out as a searing pain ripped through her skull. Then lights blinded her again, and a horn sounded deafeningly. Trembling, she changed down.

Ahead the road was clear, the ghosts drifting away. She risked another glance in the mirror. Her eyes seeing the bull bars of the four-by-four closing in on her, the silhouettes of two heads, the teeth of the grille pulling up to her bumper. Tailgating . . .

And now she could hear clearly, over the panicked whine of her own engine, the deep constant growl of a predator.

Hunting.

Waiting.

Her mind raced. Whoever was in that car could be off their heads on something; they might run her off the road at any moment. She forced herself to stay calm, to concentrate. There was a scout lodge up here, she knew, just beyond the electricity substation, some sort of activity centre where they'd be having fireworks, a ceilidh, with people dancing, celebrating the new millennium . . .

All she had to do was turn sharp left through the gates, and get up the driveway. And she would be safe.

She imagined she could even see the lights from here.

She slowed again as the road curved, her forearms aching, bracing herself for another shunt from the car behind. Nothing. Curiously, it seemed to have gone.

She breathed out, a long slow breath, dropping her full beam at the flash of a single oncoming vehicle, and slowed to forty. A volley of water broadsided her as the car swept past.

Emily drove on, muttering, *Come on, come on*, peering into the fog for the electricity pylons. Now she could see, way over to her left, the lights of Lapwing Lodge. Sanctuary.

Thirty-five . . . thirty . . . The dyke at the side of the road fell away, and she pulled sharply left, putting her foot down once she was off the road.

Crash.

Silence.

Emily realized her mistake as the strong, chained gates of the electricity substation appeared through the haze that climbed over the crumpled bonnet. She sat very still as the engine coughed and died. She closed her eyes, wishing away the scorching pain in her right shoulder where the seat belt had snapped her collarbone, the stabbing pains in her neck. She tried to unlock her fingers from the steering wheel but couldn't. Through the crazed windscreen she saw the ghosts were back, unfurling from the engine, coiling into the night air.

She had crashed her new car. Her dad would kill her.

But, at least *she* was all right. *She* was safe . . . sore, but safe.

She sighed and tried to take a deep breath.

Then suddenly the car door was opened, and cold air swarmed round her feet. Strong fingers prised hers from the wheel, the seat belt was unfastened, and then something was covering her face. She tried to move, tried to say something, but couldn't. She could taste blood. Hands were pulling her, gently, firmly, then roughly . . . too roughly . . . by the shoulders, then by the hair. She felt the roots rip from her scalp. She screamed but heard no sound, then she was on the ground, on her knees, her head forced down. A boot in her ribs pushed her over on to her back, she felt cold wet pebbles stabbing into her skin as fingers clawed at her belt, the night air icy on her exposed stomach. Then a knee on her chest, a hand over her mouth. Within the black eternity of the blindfold, she sensed rain pricking at her cheek, heard the scrabble of her heels on the stones. A voice: *Stay still, bitch*.

As the weight on top of her lifted slightly, she let herself go limp, trying to remember her self-defence classes: *Go limp, don't struggle, gain advantage*. As the weight shifted to one side, she raised one shoulder and bucked with all her strength, trying to get out from underneath him, and the blindfold slid from her face. For an instant, her eyes looked into his. A snapshot fixed in her memory. Then the blindfold was back in place, pressing on her eyes so hard she thought her eyeballs would burst.

In the distance she could hear faint music, people cheering, the shrieks and bangs of fireworks. She felt her mouth being forced open, and cold metal pressed to her temple.

Click.

I

'Nice wallpaper.'

Stuart Bannon of West End Properties turned to make sure Jim Innes was being sarcastic, and raised an unprofessional eyebrow at him in agreement.

Catriona Innes wrinkled her nose. 'It reminds me of . . .'

'That crap you had in the Indian last night. Saggy Paneer?'

She smiled at the estate agent. 'My husband's sense of humour is an acquired taste,' she said sweetly.

'As is the decoration of this flat,' Bannon agreed, with a rare touch of honesty. 'On this level, the previous owner never changed a thing, so you do have all the original features. This was the top-floor flat originally, hence the fantastic view. The attic space has been converted to give another two bedrooms up there.'

'Was the previous owner on drugs?' Innes asked wryly. 'Or were they blind?'

Stuart Bannon laughed. 'Blind, maybe; she was in her nineties.' He dunted the carpet with the heel of his Doc Martens. 'But the floorboards under here are solid. A nice wee sand, and then a good wax . . .' This seemed a good time to back off and let them think. Number 95 Clarence Avenue was proving unexpectedly difficult to sell, but at least this couple hadn't walked out after five minutes of cursory politeness like the last three had. And they were still eyeing the place up, considering.

Catriona Innes folded her arms and spun round slowly. 'I do like this room, even with that bloody wallpaper. So much light. You don't get windows that size in a new build. And we should know; we've seen plenty.'

'Well, that's the advantage of these tenements; the room size is amazing. Both this room and the sitting room have feature fireplaces, the back rooms have the original cornices and, as you can see from the schedule, the recent attic conversion is architect-designed in a Scandinavian style. They built into the roof space and used the original beams. It's even been photographed for an architects' trade magazine.'

'Yet it's been on the market for a while,' said Innes, his face quizzical.

'The beneficiaries of the will had a difference of opinion, so the renovation on this level ground to a halt. To be honest, it's on the market as a half-baked project.' Bannon gave his most candid smile.

'I think what you're supposed to say is "so you get the best of both worlds",' Jim answered.

'Do you work in advertising?' laughed Bannon.

'How did you guess?' smiled Catriona. 'He could sell Guinness to the Irish.' Then she pursed her lips slightly. 'The old dear in her nineties – she didn't actually *die* in here, did she?'

'No, she died in hospital, but she had a long and happy life. This was the family home. The executor now wants a quick sale, so it's a fixed price – £275, 000.'

'Could they be talked down?'

'They might, what with the state of the market at the moment.' Bannon's mobile rang, the trill echoing round the empty space. 'Oh, I do apologize; I've been waiting for this call. Please, go ahead and look upstairs. Take your time.'

He disappeared out on to the landing, leaving a vapour trail of Paco Rabanne.

Catriona waited until the door closed, then whispered, 'What do you think?'

'So far so good,' her husband answered. 'It's the best we've seen. Handy for the school, fixed price, slap bang in the middle of the West End, fabulous view, and Clarence Avenue is a good address. If we play our cards right, we might get a few grand off. I'd say it'll suit us fine.'

'You sound like we've moved in already.' Catriona walked into the hall, stroking the carved pineapple finial on the newel post. 'But I do like it, Jim. Look how the new stairs match what's already here.'

'Craftsmanship, that's what that is.' Her husband caressed the finial too. 'Pure craftsmanship.' Suddenly he looked up. 'What's that? I heard a creak.'

'A mouse?'

'Don't be daft! I said creak, not squeak.'

'Big mouse?'

'A rat?'

'The only rat around here is out on the landing, on the phone,' giggled Catriona.

'Bloody estate agents! He could tell us how much the executor is actually looking for and then we can stop all this faffing around.' He proceeded up the stairs, tapping the stair rail with his knuckle as he went. 'This is a sound conversion; look at the way everything's finished off. And there's no damp, no subsidence.'

Catriona paused behind him on the stairs. 'Are you sure? That creaking, it's the sound of old wood moving, isn't it?'

Jim Innes sighed. 'Might be next door's joists. We'd have to look into that. What do you think – should we have this upstairs bit as our own private floor? We could ban the kids from coming up here altogether.' He was now on the top landing, planning his pool table, a mini-bar . . . 'Look at that, they've reclaimed an old pitch-pine door from somewhere and just replaced the lock. That's attention to detail. That should be the new bedroom, with the beams. Twenty-six feet by sixteen. We're five floors up, so there should be some view over Partickhill, right over the tops of the trees.'

Catriona walked briskly across to the door and turned the key, which slid round easily. The door swung open under the light pressure of her palm. She again heard the slow gentle creak, the noise of a ship yawing on a gentle swell. Then her eyes adjusted to the dim light.

A swollen, purple body hung from the exposed beam, the blackened head almost decapitated by the noose. Caught in a slight draught from the window, it turned infinitesimally slowly round towards her. Protruding, deadened eyes stared at her, the face inclined, the ragged, blood-encrusted lips pursed to a kiss.

*

DCI Rebecca Quinn was scrolling the screen, her broken fingernail tapping impatiently on the mouse as her tired eyes looked over the most recent crime stats for the third time. The powers that be had changed the coding again, and she had to keep referring back to a photocopied chart.

She was too old for this. She had been at it since 3 p.m. and now, an hour and a half later, she was no further forward. She moved the cursor left to the referral rate and sighed. The last time she had felt this bad she was deciding definitely, definitely to get her cat put out of its misery. She was starting to feel that way about her career.

The writing was on the wall for Partickhill Station, she could feel it in her bones. The station had risen like the phoenix from the ashes after the Luftwaffe had dropped an early bomb on the way to Clydebank one moonlit night in 1941. But there was no way it could stand up to the combined uniformed might of Her Majesty's Inspectorate and the new designer suits at the Strathclyde Police Service.

Partickhill's operational capacity was slowly being eroded. It hadn't gone unnoticed that the canteen had been closed for two months now and there was no sign of it reopening. Her requests for a start date for the long-promised refurbishment had not received a precise answer, or even a vague one. The place was being stripped of resources as though a decision had already been made. DCI Quinn lost her place on the list yet again and gave up. She leaned back and yawned. The ever-growing damp patch on the corner of the ceiling seemed to be heading for the window in a bid for freedom, and who could blame it? Everyone seemed to achieve huge enhancement in their lives the minute they left this little station. Gail Irvine was now happily married with a rosy-cheeked two-year-old. Burns, the old constable who had been at Partickhill longer even than the rot, had inherited a croft in Stornoway where he was living the good life with no phone and no TV. And no computer.

Quinn envied him.

And those that stayed here at Partickhill? Their careers withered and died. Partickhill was little more than a lost property office these days, an elephant's graveyard of hopes and careers.

Of course, nobody was surprised that DC Vik Mulholland had passed his sergeant's exams with ease and immediately been transferred from Glasgow A Division to K Division in Renfrewshire – to assist in the Drug Unit at Paisley. Quinn was glad he had not been under her command for the last two years. Dedication she could cope with, but ruthless ambition ate at you like cancer. The rumour was that Mulholland would make inspector before the end of the year, and that he was gunning to get back to Glasgow and on to a murder squad. Just in time for Quinn to retire and avoid him. And DI Colin Anderson, tipped to move up to DCI soon, would be transferred too. Anderson was already spending most of his operational time at neighbouring Partick Central, a big modern station with a car park, canteen, and no damp patches, not half a mile from Partickhill. But DI Colin Anderson was a loyal kind of a sod, not one to step on her toes while she was still here and still, technically, his boss. Vik Mulholland was so ambitious he would have tipped her corpse off her seat before the cushion had got cold. Quinn missed Anderson when he wasn't here. He was the type of DI every chief dreamed of: solid, dependable, respectful and respected. A man of quiet power. She had no doubt his qualities had not gone unnoticed by those higher up the tree, and she knew she couldn't hold him back for ever.

On the other hand, the more Anderson was promoted, the less understanding his wife seemed to become. He wouldn't be the first cop to refuse a promotion to 'put family first'. Colin Anderson had still to make that decision, and nobody could make it for him.

Through the glass of her office Quinn could see Anderson in the incident room. Still looking younger than his thirty-nine years, a tiny hint of grey lightening his fair hair slightly, he was one of those lucky men who become better looking as they grow older. He was on the phone, taking some statement of great importance to the safety and well-being of the denizens of Glasgow's West End, giving it his full attention, despite the certain knowledge that it was all a waste of his time.

Quinn looked around the others in the incident room, a hotchpotch of misfits who weren't going anywhere. Littlewood, who should be the one taking that call, was nowhere to be seen. He was most likely out in the fog, sneaking an illicit fag. But like herself, he was working out the last few months of a long career, eking every penny he could out of his pension. He had recently been diagnosed with angina, which was preventing him from doing the job properly but wasn't severe enough for a medical retirement. He was bitter about it and carried his bitterness like a torch.

As she watched, PC Gordon Wyngate took careful aim and tossed a ball of waste paper towards the bin. It missed. Wyngate, known as Wingnut because of his large protuberant ears, was . . . just Wyngate. Not the brightest, but endlessly willing and occasionally capable of a stroke of genius.

Quinn pulled herself upright again, unclipping her red hair and curling it around her hand before fixing it again. Maybe she was being paranoid: after all, just this week, Partickhill's detective squad had been boosted by two. The new girl was what Quinn's mother would have called 'well built', and Littlewood called 'buxom' when being polite. She was straight out of uniform and yet to prove herself as a detective. Slightly overweight, unfit, two kids, late thirties, the worst type of rookie in a murder squad. What was her name? Black? Brown? Whatever her name was, she'd been bloody useless so far.

And then there was DS Costello. She had returned from her two-year lecturing stint at Tulliallan police training college. Her syllabus seemed to be a roving brief on CID serious crime procedures, and though Quinn was amazed she knew anything about them, her old DS seemed able to teach them most effectively, no doubt enlivened by her habit of talking before she engaged her brain, while still having the uncanny knack of saying the right thing. But usually at the wrong time.

To give her credit, Costello had some big cases under

her belt. In fact, she was what every student on that course was aspiring to be. Only Costello herself was too dense to notice. Quinn reconsidered – dense wasn't the right word. She let her eyes settle on her sergeant, watching her multitasking on her phone, trawling the computer screen, scribbling and eating a bag of Liquorice Allsorts simultaneously. As usual Costello was dressed like a scruff, her blonde hair shorter and spikier than it had been.

No, dense wasn't the right word. Costello just couldn't be arsed what anybody else thought.

The door to the main office opened and the new DC – now she remembered, it was Browne with an 'e' – sashayed in, carrying a cardboard tray with takeaway coffee and sandwiches. Quinn left them to it and went back to her crime stats.

The phone rang. Quinn looked up, hearing the simultaneous scrape of chair feet against the tattered lino. She saw Anderson get up, and then Costello bang the phone down. Quinn was on her feet even before Anderson knocked and entered without waiting for an answer.

'Two bits of good news. Browne can't count and bought you an extra coffee . . .'

'Cheers,' said Quinn.

'. . . and we have a dead body hanging in a tenement in Clarence Avenue, right behind the station here.'

Quinn felt her heart sink. 'Suicide?'

'Suspicious,' replied Anderson.

DCI Quinn could not hold back her smile as she closed the file on her computer, watching the monitor return to its lazy, writhing screen saver.

A case. A big case. And this time, it would be taken from her over her own dead body.

I flick the windscreen wiper on to clear the rain from the glass. I sink a bit lower in my seat, easing my frozen bones while keeping an eye on the door of Partickhill Station. Anderson comes out. DI Colin David Anderson. He is easy to see, even in this dank, foggy mess that has everybody muffled up to the eyeballs against the cold. He's a tall bloke – six one? Six two? You can tell he's a man who knows himself and what he is about. Not like his boss, scuttling about in her ridiculous heels. Her legs are too short to move so fast. Her navy-blue coat has the collar folded up to her ears, her hat is pulled down to her neck, but the briefcase is absent. She speaks briefly to Anderson on the way past then climbs into her Lexus and forces the traffic to halt as she does a U-turn on Hyndland Road.

But Anderson is waiting for the little fish.

My little fish.

My little Prudenza.

I turn the radio up slightly. Louis Armstrong singing 'What A Wonderful World', a song that always makes me smile at the irony. I see Anderson turn round in response to somebody's call; his gloved hands are in his pockets, his anorak zipped up to his chin.

And there she is, coming through the fog. Prudenza.

She's in a hurry, jogging along the pavement. She is carrying a drink carton; not coffee for her, it will be tea. A plump female cop comes down the steps and meets her, a congress of raven hair and blonde. The plump cop shivers, rubbing her hands roughly on the sleeves of her jumper. She hasn't even bothered putting a jacket on. Anderson is kicking his heels a few yards away, waiting. He's impatient.

To get a cop to move in this weather without an overcoat is one thing, but to get a DCI out a warm office and drive off into the freezing fog? Must be a matter of life and death. Something's rattled their cage.

It makes me uneasy.

A couple join them. The woman has her arm on her husband's shoulder. His face is ashen, and she's supporting him as if he's lost the ability to walk along the street under his own strength. The female cop with the short dark hair guides them up the steps and into the station, offering words of comfort to the man.

Prudenza and Anderson are now alone on the pavement. Anderson looks up to the sky, no doubt commenting on the weather. The forecast is freezing fog closing in. Prudenza gains his attention with a playful slap on the arm, and takes a step back. Two heads are thrown back in laughter at a private joke between old friends.

Her back is to me, but from this distance her hair looks blonder, shorter than the last time I saw her.

They move off on foot, pausing right in front of the van. They're going to go down the lane to Clarence Avenue. I turn the wipers off, to let the rain obscure the windscreen. Not that Anderson would recognize me – I was way before his time.

I flick the wiper to intermittent. Just to get a better view.

It has been such a long time.

Too long.

'What are those two doing? Waiting for an invite?' asked Professor O'Hare, rolling his white plastic suit from his shoulders. The dour grey-haired pathologist was standing on the upper landing of the tenement on Clarence Avenue. 'Should Anderson and Costello not be in here, listening to my words of infinite wisdom, instead of talking to the cop on the door?'

'Quite,' said DCI Quinn tersely. She took a deep breath and shouted, 'Are you lot quite finished chatting?' down the deep stairwell. 'Anderson! Costello! I want you up here now.' Then she muttered to her old friend, 'Those two are much easier to control when they're forty miles apart.'

'But you missed them, Rebecca; your life is too simple without them.'

'Maybe. I'm glad they're back together for this case. I think Partickhill's going to need all the help it can get.'

'*You* are going to need all the help you can get.' O'Hare stepped out of the legs of his protective suit, and checked his watch. 'No trouble at t' mill, is there? Within the ranks, I mean. If so, get rid of it now before the powers that be think you can no longer work as an effective team. It'll only be another excuse to bang a nail in the coffin.'

'Oh, there's no trouble between those two,' said Quinn. 'And how is DS Costello?'

'Just the same, unfortunately.' Quinn folded her arms, her eyes still on the stairway. 'But my days are numbered. I'm going to be retired. I can feel it. In fact, I think the

18

entire squad at Partickhill is about to be dismantled. And the building is managing to fall apart on its own with no help from us.'

'You don't look like you've done your thirty.'

'Well, I feel it in every bone.' She sighed. 'But it would be nice to go out with a big one.'

O'Hare said softly, 'Well, I don't think you're going to get any bigger than this.'

DCI Quinn frowned at the sound of two sets of footfalls racing up the stairs. 'Anderson! Costello! So glad you could join us, eventually.'

'We got nabbed outside by the guy from the estate agents on his way to the station. He wanted to tell us all about it.'

'Why was he roaming around on his own?'

'Wyngate was first on the scene and lost the witnesses in the fog. Don't ask any more,' said Costello.

'But now you *are* here, pop your collective heads in there before we go any further. Try and keep the door closed so the smell doesn't get out.'

'Fair enough,' said a blue-lipped Costello, smiling cheerfully and handing her paper cup of tea to Quinn, who had no choice but to accept it.

DI Colin Anderson nodded an acknowledgement at the Prof and approached the closed door. He figured he had seen most things in his nineteen years of service, but he steeled himself just the same as he turned the knob. When he opened the door, a rhomboid of light illuminated his feet, and the room inside was slowly revealed as a hive of silent industry. Three white-suited scene of crime officers crouched around the body, and the smell of rotting flesh wafted gently towards him.

Costello followed him in, pulling her hands up into her sleeves, and jammed her woolly fists to her mouth in an attempt to block out the smell. She narrowed her eyes and took one step further, joining him to stand on the aluminium slab that protected the crime scene – as far as they could go without shoe covers.

From the corner of the room they viewed the body, which was now slumped on the floor. It looked male, it looked young, but mostly it looked dead. The rope around his neck had cut so deep it nearly met his spine at the back, and the dark indigo serrated gouge lay open like a flowering lupin. His skin opened in a sinister crusted rupture above his chin, leaving his lips closed, pursing slightly. The other end of the rope was still looped over the exposed beam above. The SOCOs moved slowly in a tacit dance, each concentrating on their individual tasks. The only noise came from a couple of blowflies feasting at the dark wound in the throat, interrupted by the occasional whirr of the camera motor.

Costello tried to look at the face, seeking a point of recognition, but it was too swollen, too blackened. The eyes stared at the ceiling, and the flesh of the cheeks had swollen to absorb the nose. Absurdly, it reminded her of a turnip lantern, only the knife had slipped as someone tried to fashion the mouth, which looked – she searched for a word – wrong.

She tilted her head, her brain registering the brown tag hanging around his neck on a string, a simple brown label.

The SOCO lifted it with a gloved hand, tilting it for her to read. Five printed words: *My Name Is Stephen Whyte*. She nudged Anderson, who was regarding the supine figure as if it was a piece of sculpture.

'Well, I've seen enough, smelled enough,' said Costello from behind her woolly fist. She recognized Bob MacKellar, the crime scene photographer, under his plastic hood, and nodded a greeting. 'You getting all this? Can we go?'

Bob the hood nodded. 'Yip. I think the Prof wants a word.'

They both retreated, Anderson closing the door behind him.

On the landing, they found Quinn and O'Hare, still deep in conversation. The four of them shifted to let a crime scene officer pass, carrying a folded body bag, before they continued. Quinn realized she still had Costello's tea and handed it back.

It was the pathologist who spoke, slowly, choosing his words with deliberation. 'The deceased has been provisionally identified for us, by a helpful person with a packet of labels and a printer. The name is Mr Stephen Whyte. No other form of ID. Obviously, we can't take the label at face value.'

'Stephen Whyte as in . . . ?' asked Anderson.

'It's not an uncommon name. So mouths shut until I get back to you. Not a can of worms we want to open unless we really have to.'

'Could it be him, though?'

'You're the cops,' O'Hare said, looking at Anderson.

'But I think you will find that you spell his occupation R-A-P-I-S-T.'

'Pretend you didn't hear that,' muttered Quinn. 'I want no preconceived notions and no speculation. We treat this case as any other. Please.'

O'Hare ignored her. 'Anyway, that body has been hanging there for a few days. The victim was viciously battered, used for target practice with the proverbial blunt instrument. There are only minor traces of blood spatter on the wall. Dump site or kill site? If he wasn't already dead when he was strung up, I doubt he was far from it. The killer went to town on him. He . . .'

'Or she . . . ?' queried Costello, then realized she was staring at DCI Quinn. She hastily looked back at the pathologist.

'. . . had deliberately sealed the victim's lips, so as he screamed or struggled for breath, the skin around his mouth simply tore apart. You'll get the rest later, and in much more detail, from the boys. He's in his early thirties, I would suggest, well nourished. I can see that the skin unaffected by the dependant lividity is suntanned. So over to you.'

'We are working on the timeline – or the *window of opportunity*, as the modern police service calls it. DC Browne is up at the station dispensing tea and sympathy to the couple who found the poor sod – a Mr and Mrs Innes. The man seems pretty shaken up, understandably,' Anderson explained.

'You left Browne in charge of them?' Quinn rolled her eyes. 'Has she any real operational experience?'

'Not on a murder squad. She's so deluded she thinks

Anderson is God and hangs on every word he says,' said Costello.

'Must be a nice change for you, DI Anderson, to have a female subordinate who actually respects you and listens to you,' muttered O'Hare.

'Can't say I've noticed it yet,' said Anderson.

O'Hare said, 'I'm going to get him back to the mortuary. I've got a lot on, but I'll rearrange and try to take a look at him tonight.'

'We'll stay available,' said Anderson. 'Ma'am, how do you want this played? You know that the minute it gets known, the squad at Partick Central will try to pick it up.' His voice hinted at resentment.

'I don't think I'll be phoning anybody but the presently attending officers with my preliminary findings,' said O'Hare nonchalantly. 'I presume speed is of the essence here, so the sooner you get moving the less likely you are to be taken off the case. I'll be on my way.'

Anderson had subtly shifted across the landing, blocking O'Hare's path. 'So is this the new regime? The forensic pathologist himself calls a particular DCI? And they're both still here?' Anderson folded his arms.

Quinn couldn't help but smile. They were sharp, these two – annoying, but sharp. She looked to her DI then to the pathologist, and the phrase about irresistible forces and immovable objects crossed her mind.

'So, Prof, are you going to enlighten us?' Anderson persisted.

But O'Hare pushed his way past. He did a half-turn on the stairs. 'The name Stephen Whyte means to me what it means to you. The man responsible for the attack on Emily Corbett was never caught. Looks like someone else might have caught him for you.' He looked at Quinn, as if to say, *No bad thing.*

Quinn waited before following him down the stairs, and spoke softly. 'DI Anderson, please don't repeat that. The Prof and Donald Corbett are very good friends, and Donald has never got over what happened to his daughter. As soon as he heard the name on that label, O'Hare elbowed his junior out the way and took the case. But let's wait at least until we get a formal identification.'

Anderson and Costello walked back from the crime scene in silence, both remembering the case that had been messed up all those years ago. Now, ten years later, here it was again, and on their doorstep.

Anderson had to stop himself from jogging back to the station. *Something should happen now*, he kept thinking. The discovery of that body should set off a chain of events that would cascade and roll with a momentum of its own. By 5.30 p.m. it was already dark, and even in the few minutes it took them to walk back to the station, thick winter haar had silvered their clothing with crystal baubles. In a few minutes, the crystal would soak through and they'd both freeze.

Costello was slightly breathless with her attempt to keep up with the DI. 'I never knew much about that Stephen Whyte business,' she said. 'I was still in uniform on the south side. Who fucked it up the first time?'

'Paisley, K Division,' he replied, curtly.

'And how, exactly?' asked Costello. Her gloved hand rested on his elbow, asking him to slow down.

'You know, you lecture about it all the time. We can drag suspects in with no evidence and hope for a confession within the six-hour rule. But that was never going to work with a guy like Whyte, so the DCI held back until he had something concrete to work with. Never reckoned on Whyte being a flight risk, though.'

Costello nodded. 'Bad judgement call? And in a case like that? The words rock and hard place come to mind.'

'It was the worst. Come on, Costello, I'm freezing my balls off out here.'

There was some excitement as they walked back through the doors of the station. Wyngate, Littlewood and Browne had formed a welcoming committee for a wee brown dog tethered to the front desk. The dog seemed to have a few bits missing: part of an ear, part of his tail. And then Anderson noticed that Gillian Browne, who was supposed to be in charge of Reception, was kneeling on the floor, giving the dog a cuddle and a drink of milky tea – from *his* mug.

She looked up at Anderson with a beaming smile. 'I knew you wouldn't mind, sir. The dog patrol dropped him off here, because the van was full. He was being used as bait in that dog-fighting ring in Possil.'

'The important bit of that conversation, DC Browne, should have been: *When are they picking him up again?*' said Anderson, aware that Costello was about to get on her knees and join the dog appreciation society.

'Just look at the ugly wee shitface,' said Littlewood

harshly, but the grizzled old cop was tickling the dog behind its good ear affectionately. 'He's not a bad-tempered sod. Somebody's had a go at him, right enough. That ear looks sore, what's left of it.'

'We've called him Nesbitt,' said Browne, happily.

'As in Rab C? As in hairy stinky wee creature?' enquired Anderson, his voice full of sarcastic enthusiasm. He took Costello firmly by the elbow and hurried her past.

Back at his work station, Anderson sat down at his desk, the worn plastic of the seat moulded to the shape of his bum. After a month at Partick Central working a joint case, he was glad to be back at Partickhill, with its small chaotic informalities that were so at odds with the new policies of the modern police service. And he was glad that they had a case. Hopefully they could hold on to it. And if not, he hoped he wouldn't be asked to choose – to move back to Partick Central with the case or stay here and investigate housebreaking until the end of his career. His chances of promotion could depend on his answer. *What price loyalty?* He sighed.

Now, with Costello safely in view at her desk and Browne safely out of view downstairs with the dog, he could relax and get on with thinking about the information board. His intellect told him the name Stephen Whyte might just be a coincidence. That thought was immediately followed by the memory of the crime scene photograph of Emily Corbett. Some things stayed with any police officer: the first dead child, the pensioner fatally beaten for the price of a bag of chips. Glasgow was a violent city, but the image of Emily Corbett lying on New

26

Year's Day, battered and unconscious, on a blanket of dead bracken, her bare back exposed to the icy wind, her face tucked into her elbow in a bizarre parody of the recovery position, still made Anderson's stomach lurch. Paisley and the whole of K Division had mismanaged it ten years ago. There could be no mistakes this time round.

He looked up at the board as it was. A call-out. DI Anderson and DS Costello had attended – no mention of DCI Quinn. Suspicious death, the address, the time. A case number and a few smudges left from the hasty wiping-off of the coffee-break shopping list.

The victim had had all ID removed and replaced with a label. To mislead, or to make it perfectly clear? O'Hare's voice, when he said the name, had held a degree of anger, real cold anger. And his words – *'The man responsible for the attack on Emily Corbett was never caught. Looks like someone else might have caught him for you'* – had carried an unwonted degree of emotion, and an unvoiced message: *Don't mess this up.*

Of course the minute O'Hare got anything, Quinn would know. Those two were old hands at getting to the point, bypassing the paperwork and, with a bit of luck, bypassing Partick Central.

Anderson let his eyes fall on the latest update memo, about Ally the black-browed albatross. Ally, or *Thalassarche melanophris*, had been blown way off course from the South Atlantic and had unexpectedly put down somewhere near the Barochan Moss nature reserve, about ten miles west of Glasgow. It was only the third time such a thing had happened in a hundred years, so as soon as it had been sighted by a regular birdwatcher at the reserve, the blaze of publicity could not be stemmed. A red star warned that its exact location was to be kept secret in case somebody went after it with an air rifle. If Ally had landed any closer to Paisley, the locals would have deep-fried it and eaten it by now. Anderson's stomach rumbled, suddenly thinking about a chicken supper with extra chips. If he could find out roughly where the bird was, he might take Peter out and have a look. The RSPB were organizing a low-key feeding and protection rota until the weather improved. At the moment the fog was hampering their attempts to install webcams and observation platforms but, Anderson supposed, the weather was giving the bird more protection than anything else could. Though why the stupid thing didn't just fly away, he couldn't quite grasp. The tabloids were starting to cause problems, and there were rumours of a celebrity birdwatch. Give it another twenty-four hours and Strathclyde's finest would be called in to provide a protection detail for a bloody bird with all the sense of direction of a myopic drunk in a dodgem.

Anderson glanced over at the traffic report. There'd been a bad accident at the mouth of the Clyde Tunnel, which snookered him for getting home in time to see the kids tonight. He heard Gillian Browne outside the door, laughing.

She came in and the dog followed her, wagging what was left of his tail. 'He's nice, isn't he?' Browne said, arms folding across her ample chest.

'No, he's not. He's smelly and has vital parts of his anatomy missing. DC Browne, that's a job for uniform, not for us. Phone the cat and dog home and get him booked in for the night.'

'When I was in uniform we called you lot *the arses.*' She tentatively approached his desk.

Anderson tried to ignore her chest, settling his gaze on her badly bitten fingernails instead.

'Colin!' Costello's voice, as subtle as the Cloch foghorn, came to the rescue. She banged a file down on the desk. 'This is all I could get on Stephen Whyte so far. DC Browne, Reception stinks of dog shite. Quinn has her stilettos on, so get it cleaned up before she skids on it. You'll find bleach in the loo.'

Browne trotted off, and Nesbitt followed at close quarters.

'Timely intervention, Costello, but you could have been a bit more subtle,' muttered Anderson once Browne was out of earshot.

'I don't do subtle. Is this hanging man our Stephen Whyte? *The* Stephen Whyte?' she asked, ignoring Anderson's signals that Quinn was on her way.

'O'Hare suspects so. But officially we have to wait for confirmation; you know that.'

'We are *all* waiting for confirmation,' said the DCI, handing Anderson a pile of buff files.

'It's just that this is a small station. I don't know how long I can or should keep it quiet,' said Anderson.

Quinn shrugged a little too casually. 'If I'm right, and they are one and the same – oh, I don't know that I could be that lucky . . .' Her voice drifted off, leaving Anderson and Costello to exchange glances. 'Don't let anyone disturb me for the next half-hour unless something important comes in from the door to door or forensics. I'm waiting for a call from the mortuary. Oh, and shut that dog in the kennel downstairs, before it stinks the station out. It's only being held here until it gets put to sleep.' Quinn walked off to her own office, her stilettos clicking on the worn floor tiles.

'Poor dog, I bet he hasn't even bitten anyone . . .' Costello watched Quinn's retreating ankles. 'Yet.'

Littlewood looked at the single sixty-watt bulb dangling on a kinked, dirty cable. It was twisting and swinging slightly in the draught, a slow hypnotic back-and-forth, left-to-right motion. He sighed. Wyngate was doing the first interrogation and DCI Quinn had made it quite clear that he, John Littlewood, with thirty-two years' experience in the job, had to just sit there and keep his mouth shut. Wyngate had been through it all twice already. Catriona Innes had been steady and calm. Her husband was a wreck. Littlewood could have predicted that; he could read people. And he could tell Stuart Bannon was as straight as a die, nothing to do with the hanging man; he was just the estate agent who'd been asked to sell the deceased's flat.

Bannon looked as Scottish as a man could – not very tall, with fair skin and receding hair that was either strawberry blond or red fading to grey. He was slightly overweight, in his mid-forties, and wore the look of the recently divorced like yesterday's socks. His good clothes had been inexpertly ironed, and the straining buttons on his shirt suggested a recent and unwelcome weight gain.

They had got to him last, after the Inneses. Now he was going through it all again, being patient and polite, picking his words cautiously, thinking through each answer. His mobile phone had rung, and he had gone out on the landing to answer it. But the reception was poor, so he had gone down the stairs to the main door of the building. He was still on the phone when he heard pounding footsteps behind him, and was almost knocked down by Jim Innes flying down the final step and out the door.

'He only just made it to the garden before he was sick,' Bannon recalled.

'And what about her?' asked Littlewood, disobeying Quinn's instructions. 'What about Mrs Innes?'

'Well, I went up the stairs, thinking that something had maybe happened to her, but she was standing in the angle of the door and I couldn't see what she was looking at. I walked in, and it was . . . hanging there. Just hanging there. Then the smell hit me.'

'Not a smell you forget easily,' Littlewood agreed.

Bannon looked from Wyngate to Littlewood, as if wondering whether the old guy was enjoying this as much as he appeared to be.

'And before that, the last time you were in the property was about ten days ago, Saturday 30th January?' asked Wyngate, trying to regain control of the interview.

'I think so. I've been the only one doing viewings in the past few months.' Bannon smiled ruefully. 'Things have been a bit slow in the housing market, credit crunch and all that. But yes, the last few viewings were accompanied by me, and the keys were in my hands at all times.'

Littlewood steered him back on track. 'Did you recognize the deceased?'

'Look, I didn't realize that it was a body at first, that it was even human. There was just something hanging there. Then the flies started buzzing, I smelled that smell, and I had to get out. I remember almost pushing Mrs Innes out the room. I did close the door behind me. When I got downstairs, Mr Innes was already on the phone to you lot, and that's when I realized what I'd seen.'

Wyngate sat silently, as if he was thinking, thinking that he should know what the next question was. He didn't.

'And there was no sign of forced entry?' asked Littlewood, trying to get to the point.

'So I believe.'

'So how did they get in?'

Bannon looked nonplussed.

'How did they gain entry? The neighbours deny letting anybody in on the buzzer system.'

'They are very security conscious. I had to make sure all the workmen were provided with keys, not just let in by the residents,' Bannon said.

'So if there was no sign of forced entry, the killer must have had the code for the entry system, and a key for the door of the dwelling on the fourth floor.' Littlewood spelled it out for him.

'But I now have all the keys back. Three sets, to be exact.'

Littlewood watched Bannon closely. He wasn't stupid, and saw the implication of what he'd said, but his reaction was more puzzled than anything else.

'OK, you say all viewings were accompanied by your good self. But what about others who've had the keys in their possession the last few weeks? Keys only take minutes to copy.'

Bannon let his gaze fall to the floor. 'The builders put a new lock on the flat, and the digitized entry system at street level was new. Both were in by the end of November; we were waiting on it before we could put the property on the market. Since then,' Bannon bit his lip, trying to recall exactly, 'there've been a couple of surveyors, a valuation, a soundproofing survey, the usual meter readings. Oh, and an architects' magazine wanted access. I think that's about it. They were all unaccompanied.'

'So any of them could have taken the keys and copied them.'

Bannon's face paled, the first sign he was rattled. 'But the surveyors are people I use all the time; I know them well. As for the rest, there is a legitimate trail of paperwork. I certainly talked with them all at least once.'

Littlewood skimmed a piece of blank paper over the table towards Bannon, followed by a biro. 'Well, you'll be able to give us a list then, won't you?'

2

7 p.m., Tuesday 9 February 2010

DCI Quinn stifled a yawn. Her feet were like ice. She reached over and felt the radiator. Tepid. 'Is your heating OK out there?' she asked Anderson, as he entered her office, a large Manila envelope tucked under his arm.

'As good as ever.'

'Maybe I'm just cold because I'm knackered,' she said, pulling her jacket around her.

'You look knackered,' Anderson agreed, with his usual subtlety. 'Look, it's gone seven, and I have to get home at some point before tomorrow, do some daddy stuff, sign a school report card . . .'

'Of course, you're perfectly right. I'm afraid I tend to assume you're a saddo with no life, so you can just work on.' Quinn sat down in front of the computer and started typing. For a minute Anderson thought she had forgotten he was there, then she said, 'But you might be better doing the daddy stuff early tomorrow rather than later today. The fog is causing traffic chaos out there. And with that smash at the Clyde Tunnel you'd get home quicker if you swam. I'd leave it until it cleared.' It was an instruction, lightly disguised as advice. 'I thought you lived around here now.' She was fishing.

'I'm renting a cupboard just up the road in Knightswood,

but I still kip at home sometimes if the only chance I get to see the kids will be breakfast. And it's warmer.' He offered no more information about the state of his marriage, mainly because he wasn't really sure of it himself.

Quinn changed the subject. 'Did we get anything from the interviews?'

The DI shook his head. 'The Inneses have gone home, and Bannon is about to. He's giving us the names of everyone he gave access to. The other seven flats are all older folk, very security conscious. We'll finish them on the door to door by tonight.'

Quinn leaned forward; an email had just popped up on her screen. 'OK, we need to check out something here.' She reached for the phone, and used her speed dial. 'Prof? The answer to your question is three. An appendix, left knee, and a dog bite on the left ankle. And what do you have for me . . . ?' Her eyes widened slightly. 'Yes, yes.' She leaned back, checking the fax machine. 'It's on. OK. Thanks, Jack.' Quinn put the phone down and seemed to pull herself from a mild shock before she continued briskly. 'Right, the hanging man has a hole in the roof of his mouth.'

Anderson looked up. 'That sounds familiar. Sounds like –'

'Emily Corbett. Exactly what I was thinking. O'Hare says Whyte's might have a regular outline, and there's a deposit of some kind in the bony part of the wound. He's sent swabs for testing, and he'll let us know more as soon as he can. He'll send a fax.'

'And we've had an initial verbal from the crime scene manager.' Anderson recalled it verbatim. 'There's only very fine blood spatter above the height of seven feet, nothing below that. There's also a trace of adhesive at that height on the emulsion.' He looked at the wall of Quinn's office, gauging the height against his own six feet. 'That suggests he was strung up, and then battered. The killer put a tarp down on the floor, and secured it around the lower part of the wall to protect it from major spatter. So he knew blood was going to be spilled, which means the victim was still capable of bleeding. He might even have been capable of walking up the stairs under his own steam. Might he have been lured there?' Anderson suggested.

'Indeed. One thing at a time. You can open that envelope now; it's not an Oscar nomination.'

Anderson slit open the flap and removed a single sheet, trying to make sense of the jigsaw of black and white with a few shades of grey in between. Then he realized, and visibly recoiled.

One large brown eye, the smashed cheekbone, the scar of the surgeon's scalpel, had all been caught with cruel clarity. The half-bald skull looked as though it had suffered a small earthquake. Half the mouth was normal, but the bottom lip sagged to one side like a wilting rose, and a small slick of saliva ran down the chin. Anderson looked up, stricken. 'Emily,' he whispered.

Quinn nodded gravely. 'Indeed. Put it up on the wall.'

'Ma'am, if our man is Stephen Whyte, he deserved everything he got.'

'No speculation yet. We nail the bastard that killed him, no matter why he did it,' Quinn said, pulling the keyboard closer and totally ignoring DS Costello who walked in nursing a mug of tea and half a packet of ginger nuts. The DCI's fingers flew dextrously over the keyboard then stopped dead, aware of her DS's silent regard. 'Yes, I can work the computer,' she spat. 'Do you two think I sit in this office and do sweet FA all day?'

'Not *all* day,' said Costello, snapping a ginger nut cheerfully.

'We've missed you, DS Costello. But not a lot.' Quinn banged the Enter key and waited, chipped fingernails tapping. 'If I am right, we three have a lot to talk about. We need a strategy.'

'Just the three of us?' enquired Anderson, glancing to make sure Costello had shut the door properly.

'For now.' Suddenly the fax machine spurted into life, and Quinn tugged the page free impatiently. She sighed with a small smile of complete triumph. 'Stephen Whyte had three scars, so does the hanging man. We need a formal ID, and quick,' she said, looking at her watch.

Costello put down her tea. 'Ma'am, you might be interested in the door to door.' She produced a piece of paper covered in Littlewood's small block capitals.

'Go on,' Quinn nodded.

'One evening last weekend, probably Saturday the thirtieth, a neighbour heard noises through the partition wall. When asked what noises, he said: "What you'd expect – there's been a bloody racket from that house for the last six months." Then he went into a rant – unrecorded – about the building work. Bannon says he was last in the flat at lunchtime that Saturday. As far as he's aware, nobody's been in it since then.'

'The body had been strung up for about a week, according to O'Hare, so that must give us something to go on. We need to track down the last movements of Stephen Whyte. Particularly, where was he on that Saturday? And we need to know why the ID was put there *for us to find.*' Quinn sighed. '*Do* we think he was left for us? That the location of the kill site was important to the killer?'

'That's what it says to me,' said Anderson. 'But Whyte has no criminal record; he didn't stand trial for anything, and there are no prints on file. So we need a formal statement. From the family?'

Quinn's shudder had nothing to do with the cold.

'Sorry, I'm lost,' said Costello. 'Were there no prints at the scene of Emily's attack?'

'Nothing. That was one of the problems. The victim gave a visual ID – she picked out his picture instantly.'

'So why wasn't he arrested?'

'A brain-damaged, traumatized victim who admits she was blindfolded – she pointed at a picture, Costello, that's all. The fiscal would have flung it out,' said Quinn quietly. 'I'm not saying she was wrong, but it wasn't enough.'

'But Whyte's girlfriend, Donna . . . what was her name?'

'Campbell,' offered Anderson. 'A hearsay statement given to police after Stephen had left the country. "Ma man wis involved innat, you know." She was a woman scorned, so I doubt the fiscal would have given much credence to her ramblings. And she tried to sell her story to the tabloids.'

'So was there no forensic evidence at the scene of the rape?'

38

Anderson shook his head. 'You can see their problem: forty-eight hours and they had nothing to go on. Emily's picture was in every paper, the public wanted blood, and the investigating team were really up against it. Whyte refused to give a voluntary statement. They had no authority to detain him. He legged it.'

'Surely that proves his guilt? Why not extradite him?'

'You know we have no power to arrest on suspicion. We need that thing – what's it called? Oh yes, evidence!' said Anderson with extreme sarcasm, earning a filthy look from Quinn.

'It was DI Yorke who was in charge, wasn't it?' asked Quinn, rhetorically.

Anderson nodded. 'He's still at Paisley, I think. DCI now. How would he take his old case being resurrected over here?'

'Not his decision, is it?' Quinn sat back, deep in thought. 'Which leads us back to the question – why was Whyte left hanging in the nearest empty property to this station? Because somebody wants us to know they got to him first. And that suggests a degree of local knowledge or some knowledge of how we work.' She cast her eyes to the divisional map on the wall. It showed A Division, their own, as a narrow sliver, covering the west of Glasgow city centre. K Division's Renfrewshire, the adjoining sprawling mass to the west, stretched from Glasgow airport to the coast.

'Doesn't answer the question. Why us? Why not let K Division know? Why not string him up in Paisley?' Anderson asked. 'Emily was their case, not ours.'

'Maybe it's not for us. Maybe it's for Emily,' said Costello simply.

'For Emily?' reiterated Quinn.

Costello shrugged. 'Well, the body had a label on it, like it was a present . . .' her voice trailed away. Her finger rested on the map. 'Where does Emily live now?'

Quinn got up and pointed along Kelvin Avenue. 'There.' Her nail touched Costello's.

'That's way too close to be a coincidence.'

Costello leaned forward in the passenger seat of Browne's old Volvo, watching the fog hazard warning signs float past. 'Right, now we're on the M8. Stick to the inside lane; it's too foggy for heroics. Does this car have a heater?'

'Yes.'

'Does it work?'

'No.'

Costello smiled. 'You'll go far in the CID.'

'Thanks for getting me out on this,' said Browne.

'You might want to hold that thought until we're back in the warm. This fog is unbelievable!' said Costello. 'And I can think of better ways of spending the evening than driving in freezing fog to meet a family like the Whytes.'

'Bad?'

'The worst.'

'So why did you?' asked Browne. 'Change the duties, I mean. You and DI Anderson could have done this.'

'We need a relative of Whyte's to confirm the ID, just somebody to look at the scars, maybe even the face . . . if they have a strong stomach,' Costello said, ignoring the point of Browne's question. She looked at her watch. 'It's just leaving eight thirty, and this might take some time. Will your husband be OK about you being out at this hour?'

Browne flicked the indicator, letting the steering wheel slip through her gloved fingers as the old Volvo straightened on the side road. 'I'm a widow,' she said, a bit too casually.

For a minute Costello thought she had not heard. 'At your age? That's a tough one.'

'I'm thirty-six, and it can happen at any age. It's just that you think it'll never happen to you.' Browne checked the rear-view mirror and wiped it with the end of her scarf, eyes back on the road again. Then she smiled slightly. 'At least you didn't say, "I'm sorry for your loss." You have no idea how tedious that gets.'

'I can imagine,' said Costello, who couldn't. She sat forward in her seat, wiping the front windscreen, but the visibility stayed poor. *I'm a widow.* She noticed Browne hadn't volunteered any more information. 'I thought you had kids?'

'I do, two. Eleven and thirteen. My daughter is much of an age with Colin's Claire.'

'Something in common then.' Costello let the comment lie between them.

Browne moved in her seat, suddenly uncomfortable. 'Oh Christ! You've noticed. Please don't say anything to him.'

Costello sniffed airily. 'Why should I? He's big-headed enough without me telling him somebody's a bit keen on him. But it's obvious you fancy the arse off him. And as a

41

police officer, fully trained in observation of the human condition, I find it a bit hard not to notice.'

'It's not anything, you know,' Browne said, horrified.

'Nothing to do with me, even if it is.'

'He was at Partick Central with us for a while there. I mean, I didn't speak to him or anything but, well, I noticed him. Seems so nice.'

'That's one word for him.' Costello smiled to herself, imagining Browne staring at Colin, adoring him from afar. 'But you do know he looks after his kids every spare minute he gets. You'd have to pay a fortune to get those two to bugger off to the pictures if you wanted to get down and dirty in his bedsit.'

'Oh, I wish,' Browne sighed, rippling her fingers a few times on the steering wheel. For a moment or two she concentrated almost sternly on driving. Then she asked, 'Do you know how he's placed? With his wife? There were a few rumours flying at Partick Central.'

Costello was careful in her reply. 'He might end up divorced from Brenda, but he'll always be a father to his kids.'

Browne didn't enquire further.

Costello changed the subject. 'You've not been with a murder squad before, have you?'

'No.'

'So why are you here now? Tough decision when you're a single parent with two kids, I would imagine.'

'I became a cop because I wanted to do something. I was fed up with nursing, and needed a change. My sister and mum offered to help out with the kids, probably to let me prove myself wrong. But really, they're great. And I think I'm a better mum for having a life elsewhere.' A shadow of bitterness fell on Browne's voice.

'I think you're right, but you're on a murder squad now. And it's important to the team that you *are* here, when needed. Welcome to the eighteen-hour day.'

'I've always just signed off at shift change.'

'Not now, you don't. You stay until the job's done. You might want to turn off here, up on to the roundabout. So what type of nursing did you do?'

'Psychiatric.'

'That'll come in handy in our squad,' said Costello, turning in her seat to check the road behind them. 'You're clear to pull in.'

Browne indicated, and pulled slowly on to the round-about, keeping well under thirty. Once they were on the Erskine road, she speeded up a little. 'I remember another case like Emily's, a really nasty rape.'

'All rapes are nasty.' Costello tried to wipe the mist from the glass but it was on the outside. 'Emily's was horrific. God, this weather is getting worse; these fields lie very low, and we're getting close to the river. Good God! You can't even see the Erskine Bridge!'

'Fog's always worse near water.' Browne dropped her speed again.

'So when was this other case? Recently?'

'No, years ago, when I was nursing in Dundee. I was at Ninewells Hospital, on the psych ward. We had an acute admission. The antidepressants and tranquillizers weren't holding her mood steady, and she was suicidal. She was scared of the dark, and I remember her screaming nightmares – she was terrified she was going to be shot. I felt such a chill in my heart when I read her notes; so few words, but such a psychological trauma. She had a head injury, or a mouth injury, something like that, and I'm pretty certain the rape had involved a gun. There was a rumour that she wasn't the only victim. She was certainly getting a lot of police attention, which wasn't always helpful for her state of mind. It rang a bell when I heard about Emily Corbett's case, that's all.' Browne's voice drifted off. 'I like the way DI Anderson talks about Emily, as though he really cares.'

'He does. We all do,' Costello said. She pulled her seat belt close to her and shivered, knowing it wasn't the cold or the dark dangerous fog that was making her skin crawl.

As they finally negotiated their way through the endless maze of narrow streets in Erskine to number 22 Findglass, Costello found herself peering through the windscreen, trying to see the small terraced house through the fog. 'We need to tread carefully. The Whyte family do not look kindly on the boys in blue. They're a bit rough, and they are well dodgy.'

Browne said, her voice little more than a whisper, 'Dodgy enough to get their rapist son a false passport and out the country?'

'The Whytes would probably cheerfully admit to being housebreakers and car thieves, but not rapists. Either way, just remember our story is that we need an ID on a body, so we'll be as sweet and compassionate as cops can be about such a difficult request. But we may need to think on our feet.'

'That sounds like you do the talking and I just nod.'

'You get the idea.' Costello rolled the window down, her breath clouding in the fog, and looked up and down along the street, not that she could see far either way. There were cars everywhere. 'Either somebody's running a used-car business from their house or somebody's having a party,' she said.

'On a Tuesday night?' Browne asked. 'Surely even in this fog we'd hear something.'

'Drive on a wee bit,' Costello told her.

'I thought Erskine was meant to be posh,' said Browne, switching on the engine again.

'Bits of it are, just not this bit.'

'This road is a dead end.' The car stopped, and Browne slipped it into neutral but kept the engine running.

'We'll have to turn and come back. I think that house with all the cars was it, you know.'

They turned and crept back down the street, which was already narrowed by cars on both sides.

'I'll park in there, shall I?'

Costello kept quiet as Browne attempted to pull into a space that was way too small, then winced as the front wheel hit the kerb and crunched. 'Interesting interpretation of the word "park".'

Browne climbed out, and looked. 'Do you think I should try again?'

Costello got out and judged the space; the front wheel

was jammed hard against the kerb, the back end sticking out into the road 'There's room to get by. But better stick the hazards on. Come on.'

They crossed the road; the opposite pavement was only half lit by street lights that were misted to a shadowy orange by the fog. Their boot heels echoed hollowly from the concrete on to the walls of the terraced houses on either side as they counted the numbers going down, looking for 22. Costello became aware that Browne was hanging back slightly. 'Are you nervous?'

'Yes,' said Browne, honestly.

'Well, they'll be hostile. But no matter what happens, be polite. You've done bereavement counselling – if we get stuck, try a bit of that.'

There was a gap at the end of the terrace, and Costello looked through to the river. The fog was dense, giant swirls and whorls like some huge beast nestling down over the water.

'Look at that!'

'That is scary,' said Browne, bumping into Costello. 'Does it stay like that if it moves inland?'

'You can keep that question for DI Anderson; he has a degree in something, the smartarse.'

Browne narrowed her eyes. 'How far are we from the Barochan Moss? The albatross?'

'Close, but further down the river. And inland a bit.'

'I thought I might bring the kids down on my day off.'

'You're on a murder case now, so you don't have any days off. And nobody can see Ally the Albatross in a fog like this without bloody radar.'

'How can you not see a bird with a nine-foot wing span?'

'The RSPB have a squad out on the Moss to protect him, and you can see why. It only takes one idiot with an air gun.'

Browne's footfall changed slightly, less cautious, more determined. 'Is this it? Number 22 Findglass?'

Costello walked up the path and paused, checking the number.

Browne followed her. 'Those cars could be parked at any of these houses, but there are no lights in the windows either side. And I can hear chatter.'

'Yes,' agreed Costello. 'Plenty of chatter. But no music.'

'Meeting of the Temperance Society?'

'Not bloody likely, around here. Come on. Cards ready.'

As Costello pressed the bell, their ears were suddenly assailed by a tortured attempt at The Sash. She could imagine the singer – a drunken skinhead in a vomit-stained Rangers top, with a can of lager balanced on his hairy belly. She rattled the doorknob.

It took a while for the door to open. A fat red-faced man appeared, early fifties, hanging on to the door as if his life depended on it. Costello thought he was going to fall out as he swayed forward, but he was just trying to focus before shouting into the house, 'There's a right couple of burds.' Then he belched a hurricane force of cheap super-market whisky in Costello's face. 'Come away in, hen, youse two ur a bit late.'

Costello was about to show her warrant card when a slightly more sober voice called from within the house,

'Who's that, Jimmy?' An untuneful wail of *It's old but it is beautiful* wavered from the front room.

A head appeared, another man in his fifties, sober, with a tie on. Then another face, female, Tango-tanned and bejewelled.

'Whit is it?' asked the one with the tie.

Still the drunken voice struggled on: *And on the twelfth I long to wear, the sash my father wore* . . .

Costello showed her warrant card, taking a step back as her brain, just a minute too late, made sense of the cars outside, the lack of music, the tie – the black tie . . . 'Police, there's nothing to be alarmed –'

She saw the arm rise, and ducked, only to hear Browne's swearing cut short as the fist connected with her face.

3

'DI Anderson,' he said, snatching up the phone. 'DCI Quinn is unavailable at the moment. You can tell me and I'll mark it up – yes, I know it's only a preliminary examination, but we are kind of desperate.'

Anderson looked over at Wyngate who had just walked in, a file under his arm and a big grin on his stupid face, looking as if he had something. 'OK, OK, OK. Wait one moment.' He walked across to the whiteboard, squeezing through a gap in the desks. He picked up a blue marker, pulling the top off with his teeth and sticking it on the end. He then attempted to draw a floor plan of the murder room, with an X marking the spot where the body had been found. He listened carefully to what he was being told down the phone, made another two marks against the walls, one near the door, the other underneath the window. He was aware of DCI Quinn coming up and standing beside him, watching and listening. 'Can you repeat that?' asked Anderson. 'A feather . . . ? Yes, I have that. Thanks, yes, as soon as you can.'

'Was that the Crime Scene Manager, Milligan?' asked Quinn.

'Whyte was strung up alive and battered about the face as he swung. Something was rammed in his mouth, causing

49

all kinds of damage that O'Hare will confirm, then he had his lips superglued together, which would have stopped him making too much noise. It seems he ripped the skin around his lips open instead. Milligan is suggesting that he might have been left there for the blood to dry for twenty-four hours or so, as that would make the whole thing easier to clean. Just roll the tarp up and walk.'

'I can't see a man in Whyte's situation trusting anybody ... What am I saying? It would only take a few drinks, a blonde in a short skirt and the promise of a night of shagging.'

'That's what I'd do,' said Anderson, then quickly clarified. 'I mean, if I was going to lure a bloke somewhere, I'd use a honeytrap. They also found two scuff marks on the wall, as yet unidentified. Maybe one person who moved, or two people separately, leaned against the wall, one there and one there.' He tapped on the whiteboard with the tip of the marker. 'Probably watching him as he died. Which would have taken some time. Not nice, not nice at all.' Anderson shook his head and walked back to his desk. 'And there was a white feather . . .'

'A white feather? A sign of cowardice?' Quinn asked.

'Or a pigeon moulting. Only a small white feather lying on the window sill. That's all, ma'am. More interesting is this in Emily's file.' He searched a list with his forefinger. 'O'Hare said something about an oily deposit in Whyte's mouth wound. Well, the wound Emily sustained had a deposit as well. We may be able to get a comparison.'

'If I remember right, in Emily's case it was something from a gun barrel. Get to work on that.' Quinn exhaled slowly. 'Nice one.' She turned to Wyngate, making him jump. 'Make my day, Wyngate. Please tell me you have the name of only one person who had access to the place once the locks were replaced.'

'Seven of them, ma'am. There was the usual power meter readings, Devenny Electrics for the safety certificate, McKays soundproofing and Ross surveyors for the evaluation. Bannon knows them all. Two guys from the council, and Towerhill Magazines for a feature on the attic conversion. I'll track them all down tomorrow.'

'Good. Let me know when you get results.' Quinn turned and spoke quietly, head down so only Anderson could hear. 'The more I learn about this, the more I think Costello is right – somebody did this for Emily. So it has to be somebody who knows her.' DCI Quinn clenched her fist, spanned her fingers and clenched again. 'It's too personal, watching him die. And slowly, like you said. Then those injuries to the mouths – Emily's mouth and Whyte's – and Whyte's lips superglued shut . . . Close, and very personal. Very personal indeed.'

Costello stood over Browne's prostrate body, her hand on her radio. 'If I press this, you'll get every cop in the area on your doorstep. And we'll huckle every single one of you for being drunk and disorderly, assaulting a police officer and anything else I can think of. A night in a freezing cold cell. Your call.' Browne raised her head groggily; her face was pouring blood. The man with the tie was wrestling red-faced Jimmy to the ground – successfully, Costello was glad to see – and calling for calm.

Then Jimmy capitulated, allowing himself to be guided back up the path to the open front door. The man with the tie, now appearing smaller and older, looked at Costello pleadingly – *Have a heart, luv.*

'I'm sorry if this is a bad time, but the misunderstanding is on your part, not ours.'

'We've just buried my sister,' said Mr Sober.

Costello sighed. 'I'm really very sorry. But I'm afraid I'm going to make it worse. If I'm right, you're missing a member of the family?' She took a guess. 'Your nephew? Stephen Whyte.'

A look passed between Miss Tango Face and Mr Sober.

Costello pressed home the advantage and addressed him directly. 'It's freezing out here. Why don't you let them go back into the house? Then you come out, and we'll try to get this sorted in a civilized manner.' She watched him hesitate. 'Before I call for back-up,' she added for effect.

Mr Sober nodded and turned, his arms stretched out to herd the drunken gaggle back into the house. Somebody was suggesting sticking the kettle on. The angry mood was broken.

Costello clipped her radio back on to her belt, took her mitts off and bent down to help Browne up. Browne was holding on to the mess that was her face. Costello could see blood seeping through her fingers, could hear Browne's breath rasping through her nose and throat.

'Just stand there – don't try and walk yet.' Costello steadied her, holding tight on to her upper arms. 'You OK?'

Through the blood Browne said something that might have been 'I'm fine' or 'I'm dying'.

Costello rooted around in her pockets for a fresh handkerchief. There would be some type of first-aid box in her car. Then she remembered they were in Browne's car, her own having failed its MOT spectacularly. But Browne was a mum, so she would have something; kids were always bleeding all over the place. She turned at the sound of shoes on the path.

'Sorry about my brother-in-law. It's all drink and grief, he's oot his skull. Here?' Mr Sober held out a freshly laundered towel and a tumbler of ice.

'No need to ram his fist through somebody's face, though. He did just assault a police officer.' Costello tipped the ice into the towel and made a pad, pressing it to Browne's nose, which was swelling fast. 'We'll get her to hospital and . . .' She stopped as the noise of a police siren broke through the fog.

'Shite. The family can do wi'oot this,' said Mr Sober.

'I didn't call them,' said Costello.

'Bloody neighbours. Can we no jist sort it oot, between oursels, like?'

'Maybe.' Costello looked around; Browne was struggling to stay on her feet. The Volvo was parked up the street, not that she could see it. 'I get the feeling you know why we're here. I'm DS Costello, this is DC Browne, and we're from Partickhill.' She flashed her warrant card.

Mr Sober shrugged, then put his own hand out to steady Browne, who lurched, the blood starting to stream down her chin. She coughed violently, retched then coughed again. 'Moira's boy. Stevie?'

'Moira?'

'Ma sister. The one that's just passed. One of her boys, the young one, Stevie, he went oot last week and hasnae come back. That why you're here?'

'I think you know the answer to that.'

'He's been away years, that's all I know.'

'Where?'

'Just . . . away.'

'I'm trying to keep this unofficial, to make it easy for you, but I will take you in if I have to.' The fog started to strobe with a blue light, a siren cutting through the air. 'What day did he come back? Don't lie; we can check.'

'Last Saturday in January, on an early flight.' The answer was quick. 'Stevie flew in from the Canaries first thing in the morning, visited for a couple of hours, then said he'd to go out, and jist buggered off. He didn't even say goodbye to his mum properly, just upped and offed. Said he'd someone to see. He's no' been back. The family's beilin'. He knew she wouldn't be long to pass. He knew she was dying an' a'. Always was thick as shite, that one.' Their eyes met as the car stopped, and its doors opened. 'Why?'

'I think you know why, otherwise you wouldn't have told me all that. We've found a body. Can I ask you your name?'

'Archie Wallace.'

Costello held up her warrant card at the squad car and drew her finger across her throat to tell them to cut the siren. Every door on the street would be open by now. 'I get the feeling you have a more . . .' she paused for the right word, '. . . realistic take on the matter. Please come with us, and we'll have a chat. Let the rest of the family get on with their grieving.'

'Probably for the best. I'll be oot in a mo, jist let me grab ma' coat.'

'Thank you, Mr Wallace. You're very understanding.'

As he turned and walked up the steps, Browne coughed again. Sticky droplets of blood hung from her nose and mouth.

Costello helped her straighten up. 'You OK?'

'Aye. But I wasn't expecting that.'

'You have to be quick,' said Costello, for once thanking her drunken mother for her own lightning reflexes. 'Or learn to box. Stay upright, will you?' she said under her breath. 'Or one of these bastards will offer to run Archie Wallace in for us and that'd be a triumph for K Division. We can't let that happen.'

'What's the score?' asked the uniform, getting out of the car, swaggering like John Wayne with a double hernia, with his thumb tucked inside his utility belt as if ready to draw. Browne started to giggle through the oozing blood.

'Partickhill CID. DS Costello.'

'Oh, the Toytown cops. All OK?'

'It is now. Just stay around until we get one of them away safely. He's helping us with a difficult ID. There's a funeral on, feelings running a bit high, a bit too much to drink, that's all.'

'She OK? She's bleeding all over the place.'

'DC Browne was injured in the line of duty. Like I said, we called at a bad time.'

'Stevie Whyte's house? Anything to do with the body you have up at Partickhill?' asked John Wayne, casually.

'News travels fast,' answered Costello, equally casually.

'Aye, well, if you get the guy who did it, pat him on the back for us. We'll go up and turn, but we'll stay till you give us the nod.' He turned round and swaggered back to the car. 'Two women! Christ!' he added when he thought he was beyond earshot. They watched as the car pulled away, then stopped. John Wayne got out and walked slowly round Browne's Volvo. He then walked back towards them.

'That your motor?'

Costello pointed at Browne.

'Well, she kerbed. You've got a flat.'

It was at that moment Costello decided brains were the better part of feminism and fluttered her eyelashes.

Anderson handed the plug to Wyngate, who rammed it into the wall socket with the heel of his hand. The computer monitor flickered to life.

'Thank God for that. Right, are we under control here?' asked Quinn.

'Yes, ma'am, seems like it.'

'It's past ten now. Where have they got to, Cagney and Lacey?'

'No word as yet.' Anderson checked his mobile.

'Well, if Wyngate sniffs anything at all on the list of key holders, then bring them in for Littlewood to question tomorrow,' barked Quinn, making Wyngate take a step back. 'Anderson? Track down the crime scene photographer and chase him up; we want those pics asap. We need to know whether Whyte walked in there on his own two feet, willingly or under duress. Just keep that in mind.'

Quinn went into her office, accidentally slamming the door behind her. Anderson sighed. His phone rang. A man's voice asked for DCI Quinn, a voice that clearly thought it was superior to Quinn. Anderson politely asked who was calling. Somebody from K Division; again just a surname, as though Anderson was expected to know. Anderson put him through and clicked the line off. He waited for a slow count of ten before he heard Quinn explode in her office.

Behind him the incident-room door opened. Costello and Browne stood there like two refugees from an earthquake, Costello supporting Browne who was covered in blood, the white padding at her face blotted deep red like crimson roses in snow.

'Good God!'

'Now, right – from the top again,' said Quinn, closing the door of her own office and gesturing that maybe Browne should sit down. 'No, don't bother; it was bad enough the first time. So there was a fist fight. And we have DC Browne here . . .' Quinn looked at the constable's swollen and bloody face, and her clothes covered in blood and mud, '. . . injured in action. Then a patrol from K Division had to change your tyre for you. And this debacle was witnessed by the entire street.'

'We did attempt to change the wheel, ma'am, but the nuts were on too tight for us to get them off with the big crowbar thing.'

'Wheel brace,' Costello corrected Browne, passing her another handful of tissues. 'One of the two patrol guys had to jump on the cross brace several times to get the nuts to budge. But on the plus side, the fog was that bad nobody really saw anything. And the body at the mortuary has now been identified as Stephen Whyte by his uncle who is downstairs having a coffee. It wasn't easy but he confirmed the scars and the mark of an amateur Rangers tattoo. Definitely, ma'am.'

'And we used the time it took the patrol to change the wheel to talk to the sober members of the family,' added Browne nasally through the wad of blood-soaked handkerchiefs pressed against her nose.

'Well, I've just had a call, and it seems the patrol that attended has reported . . . shall we say *rather adversely* on your handling of the situation. It's not going to look good when –'

There was a knock at the door and DI Anderson came in without waiting to be told to enter. 'Gillian, I really think you should go to the hospital,' he said. 'Look at the state of you.'

'She's fine,' snapped Costello. 'Look, the family say they've had no contact with Stephen for years. Stephen's mother, Archie's sister Moira, was terminally ill, and went into a coma on the first of Feb. She died last Thursday and was buried earlier today. Now, according to the family, nobody spoke to Stephen to tell him his mum was poorly as nobody knew where he was, but he suddenly turned up on their doorstep, bright and early from the Canary Islands, had a quick chat with his mother, who was lying upstairs on her deathbed, then some mysterious phone call took him away – probably to his doom. That was the morning of the previous Saturday, 30th January. The date of the noise in the attic.'

'And O'Hare has confirmed that bruises have come out on his arms and legs, less severe than the bruises caused by the battering, and therefore possibly consistent with him having been forcibly restrained. However, I've checked with the SOCOs – no scuff marks, no signs of a struggle on the stairs or the landing. The upper floor was a new build remember,' added Anderson. 'So it looks as though he went into the flat willingly, and was attacked when he got there.'

'But what Archie Wallace doesn't know is who told Stephen his mother was dying,' Costello put in. 'So who stayed in touch with him all those years?'

Browne was making a peculiar sound, like a mummified puppy. 'Ma'am, I'd say we're looking at the mother. According to Archie, she was diagnosed with pancreatic cancer eight months ago, and they were told just after Christmas it would be a matter of weeks. If she knew she wasn't long for this world, she would want to see her wee boy again, no matter what he'd done. I'm a mum, and that's what I'd feel. So maybe she said something to him that brought him back.' She wiped a smear of blood across her face. 'No matter what an evil little sod he was, he'd still be her wee boy.'

Quinn ignored her. 'I've been looking at the reports K Division did ten years ago. Whyte apparently just disappeared off the face of the earth, probably got out the country under a different name. Though I'd say that while a bit of receiving is acceptable in that family, rape and attempted murder are outwith their code. So seeing the back of Stephen was probably good riddance to bad rubbish.'

'Uncle Archie certainly isn't a fan,' muttered Costello.

'Whatever, Paisley – the whole of K Division for that matter – at the time didn't pursue it tactically as they should have done. So he did a runner before the cops could get to him.'

Costello said, 'Archie suggested that somebody gave him the money to go, as if he'd been thinking along the same lines as Gillian here. Maybe Whyte's mother stood up to interrogation by the DI in charge, Neil Yorke. Though that wouldn't be hard. I've heard it said his interrogation in those days was about as effective as being mauled by a teddy bear.'

'And the dad?'

'Don't think there is one. The mum had a husband, though, the one who thumped Gillian. I also get the feeling there wasn't any love lost between him and his stepson.'

'So Stephen's mum gave him money to piss off – probably on condition that he stayed away – he comes back to see her before she dies and promptly gets murdered.'

Quinn nodded, the theory appealing to her. 'Did the mystery phone call come through on the home phone number?'

'No, his mobile. Archie can't remember what time it was exactly. Stephen got a call, and just upped and offed, like he was going to meet an old pal down the pub. He failed to come back, so they just assumed he'd done a runner again.'

'And we don't have the mobile,' Quinn mused. 'Because they stripped him of all his effects. That's a dead end then. Can you get all that up on the board, Anderson?'

'Consider it done.'

'I'd say we need to dig a bit more in Whyte's background. How were things between him and the ex-girlfriend?' Costello pondered. 'Would she have his mobile number?'

'I doubt it. Donna Campbell shouting her mouth off in the pub about his involvement in the rape was how Whyte came to the attention of K Division in the first place. And why he buggered off. I'd imagine no love is lost there. No, not her. I think there must be somebody else close enough to have his mobile number.'

'Well, he certainly said something to Donna about what happened on millennium night,' said Anderson. 'I'll go through it at the briefing; it's important. Oh, and O'Hare said there might be swabs still in storage from Emily. He suggested we check them again. Ten years on, forensics have progressed so much there might be something the lab boys can retest.'

'Of course.' Quinn looked out the window, at nothing but thick cloud. 'It's really closing in out there.' She sighed. 'Littlewood is typing up the statement under duress, and we'll thank Mr Wallace for his help and send him home in a taxi. Ask him if his sister had a book of phone numbers or a phone of her own where she stored numbers. If he looks like refusing, threaten him with a warrant. We need to trace Whyte's phone number. Otherwise there's nothing here that won't wait until tomorrow, and my brain is starting to hurt.'

'I'd like to stay and look at the intelligence log on Emily's rape,' said Anderson.

'I'd like a look at that too,' said Costello.

'Why? I can manage.'

The only answer Anderson got was a slight shake of the head.

Quinn wasn't really listening, her mind elsewhere. 'OK,' she went on. 'See if you can have something drawn up for the briefing at seven a.m. tomorrow morning. I'll stay on for an hour, give you a hand. Browne, wash your face before you frighten somebody and then go and get yourself checked out. I think there's a crowd of journalists hanging about out there, waiting for a sniff of developments on Emily's case. I don't want them reporting that we're practising police brutality.'

Browne got unsteadily to her feet, and Anderson held the door open and steered her carefully out.

'How was she out there?' Quinn asked Costello as soon as the door had closed.

'Well, she's a good partner, a good cop. She just needs a bit of experience, ma'am,' Costello answered. 'And quicker reflexes.'

The phone rang, and Quinn lifted it up. 'Oh, hello, you've got more for us –' But she was cut short. 'Who?' she demanded, and sat bolt upright in her seat. '*Who?*' she repeated.

62

Costello leaned forward, trying to eavesdrop.

'Shit! Yeah, I've got that. And Jack . . . thanks.' She put the phone down. 'Costello, you've still got your big jacket, haven't you?' She scribbled a few notes on a pad. 'Get Anderson, tell him I said to use his car; and he needn't worry, I'll make sure Browne gets medical attention. But there's a dead body out on the Barochan Moss, and you two have to get out there asap. O'Hare's already there.'

Costello looked at the notes. 'Why, who is it?'

'Just go!'

Costello looked at the location scribbled on the Post-it note. 'Why us? That's not our jurisdiction. That's bloody K Division again!'

'Please, Costello, just do as you are told, for once.'

'So you want us there, down on the Moss? The fog will be awful. It was bad enough in Erskine.'

'Well, drive carefully then,' said Quinn.

'It'll be a thousand times worse now.'

'So drive *very* carefully then.'

'But why us?' Costello asked again. Then her face relaxed as if a penny had slowly dropped. 'It's connected, isn't it? With the Whyte case?'

'O'Hare has phoned me. And I am telling you. I won't tell you again. On your way.'

It's late. It's very cold. And the wee one is still missing. It's not like her to be away so long – somebody usually finds her and brings her back – but in this weather? Who knows what might have happened to her?

But, as they say, it is an ill wind that blows no good.

It's happened twice in one day. I saw her, my other wee one. Prudenza, the little fish.

After so many years, twice in one day.

But it was by chance this time. I was taking a little extra time at the traffic lights as any good citizen would, taking care not to dent the works van, when I saw them, Costello and Anderson, coming down the stairs of the cop shop as if the taxman himself was at their heels.

They paused in the overhead light before stepping into the gloom of the fog. Anderson pulled on his gloves, wriggling his fingers. Even from the road, I could see he was shivering, as if he needed an extra layer to keep him warm. He walked towards me, with her trotting alongside him, her rucksack over her shoulder, one hand behind her to steady the weight on her back.

They were being businesslike, no chit-chat like before. Anderson in front, her keeping up, both looking bulky in their winter jackets. The thermometer in the van was rising slowly to zero and I'd been driving around for a good ten minutes, so God knows how cold it was out there.

They came closer, caught in the subdued street light. Her face looked pale. She must have been tired, yet she had that energy still in her step, like a Jack Russell with the scent of a rat. They crossed the road, engulfed in the fog. Before I lost them I noticed him put his arm out, not touching her but slightly around her to protect her, ushering her across the road. Like a brother.

The traffic lights changed, I let out the clutch and squeezed the accelerator, driving closer to them. He dropped his arm when they got to the pavement. She was holding a bit of paper, her rucksack slung down from her shoulder and now in the crook of her elbow. The brief conversation finished, the lights on his Honda Jazz flashed as the alarm clicked off. He got into the driving seat, she into the passenger seat.

I saw him hand her the seat belt before I pulled out to pass them. I must have been within feet of them.

I didn't look back in the rear-view mirror.

She is in safe hands for now.

My little Prudenza.

'Just use the bloody sat nav!' Anderson snarled.

'According to the bloody sat nav, we should still be on the M8!'

'And instead we're bumping down a single-track road at the arse end of nowhere in a pea-souper.'

'A pea-souper?' Costello laughed. 'My God, you've been watching *Mary Poppins*. A roight pea-sooooooper!'

Anderson leaned forward, his eyes screwed up to concentrate, trying to see through the murk in front of the car. 'Why don't you try looking at the map, Costello? Then you might have some idea where we're supposed to be.'

'Oh, I know where we're supposed to be,' she said, turning the map through ninety degrees. 'I just have no idea where we are. Being able to see the road might help. Never mind a sign.'

Anderson was about to make an ill-advised comment about women and map-reading; instead, he couldn't help smiling. It was good to have Costello back, rubbing along together, being able to say what he thought, not watching his words. He just wished she had some semblance of a sense of direction, and said so.

'Look, even Ally the Albatross got it a bit wrong – the Falklands to Brazil via Barochan Moss? Anybody could make that mistake.'

'It wasn't his fault. The prevailing wind was in the wrong direction. They don't fly all those thousands of miles, you know. They just float about up there, and if the . . . shit!' He swore as the Honda bumped badly on the invisible grass verge and slammed to a halt. 'And this road is in the wrong bloody place.'

'That'll be my fault as well,' said Costello easily, still fighting with the map. 'I think we follow this road round . . .' she stabbed at the map, '. . . and it'll take us round the outside of the field where the body is . . . and surely to God they'll have somebody on the road with a light. My notes say the body is far down the field in a copse, low-lying, not visible from the road, so they've stuck an officer at the top of the lane. I can't see anybody.'

Anderson thrust the map back at her, a tacit agreement that she might be right. Costello unclipped her seat belt, causing a small alarm to beep irritatingly, and wiped the front windscreen, shielding her eyes with her hand and peering through the glass.

'That won't help you see any better,' said Anderson, trying not to keep deviating into passing places, thinking the road was bending. 'If I have to do an emergency stop, you'll be joining Gillian in A & E.'

'Oh, it's Gillian now, is it?'

Anderson knew the warning signs of that as a topic of conversation, and was relieved when Costello said, 'I think I can see some lights over there to our left; I'm sure we're nearly there.'

The Honda crept forward, the only noise the small bleep of the seat-belt alarm. Costello looked at the height of the wall they were driving past, the dense fog, the jigsaw of the drystane dyke floating in and out of focus. A foggy night and a killer on the loose – that alone would scare the intake at Tulliallan shitless. No amount of lecturing could prepare you for the adrenaline rush a case like this gave you, the sleepless nights, the strange light-headedness of the chase. She looked at Anderson's black-gloved fingers on the steering wheel, guiding them through the fog, and resisted the temptation to reach out and pat him on the forearm. 'Some of the recruits I taught would make you laugh; five stone and the height of nothing,' she said.

'Not exactly built like a brick shithouse yourself.'

'Yes, but I punch above my weight.'

'And with a tongue like a scalpel, Costello, you never need to punch.'

'Shut yer face.' She wiped the window again, after clouding it with her own breath. 'So what about you? And the rather ample DC Browne?'

Anderson sighed. Bloody Costello.

'I'm coming round to the fact I'm destined to wake up alone in a rented bedsit somewhere in Knightswood, with a damp patch on the ceiling and a stinking threadbare carpet composed of the dead skin cells of previous inhabitants, and fleas. I'll have to share a toilet with the incontinent old guy from the room next door, and I'll spend my aimless days wandering round Lidl buying tiny cans of baked beans and sausage for one, Cup-a-Soups, and bottles of Thunderbird.' Anderson looked over to his left, where he too could see lights. 'I'll spend all my pension on 0898 phone numbers and fantasize about the lollipop lady at Rowan Hill Primary.'

'I'd say you have three other options. You can get back with your wife and support your family, which will be cheaper than the current arrangement. You can wake up in the arms of the delectable Gillian Browne and end up supporting her, her dysfunctional kids, your own dysfunctional kids and, by then, your own embittered wife. Or you can live in luxury with jacuzzi baths and two cleaners with Helena McAlpine, and Alan's ghost will stalk you for ever.' The car ground to a halt and they sat for a moment, as memories of three years ago crowded the car. Costello shivered, then laughed. 'Colin, just settle for the bedsit and the 0898s.' Then she said, 'Look, I think there's a man flashing in the road.'

'Brave man, in this weather. It's so cold it'll fall off.'

'With a torch, you arse! Come on.'

Costello looked out of the side window as Anderson parked as high on the verge as he could, tucking in behind an Audi. All she could see over the top of the dyke was a carpet of white spiky grass disappearing into a low bank of dense fog.

'So who found a dead woman out here in the middle of nowhere?' Costello grunted, squeezing out of the car in the gap between door and wall.

'One of the albatross protection squad, I bet. Who else would be wandering about here at this time of night, in this effing weather?' said Anderson, opening his own door. 'Watch yourself here, it's slippy.'

It was bitter, bitter cold. They could see nothing, their only clue the sole police patrol on the road, jigging in the cold in an effort to keep his circulation up. He gave no more than a brief glance at their ID. He nodded and pointed them down a narrow single-track road in the direction of the sloping lower field.

They clambered over the wall then fell in one behind the other as the path narrowed down a slope. Anderson held his hand out to steady Costello, who immediately shrugged free of him.

'I'm not a helpless little girlie, you know,' she said.

'Yes, I noticed,' replied Anderson dryly, as Costello slipped on the icy grass and grabbed his sleeve.

She sidestepped off the track for a better grip, the frost crunching under her boots as they walked towards the copse.

'Watch out, Costello. This whole place has been cleared recently; there are wee sapling stumps everywhere.'

She hopped back on to the path again. 'I wonder why O'Hare called us out. A woman frozen to death out here . . . Maybe she's had her head bashed in and has been left hanging from a tree somewhere, mouth glued shut. There must have been something that made a connection in somebody's mind.'

Anderson shivered against the intense cold.

'Look, there are the lights, over there,' said Costello, her pace quickening. She risked a look round, her arms out like a bad tightrope walker trying to keep her balance on the icy path. They were a fair way from the road.

They hurried towards a cluster of lights struggling in the mist. The scene of crime officers were hanging around, and a tall figure in a white protective suit was standing, slightly stooped, talking to someone a good bit shorter. The taller figure raised a hand as Anderson approached, then waved to the side, telling him to come in the way everybody else had so as not to contaminate the scene any further. But it was difficult to see the yellow markers against the icy white grass, the fog, the darkness.

Behind them, far away, the noise of a diesel engine died as soon as it was born. Anderson turned in the direction of the sound. 'I bet that's the van with the generator getting stuck. It'll never get round the corner and down that lane.'

'Like any light will help us in this soup,' said Costello. She pulled out her torch, and switched it on, lighting up only an impenetrable wall of fog. She wiped the glass and tried again. No difference. 'No light, no sound, no visibility. And dead quiet. A perfect killing ground.' And a lonely place to die.

The only perceptible light was the irregular flash as the scene photographer tracked along the yellow flags on the grass that marked what may or may not be the suggestion of footsteps in the hard frost. He was ghostly in the fog, seen and unseen. This was a bleak scary place at the best of times, but now, at midnight, in swirling ground-lying murk, it was the haunt of nightmares. And somewhere among it all was a body.

Costello picked her way round the clearing, towards the partly illuminated scene she could see through the fog. It looked as though a herd of migrating wildebeest had arrived at a watering hole. There were cops everywhere.

Briefly she turned her back on the lit-up crime scene to look out at nothingness. 'Look around for a moment, Colin,' she said wonderingly. 'Out here, in the middle of nowhere, with all the snow and fog, it's as though we were between worlds, as though we'd died and didn't know it. It's so beautiful, the realm of the Ice Queen, don't you think?'

Anderson looked around him and shivered.

'DI Anderson?' The clipped Newton Mearns tone sounded loud through the fog. 'DS Costello?' the voice added as an afterthought. 'I thought you were away.'

'Well, unluckily for you I'm back,' Costello responded before she twigged who had called to them. She raised her hand in a tentative greeting, noting how the 'S' had been emphasized, as if reminding her of her rank. She saw a figure emerging from the mire and the fog, recognized the designer cut of the coat, the precise tuck of the scarf, the hat, the gloves. The clean wellies.

Detective Sergeant Viktor Mulholland.

'Hello, Vik,' said Costello, annoyed as he flicked her his Johnny Depp smile. He didn't look any older, still drop-dead handsome. Still an arrogant sod. Still Vik the Prick.

'DS Mulholland, now.'

'Hello, Vik,' Anderson echoed, and walked right past him. 'Is it this way?'

71

But Mulholland had moved in front of Costello, knowing she wouldn't step out of the designated access to the scene. He turned his back to her. 'Look, Anderson –'

'DI Anderson to you,' he corrected, pleasantly.

'DCI Quinn knows, as well as I do, that this case is ours, K Division's. This is not your jurisdiction. You should not have been called out to this.'

'You know, you're right, DS Mulholland. DS Costello and I had nothing better to do tonight but wander down here just to piss you off. Or maybe, just maybe . . .' Anderson held up a finger, '. . . our superior officers know something that we don't. Do you think that might be the case?'

'Nobody's told me anything about it,' grumbled Mulholland, still in Costello's way and not looking like budging.

'That's because you're only a sergeant, and not paid to think. You're paid to do. I am the senior officer present, I was asked to be present, and therefore I am in charge.'

'Well, I'm not happy.'

'Oh, get out my bloody way, you moron! You two can play Power Rangers in the canteen later, but there's a dead body out here somewhere,' said Costello, stamping past Mulholland to walk into another figure, a smaller man, rotund, scruffy in an anorak, red-faced with the cold, his nose running. He was holding up a handkerchief, like a child scared to blow while the adults were talking.

He looked past Costello to Mulholland then to Anderson and back to Costello, trying to work out where the power lay. The scruffy anorak with the torn collar like his own? The foul-faced support act that was looking daggers at him? Or the pristine cashmere vision that was his colleague? Costello didn't feel like enlightening him.

'If this is connected with another case you have, we were not made aware of that,' said Mulholland, fishing.

'We're all pawns in the game, Vik,' said Anderson. Then he nodded amicably to his fellow anorak. 'I'm sure DS Mulholland will remember his manners and introduce us in a minute.'

'Sorry,' said Mulholland, his mood broken. 'DI Anderson, Partickhill. DS Lambie, Paisley, Mill Street.'

'Colin.'

'David. Did you find it OK? We never heard your car. But fog can blanket sound very strangely. It's a long way across the field, and there's a fair way to go yet,' said Lambie.

'So who found the body – a twitcher looking for Ally?' Anderson enquired.

'An ornithologist.' Lambie turned and walked them back up the slight hill, towards the heart of the activity. Costello and Anderson followed, leaving Mulholland to fall in behind them, his boots slightly out of step with theirs.

'And where is Bill Oddie at the moment?' continued Anderson, shouting along the single file of four.

'We've sent him home,' said Mulholland from the rear. 'We got a statement. His name is Ernie English, and he's apparently a well-known expert in all things feathered – the bird man of Ailsa Craig. He was wandering around looking for the albatross and heard something. A scuffling noise, is how he described it. He went closer to investigate. He was walking around in the copse for about five minutes, just waiting and listening, before he actually tripped over the body.'

'So can we fix a precise time of death?' asked Costello over her shoulder.

'Not yet. We know the call came in at 9.17 p.m., but he'd had to walk up to the road to find a signal. So time of discovery ten or fifteen minutes before that. I've asked him to come back down here tomorrow and re-enact it backwards. I don't want to disturb the scene any further tonight.'

'I'll come along on that re-enactment, if you don't mind, DS Mulholland,' Anderson said smoothly. 'I might want a word with Mr English.'

'If you think that will help. But I did the right thing sending him home; he'd already been waiting forty minutes while we were trying to find him. And it's minus twelve out here.'

'Poor bloody albatross, why does it not bugger off to the Arctic? Must be hotter there,' said Costello.

'Antarctic,' corrected Mulholland.

'Arctic's just as cold, but nearer,' snapped Costello.

'Have you been informed of the ID of the victim?' asked Lambie quietly from the front of the column.

'Not confirmed,' evaded Anderson.

'It's Marita,' said Lambie. '*The* Marita. Or Mrs Iain Kennedy, as she is in private life. Interesting set of injuries.'

'We're trying to keep that from the press as long as possible . . .' said Mulholland from the back, just as somebody shouted his name.

'You go, I'll fill you in later,' said Anderson with the easy grace of one used to being obeyed, and he walked off quickly, following in Costello's wake now she had moved ahead of Lambie. He was glad of the quicker pace, glad to have the blood pumping some warmth to his muscles and thinking how fit Tulliallan had made Costello, who was moving much faster than him, shape-shifting through the eerie fog, her figure fading to a ghost as she strode towards the light.

'Why did you call us, Prof?' asked Costello as she approached the crouching pathologist.

'Good evening, DS Costello,' O'Hare replied automatically without looking up. 'As they say, I saw this and I immediately thought of you. Where is DI Anderson?'

Costello looked round. 'He's back there, talking to Mulholland and Lambie.'

O'Hare made a soft little noise. 'Do you know it's Marita?'

'We've just been told.' Costello crouched down, looking at the terribly damaged face. 'Bloody hell! It really is!'

Marita had been Miss Caledonia twenty years before, and ever since then her controversial love life and her relentless self-publicity meant she had rarely been out of the headlines. Now she lay curled on her side, arms folded as if in prayer, her duffel jacket fastened snug up to her neck. She could have been asleep, were it not for her bloodied hair and the messy pulp of the lower part of her face. There was something wrong about her mouth; it had no boundaries, just a dark ragged hole. Costello bent down to see uprooted teeth, deep sockets exposed and bleeding, as though something had been viciously rammed in. 'From *Celebrity Big Brother* to this,' she said quietly. 'Prof, are these injuries the same as Whyte's?'

'She has a wound to her mouth, and a wound on her head,' said O'Hare carefully. 'The wounds appear to be very similar to Emily Corbett's. And she's from Partickhill.'

'Oh.' Costello had not expected that. She was surprised at the punch of emotion she felt in her stomach. *For Emily.*

But Marita needed her now, needed her to do her job. She pushed the emotion from her mind and observed. The famous titian hair was black and stiffened with blood, moulded on to the dark material that lay under her head. A hat? A scarf? Costello looked round. The police photographer was snapping away. Something was nagging at Costello's mind; she wanted to say to him: *Do this – make sure you get that.* Something was not right. She saw the victim's woolly hat lying some three metres away on the snow, marked by a numbered yellow fluorescent tag. Of course they wouldn't have missed that. She was panicking; she'd spent too long in Tulliallan, standing in a room with no fresh air, talking shite. She had to do the right thing now.

But what was it?

She looked again at the victim, catching the nacreous pallor of the face in the brief flash from the camera. She could see what the dark material was now. A scarf, a rich beautiful red, soaked and blackened with blood, had been folded carefully, placed under the dead woman's head, and tucked under her neck.

O'Hare was trying to open the mouth, a wooden spatula in his gloved fingers. He was talking, but Costello wasn't listening. Surely he could do that in the lab, she thought. And there was something else here that she needed to ask about, to know, and it was going to be lost.

She looked down at the victim's feet, at her Ugg boots, one on properly, one stuck crookedly on the heel, causing the suede to bulge like an overfed snake. The warm padded trousers were tucked into one boot, but half out of the other – why should that be?

She gripped her own mitten, and tried to think calmly. She was trying too hard.

'Oi! Costello? Are you listening to me?'

'Sorry, Prof. I was miles away,' she answered and pointed at the scarf. 'Has that been put there?'

'Don't jump the gun,' said O'Hare, turning the body slightly, then pausing and leaning close as if listening intently.

'Oh, shit, shit, shit, shit,' he muttered. 'Her airway has closed. Hand me that, will you?' He pointed quickly at a black zipped folder in his bag. Costello pulled off her mittens and unzipped the wallet, which opened like a book. O'Hare selected a scalpel handle. Instinctively she picked up the tinfoil sheath of a fresh blade, unwrapped it and offered it to him; she had seen it done often enough. All the time O'Hare was softly cursing and swearing. In all the years she had known him, she had never heard him swear.

'Come here. I need you to hold on to her.'

Costello knelt down and gingerly took the victim's head

between her hands. As she lightly touched the left cheek, she felt the bone sink beneath her fingers.

'Oh, shit,' she muttered in her turn, watching as the pathologist undid the first toggle of the duffel jacket, carefully moved the blood-soaked hair aside, and felt for the Adam's apple. He prodded once, twice, then nicked the skin with the blade. There was a faint bubbling noise.

He kept his finger there, silent now. Costello looked from the woman's throat back to the pathologist's face . . . O'Hare cut firmly.

There was a noise like a piglet grunting, like water gurgling through a disused pipe. The hole cut by the blade opened a little, then closed, then opened again. O'Hare's face and her own were very, very close, clouding each other with their breath in the freezing fog. She could smell him, the smell of soap, like a mild carbolic.

'Good girl,' said O'Hare, to either of them or both. 'Right, Costello, hand me that wee pipe, the tiny tube, front pocket. It'll do her for now.'

Costello handed it over, unpeeling the plastic sleeve. With infinite tenderness O'Hare slid it into the hole. He leaned forward, placing his cheek to the open end, feeling for a draught of warm breath. He sighed with relief.

Costello tried to blot out the cold, and the pain in her thighs as she rested on her hunkers. O'Hare handed her a thick swab and placed her hands on either side of the victim's face. She felt him apply a gentle pressure through her own hands before removing his own. He was looking straight at her, deep into Costello's eyes, as if noting the colour of them, marking each feature in her face. Then he lifted her fingers and exchanged the soiled swab for a clean one.

'The ambulance is coming. Let's leave the others to it. They can fight about the jurisdiction until the cows come home, but we have one advantage they don't.'

'And that is?'

'Just the small matter of the victim. She's coming back with us.'

Costello looked at him enquiringly.

'Victim with a nasty head wound, and a second wound to her mouth that might prove to be penetrative. Similar to Whyte, but exactly like Emily. As far as this investigation is concerned, we have two in twenty-four hours. I'm erring on the side of caution, just in case they are connected.'

She could hear, in his voice, that this was important to him. 'OK,' she said slowly, trying to ignore the way her heart was pounding. 'Can I ask you something?'

'Mmmm?'

'You're not doing the things that you normally do for the dead.'

'That, DS Costello, is because she is not dead.'

'You sure you want her taken to the Western?' the paramedic asked. 'We had instructions to go to the Royal Alexandra Hospital in Paisley.'

'The Western, please, and as quick as you can,' instructed O'Hare. 'I'll sign for it if you want authority. Just radio them, and tell them that I said so.'

'And you are . . . ?'

'Professor O'Hare.' Then, when that clearly meant nothing, he added, 'Forensic pathologist.'

The paramedic looked up, and Costello saw the driver's head turn round.

'A pathologist? But she's not dead.'

'Not yet she's not, but she will be if we keep having this conversation. So can we get a move on? I know the facilities we have at the hospital, so let's get her up out of this field and on the bus.' O'Hare's voice had a tone that said distinctly it was best not to argue.

The paramedic nodded, acknowledging that the change to the initial call now made sense. He looked down at the body, the shattered face, the immense amount of blood, and nodded. 'Better be the Western then. We're going to have to carry her up on to the road.'

'There are four of us,' O'Hare said. 'We'll manage the board up to the ambulance.'

'I'll radio it in once we're back in the bus. We'll take our time. Bloody fog.' The paramedic placed the spinal board down beside the victim, planning to pull a mat underneath to get her up. O'Hare spoke to one of the crime scene officers, explaining how they were going to disturb the scene.

Costello watched as the woman was loaded on to the board with extreme care, the paramedic talking to her all the time while O'Hare steadied her head in his gloved hands.

Mulholland and his colleague had retreated to a sheltered place under a tree. They watched but did not comment as the slow procession passed silently by like a funeral cortège in the fog.

*

The ambulance juddered violently as the driver changed down a gear to gain some grip on the ice. Costello held on to the steel bar that secured the trolley and listened as the tyres spun then crunched and she felt the vehicle lurch forward. She released her grip a little.

'So who was the police surgeon who pronounced her dead? Shouldn't they know the difference?'

'It's not always as easy as that. Could you hold her head back, as steady as you can? Don't put any pressure on the side of her skull; she has a nasty fracture there. She's bleeding into her brain.'

'Any idea what she was hit with?'

'The SOCOs will find it if it's still at the scene; whatever it was, it'll be covered with blood.' O'Hare manoeuvred Costello's gloved hands over the blood-soaked head. He then started to cut the sleeve of the victim's duffel jacket with a sharp pair of scissors, keeping the path of the scissors straight and true through each layer of clothing, the sleeve of the duffel, then the sleeve of her cardigan, then – strangely – a flimsy flesh-coloured top with a pattern of sequins and small stones at the wrist. He wrapped a cuff on her arm, then clipped a peg on her finger. A vein found, a needle in, a tap turned, fluid beginning to drip down a tube. Life being fed back into her. O'Hare opened each eye, flicking back the lid with a fine pressure of his thumb, shining in the little torch the paramedic held out for him. He pulled a doubtful face.

The ambulance pitched; Costello shifted her weight on her precarious perch at the top end of the stretcher, and the makeshift trachea tube waggled from side to side.

O'Hare changed his gloves, and with one hand he gently prodded the victim's face, and her head fell to one side. Costello put her own gloved hand out, fingers spanning the face, and again felt the shattered arch of the cheekbone grate under her fingers. She averted her eyes as the Prof undid the victim's coat and cardigan, slicing up the front of the sequinned top, then under it a T-shirt, and a vest – an old woolly vest – to reveal small pale breasts. Then he began to play about with a set of wires with discs on the end as the paramedic unfolded a tinfoil thermal blanket to cover the victim's lower half and pulled her arms back to her sides to tuck them in. The waist of the padded ski trousers had been pulled down around the woman's hips, but from her vantage point, Costello could see no marks of violence.

Then her eye was caught by a mitten, dirty and soaking wet, dangling from the end of a cord which disappeared up one sleeve of the duffel jacket and down the other to meet its neighbour. Then she noticed the ringless fingers, the dirty fingernails – short, dirty fingernails . . .

'Costello, can you hold her still?' said O'Hare again, his voice curt with impatience. Again he moved her fingers under his, moving her grip away from the fracture site. Even through the gloves his fingers were warm, not cold like she had always imagined. O'Hare then slipped his fingers under the victim's head, frowning in concentration, keeping his eye on the tube that wriggled from the hole in her throat.

'Prof, do me a favour while you're under there – is there a name on the back of the coat collar?' asked Costello.

O'Hare picked up his torch and shone it under the victim's neck. 'Hmmm. It does say something.' He tilted his head round to get a better look. 'Handwritten. It says I-T . . .' O'Hare turned his head the other way. 'It says . . . Itsy.' He sat back down on his haunches. 'Bloody hell, this is Itsy Simm. Marita Kennedy's sister. I never realized. I never knew they looked so alike.' He shook his head in disbelief. 'It is remarkable.'

'Do you know these people then?'

'Iain Kennedy is a friend of mine. That's why I wanted her at the Western,' said O'Hare with a hint of reproof. 'These two could almost be twins. *An apple, cleft in two, is not more twin.*'

'God, I wish I'd gone to private school . . .'

O'Hare's hand hovered over the unlined marble-white forehead and the fine golden eyebrows. 'What we're looking at is the wreck of a very beautiful face. And whatever her sister is, Itsy here is an innocent.'

Once they had hit the motorway Costello phoned Anderson, who snapped, '*I've heard,*' and the signal went dead. She then phoned Quinn and heard the DCI's voice go through every emotion; horror at the similarities of the injuries, relief that it was not Marita, despair that it was Marita's sister, annoyance that she might be forced to carry the can for the ID being wrong, then relief that it was one of her team who had corrected it. It was some small consolation to her that the entire team, including O'Hare who knew Marita's husband well, had been wrong. All this was tinged with the knowledge that any involvement of

Marita, the tabloids' darling, would attract a huge amount of media attention.

'Do you think the attacker made a mistake? Went for Itsy mistaking her for Marita?' asked Quinn. 'It's not outwith the realms of possibility.'

'Who knows?' Costello answered. 'We're taking her straight to surgery at the Western. We'll hang around and I'll get her clothes for Forensics.'

'Good. No more cock-ups on this one, Costello, not this time.'

'It wasn't us who cocked it up before . . . ma'am.' She snapped her phone closed.

It rang immediately, and Anderson's voice said, 'Sorry, bad timing before.' He sounded strangely subdued. 'I'm still at the scene,' he said. 'I'd better inform K Division officially about the identification, as a professional courtesy.'

'Just wanted to confirm you knew. Bye.' Costello slipped her phone into her pocket.

'This is big, isn't it? If it turns out to be connected to what was found at Clarence Avenue, this is very big,' said O'Hare, contemplating the drip. 'Not sure the powers that be will think Partickhill is up to it.'

'They won't get either case off Quinn easily.' Costello sighed. 'Have we done everything we can do? For Itsy, just now?'

'We're trying to stop her bleeding, but I think a lot of it is internal. We need to minimize her blood loss and keep her circulating volume up. The tube has established a clear airway. Why? Do you have something else in mind?'

'Can we try and take some samples before she goes to surgery? They'll wash away any trace evidence. Can we get some swabs, scrape her nails? And, basically, was she raped?'

O'Hare backhanded a loose lock of grey hair from his forehead. 'Oh, I remember. I was a forensic pathologist once,' he said, with a touch of granite humour.

'So pretend she's dead and get on with it then, eh?'

4

She was in the womb again.
  Floating.
  Turning the clock back.
  Eyes closed. Ears muffled. Floating.
  No sound, no vision.
  Tethered and secure, she floated. Cushioned. Warm.
  She could feel her hair like filigree on her cheek, ten-
drils of seaweed dancing free in the water.
  She breathed. Then she sank and exhaled, breath
bubbling through the water.
  She was safe down here.

So here he was, sitting in the Honda Jazz, with the lights
on, and the clock showing 1.05 a.m. Count Basie was giving it his all with 'Splanky' on the CD. The car's interior
was spotless, Anderson realized, and his heart gave a little
jolt. There should have been some detritus, some waste
from the children, a CD of some prepubescent manufac-
tured boy band he had never heard of, or a collection of
Peter's cartoons kicking around the floor. But the floor
was immaculate.
  Not that Peter was drawing much nowadays. He really
didn't do much of anything; he just clung to his mother's

hand and glared at his father through dark narrowing eyes.

The fog was getting worse. When Anderson had arrived outside Strathearn House, home of the Kennedys, he'd been able to see the gable end of the gatehouse clearly from here. Now, only fifteen minutes later, he couldn't even see the gates on the far side of the road. DCI Quinn had been specific: *Wait for me in the street.* He was glad she had taken it on herself to break the news to the Kennedys.

He pushed his fingers deeper into his gloves. There was a malevolent quality about this fog, the way it encased you, disabled you, disorientated you. Whether it was physical or not, the sheer density of it made it difficult to breathe. There could be anything out there, stalking him, creeping up behind him. He turned down the CD a little, then turned it off, then he flicked the door lock of the car.

Just in case.

God, he was cold.

It crossed his mind to phone Brenda and tell her to be careful. The family home, her home, was on the south side but only just. The small housing estate behind the Southern General Hospital was low-lying; the fog would creep up the river first, and the house was less than half a mile from the river bank. Then he remembered – it was the small hours of the morning. She would be in bed, in her bed, with Peter. The psychologist was having a field day with that one. Fine for a four-year-old, not so fine for a nine-year-old. Take him back to his own bed, firmly and calmly, the psychologist said; comfort only reinforced the fact there was something wrong.

But of course there was something wrong. Daddy wasn't there.

Anderson looked up as the fog behind him swirled, clouding and corrupting the orange light from the street lamp. He only actually saw Quinn's Lexus when it was grille to grille with the Jazz. Quinn was on the phone and as she walked smartly to the passenger door of his own car, she was talking, constantly, incessantly.

'With all due respect, sir,' she was saying, in a manner that suggested no respect at all. 'You don't get to my age without amassing a certain amount of experience. And *yes* I can bring something to it – I can bring my team.' She fell silent as the other end of the phone chattered away, and rolled her eyes at Anderson as she climbed into his car. '. . . And now there is another victim with similar injuries, who lives a few hundred yards from the station . . . the body was out at the Barochan Moss. Yes, I appreciate that lies in K Division jurisdiction, sir . . . I feel at this point, sir, I have to say that it was one of *my* officers who correctly identified the victim . . . Yes, and the suspect of *that* name was found dead in a property directly behind our station. My officers and myself have already established a supportive relationship with the Whyte family – notwithstanding the small matter of the previous investigation by K Division . . . Indeed . . . thank you, sir.'

DCI Quinn sighed and closed the phone. 'To say nothing of the small matter of us having the body of Incident One in the mortuary and the victim of Incident Two in the Western Infirmary, both on our doorstep.' She reclined back against the headrest and closed her eyes.

'Costello was wondering why O'Hare was so insistent on that,' said Anderson.

'Don't forget that O'Hare knows Donald Corbett well. I don't think the case of Emily Corbett has ever been far from the Prof's mind. So if he saw something there, a connection . . . well, let's leave it at that.'

'So how did it go? Are we getting the case?'

DCI Quinn shrugged. 'The ACC Crime is away to talk to his boss. They'll have to come to some arrangement soon. And Marita being who she is, nobody's taking a decision without getting it in triplicate; they're all so scared these days.'

'Messy if K Division get it, ma'am.' Anderson started to drum his gloved fingers against the steering wheel. 'But Mulholland was all over the scene right enough.'

'The ACC was quite clear; Vik has all the credentials to be the public face of the new police service. Yes, I am totally aware of what you're thinking, but you're not the one who makes the decisions. Vik is bright, attractive, charismatic. And he's an incredibly focused young man.'

'And we are not focused?'

'You're certainly not. You've been sitting here thinking about your kids getting around in this fog. Don't lie to me, Anderson, I know you too well.'

'Well, Mulholland is a warped . . . sod.'

'The word you were going to use rhymes with banker, but you're too polite. He took six months' leave of absence after that debacle three years ago, went to Russia to visit his mother's relatives, and got his head together. Since then he's been totally driven, a career cop. And there's something else.'

'I guess I'm not going to like this.' Anderson leaned forward over the steering wheel, bracing himself for bad news.

'There's a photojournalist around, recording the work of the Strathclyde Police Service for the visual arts exhibition in the summer. He's at Govan at the moment.' She looked at the dashboard clock. 'Well, he was, but I bet he's just had a phone call and is on his way to the Moss. They've been waiting for a good story, a week in the life of the murder squad.'

Anderson almost laughed. 'There's no way the victim's family will agree to that.'

'If we were talking about a normal family I would agree, but Marita might. She's a professional celebrity, so it's profile and money for her. Her husband Iain, her new husband – is he number three?'

'Or four. I've lost count. Rumour has it that's why she's only known by her first name. She changes the second one so often.'

'Anyway, Iain Kennedy is a respected man in this city, and she will have the full weight of the press on her side. She'll be on the front of every tabloid tomorrow, and if we're not careful so will we. And if we're not *very* careful we could find ourselves being part of a terrible docudrama. So we're getting off lightly with a photographer who, as far as I'm aware, is a half-decent human being. Some guy called Harry Castilia? Castigilia? I've seen some of his stuff in the art pages of the *Herald*, all black and white and moody. It said in the memo he'd done some award-winning stuff in Somalia and Darfur. God knows what he'll make of this lot. At least he and his sidekick have a respected track record and better them than a Channel Five camera crew following us about,' Quinn explained. 'Oh, I meant to mention – Browne's at the hospital now, being checked over.' She rubbed her nose between thumb and forefinger. Tiredness was setting in. She sighed. 'Thank God we didn't jump the gun and tell Iain Kennedy his wife was dead, just as she was coming down the stairs looking rather marvellous and with a steady pulse. We're going to play this very carefully.'

'So we're working the case as if it's ours? Attempted murder? Grievous bodily?'

'Until we're told otherwise. Come on.'

Anderson fired up the engine, reversed and turned into the short approach to the gate. An electric sensor on the metal stanchion flashed, and Anderson pressed a button to open the driver's window, ready to speak to the intercom which crackled in readiness.

'Go ahead,' said Quinn. 'The gates are opening.'

'Must work on a sensor.' He drove slowly forward, passing the little gatehouse, its lights trying hard against the fog. He continued slowly up the drive, following the verge on the right, up the gravel drive towards the main house. The dense shrubs on either side glittered with frost, Christmas-card pretty.

The driveway opened out into a cobbled parking area in front of the big house. Small lights around the big front door struggled to look welcoming in the fog. Anderson pulled the Jazz up beside a BMW and an XK8. 'And are you handling this, as SIO?' he asked, as they approached the door.

Quinn looked up at him. The grandeur of the surroundings, the size and age of Strathearn, made the moment seem intimate, as if they were physically closer than they actually were. Anderson's blond hair, with its faint trim of grey, was all over the place. His worn anorak was soaked at the shoulders. But she felt safe with him, totally safe. 'Do you want me to act as SIO? I know you are, but . . .'

'Please, no argument from me, ma'am.' Anderson was relieved.

Quinn walked up the stone steps of the house and rang the bell. They heard it sound deep within.

'Some place this, isn't it?' Anderson stepped back to look up. The house was imposing, built in a Scottish baronial version of the Italianate style a hundred and fifty years earlier. A rich man's self-indulgence. 'It took Iain Kennedy two years to restore the place; they've only recently finished. Must be worth a few million. How many bedrooms, would you say? Twelve?'

'And the rest! Straighten your tie a bit, will you?'

'You'll be asking if I have a clean hanky in a minute.' But he did as he was asked. He knew Quinn was right, and that she had every reason to be more annoyed than she actually was. He was here doing a DC's job, but she was a DCI doing a DI's job. It was that kind of case.

As he had said, Marita Kennedy was not just anybody.

Water.
   Her face underwater.
   She was free.
   Weightless.

Cocooned from the world.

Not yet born.

She was a floating bubble, a drifting cloud.

The gentle nudge of the water caressed her. Her fingers opened, her hands rose to the surface, drifting like leaves. Then they sank once more.

She could see nothing but the map of veins on the backs of her eyelids, threads of red and gold, outlined in silver, as she too sank.

She could hear her lungs protest, a crackle deep and muffled under the water, the faint prickle in her throat as the air fought to escape, the pressure building, the need to breathe. She pursed her lips, holding it all back.

Her eyes closed tighter, sharp needles of pain in her head, her brain pounding with the lack of oxygen, her heart thudding faster and faster, louder and louder.

So this was what it was like.

Strange, that she had never thought about it before.

An efficient blonde wearing navy wool trousers and a matching twinset opened the door, confusing them for a moment until they remembered that in a house of this size there would be staff. She smiled, displaying perfect teeth. She did not seem at all unnerved; instead, she opened the door wider, tucking her short hair behind her ear and peering over their shoulders as if looking for a third person. She frowned slightly, and gestured to them to come in, then the smile flicked back on. She had not asked who they were, had not asked to see their ID, and she was definitely not surprised to see them.

As they walked past her Quinn noticed the blonde was older than she had first thought – more late thirties than the twenties suggested by her model slenderness and immaculate grooming. Quinn followed Anderson across the carpeted floor of the massive entrance hall. Despite being impressed by the highly ornate ceiling and the gleaming wood panelling, Anderson thought it felt like a film set, a director's idea of what a grand Scottish house should look like. Everything was that little bit too perfect, not like a house that people actually lived in.

They halted at the bottom of the wooden staircase with its central run of thick Axminster. Another stairway ran down – to a garden-level floor, Anderson assumed. This house had once been famed for its beautiful gardens.

'I'm DCI Quinn, and this is DI Anderson . . .' Quinn said to the woman at last.

'Good, glad you're here.' The woman smiled, not even glancing at the warrant card. 'Iain will be with you in moment. We've been expecting you.'

'How?' asked Quinn, slightly wrong-footed.

'The gate has a sensor, for security. Nobody can get in or out without us knowing. Just as well, as the cameras are picking up nothing in this fog.'

'But how did you know it was us?'

'Well, it's not like this is the first time, is it?'

Quinn nodded slowly. 'And you are . . . ?'

'Diane Woodhall. I'm Marita's PA.'

'So you have CCTV in the grounds?'

'Yes. Well, with people as important as Mr and Mrs

Kennedy you can't be too careful, can you? Both cars and pedestrians have to buzz to get in and out.'

'We didn't.'

'Yes, but the sensor on the gate told me you'd arrived, and we *were* expecting you.'

Quinn nodded understandingly again. They must have reported Itsy missing, but the report had got no further than Partick Central.

'I presume you haven't found her?' Diane's voice carried no hint of worry. 'She really is a case and a half, that one. I think she sees getting out of here as a challenge. We should put one of those trackers on her – you know, the ones that fit around your ankle . . . Oh, here's Mr Kennedy now. It's the police, from Partick,' she announced inaccurately.

Quinn took the initiative. 'Good evening, Mr Kennedy. I'm DCI Quinn.' Now that she was face to face with him, Quinn had to admit that she did recognize him immediately – one of those tall strong men, with chestnut hair tinged with grey, and an open friendly face. She had seen his picture many times in the gossip columns since his marriage to Marita. He must have been in his fifties by now, the same age as herself, she thought idly.

He shook her warmly by the hand. 'I think our paths have crossed already, but I would be lying if I said I remembered. I tend to leave all that type of thing to Marita. I've a terrible memory for faces.' He turned to Anderson, eyebrows raised enquiringly.

'DI Anderson.'

'Pleased to meet you.' Kennedy indicated the way

downstairs. 'Please come down to the living room; it's a lot warmer down there.' He turned to the PA. 'Thanks, Diane. I'll let you know the score.' He led them down the stairs, the thick carpet runner on beautifully polished treads soft beneath their feet. 'I really do appreciate you coming out so late on a night like this. I can't fault the support we get from the local police, but I know we're going to have to do something about Itsy.'

The stairs led down to a cheerful, comfortably furnished room with a welcoming fire. Kennedy gestured that they should take a seat on one of the opulent leather chesterfields. 'We've been lenient with her,' he went on. 'She's coming on so well and gaining her independence, but with that she has to learn responsibility for herself and that, I'm afraid, is a difficult lesson to teach. Maybe she'll get a fright from this and take it on board. So, have you found her?'

'So Itsy's missing?' Quinn asked blandly.

Iain Kennedy's eyes darted from one to the other, taking in the fact that they were still standing, still official, as their senior rank filtered through to him. 'This *is* about Itsy, isn't it? Please don't say something has happened to her.'

'There's no easy way to tell you this, Mr Kennedy. We are not from Partick Central Station, and we weren't informed that you had made a missing person report. We are from Partickhill Station, and a woman answering Itsy's description was found a little while ago at the Barochan Moss.'

'The Moss? She got out to the Moss? That's – what – ten miles?' Kennedy's concern was suddenly acute. 'And . . . ?'

'She's . . . hurt. She's at the Western now. I strongly suggest you and your wife come along with us.'

'Right.' The colour drained from Kennedy's face. He took a deep breath, then another, as though he was having difficulty thinking. 'My wife's upstairs having a bath. They were all out looking for Itsy and Marita got so cold . . .' At last logical thought seemed to be working its way through his panic. 'I'm just thinking – DCI, DI? How badly hurt is she? We're not talking about a sprained ankle, are we?'

Quinn nodded. 'I'm afraid badly injured is what I mean. Professor Jack O'Harc asked us to come and speak to you. I think you know him.'

'Jack?' Kennedy said, distractedly. 'Yes, he's a good friend.' Then he looked up, totally focused. 'But he's a pathologist. Why was he there?' His hand went to his mouth. 'Oh my God, please no . . .'

'She's alive, but it's a long story and we would like to get you and your wife to the hospital.'

'Right,' he repeated. 'I'll call Marita and we'll get on our way.'

Quinn nodded encouragingly.

Kennedy paused. 'I'm sorry, I still don't quite understand what's happened . . .'

'There was an incident and she has a serious head injury.' Quinn's tone was reassuring.

Kennedy misheard. 'An accident?' he repeated. 'OK, OK. So we have to get to the hospital.' But still he seemed incapable of action, and simply stayed there distracted, in shock.

Anderson glanced at Quinn, who gave a covert nod of

the head in response, and handed him the keys of the Lexus. 'We have a car waiting for you outside. If you want to bring your wife, tell her to wrap up warm.' Anything to get Kennedy moving.

He gathered himself together, and picked up a cordless phone. 'Diane? They've found Itsy. Can you call Tony and Bobby and tell them to go back to the gatehouse? Yes, she's in the hospital, a bit of an accident . . . Of course, I'll let you know as soon as I can.' Then he jumped up, muttering to himself as if rehearsing his lines. 'I'll go and tell my wife.'

She raised herself up through the water, letting the water run from her face, feeling her hair clamp to the back of her neck. She looked at her reflection through the fog of steam, and lifted one foot from the water, admiring her beautifully manicured toes, red varnish peeping through the bubbles that slid slowly down her slender instep. She slid down, stretching her foot to reach the mirrored tiles at the end of the bath, swiping her big toe back and forth, back and forth, until her face came clear, with its perfect features and arched eyebrows, framed by wet, dark red hair. She blinked, and a droplet of water ran down her cheek from her eye. She wiped it away and sank back into the foam.

She lay there, under the water, listening to the echo of her own heartbeat, letting her mind drift, a fog falling on her brain. Then, through the water, she heard the deep echo of a door closing.

She raised herself out of the foamy water, listening.

But minutes passed, and there was no more to hear. She submersed herself again, in stillness, in silence, water closing over her face, swirling into her ears.

She felt rather than heard the hurried footsteps of her husband coming up the stairs.

Quinn cast her eyes around the room they had been left to wait in. 'No expense spared here,' she observed. The split-level floor was solid wood. The wall opposite the fireplace was covered with generously swagged curtains, presumably drawn across a series of patio doors that opened on to a terrace and the garden. 'Imagine having all this to yourself.'

'How the other half live, eh? There'd be some view of the gardens out that window if we could see it. I remember there's a lake – well, a boating pond – out there somewhere; at least, there was in the old days. The park was sort of unofficially open to the public back then.' Anderson was prowling the room, taking in the papers neatly arranged in a wicker basket, the baby grand on a raised platform, the six-foot-square coffee table laden with bowls filled with crackers, almonds and something covered in chocolate. Above the fireplace hung a silver-framed black and white photograph of Marita, which dominated the room. She was smiling coquettishly over her bare shoulder, and the famous hair was a black snake winding down her milk-white back. It was a beautiful yet unattractive picture, more suited for a magazine advert for French perfume than a living room. Anderson studied it, transfixed.

Quinn prodded him gently, and indicated the sideboard

and its display of photographs: Marita Simm, as she was then, being crowned Miss Caledonia in 1990; then 'Marita', as she decided to be known, posing with endless celebrities, footballers, singers and a few Anderson recognized as actors from the soaps. Mrs Iain Kennedy gracing exclusive charity events alongside the great and the good. 'Look at that one,' said Quinn, pointing to the only one of the sisters together.

Anderson glanced over his shoulder, checking that Kennedy was not about. Then he lifted the picture up. 'This was taken recently; this place has only been refurbed in the last two years. Say Marita was eighteen, nineteen, when she won Miss Caledonia – she'd be nearly forty by now. But she doesn't look it. Was Itsy the younger one?'

'So I've read in the papers, but you can't believe everything you read,' said Quinn dryly. 'I bet Marita's been having Botox to look more like her wee sister. She certainly can't grow older; her PR consultant wouldn't allow it.'

Anderson looked closely at the photograph, moving it slightly to take the glare from the glass. Two almost-identical faces, heart-shaped, snub-nosed, titian hair – but one was a closed book, the other an open one. Marita was like a polished diamond, elegant, calm, self-conscious. Itsy glowed with mischief, her smile one of genuine happiness. Anderson could see the attraction of her liveliness and warmth. 'I heard, read, that the sister is a bit . . .' Anderson tapped a finger to his temple. 'But do we know how bad she is?'

'I only know what I read in a magazine while I was waiting for a root canal treatment. The article was all about

Marita being so lovely and how she was spending her fortune looking after her special needs sister.'

'Nice of her,' said Anderson with sincerity. 'It can't be easy.'

'Not bad for publicity either,' replied Quinn acidly. 'But the sister looks normal, as you can see from that photo.'

'I'd say she's really pretty. But the more I look at it, the more I wonder about this case,' he said. 'Marita could easily have been the intended victim.'

'Or it could be a random attack, some loony hiding in the bushes,' said Quinn, not even convincing herself.

Anderson looked up sharply. 'Out on the Moss? I don't think so.'

'That bloody albatross means there are all sorts wandering around out there. So Ishbel Simm is officially the victim of a random attack, DI Anderson,' said Quinn, her tone hard and insistent. 'Please.'

Anderson nodded and carefully put the picture back.

'Are you up for driving my car?'

'Of course, ma'am.'

'Good. I can't drive through this fog and earwig on their conversation. And I do want to earwig; we have to know how she got out there.'

Quinn and Anderson locked eyes grimly at the sound of a shriek from upstairs.

The hospital was quiet, eerily quiet. Costello took up residence in an empty examination room, where a single white fluorescent tube hummed quietly to itself. Itsy's belongings had been roughly stuffed into a green plastic bag, the space for her name filled in with just the four letters, as though nobody knew what her real name was. Yet the patient number had been scribbled in, in black marker pen, her admission date and time, and a note that the contents were contaminated with bodily fluids.

O'Hare had been a star, walking swiftly alongside Itsy's trolley, through the swing doors that banged noisily behind him, talking to the doctors using technical terms, so the trolley had hardly halted to take on more bells and whistles. Then came a succession of ever more important-sounding doctors, each looking as though he had a lower golf handicap than the last.

Costello pulled on a pair of latex gloves and covered the examination couch with paper roll to catch anything that fell. She unpacked the bag, starting with the Ugg boots – original, expensive. She flipped them over; the soles were unmarked, with no scarring or cuts that might differentiate a print. The beige suede was not yet ringed with rainwater, so they were clearly very new – or a Christmas present hardly worn, perhaps. Marita would know where Itsy had got them from. She looked at the socks, Tigger socks that felt as though they had had the life washed out of them. Such thin socks, on a night like this. On her own feet she had a thinner pair then a thick woolly pair, yet her feet had still been like ice cubes by the time she'd walked from the car to the copse. Itsy's feet would have been frozen out there.

There was an incongruity too about Itsy's clothes. The silky top, peach in this light, and now sliced up the front, had a Chanel label, but the duffel jacket was from Primark.

And the cardigan was cashmere. Under those Itsy had been wearing a washed-out T-shirt, also now sliced and sodden with blood, and an old thermal vest that was bobbling under the arms. Was Itsy in the habit of stealing or borrowing her sister's clothes? The tinfoil blanket was in there as well, but Costello didn't open it. She looked carefully at the big sensible Sloggi pants, but found no blood, no sign of tearing or violent removal. Then she found what at first she thought was a hanky, and opened it out – a tiny pair of knickers. La Perla, silk, the kind of knickers you wore knowing they would be taken off soon, the kind you would want a man to remove with his teeth. Two pairs of knickers? Why? Costello thought for a moment, looking at the expensive silk. A secret life? One for 'public' view, one for her? Or him? More likely just another theft from her sister who 'had it all'.

She checked them quickly; there was some staining, but no blood. So no rape?

Costello folded them carefully. Had Itsy – nice innocent little Itsy – gone out to meet somebody? She was, after all, an attractive woman. And then there was the scarf, the expensive red scarf, folded with care like a pad or a pillow under the victim's head. Arranged with love? Remorse? Costello spread it carefully. The bloodstains had cleanly defined edges, and the pattern was repeated several times, where the blood had soaked through the folded layers. So had it been put in place while she was bleeding? One for the forensic boys. Costello cast her eyes over the padded trousers, checking back and front. No sign of scraping or tearing. The only damage had been done by O'Hare and his scissors. Costello suddenly remembered what it was that had been nagging at the back of her mind. She had been looking down at Itsy, or Marita as they thought she was then, thinking there seemed to be something odd, as if her clothes – specifically, her padded trousers – had been disturbed, but O'Hare had said or done something that had distracted her. She made a mental note to check the official crime scene photographs. In fact, she'd phone Bob MacKellar shortly, and make sure they were there for the briefing tomorrow. Had somebody grabbed Itsy, pulled at her trousers? Had a potential rapist been disturbed? Had Itsy struggled too hard, earning her a blow to the head so severe that her brain was bleeding? *Nothing about this makes sense*, Costello muttered under her breath.

'When did you notice she was missing?' Quinn asked, twisting round in the passenger seat to talk to the Kennedys, who were sitting in the back. She noticed that Anderson was going the long way round. Good man – he was giving her another few minutes in the car with them, just in case they later tried to get their story straight. But Quinn was not going to give them that time. Marita had come downstairs in hysterics, but had calmed down quickly; it was Iain Kennedy who was badly shaken. Now Quinn was itching to separate them but couldn't think of a good reason.

Marita sniffed, and dabbed her nose with a spotless white handkerchief. 'I'm sorry, all this is so much of a shock,' she said. 'Itsy was being a pest earlier – wasn't she? – about being taken to see that albatross out at the Moss. I kept telling her that we weren't allowed, in case it took fright, but Itsy could go on and on, you know, like a child.'

'Our gardener, Wee Tony –' started Kennedy.

'Wee Tony?' Quinn asked.

'Abbott, Tony Abbott, but everybody calls him Wee Tony. He was out looking for her when you came. They'd taken Itsy down to the Moss to look for the bird once or twice before. But tonight they told her it was too foggy.'

'They?'

'Tony and Bobby – Bobby McGurk. He's the . . . well, I don't know what you would call him.'

'He does the heavy work in the garden for Tony,' Marita put in. 'He has learning difficulties.'

'No, he doesn't, darling.' Kennedy's voice had a reproachful edge.

'Well, he's not exactly Einstein, is he? Just muscles. And more muscles. But the three of them are as thick as thieves. What actually happened to Itsy? Do you know yet?'

Quinn noted how long it had taken Marita to ask the question. She was glad when Iain Kennedy answered it, talking words of comfort rather than fact.

'They don't know yet. She could have fallen and injured her head; it might be one of those head injuries that starts bleeding and they lose consciousness. Jack O'Hare was there, and you know how good he is, so please don't worry, darling. We'll know more once we get to the hospital.' Iain hugged his wife, but the gesture was stilted, wooden. He looked up, noticing the route they were taking. 'Where are you going? It's much quicker to go straight down Hyndland Road from here.'

'Yes, but the fog is causing trouble at the junction,' Anderson replied smoothly. 'I've checked with Traffic; they've had three prangs there tonight. Trust me, we're a lot quicker going this way.'

Anderson had the kind of honest face you would believe no matter what he said.

Quinn could have hugged him. 'Could you put a time on any of it?' she asked. 'Any kind of timescale will help.'

Marita shook her head, and tendrils of wet hair escaped from under her hat and hung like rat-tails. 'I noticed she wasn't around at about six, I think. I spoke to Iain and then I asked Diane to go and find her. I was worried that she'd persuaded Tony to take her out to the Moss after all. But Diane rang to say Tony and Bobby were at home in the gatehouse and that Itsy had been there but left. I never gave it a minute's thought; I presumed she was on her way back to the house. That would have been – oh, about quarter past. Anyway, I had a lot to do upstairs. Then later, maybe half past seven, I spoke to you again, darling, didn't I?'

'Yes, and we realized she wasn't with either of us. I thought she might not have the sense to come in out of the cold,' Kennedy explained.

'So I rang Diane again, and Tony, to get them to track her down. Tony said he'd go down to the pond; she was always going down there to look for those bloody nightthing birds . . .'

'Nightjars,' Iain said quietly. 'Tony phoned me after

about half an hour, when he got back to the gatehouse. That was when I phoned the station, Partick Central.'

'And I went out with Bobby to look, but Tony stayed in because he'd got cold. He has a bad heart.'

'And how long were you out for?'

'We looked all round the pond, and up the far path. I can't remember how long for. But I got chilled through, and I got one of those terrible cold headaches so I had a lie-down and then a bath. All I remember is being so cold.'

'What about your security cameras, Mr Kennedy?' Quinn asked.

'I doubt they'll tell you anything. You're welcome to look but we had the engineer out yesterday to see if he could make the cameras work better in the fog, and he said he couldn't,' Iain explained. 'The sensors on the gate are fine, though.' Kennedy's gloved hand rubbed his wife's arm, giving more comfort to him than her. 'But I'd already phoned the police. She might have got out of the door and then past the gate. It's supposed to be security locked but she's a determined wee —' He stopped talking as the car swung into the hospital car park.

Quinn got out and opened the door for Marita, then leaned back in to speak to Anderson once the Kennedys were out of earshot.

'I'll stay with them. For now, I want you to find Browne — she'll still be here getting her faced looked at — and go back to Strathearn. You get that housekeeper woman's story — off the record for now, as we don't want to alienate these people — and I'd like Browne to have a look round Itsy's room, see if there's any reason why she was out on the Moss at that time of night. When you've done that, bring Browne back to the station, and persuade her to go home if you can. Then take my car back out to the Moss. We'll work out how to reunite you and your own car in the morning.'

Anderson looked at the clock, his heart sinking. 'Back out to the Moss? Tonight?'

''Fraid so. I want you to keep an eye on Mulholland for me. I don't entirely trust him to pass on all that he should. And ask the team if they've found any signs of rape. Or blood. A weapon. Anything. If you feel they've covered everything of good evidential value, then they can withdraw until tomorrow, but that is your decision not theirs.'

'What do you expect them to find? The proverbial blunt instrument?'

'And some footprints would be good. Something uncontaminated. We have two attacks, two head wounds, two mouth wounds. One victim in High Dependency and the other in the morgue. And all the time I'm thinking about Itsy, in my mind's eye I'm seeing Emily.'

Anderson had the car door closed on him before he could argue.

In the hospital waiting room Costello flicked through a magazine until she came to what her mother would have called the society page. Some footballer was standing with his arm round the Page Three floozy he had left his wife for. Two newsreaders and a pop star at a hospital benefit were holding on to some poorly children, whose small faces were etched with smiles while doubtless wishing they were back in their beds. She recognized a shot of Iain Kennedy and Marita at some charity fund-raising ball. Costello peered closely at the snub-nosed, cat-eyed face. Any more Botox and Marita Kennedy wouldn't be able to smile without using a crane. How a woman like that got a man like Iain Kennedy to leave his wife and set up home together was one thing. How she did it without being pilloried by the press was way beyond Costello. Of course, the 'tragic secret' – that the apparently blessed Marita had a brain-damaged sister – was out, 'accidentally' brought to light during a TV telethon for charity. The cynic in Costello knew it was ideal timing; the tabloids were ready to turn Marita into a home-wrecking bitch when up popped a career-saving, pretty-faced younger sister with special needs and public opinion swung back in favour of Marita. And now, with her sister lying in surgery, a tragedy in the true sense, Marita was undoubtedly going to wring every drop of pathos out of the situation. Costello turned the page to the light; just what did Marita have that had netted her fame, fortune and a series of husbands? And this one a millionaire several times over?

And what did she – Costello – have? Her idea of a good time was a night curled up on her sofa with P. D. James and a caramel log. She turned over the page, and there was a montage of colourful pictures of Helena McAlpine. One photo of her in some Moroccan souk choosing reams of dyed silk, short slightly spiked hair tucked under a headband. She'd had her glorious auburn mane cut after losing her husband and had never grown it back. The bigger picture was of her with a bearded man at a charity ball, wearing a long dress made from the silk she had brought back. Now there was a good-looking woman, Costello had to admit. Helena had aged since DCI McAlpine's death more than three years ago, and had been operated on for cancer which was now in remission. But her face was chiselled, beautiful, marked by her strength of character, sculpted by her life. Costello didn't need to read the caption, knowing it would say *the renowned artist Helena Farrell and her business partner . . .* And there would be the inevitable speculation about a romantic relationship between Helena Farrell and Terry Gilfillan. She wondered if Anderson had seen it. She hadn't heard him talk about the old Boss's wife for a while, but she knew he was still keen on her.

Oh well, the Maritas and Helenas of the world got the Kennedys and the McAlpines. She and Anderson would have to be content with a good book and amply proportioned female cops who couldn't park.

Costello jumped as a door slammed outside in the corridor, and heard running feet. A drama was kicking off elsewhere in the hospital. She squeezed her feet against the green plastic sack that was stowed under her seat, bulky with Itsy's clothes. She had the eight samples O'Hare had managed to get from Itsy in the ambulance – vaginal, three fingernail scrapes, head and mouth wounds, injuries to lips and cheek – all safe in sealed sterile plastic bags and bottles, ready for Forensics to work their magic. How much use they were going to be, she had no idea, but the chain of evidence was complete, and anything they had could be produced in court. She had done her job. Itsy wasn't dead, but she'd be as sterile as the operating theatre by now; there would be no second bite at this cherry. She squeezed the bag a little harder.

She looked at her watch and wondered if she had a cat in hell's chance of getting a cup of tea. But Quinn had told her to sit tight, and Quinn would have her reasons. The admitting doctor and the neurosurgeon had not been hopeful; in fact, they were amazed Itsy was alive at all. Severely injured, with massive blood loss, in a ground temperature below freezing and dropping ... Costello shivered at the thought.

She tried to turn her mind to her job. They needed to know the nature of the injury to Itsy's mouth. How did it compare with Stephen Whyte's? With Emily's? Were they all three connected somehow, maybe as people rather than victims? Or perhaps the connection was with Marita rather than Itsy? Where, and who, had Marita Kennedy been ten years ago, the year Emily Corbett was raped? Hosting that stupid TV show where talented pets did stunts like breaking wind to the theme tune of *Coronation Street*? That was something they needed to look into, but Costello was far too tired to think about it just now. She wondered if there had been any progress down at the Moss. She felt for her mobile and found it in the pocket of her anorak, at the same time realizing she had left her rucksack somewhere. She didn't remember having it in the ambulance. She must have forgotten it as she helped carry Itsy's stretcher up to the road. She knew she'd had it when she left Anderson's car – or had she? Her flat keys were in it. She swore out loud.

She phoned the station. To her surprise Wyngate answered.

'You still there?' she asked.

'All hands to the deck.'

'Good. Look, Wingnut, I need to get in touch with somebody at the Barochan Moss. Mulholland would do.'

'Aye, I've his number right here,' Wyngate said, and gave it to Costello with uncharacteristic efficiency.

'Costello, I've no idea where your bloody rucksack is,' Mulholland snarled when he answered. Clearly his designer cashmere was losing the battle with the freezing fog. 'No one's mentioned picking it up. Anyway, why is the victim at the Western? She should have been taken to the Royal Alexandra at Paisley; that's K Division's patch.'

'Because O'Hare said so,' said Costello, feigning the innocence of the slightly stupid.

'And does the world do what O'Hare says? Is he God? Don't think we won't take the matter further. Anyway, that photojournalist, Harry Castiglia, is on his way over to you.'

'Who?'

'You'll find out.' Costello could hear the smirk in Mulholland's voice as he continued. 'He's recording your work for the mission statement of the new service. God knows why Partickhill was chosen but the ACC was keen.'

'He'll need permission,' Costello snapped.

'The Kennedys are friends of the ACC, so it'll all be arranged. The ink won't be dry on the deal with *OK! Magazine* for exclusive rights to the funeral of Marita's sister. She looks good in black.' He paused as though he was taking a drink of something, probably a mouthful of nice hot tea from some hapless subordinate's flask.

'He'll still have to get past me, though.'

'Costello, do you want to be a sergeant all your life? You're going to have to play the game on this one. Marita Kennedy will waste no opportunity to get her picture in the paper and Harry Castiglia is the man to do it – and with taste and respect.'

'Surely Marita'll just tell him to bugger off. For Christ's sake, Vik . . .'

'DS Mulholland to you.'

Costello ground her teeth. 'Well, DS Mulholland, have a look for my bag while you're doing media liaison and clearing up *our* crime scene, will you?' She snapped the phone shut.

The door opened, and Costello looked up expecting Quinn or Anderson, but she didn't recognize this guy at all. And there was no way she would have forgotten him if she'd ever set eyes on him before – over six feet tall, longish black hair swept back, a sprinkling of designer stubble and a padded bag over his shoulder. And in his hand, a cup of tea.

'Hello?' he said, smiling almost nervously, and hovering in the doorway.

'The night Reception is down there; I think the main one is closed,' she said, staring at the steam rising from the tea. She felt her stomach churn.

He made no move to leave; if anything, he opened the door further. 'I'm looking for a DS Costello . . . would that be you?' His voice was from south-east England, polite.

'I think you know that it is me.' She eyed him suspiciously. 'Who sent you? And is that tea mine?' Instinctively she shuffled the sack with Itsy's clothes closer to her feet, like an overprotective bag lady on the last bus home.

'I was told it was a good way to make friends with the natives.' He walked into the room, holding his hand out for her to shake. 'I'm Harry, Harry Castiglia,' he said. 'I've been all over the place tonight. Good to get a seat. I thought you might be in need of some refreshment. And I was going past the machine anyway.'

'And?' She shook his hand but didn't stand up, then took the proffered cup and had a sip. Perfect, black with no sugar, just perfect. She said nothing.

'I'm the photographer.'

'So I gather, but this is not the time or the place. There's been a serious incident and the family haven't yet been –'

But he was paying no attention. He swung her rucksack off his shoulder. 'I think this is yours too.'

'Oh, thanks. I thought I'd left it down there, but Mulholland said –'

'DS Designer Cashmere? He could almost turn me gay, that one. Almost.' He had opened his own bag and was pulling out the body of a camera. 'It was he who tipped off the ACC about this case. I think he thought I was going to follow him around photographing his pretty face and do a feature on him. However, he got the picture . . . if you pardon the pun.'

'You must have been really on the ball, getting there so quickly. Or are you one of those ambulance chasers?'

If Castiglia was offended he showed no sign. 'Our brief is to follow the work of the Strathclyde Police Service, showing you in your new light for the new decade. Ostensibly it's for the visual arts exhibition in the summer but actually they want a huge PR success – Strathclyde on a big case. However, so far we've covered nothing but drug deaths, alcohol deaths and a few suicides. I was over in Govan earlier tonight and it's all a bit samey. But this has real human appeal and it'll show a good murder squad at work. Value-for-money policing.'

Costello glanced at her watch, demonstrating her disbelief.

'I bet I was called out before you, for the picturesque location if nothing else. Remember you have to think like a PR expert, not a cop.' He looked through the viewfinder of the camera.

'Why you?'

'I was born here so I suppose the powers that be think I'll understand the natives. But I grew up in London, still live there. Nowhere else to be in my line of work.'

The camera swung in her direction. She reached out and placed her hand on his arm. 'Didn't you hear me? You can't start taking photographs in here.'

'Yeah, I heard. But don't worry. I know la Marita. However, my remit is to photograph you lot as you go about the case. No need to mention what you're actually working on. Anyway, it's you I'm interested in.' For a moment his eyes held Costello's and she felt a frisson down her spine. This guy had charm and he knew how to use it. He carried himself as if he came from the world of the

McAlpines and the Kennedys, not the world of the Costellos and the Andersons. But she could look. And dream.

'However, you do have to agree,' he said, a shy smile crinkling his eyes.

'Well, I don't, so bugger off. But thanks for the tea.' She crossed her legs in a gesture of dismissal, then turned her head at a noise in the corridor. Footsteps, and a flash of reddish hair seen through the glass door panel. 'Excuse me a mo. Don't go anywhere, and don't touch anything,' she said to Castiglia. 'Or photograph it.'

5

After dropping DCI Quinn and the Kennedys at the hospital, Anderson stayed in the Lexus in the car park, waiting for Browne to emerge from A & E, with the heater on full. He closed his eyes, letting them grow heavy, trying to think about Itsy lying out on the Moss and how she got there.

A sharp rap on the window made him jump. Browne's bruised face smiled lopsidedly at him as she sank into the passenger seat.

'How did you get on?' he enquired.

'No fracture, but it hurts to talk.'

'Well, keep quiet then,' said Anderson. He offered up a small prayer of thanks, and concentrated on driving through the car park in the fog.

But Browne started talking immediately, making it clear she was still on the case, and Anderson didn't have the energy to argue.

They passed another two prangs on the five-minute drive up to Strathearn, though the roads were mostly devoid of moving traffic. They could have been on another planet. All the time he was aware of Browne's eyes on him, and longed for Costello and her hopeless map reading, and that easy silence of a well-worn partnership.

The gates opened on their approach, the sensors

picking up the presence of the car. The gatehouse was invisible, consumed by the fog; Anderson hardly saw his own frost-dusted Honda until he caught it in the powerful headlights of the Lexus. A rectangle of light fell on to the driveway as the door opened. Diane was waiting for them, her hand clasped tight around a mug of coffee.

'Come in, do.' She gave them both that smile again. Her gaze passed over Browne's swollen face without comment. 'How's Itsy?'

'All we know is that she's in surgery – well, neurosurgery. There was a bleed in her brain. Her skull's fractured.' Then he added, 'Among other injuries. DC Browne here would appreciate a wee look round Itsy's room, in case she had a diary or something . . .'

'That one?' Diane snorted. 'She can't spell.' She looked at Browne's swollen, bruised face again then said dismissively, 'Down there. Third door.'

And off Browne went.

Anderson cursed inwardly. He was very aware he was talking to a suspect, or – at least until they found out about the timing of the attack – a potential witness, and the fact that he was now on his own left him with a problem.

'Shall I call the boys in from the gatehouse?' Diane offered. 'Bobby's very upset, so he won't be getting any sleep tonight, him being the way he is.' She seemed keen to talk so Anderson decided to sit down and listen. He was shown to a comfy chair in a small cosy sitting room with a warm fire, and was offered fresh coffee from a percolator that sat gurgling in the tiny galley kitchen next door. And chocolate biscuits – Belgian chocolate biscuits.

He took one, eyeing up the rest. The coffee would keep him awake, but it was good. And being wide awake might not be a bad thing. It was starting to look as though he was destined to spend the night at the station. Again.

'Tell me about Itsy,' he probed.

Diane sighed. 'Itsy has the reading age of an eight-year-old if she's lucky. Bobby is . . . odd. A strange boy. He never says much, so it's easy to assume he's a wee bit lacking, like Itsy. But it's hard to tell. He's . . . he and Itsy are very close . . .' She shrugged.

Anderson noticed the immediate connection Diane made – Bobby and Itsy, Itsy and Bobby – and raised an eyebrow encouragingly. 'He's . . . ?'

'Different.' Diane dunked a chocolate biscuit in the coffee. 'He talks to plants. He talks to birds. He's a Partick Thistle fan. I suppose that might be a form of mental illness.'

'You said "boy". What age is he?'

'Oh, late thirties maybe. I really have no idea.' Suddenly Diane was bored with Bobby as a topic of conversation. She flicked over a dark chocolate biscuit to get to a milk chocolate one. 'But what concerned us was the stalking.'

'Itsy had a stalker?'

'No, Mrs Kennedy. But I expect you'd know all about that.'

Anderson nodded.

'And of course, she's a very busy woman. Very few folk realize how hard she has to work.'

Anderson nodded again, letting her ramble on, knowing that sooner or later he would catch up.

'She's tremendously generous, taking on Tony with his heart, taking on Bobby with him being the way he is. Well, I suppose you would expect her to take on Itsy, with them being sisters . . .'

'Take on . . . ?'

'Itsy had to go into a home after the mother died. When she came out, she was quiet, obedient and without the sense she was born with. Well, she was here for two minutes and turned out to be as crafty as a box of monkeys. Not in a bad way, but it makes you wonder.'

Wonder what? 'So what is Itsy's problem?' Anderson asked.

'Oh, brain damage. Something like that.' Diane gave a dismissive wave of the hand. 'But it doesn't stop her playing us all up. She tries my patience often enough, I can tell you.'

'I know what you mean. My son is a handful,' said Anderson encouragingly, remembering the old days when Peter really *was* a handful.

'She's always getting up to mischief, playing the fool, cartwheeling on the front lawn – it was Bobby that taught her how to do that. Well, it's all right for a little girl, but not the kind of thing a grown woman in her thirties should be doing. And especially not Mrs Kennedy's sister.'

'Suppose not,' said Anderson, rather liking the mental picture he had of a free-spirited Itsy annoying the disapproving Diane.

'And then,' Diane leaned a little too close, 'all this running away nonsense. The boys just encouraged her, taking her birdwatching, teaching her how to do bird calls. And always doing things down in the greenhouse, the three of them.'

'What kind of things?' Anderson asked, faint alarm bells calling him from his reverie.

'Oh, planting things for the kitchen, bringing things on from seed. Itsy likes to help, and Mrs Kennedy's happy with that as it keeps her occupied. I say "help", but really – wheelbarrow racing! You never heard anything like the shouting and laughing. It drives Mrs Kennedy mad, since they're supposed to be working. I mean, there's taking advantage and taking advantage, isn't there?'

'Bobby, Tony and Itsy?' Anderson acted confused. 'What age is Tony?'

'Oh, he's in his sixties, old enough to know better. You could talk to Bobby and Tony but you'd get bugger all sense out of them. They're as daft as each other.'

It was beginning to dawn on Anderson that he could sit here all night, and get no more than opinionated chatter out of Diane. Half of him thought that if she kept perking nice coffee and maybe opened another packet of chocolate biscuits that might not be such a bad thing. But he had to get back out to the Moss, and the longer he left it, the longer before he could even think about getting some kip. So he heaved himself to his feet, and set about taking his leave. 'Can I just confirm when you last saw Itsy?' he asked, as if he'd only just thought about it.

Diane thought. 'Oh, I suppose it might have been about five thirty; maybe a bit before. She was all dressed up in her warm coat, talking about going out. Down to the gatehouse to pester Tony and Bobby to take her to the Moss, no doubt.'

'Thank you, you've been very helpful,' Anderson said.

'I have to make a couple of calls. Can you ask DC Browne to join me in the car when she's ready?'

'Any time,' Diane said flirtatiously.

Anderson let himself out and walked across the drive towards Quinn's car, a mere outline in the fog. The icy cold in his lungs made him feel alive. And he could understand the sudden impulse to do a cartwheel; there was something oppressive about that house, something inhibitory. It might have grand plaster ceilings and nice carpets, but there was no soul to the place.

He zipped his anorak up to his neck and shivered slightly. He walked towards the car, thinking about the quickest way to drive the ten miles out to the Moss at this time of night – Clyde Tunnel, then the motorway? – and wondering how in heaven's name Itsy would have got herself all the way out there. He pressed the button on Quinn's car key, and paused. Was that an animal moving in the undergrowth, or a strange echo in the fog? He reached for the handle of the driver's door, and jumped as another hand clamped over his.

Costello stopped DCI Quinn in the corridor and took her by the elbow away from the visitors' room where Castiglia waited. 'Do I really have to put up with him?'

'Who?'

'Harry bloody Castiglia.'

Quinn stood on tiptoe and viewed him through the glass panel. He had his back to them, doing something with his bag.

'Is that him?'

He turned round and smiled his easy smile.

'Well, I don't think many folk would chuck him out of bed. Is he causing you problems?'

'He's not really causing me trouble at all. But Mulholland got in touch with the Chief and suggested that this might be a good case to cover and —'

'Mulholland did?' said Quinn, quietly. Too quietly.

'I didn't know what to say. I didn't know if it had come from you.'

'No, it certainly had not. I was told he was there, but that was all. I'll sort DS Mulholland out later. But Mr Castiglia hasn't caused you any problems yet?'

'Not really, I suppose. In fact, he's been quite nice so far. Brought me a cup of tea. I just don't like the thought of being watched all the time.'

'Give it an hour, you'll forget he's there. Just remember that he's very good at his job, and has a reputation for — to use an old-fashioned word — integrity. I've seen the stuff he's done; it's hard but it's honest. He'll want to show it as it is. The cold lens of the camera can't lie, can it? He will show us in a good light and that could put an end to all kinds of gossip about our station and our wee unit. I don't like the idea any more than you do, but better to have him in the boat pissing out than out the boat pissing in. So you do your job and let him do his. The only thing I'm wound up about is Marita Kennedy and the sort of media attention she'll attract. I can see us trying to keep a lid on this while she organizes photo opportunities all over the place.'

'How is she — Marita?'

'Devastated, apparently. Though to be honest, I think Iain is more upset than she is. He seems to be the responsible one of the two. Itsy Bitsy, they call her, innocent, cute and not very bright. Losing her must be like losing a puppy. She's still in surgery, and I don't think it's going well.'

'Do we have any more of the story?'

'Anderson's with Browne, doing Strathearn House now. Seems they noticed Itsy was missing at about six last night. They all thought she was somewhere else – well, it's a big place. But it's a long time for someone like Itsy to be AWOL.'

'But how did she get out to the Barochan Moss? It's ten miles.'

'That's what I'd like to know. I told Anderson to take Browne back to the station – well, she'll be full of painkillers and minus a car anyway – and go back to the Moss once he was through at Strathearn. He'll see if they've come up with any signs of rape. I'm just worried Mulholland will snaffle evidence that I want to have the first bite of.'

'I couldn't see any tearing, blood or semen on her clothes, if that's any help. But the head and mouth injuries – is there a connection to Emily? Are Itsy's injuries consistent with Emily's, with Stephen's?'

'Costello, that really opens a new avenue of investigation. Possibly some fine upstanding citizen did to Stephen what Stephen himself did to Emily. But if Emily Corbett's attacker is still out there and has just attacked Itsy, where does Whyte come into it then?'

'Ah,' Costello said quietly. 'The original team put a lot

of faith in Emily's statement. They were sure, but they just couldn't prove it. What if they were wrong? We have to consider that.'

'We'll consider it tomorrow morning.' Quinn rubbed at her eyes. 'Anyway, Mulholland has been down at Barochan all night so that should freeze his ardour a bit. Was he OK with you? Just remember, he wants a transfer back to Glasgow, so he may be one good collar away from being your boss.'

Costello pulled a face. 'That'll be the day the Devil iceskates to work.'

'Just make my final year a bit easier, Costello. This is a difficult case, and I have enough shit from above without getting it from you as well. Be nice to Mr Castiglia. Shouldn't be that difficult; after all, he's very easy on the eye, isn't he?'

Anderson should have been getting more than a little pissed off driving around in the fog in the small hours of the morning. But he had to admit he wasn't. Cruising on the M8, heading west, he was almost happy. Compared to lying in the freezing shithole that was his bedsit, or climbing between cold sheets at Brenda's house, Quinn's Lexus was sheer luxury.

On the way back to the station, Browne had commented how austere Itsy's room had seemed – no posters, no pictures, no mess. Nothing that was 'of Itsy', was how she had put it.

'What, nothing?' prompted Anderson. 'Nothing personal?'

'One photograph of the Kennedys on their wedding day, one drawing book, and a bird book. Her clothes were all . . . functional. No pretty dresses.'

Anderson smiled. No pretty dresses. He would have missed that. He asked Browne to write it up, and she nodded.

Now he was driving out to the Barochan Moss – his foot down, full fog lights on – and the big engine ate up the darkness. He messed about with Quinn's multi-change CD player, and stopped at a Beach Boys track, the *Light Album*. It was totally incongruous with the weather outside but it suited his lightening mood. He was beginning to warm up.

He had got bitterly cold talking to that wee guy in the drive at Strathearn. Once he had overcome the initial fright that had nearly stopped his heart, Anderson realized who the small grey-haired man must be. Wee Tony had on an old overcoat, a woollen hat pulled down over his ears, and underneath the old lined face of a man who has lived a few lives, none of them easy, and strange grey eyes that sparkled with a streetwise intelligence. There was something disturbing about the way the hard little fingers in their woolly gloves had clamped over his, something even more sinister about the way he had been waiting outside in the dark, in the cover of the fog and the shadow of the trees. Anderson's cop's instinct told him that this was a man who had learned to stay hidden.

It had been an unsettling exchange, and Anderson had not been in control of it. He had felt himself questioned, interrogated even, about Itsy – how she was, who was there, did they need anything? The small man had paced up and down the length of the car like a caged animal as Anderson tried to engage him in normal conversation, but to no avail. Then he'd nodded goodbye, and disappeared into the darkness. Anderson had felt himself summarily dismissed. By Wee Tony.

But as he got into the car to wait for Browne, he had been struck by one thing. Behind that apparent aggression, the man was scared, very scared. Scared of what? As Anderson drove along listening to the Beach Boys, another thought struck him – Wee Tony was the only one so far who felt strongly enough about what had been done to Itsy to get really angry.

Fifteen minutes later, he was pulling up outside the tape placed across the entrance to the lane that ran alongside the dyke at the Moss. There was a van and a police car parked at the tape, and he could see the dim lights of another two vehicles too far down the lane for him to identify them.

He sat for a moment or two, taking in the silence and the raw natural beauty of the place. Remote. Out here, Itsy could have screamed and screamed, and nobody would have heard a thing.

Usually, he reminded himself.

But the Moss was not usual at the moment. With an albatross on the loose, with sightseers trying to get at him and protection teams trying to stop them, the place was unusually frequented. Birdwatchers were out in their dozens, and all sorts of photographers. Sealing off the roads did no good; they tramped across the fields instead.

Itsy had wanted to come out here; the bird was the reason she had wanted to come. So was she followed? Did the person who brought her here attack her? Or had somebody stumbled across her and attacked her? Anderson got out of the car. He marched briskly down the lane, sure now of the direction of the common path of access, and climbed up and over the dyke.

He nodded a hello to the two SOCOs and made his way over to DS Mulholland who was talking to a tall man with a cap on. Another K Division cop? But the body language was wrong. Mulholland was being ... Anderson's mind searched for the right word through the tiredness that enveloped his brain. He had known Vik Mulholland for a long time and this behaviour was unusual. He was preening, showing off to his guest. The tall stranger had a large padded bag hanging on his shoulder. Anderson's brain clicked into gear, and he tried not to smirk as he approached.

'DS Mulholland,' he said in greeting.

'Oh, Anderson,' replied Mulholland.

'You'll be DI Anderson,' said the man in the cap, stressing the rank. Their eyes met in a split-second acknowledgement.

Anderson noticed the jacket with multi-pockets, the notebook, the good padded gloves, the standard police-issue map of the Moss. 'And you'll be Harry Castiglia?'

'I wish I was. I have half his income and a third of his talent. I'm Ronnie Gillespie, his assistant.' He pulled his cap from his head, spiking his brown hair, and Anderson was struck by how young Gillespie looked; his jowls still appeared to hold some puppy fat, or maybe too many late-night takeaways.

'Mr Castiglia has already been down here. He's gone up to the hospital now to see what's happening up there,' said Mulholland, as if he had just spoken to God.

'I'm just scouting about. It's some sight down here, isn't it?' Gillespie looked up to the sky, his breath billowing in the night air. 'It could be the end of the world, any planet in the universe.' Then he said to Anderson, 'You know the Kennedys have already given Harry permission to shadow you fully in their part of this investigation? But for now, I'd like permission, you being SIO, to do some shooting here. Harry's given me a good briefing – I'm to shoot the SOCOs doing their job. Are you OK with that?'

'Fine. I'm sure DS Mulholland will give you all the assistance he can. Has he been helpful so far?'

'If I can be of help, or if you or Mr Castiglia need anything at all, day or night, please call me,' said Mulholland, who looked as though he was not only going to invite the photographers for a drink but was willing to climb into bed with them. 'Here's my card.'

Gillespie placed the card carefully in a wallet, then he tactfully walked a few yards away, leaving Anderson slightly more free to talk.

'Any progress, on the case I mean? How are the boys doing?'

'The SOCOs have gathered some stones from the discovery site. One of them is stained; it might be blood. There's a remote chance that might explain the head injury, but not the injury to her face. That was made with something narrower, longer.'

Anderson recalled Quinn's words about the dangers of speculation as he noticed out of the corner of his eye that Gillespie was very obviously not listening, not eaves-dropping. Maybe Quinn was right about Castiglia and his assistant having a good reputation. But then it was in Castiglia's own interest to gain trust, for his team to become part of their team. 'What else do you have?' he asked quietly.

'There are signs of a struggle, somebody thrashing around. There are marks on the frost of somebody moving at speed from over here; but over there, where she was found . . .' Mulholland gestured to the bottom of the field, '. . . the twigs and bark and brashings from when they cleared this bit mean you can't make out any footprints at all. Otherwise, the strange thing is that apart from the very distinctive boot prints of the guy who found her, there appears to be only one set of prints, alongside the path over there. They go back and forth as if someone was walking up and down. They're all the same size, about a four. We're checking whether they match Itsy's Ugg boots.'

'Anything else . . . ?'

'The bloodstained stone we found – it was sitting in a small hollow with no frost underneath. Which suggests it had been there for some time. And probably had not been moved.'

'So she struck it rather than it struck her? Meaning she fell? Well, bag up anything else that might be useful.' And Anderson walked back up the path, chewing over this new information while wondering how long he could hold on to Quinn's car.

Castiglia sat down opposite Costello, screwing a lens on to a camera body. 'Was that DCI Quinn? She has a great face. Forceful. She'll photograph well.'

'You'd know.' Costello sipped her tea; it was lukewarm. 'There's a cop on our team who was X-rayed earlier, busted nose; you should take a snap of her too, before the bruising dies down,' she said sarcastically.

'Oh, I shall. She sounds like the sort of thing I want – police in the firing line. I'm focusing on the crime and the real people involved. This case – *My nightmare terror, my personal anguish. Marita tells her harrowing story.* Think how many magazines will pay good money for that crap.'

'I suppose we all have a living to earn. But of course, you are squeaky clean.'

The returning smile was more than flirtatious. 'I promise I have never sold any pictures of anyone in a compromising situation. Not sold – just used them for blackmail. Much more profitable.' He winked. 'Seriously, though, I'm too talented to sink to the depths of the tabloids.'

'Are you always this modest?' asked Costello, smiling despite herself.

'I don't have much to be modest about,' he said, without smiling. 'I don't find life difficult. I certainly don't find women difficult.'

'No, I bet you don't,' she said dryly. He was probably right. Did that make him an honest realist or a big-headed bastard? He couldn't have got through life without being told he was gorgeous by every woman he met. But his charm would not work on her, no chance. She moved slightly along the seat in an effort to create some distance. 'I'm thinking of going for a refill. Do you want a coffee?'

'Thank you. Yes – white, no sugar.' He handed over some loose change, and she took it carefully, making sure their hands did not touch. He smiled up at her. 'I reckon we're going to get through this without killing each other,' he said. 'Could you just sit down for a minute?'

'I thought you wanted a coffee,' she said but she sat down, as he messed about in his bag.

'I want to set this up. How long have you been on duty for?' He waved something in the air, a secondary light source.

'A long time. But if you're going to go flashing about the hospital, I really don't think Marita would want to be pictured without her hair done and her full face on.'

'Not my kind of market,' he grinned, as the flash went off. 'I get much better money for real stuff.'

'Real stuff?'

'Just testing.' The camera flashed again, then he leaned his arm along the back of the chair, one leg crossed over the other, black denim stretching tight over his long thigh, a casual flick of his black hair away from his eyes. 'You can delete that if you want.' He handed her the camera. 'But I'd like to use it – it's good.'

She looked at the small image on the back of the camera. She had to agree, it was a terrible picture of her, Costello, but her pose said it all. She looked like a middle-aged woman with bags under her eyes, tiredness seeping from every pore, wearing worn boots and trousers, sitting on a hard plastic chair on cold lino. The fluorescent overhead light made everything look hard and harsh. The only soft-looking thing was the bag full of bloodstained clothing that her curled ankle held protectively under the seat.

Harry was talking, long fingers circling in the air. 'I know it's a bad picture of you – you're much prettier and fresher faced – but this is filtered in a gentle grey, which makes it look impersonal. It gives you a hard edge.'

'Cheers,' said Costello, sarcastically.

Castiglia talked on as if he didn't care what she thought, his enthusiasm for his job carrying his conversation. 'What I wanted was to freeze one split second in time that says everything about your dedication, your passion for the job. And behind you, there's the clock on the wall. Look at the time. Nearly half past two. It speaks for itself.'

'It's good.'

'Do you want a copy? I'll drop one in to the station. It's not the big posh station at Dumbarton Road, is it? It's the wee scruffy one in Hyndland Road?'

Their eyes met, and she saw something conspiratorial at the corner of his lazy smile. 'I'll go and get us a hot drink, eh?'

It was half past three when Anderson parked the Lexus in his driveway. Brenda and the children would be asleep. He kicked off his shoes before going into the living room and picking up Claire's report card and two opened envelopes: one bank statement and the other a final demand, no doubt. He then padded up the stairs in damp socks, heart and legs weary with the day and night that had been. But the approaching morning would be just as difficult. He needed to talk to Quinn before the morning briefing. O'Hare wanted a word with the investigation squad re his update from the surgical team, and Quinn had forwarded the text to Anderson. The tone of the text was *be cautious* – something needed to be explained about Itsy Simm's injuries. Anderson knew in his bones it was bound to throw up more questions than answers. Just like the footprints and the blood-covered stone at the Moss.

He stepped on to the upper landing, and silently opened Peter's bedroom door. Peter's bed was empty. Winnie-the-Pooh lay spreadeagled on the pillow, with only Peggy Steggy Saurus for company. Everybody else had joined Peter in the insidious drift from his own room to Brenda's. Anderson didn't have to look to know that his son would be in bed with his wife, thin arms coiled around his head to fend off unseen demons. He sighed, and flopped down fully dressed on his son's bed, his feet hanging over the end. He looked at the model 1926 Gypsy Moth hanging from the ceiling. It had taken him bloody ages to build it, with Peter getting the glue everywhere but where it was supposed to be, and trying to stick the propeller on the wing – like the plane that took them to Benidorm on holiday – rather than the nose. All that seemed so distant now.

He watched the plane undulate in the gentle draught, thinking. He picked up Peggy Steggy Saurus and held it to his nose, hoping it would smell of Penhaligon's Bluebell, the scent of Helena. It had held the scent of her the day she had given it to Peter, but not now of course. Not after all those washes, the dip in the sea at Largs, and even going head first down the toilet if memory served him right.

He switched on the *Thunderbirds* bedside light and read through Claire's report card. He'd spent the few days he had off at Christmas decorating Claire's room, changing it from girlie pink to a very grown-up magnolia, which was now covered in posters of the latest pop sensation. Her school uniform would be neatly hung up on a hanger on the wardrobe door, the hair straighteners she had got for Christmas would be on her dressing table, Barbie in a box under her bed. Quite the little lady now. No longer a messy, mouthy, lanky girl with skinned knees. She was growing up.

He folded up the report card, and remembered suddenly how concerned Browne had been after looking through Itsy's room. 'It was a pokey wee cupboard of a room,' she'd said. 'It had no personality about it. Nobody'd made it nice for her.'

He thought about Itsy, who loved the garden and living things, being kept in a 'pokey wee cupboard', shut away from the sun. He recalled the deep, deep concern in Wee Tony's voice. Real concern, compared with Kennedy's quiet panic and Marita's initial hysteria that had quickly settled to pragmatism, as most women's did.

Anderson switched off Peter's bedside light. He breathed hard into Peggy Steggy Saurus's thick velvet neck, trying vainly to summon the bluebells. God, he was tired.

'Are you still here? I thought you'd gone home,' said Browne, slinging her bag on to the bare freezing floor tiles of the female staff toilet at Partickhill.

'I was at the hospital, waiting for Itsy's clothes to be picked up and taken to Forensics.' Costello peered at herself in the toilet mirror. 'Where have you been? Did they not send you home?'

'Well, yes, but my car has no spare tyre.' She looked out at the fog, and shivered. 'So I'm not legal to drive. With my luck, I'd get a puncture.'

'What about that?' Costello pointed to Browne's face.

'Oh, it's fine. I had it X-rayed. Then I went to Strathearn with DI Anderson . . .'

'Why were you at Strathearn?' demanded Costello, immediately jealous.

'I'd to look round Itsy's room, then do a report. But I don't know what to say. It was like a child's room. Everything's thrown together, and she's got no nice clothes, just horrible dowdy stuff. And there was no diary, no calendar to say she was going anywhere.' Browne stared forlornly at the mirror, patting the red swelling under her right eye that was threatening to close it completely. 'I don't think she likes her sister much.'

'How do you mean?'

'There's a wedding photo of Marita and Mr Kennedy, and Itsy's stuck a little photo of herself in the frame. It looks like she's sticking her tongue out at Marita.'

'Good for her!'

'She's got this drawing pad,' Browne went on. 'On the back she's written Iain's name over and over, in big letters all coloured in, like my daughter does.'

'But not Marita's name?'

'Not once. You know, she's done loads of lovely bird

drawings. There are dozens of them in her drawing book, all labelled, but I think it's someone else's writing. She's really talented.'

'Well, put that in your report,' Costello said. 'But that room – it doesn't sound like a room for a well-loved sister, more like a kid that nobody's bothered about.'

'The only thing was her wee Snoopy dog. It was really scruffy, as though she'd had it for years. But it was real; it was something of hers. Otherwise it was all cheap and . . . impersonal, somehow. Not quite the story we read about in the magazines, is it?'

'Indeed. And that house is a bloody palace. Where do you live, Browne?'

'Jordanhill. The poor part of Jordanhill.'

'My car's failed its MOT, you've got no spare,' said Costello, rooting around in her rucksack, remembering the casual way Castiglia had swung it from his shoulder. 'So tell you what, I'll shout you a taxi.'

'But the kids are at my mum's, in Balloch.'

'There's a briefing first thing tomorrow, so I think the kids will be staying in Balloch.' Costello swore with exasperation and rummaged further. 'Welcome to a murder squad.' Costello pulled a face. 'Shit!'

'Have you lost something?'

'My flat keys. I thought they were in my rucksack . . . and I bet they fell out my bag somewhere on the Moss.' She tapped her fingers on the top of the flap, thinking. 'My neighbours have a spare set but they're about a hundred and ten years old. There's no way I can get them out their bed at this time in the morning.'

'Well, my mum will have my kids for another twelve hours, so you can kip on my sofa. You do the transport and I'll do the B & B. Deal?'

'Deal.'

Browne slumped on to the floor and sat in silence, staring straight ahead of her, exhaustion hitting home. Costello slid down the wall to join her, her phone open, scrolling through for a cab number. Once she'd ordered a car, they sat for a couple of minutes, their silence accompanied only by the ticking clock. Costello became aware that Browne was breathing unsteadily. She was crying.

'What's up? Your first time on a case like this, it can be tough, you know, Gillian. Nothing to be ashamed of.'

'It's not just that.' Browne sniffed loudly. 'It's the weather, that fog. I hate it; I feel I'm being watched, followed. It's really starting to spook me.'

'Just your mind playing tricks on you,' said Costello, nipping into a cubicle and coming out with a few sheets of toilet roll. 'Here, blow on that, as my mum used to say. And if you're going to cry a lot, you should transfer back to Partick. The rumour is they have soft toilet roll up there.' She smiled at Browne, then looked out at the yellow fog which seemed to be eating up the street lamp, devouring it. She knew exactly what Browne was feeling, that sensation of unseen eyes, watching.

She was feeling it too.

6

DI Anderson got back to the station at six o'clock, after a restless couple of hours in Peter's room. His brain had not let him sleep, but his mind felt clearer. He had left a note for the kids, he had reread and signed Claire's report card. He had spent a long time in the shower and he had called in at the 24-hour McDonald's for breakfast. He was feeling so good, he texted Littlewood to see who was on duty and ask did they want anything.

Littlewood was on the front desk. 'Couldn't be arsed,' was his reply when Anderson asked if he'd managed to get home. The question had been prompted by rumours that Littlewood was spending more time at work than anybody else. For someone who insisted he was desperate to leave the job, he seemed very reluctant to leave the station. He handed over Littlewood's breakfast without further comment. He wasn't sure Littlewood's advanced arteriosclerosis would appreciate the double bacon burger, two hash browns and large black coffee. On the other hand, a heart attack might not be an easier death than hypothermia, but at least it was quicker.

Littlewood gave him a rare smile as he handed the DI a file which had been couriered over in the small hours.

There was a pause, each man with his hand on the brown cardboard.

'It was the old boy network that got you this at such an ungodly hour. We come in helpful, we old boys,' said Littlewood.

'You've had a look, haven't you?' Anderson asked him.

'I was on the outskirts of the initial investigation of Emily Corbett's rape,' said Littlewood. 'I want to be involved.'

'You know if I could I would.'

'Then do it! Quinn can't carry this on her own. There's only one way she can do this – get every man in this station on the ball 24/7. Anything less than that and the case will go elsewhere; you know it and I know it. Just make sure she knows it. Costello's not been operational for two years, and that new girl's so top-heavy she'd wreck the bar in the Three Judges just by leaning on it. I was in Vice for years, I know more about sex crimes than the rest of this squad put together, I know this case.' Littlewood's grip on the file tightened. 'You know bloody well I do.'

'Don't doubt it for a minute. Your experience would be valuable, and Quinn knows that. OK, we're ready to roll at seven. Why not wander up and join us, see if anybody dares to fling you out?'

Littlewood's grip on the file relaxed. 'Fair dos,' he grunted.

As Anderson sat waiting in the main incident room for the computer to boot up, a wave of tiredness hit him. His early morning energy spent quickly, his brain meandered back to how shit his life was, and he dropped his head into his hands. Something else was nagging at him, something he needed to attend to, and it wasn't Itsy. Brenda had left him the bank statement with good reason. A moment's glance had been enough. Brenda had given up her job to be at home with Peter, and the rent on the bedsit from hell was eating into Anderson's salary at an alarming rate.

They were skint.

Suddenly he could see Littlewood's point of view; it was much easier being here and dealing with someone else's nightmares than having to face your own.

The computer screen flashed to life. Grateful for the distraction from his private thoughts, he read the emails and attachments that had come through, and made notes for the briefing. He had Quinn's authority to access the crime database. This allowed him to go further than his own authority could. It was a sign of trustworthiness to be permitted to look at highly confidential and sensitive material that might have no bearing on an ongoing enquiry. He typed in the code for Rape. The code for Gun. Then he noticed something interesting, a familiar name on the log. Someone had been here before him. He typed in the code for Blindfold.

Then pressed Search.

Five minutes, and he had all he needed to know.

Detective Sergeant David Lambie was raking over the same ground, using his privileged access from his time on the original case. Everywhere Anderson went the quietly spoken sergeant from K Division had been there before him, sometimes years before. Was that why K Division were so keen? Were they searching for signs of Emily's rapist being active again? But why, if they knew it was Stephen Whyte? Had they been waiting for him to come back and strike again? But no, it didn't look like it, Anderson realized; the only name was Lambie's. The man was working on his own. He made a mental note to talk to Quinn.

He slid open the envelope in the file Littlewood had given him, and a pristine black and white photograph slid free of its cardboard backing. It had been preserved in a protective polythene cover; that in itself was unusual. He sipped his cold coffee, waiting for the caffeine to hit his arteries and wake him up.

The face was Emily Corbett's. Shiny dark hair, perfect skin, perfect smile. A friendly face, but even at eighteen she had a slight glint in her eye, as if she was going nowhere but the top. She had been head girl of her school, winner of a Young Scot of the Year award for her work with old folk in the community, and was going to study law at Glasgow.

Anderson's brain jumped a synapse. Could there be a connection there? Her dad was a lawyer; did he move in the same circles as Iain Kennedy? Alan McAlpine used to moan that all those folk in the Rotary Club and on the board of the hospice were as bad as the Masons.

He looked at the Corbetts' address; Emily had been brought up in Kelvin Avenue, only a mile from the station and less than half a mile from Strathearn. It had been confirmed that she still lived there, with 24-hour care. That was one interview Anderson was not looking forward to. He imagined a room like an orthopaedic ward, a bed with a ripple mattress to stop bedsores rotting her skin. He remembered hearing that the mother had died a few years back, of some kind of cancer. After a brief flurry of unwelcome activity, Donald Corbett had returned to his job as a corporate lawyer, based in London but coming home to Glasgow at weekends. No one seemed to know what had become of the elder daughter, Emily's sister. In fact, in all these memos and faxes, Anderson could not recall seeing her name anywhere. Always 'Emily's sister'.

He looked at the other picture of Emily, her pretty face beaten beyond recognition, the bruising black, her left eye closed. She had never regained sight in that eye and the bleed in her brain had removed her speech and much of her motor control. But she was alive – at least, her heart was still beating. What her quality of life was like was another matter. He scrolled through to find the initial victim statement and realized with horror that Quinn had not been paraphrasing when she said, 'She pointed at the victim.' The interview, if he could call it such, had taken place in a side ward, when Emily was only hours out of surgery. On the basis of Donna's statement, DI Yorke had given instructions that Emily was to be shown four photographs – of Whyte and three others. On seeing the picture of Whyte she had reacted violently, so violently they had had to sedate her. Two days later they tried again, using a blackboard. She had pushed herself to exhaustion trying to explain – two men, one of them Whyte, and a gun held to her head – and her story had never wavered. No wonder DI Yorke had been convinced at the time.

Anderson flicked through to the medical report, a

photocopy, heavily scribbled on. The notes were brief —
they usually were when the victim survived – with far less
content than a good post-mortem report. Emily had been
admitted with a depressed fracture of the left temporal-
parietal junction, and the CT scan showed a penetrating
injury directly to the hard palate, caused by some narrow
blunt implement being thrust into her mouth with great
force. In the margin was scribbled a note that the surgeon,
on cleansing the area with a view to putting in a bridge to
stabilize the roof of her mouth, had found an oily black
substance on the inner surface of the bony palate. O'Hare
had mentioned that. X-rays had been taken, but Anderson could tell from the feel of the file that they were not
included – the living had a right to confidentiality that the
dead did not. The initial conclusion was that a gun had
first been placed against the side of her head, then the
barrel had been rammed through the roof of her mouth,
chipping her teeth and shattering her nasal septum.

Involuntarily he ran his tongue along the roof of his
own mouth. The inner surface of the bone? That meant
uppermost, he assumed. So did that mean the oily black
substance had been deposited as the weapon was pulled
out? The substance had been analysed and identified as
dirty Silicolube. Among other things, Silicolube was used
to prevent deposit in gun barrels. He flicked through the
rest of the file. All the while his tongue rested against the
roof of his mouth, so tender, so brittle. He couldn't
imagine the pain.

He looked back at the first picture. Emily had been only
six years older than Claire was now when the rape had

happened. He would kill anybody who did that to his daughter, no question. Had one of Emily's family felt the same, and waited – for ten years – for Stephen Whyte to come back? He shook himself again, to dislodge that train of thought. No good detective got carried away with his own theories; that was dangerous, especially theories rooted in emotion and not fact.

They needed to get the wall organized, pictures up, a map for the presentation, larger-scale maps of the Moss and Clarence Avenue; they needed to pool their information and ideas. And it would be good to know what Lambie knew. And what Lambie merely suspected.

And why he was still so interested.

DCI Quinn dropped her handbag on Anderson's desk and tentatively slid her coat from her shoulders. Then she thought better of it and pulled it back up. She looked at the clock; moving on to 6.25. It was deathly quiet outside.

'It's going to be a difficult day today. You had any sleep?' asked Quinn.

'A bit. Enough,' yawned Anderson.

'More than I did. How's it going?' She reached across to pick up the file Anderson had been reading.

'I can see why you insisted on waiting for the formal ID before ploughing into the Whyte case. I've just read the report on Emily's questioning, and I'd have killed the bastard, so no doubt more than a few others felt the same way. We're going to have to be very careful indeed.' He yawned again and stretched.

Quinn resisted the urge to yawn herself. 'Ever since Itsy got attacked the whole upper echelon have been falling over themselves to help. Emily Corbett's father, Itsy's sister, both have connections. So nobody's taking any chances. I got a phone call in the early hours. We have the Itsy case to investigate along with the Whyte case. But the condition is that we take two as yet unnamed DSs from Paisley,' she growled.

Anderson nodded slowly, like a man given a bad prognosis. 'Fair enough. Better that than two separate investigations. I don't imagine they're going to let us get away without taking Mulholland on board. He is their golden boy, after all. And I need to talk to you about DS Lambie.'

'Don't worry, I've seen his activity on the database. I know about DS Lambie. I'm going to check with Neil Yorke that he really should have that level of clearance. You don't – officially. And he's acting as if Emily's file is operationally active, and it's not.' Quinn pressed her lips together. 'This is all very complicated, so I'd like you to prepare the wall right away – both cases.'

'Three cases,' corrected Anderson. 'Itsy, Whyte and Emily.'

She picked up the two photographs of Emily – before and after – pinned them up in a space speckled with pinpricks, and sighed. 'Three cases.'

'Should you not be in your office, ma'am? No disrespect, but you're not paid to pin things on the wall.'

'Neither are you. But we're the only ones here, and I do need to be aware of every single bit of this. We need to know what K Division have been thinking. They'll be sending over their dream team and that, as you say, is bound to mean Vik Mulholland. Look what we have. You, good but knackered and distracted. Costello, good but not been operational for two years. Browne, psychologically challenged and with a face fit to frighten people in the street. Littlewood, walking dead. Wyngate, enthusiastic but thick. And me? About to retire. And a one-eared Staffie with a flatulence problem.'

'The not-so-magnificent seven.' Anderson picked up what was left of his coffee. Then he put it down again. 'What do you mean, Browne is psychologically challenged?'

'My other call, at three this morning, was from Costello. She wanted me to chase up Bob MacKellar for some blow-ups of Itsy. Then she asked if I knew Browne was a widow. I confess that I didn't, though I knew she was a single parent. It turns out Frank Browne was a Good Samaritan who tried to break up a fight, got stabbed and died at the scene.'

'Christ,' said Anderson.

'Seems Browne and Costello had a cosy chat into the small hours this morning over the Ovaltine. I don't know what was said but it concerned Costello enough for her to phone me and wake me up. I don't want one of my team cracking up, Colin, not on a case like this. It's too important.'

Anderson took a mouthful of cold coffee. 'Did they get anybody for Frank Browne's death? Does Costello think Gillian has an agenda?'

'Nobody stood trial for it. Gillian was left with two

kids. She quit her nursing job and joined the force. And Costello's worried that a murder squad may not be the best place for her. She might lack a certain professional detachment.'

'She seems OK.'

'You think so? Look at her determination, to get back out there and get on with it even though she'd had her face smashed in. That's taking risks. And it's dangerous.'

Or just dedicated. Costello would do the same and you don't complain about her, thought Anderson. He asked, 'So you think she'll fall apart when the pressure is on?'

Quinn pulled a slight face. 'She and Costello obviously had a heart to heart. Costello is a good judge of people and she's the one who suspects something. So something must have been said. Which means, if Costello is right, that fifty per cent of my reliable investigative team is partnered with an emotional time bomb. One mistake, and K Division will be on us like wolves. Having Browne on the team could cost us a lot. Everything, maybe. Keep an eye out, will you? And bearing in mind you are SIO, can you cope with Mulholland being sent here? If not, I need to know now.'

'I had a wee run-in with him at the Moss, ma'am, but nothing that we can't ride. Have you spoken to him?'

'No.'

'And DS Lambie?'

'Leave him to me. I doubt Mulholland's motives in pursuing this case are altruistic, but I bet Lambie's are. He was a young cop at the time he worked on Emily's case, just out of probation. He wouldn't be human if it hadn't affected him. Remember what happened to Alan McAlpine.'

Their eyes met as they remembered. A vulnerable young cop, and a beautiful female victim with a face that had haunted him for the rest of his life. A lethal combination.

'So we'd better go easy on Lambie then,' said Anderson quietly.

The high dependency unit of the Western Infirmary was quiet. A cleaner was silently mopping the floor at the far end of the corridor, making fan patterns on the blue lino. Behind a glass screen Itsy lay in a shroud of dim light. O'Hare approached quietly, his professional eye assessing the technology that was keeping her alive. Iain Kennedy was leaning against the wall, arms folded, gazing at her intensely. Marita sat close to the glass, a blanket around her shoulders, staring blankly in front of her.

At O'Hare's approach, Kennedy briefly touched his wife's shoulder and came out to join him. 'Jack, Jack. Great to see you.'

'I wish it was in other circumstances.'

O'Hare and Iain Kennedy shook hands, the firm grip of a long-established friendship.

'Do you have any news?' asked Kennedy.

O'Hare looked at his watch. 'Six thirty. She came out of surgery less than two hours ago. It's early yet.' He guided Kennedy off to a corner with a gentle grasp of the elbow, and nodded in Marita's direction. 'How's she bearing up?'

'As you would expect. Do you think there's any point in moving Itsy to a private hospital? I want the best for her.'

O'Hare smiled slightly. 'She's got the best, Iain. McNee is the best neurosurgeon in Glasgow. And he's a good mate. All I've done is save you a few bob.'

Kennedy smiled wryly. 'It's really difficult coming to terms with a problem that I can't throw money at to make it go away.'

Like Sarah. The image of Iain's first wife crossed O'Hare's mind. She got a good settlement after twenty-five years of marriage, but no compensation for the pain of rejection and the humiliation of watching Iain flaunt Marita in the same circles that she was now excluded from. 'I think you have to be prepared for the prospect that this might not go away at all. Itsy lost a lot of blood out there, Iain. If it hadn't been so cold, she wouldn't have survived at all; it was only her circulation going so slowly that kept her alive. In some ways, it's a miracle she's got this far.'

Iain held his hands up to his face.

O'Hare did not relent. 'And if she does survive, I doubt very much that she'll be the way she was before. The brain will have suffered oxygen deprivation as well as actual damage from the fractures. And I don't need to tell you the consequences of –'

'No, you don't. But you're not a neurosurgeon, are you? Have you spoken to McNee? I mean, do you *know* any of this? Or are you just giving it your best guess?' Kennedy was angry, and his voice had risen to a tortured hiss.

Marita looked over, but turned back to her vigil.

O'Hare kept his own voice low and empathetic, recognizing the anger of guilt. Itsy was mentally a child, and Kennedy had failed in his duty of care. 'I only know what you know. I just didn't want you thinking you were going to get your old Itsy back.'

A look flashed across Kennedy's face that O'Hare couldn't quite read. 'I'm sorry. The way she was . . . Life was just opening up for her, and then this has to happen. Jack, I want to nail the bastard who did this to her.' He backhanded a tear from his eye. 'I mean it – I want that scumbag by the balls. You know how lovely she was . . .'

'I'd never met her, Iain. When I saw her I thought it was Marita.'

Kennedy did not react at all; he just kept talking as though O'Hare had not spoken. 'She was really coming out of her shell, as if some switch in her brain had clicked on. Take this albatross business – when she first came to live with us she wouldn't have remembered that from one day to the next. But she was interested in it, drawing pictures, asking questions – surprising questions. It's so cruel – she was coming out of a sort of darkness, and now she's been shoved back into it again.'

'The cops will want to talk to you again today. Iain, I have known you a long time. And I know the investigation team well. Colin Anderson is a good guy. Don't hold anything back from him.'

'I don't have anything to hold back,' said Kennedy, his voice offended.

O'Hare looked his old friend straight in the eye. 'You sure? I'd think hard about that. They're not stupid people, and you will not pull the wool over their eyes, not for a minute. I'll say goodbye to Marita before I go.'

*

It's been a lifetime habit of mine to get up early in the morning. I like seeing the world before anybody else; I like the feeling of having it to myself.

Recently, I've been taking an early morning stroll down to the Hazbeanz coffee shop, getting used to the old town again after being away for so many years. Remembering the way it used to be, the mornings in the rain, mornings in the fog.

Glasgow is a city of its weather. That hasn't changed.

And Hazbeanz is good. They know how to do a *caffè Americano*. And the French toast is excellent. It's a bit of a habitual haunt these days for the early risers of the west side of Byres Road. And of course for the cop shop. Most of them pop in here in the course of their working day. Easy to get to know them when the girl behind the counter calls them all by name, usually followed by some soap opera gossip shouted over the noise of the coffee grinder. It's bitter cold this morning, the fog is still low, and Hazbeanz is a cosy beacon of light in a dark and depressing urban landscape. The smell alone – a warm aroma of freshly baked croissants and ground coffee – is enough to cheer the soul.

I stand in the queue, order my usual, have a wee bit of chit-chat with the girls, especially the one I call Screeching Rita. She has a voice you could drill teeth with. They know I like to read my paper while the bread is soaking for my French toast. I like it well soaked, and well cooked. It gives me time; that's why I order it. *The Daily Record*, opened at the Just Joan agony page, gives me cover for my face. And a good laugh.

Bannon the estate agent comes in, says hi to the girls, and orders his usual – bacon roll and large white coffee.

I nod to him in greeting, then go back to the problem page. Somebody's fed up paying for their daughter's chaotic lifestyle. They don't know how lucky they are having a daughter.

Rita shouts from behind the counter. She's been rushed off her feet this morning. The cop shop was open early. Bannon nods. Rita shouts that it's all to do with that body that was found down the lane back there. Bannon nods again, slightly more tentatively.

Rita goes on: 'Still, it's an ill wind, them not having a canteen over there, and them working all hours, needing lots of sausage rolls to keep them going.'

The door jangles, and another man comes in. He's on his mobile, smiling. 'Black tea no sugar, right?' he says down the phone. He turns his charming smile to Rita.

Rita wipes her hands on her apron, dismissing Bannon. 'Good morning, sir, can I help you?'

I look round the side of my paper.

And somehow it all stops.

Dead.

By quarter past seven the entire squad, such as it was, was assembled. So far there was no confirmation about who exactly was coming over from K Division.

Anderson stood up, taking in a view of the team. Then he corrected himself – of the Partickhill branch of the team. The swelling on DC Browne's face was starting to darken, making her look like a panda. He watched as she turned her gaze to the pictures of Emily, eyes full of pity. Emily Corbett's case was highly emotive, and Browne was new to a murder squad and she hadn't yet had time to develop the skill of detachment. If she was emotionally vulnerable, this case could test her. And what of Lambie, who seemed to have some emotional agenda of his own? Anderson was keeping his fingers crossed that whoever K Division sent over from Paisley, it wouldn't be him.

Wyngate knocked over a pile of files and scrabbled on the floor to rescue them. While he was on the floor the fluorescent light flickered.

'Oh, Christ,' muttered Littlewood, willing the fan heater to hang on to life.

At the back of the room, Costello was sitting hunched up beside the radiator, her arms around her knees, her heels on the seat. She looked frozen but deep in thought. The door opened, and Ronnie Gillespie, the assistant photographer Anderson had met at the Moss, came in carrying two heavy bags of equipment. Behind him was another figure. Anderson couldn't help but compare them. Both men were tall, dark and slim, but the gods had smiled on the second while merely giving Ronnie Gillespie a quick pat on the way past. This must be Castiglia, the man himself. He was carrying a cardboard tray of coffee, tea and hot croissants.

'Don't thank me,' Castiglia said. 'They're from the girl at the coffee shop.'

The team fell on the food like starving hyenas.

'Cheers, Harry,' said Costello. Anderson had noticed that her tea was handed to her, specifically to her, by

Castiglia on his way past. Had there been a bit of communication going on between them? His suspicion was confirmed when Castiglia put a tin of Chappie dog food on the desk and muttered, 'As requested.' Anderson knew exactly what the man was up to. Harry Castiglia was well versed in charming women to get his own way. He might have met his match in Costello, but Nesbitt the wee brown Staffie was one way in.

Harry walked up to Quinn with an energetic stride, his roguishly handsome face smiling, and Quinn smiled back. Then Castiglia introduced himself and Ronnie Gillespie to the squad, commanding the room with an ease that Anderson wanted to find sickening, except the charm was working on him as well. 'We'll push off elsewhere during your briefing,' Castiglia was reassuring Quinn. 'We understand about full consent only being given for Ishbel Simm's case, not Emily Corbett's. But we are still detailed to follow you.'

As he spoke, Anderson noticed him glance in Costello's direction, twice. Costello looked up in Castiglia's direction, and a shy smile passed between them.

Castiglia then turned his charm directly on to Anderson. 'Good to meet you, DI Anderson. The man in charge.'

'Colin. Hello.' Anderson shook the proffered hand.

'You've already met my assistant, Ronnie.'

'Yes, either late last night or early this morning, I can't remember.'

Castiglia nodded. 'Well, that's something I really want to get across, the hours you guys put in.' He clasped his hand around his own neck, and rotated his head; Anderson could hear the bones crack. 'I'm knackered and I've only been shadowing you for twelve hours.' He noticed the prints Quinn was now pinning on the wall, and dropped his voice slightly. 'I think we'd better push off. No problem if we dump some stuff in the corner while we scout outside? I don't fancy leaving it in the car.'

'If you did it wouldn't be there by lunchtime.'

'We'll be back after the briefing then.' Castiglia nodded a general goodbye and retreated, picking up the can of dog food on the way out, tossing it from hand to hand. He clicked his tongue and Nesbitt trundled out from somewhere.

As the door closed, the light went out.

The board was busy, divided into three sections, with headings and subheadings. Before and after photographs of Whyte, Emily and Itsy had appeared, with one of Marita tagged on the end for comparison. There was a drawing of Strathearn and a list of who lived there, including Robert 'Bobby' McGurk and Anthony Abbott. There was an Ordnance Survey map of the Moss that clearly showed the triangle of flat land tucked between the Clyde and Black Cart Water. The photograph of Emily lying in the bracken had an arrow going to a map of Paisley and the Gleniffer Braes. For the benefit of anyone coming in from K Division, Wyngate had added a simple street map of Partickhill showing the station, number 95 Clarence Avenue, the Corbett family's house, and Itsy's home at Strathearn. All so close. Greater Glasgow covered more than sixty-two square miles; it seemed too much of a coincidence.

Wyngate had to stand on a chair and belt the end of the fluorescent light with a broom handle before the light eventually buzzed and flickered back into life, while DCI Quinn gave them a résumé of who Harry Castiglia and Ronnie Gillespie were. She had read from a printed email, '. . . not to shadow the investigation as such, or to document it, but to record the human side of the modern police service as it faces its biggest challenges in today's society . . .'

She stopped reading and wrinkled her nose as if she had just smelled bullshit. 'Just be nice to him, and don't give him any excuse to complain about us being obstructive. It's important we don't screw up in front of HQ.' Quinn relaxed a little and perched on the side of the front desk. 'On a personal note, I think we all agree it's in the public interest that we catch who is responsible for this. By "we", I mean I think it should be us. Here, in this station. We are threatened with closure, but success in this might sway the decision in our favour. We all have a vested interest here, we work well as a team, and we don't want to be transferred to Oban. So I know I don't have to ask – every effort until we get these guys. Thanks. Over to you, Colin.'

Anderson coughed gently, bringing the assembled team to order now that the lighting had been restored. He thanked everyone for coming in early, aware that all eyes were focused on the faces staring out at them from the whiteboard.

'Background first,' he began. 'Millennium night, ten years ago. There was mist on the hills and a ground-lying fog on the Gleniffer Braes road. And I'm sure you can all remember where you were at that time.'

'No fuckin' idea. I was too pissed,' said Littlewood, and the tension in the room snapped. Even Quinn smiled.

'I don't doubt it. But for Paisley cop shop, it will always be the night Emily Corbett was raped and left for dead. It wasn't our case, so no matter how much you think you know, I want you to read the printout.'

Quinn took over seamlessly. 'Emily's father is Donald Corbett, the corporate lawyer. He has friends in high places and enough money to buy more if and when he needs them. I am going to have to tell him that this case is being reopened and that we need to re-interview his daughter. But nobody goes near that family without my specific consent.'

Anderson tapped the photograph on the board. 'This is the family home in Kelvin Avenue, under a mile up the road.'

'You probably all know the house,' Littlewood put in. 'It's that one on the corner with the big conservatory; it has a long beech hedge about twelve feet high. And huge security gates, come to think of it. I think they built on an extension for the lassie – she's bedbound now, isn't she?'

'I believe so. You'll see that Emily's car was tailgated and rammed repeatedly, until she crashed into the gates of the electricity substation up on the braes. She was dragged from the car, blindfolded, and had a gun held to her head; she was raped and beaten. Please note the injury to the roof of the mouth; that's important. It was probably made by the barrel of the gun being rammed through the bone, there. A parody of the rape, the psychologist said at the time. Traces of lubricant left in the wound have now been identified as Silicolube, which is used on gun barrels, among other things. During the attack the blindfold slipped, and she caught sight of one of her attackers. The investigation team at the time had no leads or evidence as to who the other guy was. But she was adamant that there was another person present. It is clear that one of Yorke's logical reasons for later thinking Emily had made the wrong ID, or was mistaken, was that there was nobody in Whyte's circle – no likely candidate – to be his accomplice. No friends or acquaintances that weren't vouched for or alibied. After being raped, Emily was put in this four-by-four . . .' Anderson held up a photograph of a burned-out vehicle, '. . . driven to the hairpin bend at the top of the braes, and kicked out down the hill.'

He pointed to the colour photograph, a tangle of pale limbs in dead brown bracken, the angle of the ground dangerously steep. A red ribbon hung from Emily's black hair, coiling across her back like rose petals. Anderson was aware of Gillian Browne sitting with her hand over her open mouth, a tear moving down her cheek. 'Fortunately she landed head first, downhill. That helped keep her airway open, otherwise she would have choked to death on her own blood. This vehicle – a stolen Isuzu – was found burned out in Easterhouse later, on 1st January. Identified by tyre marks left on the road. Emily indicated, very firmly, that there were two people in the vehicle that rammed her, and the fact that she could be thrown from a moving vehicle suggests there was indeed more than one attacker. There was no forensic evidence at the scene, nothing at all. It was a well-planned and well-executed attack.'

Using the penlight, Anderson pointed next to a bad black and white photograph, all stark peroxide hair and glowering black-lined eyes, obviously taken from police records for some previous arrest. 'This woman is Donna Campbell. Her drinking buddies in the Clansman pub in Greenock the following evening, 1st January, later reported her as telling the following story. Her man . . .' Anderson pointed to the picture of an acne-scarred young man with a bad mullet, '. . . Stephen Whyte, failed to meet her for the millennium bells. Instead, he came home some hours later. He was quite sober at that stage, but then he started drinking. He said he'd been with friends, though the friends later denied being with him as far as they could remember. Donna didn't believe a word of it, and accused him of messing with another woman, which led to a drunken fight. In the morning, still drunk from his early-hours session, Whyte caught a report of Emily's attack on the TV news and boasted to Donna that he'd been involved. How involved, he didn't specify. And Donna had no idea who the other man might have been. Donna was well pissed off, having got a lovely black eye in the fight, and she repeated his story in the Clansman. Well, people know other people, and they talk. By midday on the third, that intelligence had reached K Division. They started enquiries in Greenock, including a visit to Whyte that same day at his home in Erskine. That evening, when

Emily came out of surgery, she was shown this picture of Whyte and identified him. K Division set out late that night to have another word with him, only to find he'd already legged it. DI Neil Yorke was the senior investigating officer. As you'll remember from your law classes, we cannot arrest on suspicion; so there was then, and is now, absolutely no physical evidence that Whyte was involved.'

Anderson then indicated the second section on the wall. 'Yesterday, Stephen Whyte was found dead. He'd been battered to death or near death, and strung up, his lips superglued together. Later investigation revealed a significant wound to the soft palate, as though something had been rammed in, hard. Swabs have been sent for analysis.' He paused to let those writing notes catch up. 'Now we need to track Whyte's movements from the moment he landed at Glasgow Airport on Saturday morning 30th January until the Inneses discovered him yesterday, Tuesday 9th February. In particular Saturday the 30th. According to the statement from the uncle, he got off an early flight at Glasgow and went straight to the family home, which is ten minutes at most from the airport. He had a cup of tea and a shower, and a chat with his bedridden mother.' Anderson paused. 'Then he said he had to go out, and he simply buggered off. Mid to late morning is as far as we can narrow it down. We need to know if anybody saw him after that, because that is the last we know of his movements until he was found hanging yesterday. We need to speak to Donna Campbell, in case she knows more now than she did then. Interestingly, the preliminary findings show that Whyte's body had been battered mostly on the left parietal area, the left side of the face and the left temporal area to produce injuries that might be seen as mimicking exactly those inflicted on Emily.' Anderson swung the penlight beam back and forth between the photograph of Emily's shattered face, and the bloated obscenity that had been Stephen Whyte's. 'However, let's stick to what we can find out. For instance, who knew he was flying home, other than possibly his mother?' Anderson paused. 'Please do not let who this man is, or what he might have done, influence the way you investigate his death. That is not our judgement to make.'

'Fair dos,' said Littlewood, nonchalantly, and blew a bubble of gum that burst with a loud pop.

The rest of the team ignored him.

'Now we come to the events of last night, the case of Ishbel – known as Itsy – Simm. Most of you are up to speed on this one. She sustained blows to the side of the head; the left parietal area. She came out of surgery just before five this morning – alive, but only just. She now has a steel brace at the base of her skull to stop her head falling apart like a split coconut. So she will not come out of this well. And she also sustained a separate penetrating injury to the roof of the mouth, the extent of which is as yet unconfirmed. So, is there a connection?

'To make matters worse, I don't need to tell you who Itsy's sister is and that the media attention so shunned by Donald Corbett will be actively encouraged by Marita Kennedy. The media attention at the time of Emily's rape was very hard for the family. One journalist was even threatened with legal action. So please avoid all contact with the media. And all approaches to the Corbetts will be made through DCI Quinn, as she said. I think you should all read the statement Emily made after her attack. It is not an easy read, especially when you see how many hours it took to get those few facts, but I'm sure you will agree that it is —'

'A testimony to the bravery of an extraordinary young woman.' The voice drifted in from the back of the room. All heads turned to the two men who had come in unnoticed. DS Lambie stood slightly behind Vik Mulholland, his chin up, as if proud to have spoken out.

'Indeed it is, DS Lambie,' Anderson said courteously. 'Everybody here is aware of the tragedy that unfolded that night. DS Mulholland, good morning.'

Vik nodded in acknowledgement. 'Partickhill! My God!' He looked around him. 'Abandon hope, all ye who enter here, eh? Even the rats have deserted this place!'

Anderson glanced at Quinn, who gave him the slightest nod to proceed. 'Good to have you on board, Mulholland, even if you do see us as the *Titanic*. Please take a seat. As you see, we are in the middle of a briefing. DS Lambie, you worked on this as a youngster, didn't you? Have you anything to add?'

Lambie was caught slightly unawares. Then he found his voice. 'I know you might have some doubt about Emily's ability to recall the events of that night. But she identified the make of the four-by-four from a selection of photos we had by the distinctive grille and the lettering — she indicated it was an Isuzu we were looking for. If she was so accurate in identifying the vehicle, why should anyone doubt her insistence on there being two men in it? Why should we doubt her ID of Stephen Whyte? I know she couldn't speak and was only pointing, but she was absolutely, unshakeably, certain. You can't begin to imagine the effort and courage it took her to tell us as much as she did.' He pointed at the photograph of Whyte. 'Make no mistake – he raped Emily Corbett. She saw his face.'

Quiet words, strongly spoken.

Anderson nodded. 'Thanks, David, it helps to have that perspective on it. What did you make of Whyte's girl-friend's story?'

Lambie blinked hard and shoved his specs up on the bridge of his nose, as if his confidence had gone again. 'I spoke to Donna Campbell, Donna McVeigh as she is now, many times. She has six convictions for breach of the peace and shoplifting, and she's not easy to deal with. She was eighteen years old then, and bitter with Whyte for two-timing her, as she thought. So she badmouthed him in the pub. We heard about it a day or so later, on the third, but she tried to hold out for some kind of reward in exchange for confirming it all to the police. She certainly wasn't going to get one, but it cost us time. We went to see Whyte immediately, but we were hampered by having only Donna's word to go on. And several more hours elapsed before we could get an ID from Emily, by which time Whyte had disappeared. We had no actual evidence to link him directly to the rape, just Emily's statement and Donna's. I don't think Donna has changed her story at all over the years.'

'But what about the other guy in the car?' asked Costello.

'I mean, they stole a car, attacked and raped Emily, burned the car and separated – they must have known each other well. That is teamwork, a plan. But as nobody seems to have come forward to say, "Oh yeah, Stephen Whyte and Mr Other are the best of friends," there seems to have been a degree of secrecy about their liaison. The same secrecy that has hidden any connection with Whyte all these years? Was it Mr Other who lured Whyte away? Then killed him?'

The room fell silent.

Anderson said. 'Which might suggest the death of Whyte was not to avenge Emily, but to silence Whyte. That would fit with the superglue.'

Lambie asked, with the same quiet intensity, 'Do you think we can trace the other man, after all this time?'

'Hope so. I don't want to cast doubts on your approach at the time but we need to talk to Donna McVeigh again.' Anderson pointed to the sour-faced peroxide blonde in the photo. 'She might have had some knowledge of him coming back. We'd need to send somebody non-threatening, chatty, female . . .' His eyes rested on Browne.

Browne looked chuffed, and nodded. 'I'm game.'

Lambie spoke up, his eyes twitching behind his glasses. 'Whoever carried out this attack was forensically aware. Nothing was left at the scene of the rape, and the vehicle was destroyed by fire. The lab went over everything else. But that was ten years ago. I'd like to suggest we should ask to get anything we have retested. Emily's clothing, anything.'

'We're a wee tad ahead of you there,' smiled Anderson.

'Good,' said Lambie, genuinely impressed. He looked at the female cop with the spiky hair. 'Personally, I'm convinced we had one of the right men in Stephen Whyte. But he had a low IQ, not the skill or the patience to plan an attack like that. There was a bigger intelligence behind Emily's attack.'

Mulholland stood up, running his forefinger through his designer haircut, and a look passed between Browne and Costello. The look didn't go unnoticed by Quinn.

'So,' Mulholland began, casually undoing the buttons of his designer jacket, 'ten years ago we have Emily battered, with an injury inside the mouth. Raped. We now have Itsy, battered, with an injury inside the mouth, but was she also going to be raped out at the Moss?' He picked up a black and white picture showing Itsy lying curled on her side, and pointed to her waist. 'Look at the way her trousers appear to have been pulled down here. Somebody might have been disturbed in the process of attempting rape, but I don't think that has been considered.'

Costello got to her feet. 'He's right,' she said reluctantly, holding up one black and white twelve-by-eight that MacKellar had delivered that morning and one, much enlarged, obviously taken later at the hospital. 'The trousers were cut off her at the hospital and indentations on her body show that the waistline of her trousers was not at her waist, but down over her hips. The zip was still up, so had her trousers been tugged down? Was she about to be raped? Or was her attacker disturbed? As far as the surgical staff could see, there were no signs of actual rape on the body. However, bruises are starting to show on her lower legs and upper arms so there is some suggestion of a struggle. Her boot was half off, as if she had tried to run and caught it on something. The usual body samples and her clothes are away being tested for fluids, et cetera. And –'

'None of that matters if he was disturbed before he finished what he'd set out to do. The birdwatcher did hear a struggle –'

'*And*, she'd scream her head off if she was about to be raped,' said Costello coldly. 'He would have heard a lot more than that.'

'Difficult to scream with a gun rammed through the roof of your mouth,' said Mulholland. 'So we should treat this as an attempted rape. The assault was the rapist silencing his victim *before* a sexual attack that was interrupted.'

'Or maybe not,' said Costello, sniffing haughtily. 'What's not consistent with that is that Itsy had been . . .' she floundered for the right word, '. . . arranged, in the recovery position almost. So I don't get how that fits in with the attacker being disturbed. He'd surely just bugger off, not wait about and arrange her.' Costello gestured to the photograph of Itsy's head. 'Look, her jacket's done right up. She's lying on a folded scarf, a scarf that was carefully tucked under her head like a pillow, *after* she started bleeding – the bloodstains confirm it. Somebody else did that.' She stabbed the board with her finger.

'So she was made comfortable, and then left to die,' said Anderson, his quiet words drifting over the silent room.

'It would seem so,' replied Quinn. 'A psychologist would say that showed a degree of care. Or remorse.

Maybe you're both right; maybe she was attacked, but by somebody who had feelings for her.'

Anderson looked up at the board, at the name Robert 'Bobby' McGurk. *Him being the way he is.*

'You got something to add?' Quinn asked him.

'No, sorry.'

'So who was doing the background on Itsy?'

Wyngate stepped forward, coughing nervously. 'Itsy – Itsy Bitsy to her friends – Ishbel on her birth certificate. Brain-damaged as an infant. Reported mental age of eight. Lived with her mother until the mother's death five years ago, when Itsy was thirty. Then she was in a home for two years, which caused marked deterioration in her physical and mental well-being. Her sister, Marita Kennedy, took her to live at Strathearn after she had broken up Iain Kennedy's marriage and was in need of some good publicity.'

'Wyngate! Facts only,' chastized Quinn.

Wyngate went back to his notebook. 'Itsy was last seen sometime before six p.m. yesterday at Strathearn House. It would appear that nobody from Strathearn took Itsy out to the Moss. Mr Kennedy has good security and vehicles have to go through a controlled gate. No cars went in or out that evening.'

'So how did Itsy get from the house which is – what? – five hundred yards from us here, to the Barochan Moss which is about ten miles?' asked Mulholland, trying to gain control. 'Not an easy place to get to; you have to *know* it. And it was exceptionally cold last night.'

'From the wrong-victim angle, it might be worth noting that Partick Central has reports of somebody trying to intimidate and harass her sister. We've asked for those records,' said Anderson. 'I've already allocated a task list, but I didn't know who was being sent down from K Division. Lambie and Mulholland, you can each team up with one of our lot so you miss nothing. Meantime, DS Mulholland, you and I are going to interview Mr English once we're through here. We'll walk him through the sequence of events – try and establish a timeline which we can work backwards from the 999 call that came through to the control room at nine seventeen.'

DCI Quinn got to her feet. 'Right, that's it, I think. DS Lambie, can I have a word?'

Mulholland spoke out. 'Actually, I want a word.'

'Why? Is your name Lambie?'

Mulholland picked up a leather folder he had left on the desk, and let it fall open into his palm. It held a series of black and white A4 photographs. 'Ignore this at your peril, DCI Quinn. This case is too big for you.' He turned the photographs over, one by one, reciting a litany of names with determined clarity. 'Emily, Janice, June, Vivienne, Joanne, Iris . . .' His face was distorted into a vengeful sneer. 'You've no idea about this, have you? Nothing!'

With the skill of a pickpocket, Quinn tipped his folder closed with one finger, and the spine of clips securing the photographs flipped over with a slap. Taking the folder from him, she said, 'Thank you for drawing this to my attention. My office, please, DS Lambie.'

'Excuse *me*!' said Mulholland, stunned.

'Why, what have you done?' asked Quinn. 'I'll speak to you later. Now go out and interview Mr English. Find out

what he actually heard. That's an order, DS Mulholland.'
She guided Lambie into her office, abruptly slamming the
door and closing the blinds.

Mulholland stormed out and tripped over Nesbitt, who
was trying to sneak in. Costello, Browne and Wyngate all
exchanged glances as they heard Mulholland retreat down
the corridor, swearing loudly that he was away to get his
bloody car.

'Jesus Christ!' said Littlewood. 'I'd better have a puff of
my stuff. Too much stress.'

Quinn spent a few minutes flicking Mulholland's notes
back and forth. At one point she slipped her specs on,
examining a few dates more carefully, then she closed the
file and placed it on her desk. 'Well, DS Mulholland was
right about one thing – I had no idea about any of this,'
she said. 'So do you want to enlighten me, or will I ask
him? It's obvious to me that you've been working on this
longer than he has. And you are the one with the legitimate access.'

Lambie sat, his glasses slipping, his mouth opening and
closing like a dying fish.

'Oh, Lambie, stop looking so shocked. Did you really
have no idea that Mulholland might have an agenda of his
own? You know how ambitious he is, always has been.
He's not above standing on a colleague's head to get promotion. He'll happily take credit for the hard work of
others. It wouldn't surprise me to learn that he's been
making use of your privileged access. For heaven's sake,
you look as though you're about to faint.'

Lambie did indeed look as though he was going into shock.

'I was joking about the fainting, DS Lambie, not suggesting it.'

'Sorry, ma'am.'

'Do you need a cup of tea?'

'No, thank you, ma'am.'

'So do you have anything to add?'

Lambie pulled an old notebook from the inside breast pocket of his jacket, opened it and handed it to Quinn, who began reading. In small precise handwriting was a list of names and dates, followed by a line of symbols after each. 'Emily Corbett, 01/01/2000,' she read at random. 'Lucy McCallum, 07/11/08. Iris Everitt . . .' She paused.

Lambie knew the list off by heart. 'Tuesday 30/08/05,' he continued. 'Iris was twenty-two, a design student, raped on her way home from university —'

Quinn held up her hand, halting Lambie mid-sentence. 'Even after only a few minutes, I can see that these two lists — the one in Mulholland's file and the one in your notebook — are by no means the same. Surely, if you were using the same search criteria, they should be.'

'I don't know anything about Vik Mulholland's list. I didn't even know he was making one. But I was very careful in my search. The MOs involved a gun, penetrating mouth wound, rape, blindfold, evening or night. Combinations thereof. I've tried to keep it really tight, ma'am.'

'And you've been doing this all the time you've been at Paisley. Ten years?'

'Yes, ma'am.'

'Ever since Emily?'

Lambie hesitated. 'Yes, ma'am.'

'And not just here in Strathclyde. These cases occurred all over Scotland.'

'There have been huge changes in the databases over the last ten years. They are compatible now, ma'am; it's truly national. Some of these are cold cases, and some are solved cases ...' he pointed at the notebook, '... but they're all the work of the same perp or perps; I'm sure of it. I've been waiting for a DCI brave enough to take this on,' said Lambie.

Quinn regarded him over the top of her glasses. 'Don't goad me, Lambie. So you think there is a serial sex attacker operating in this country? You are under DCI Yorke? I know Yorke; the Corbett case was a low point for him, personally and professionally. If he thought there was something in this, he would have moved on it.' She paused to consider. 'Look, I'm prepared to phone him and get his take on the matter. He's not a fool. He might already have tried to move some of this forward, and been unable to for some reason that we don't know. No doubt each incident was thoroughly investigated at the time.'

Lambie's face remained impassive, but he was working hard to maintain it. Quinn was used to the lower ranks talking back. Costello did it on a near-daily basis – and Anderson wasn't all that far behind, though in a more subtle way. But there was a deep, slow-burning passion here, she sensed. What happened to Emily would have been shocking to a young cop. It would haunt him. It looked as though it still did.

She tried again, her voice softer. 'David? You've been working on this almost since you joined the force. All your searches on the database are time-stamped, so where did Mulholland get it all? Did he think you were on to something and try to hijack it from you?'

'Obviously.' Lambie slid his specs from his face; he was just a chubby-faced youngster without them. 'When he joined us about three years ago, he was described as a real high-flyer. He was teamed with me, and I thought he was a good mate. Initially I just asked his advice, figuring two heads were better than one. I didn't realize he would use it for his own advantage. But I reckoned whoever did, or planned, what happened to Emily would do it again.'

'Do you have any close connection with Emily?'

'No,' he said brusquely. 'I was just on the original case. But this man, or men, has struck again. I am not wrong.'

'But Whyte did it to Emily. You know that.'

'We knew it then too. But Whyte disappeared. I thought he might reappear, so I watched for his activity on the national database. Then I realized I was stumbling on all those other rapes over the years with a similar MO. I thought it might be the other man. It keeps happening. Some have been solved, but not all. Nobody will listen to me.' He dropped his hands to his sides, a gesture of defeat.

'I'm listening, David.'

Lambie stretched his fingers out, staring at the palms of his hands, as if rehearsing. 'I think it needs a task force.'

'You said yourself, some of them were solved. Do you think we have the resources to —?'

173

'That's all I keep hearing. Solved! Not our jurisdiction! We don't have the money.'

'It's not bloody surprising they're not going to be re-investigated, is it? No connection has been established.' Quinn became thoughtful. 'Tell me, David, hand on heart, do you believe that all the attacks are related? It's a big geographical and temporal spread. Ten years is a long time.'

'I've read everything available,' Lambie said tiredly. 'I've been thorough and careful. If I hadn't, the list would have been a hell of a sight longer.' He leaned forward, his hand outstretched. 'Can I look at Mulholland's list?' he asked.

'Not just now. Go out and talk to Anderson and Costello. Talk to any of them, but not to Mulholland. I'm going to make a few calls.'

Quinn waited until Lambie had left her office. Then she picked up the phone to call DCI Yorke at K Division.

7

'Come over here a minute, out of Quinn's earshot,' said Costello, pulling out a seat so Lambie could sit down. 'I've been giving Gillian here the low-down on Mulholland, and what an arse he is.'

'I don't think we should be so hard on him,' Browne volunteered. 'He lost somebody he loved, you said. Who knows what effect that might have had on him?'

'I think we all know what effect it had on him. It turned him into a complete wan –' Costello was silenced by a glare from Anderson.

'You're right, Gillian, we should make allowances,' he said, earning himself a subtle two-fingered salute from Costello. 'Right, Lambie, talk us through it,' he said.

Costello turned the Anglepoise to dazzle Lambie's eyes, and they laughed.

'Seriously, David, we heard every word. The door wasn't properly closed, and we were listening carefully. If you really want us to follow this through, then we have to come up with better reasons to run with it than Yorke will give Quinn not to. There's more to this than meets the eye. Your instinct tells you so,' Anderson reasoned.

Lambie pulled his specs off, as if they were annoying him. 'DS Mulholland and I were about to request that we head up a special task force. I was trying for a national squad. There are a lot of unsolved rapes which share some common features with rapes that have been solved. But only some; they're not all absolutely the same. And I think I can see a pattern emerging. There seem to be a few attacks in one area; then they stop. Then a few more somewhere else; then they stop too. I know what you're going to say: each incident has been thoroughly investigated. But they've been looked at individually; they haven't been looked at as part of a series of incidents. There's evidence to suggest two people are involved in every one of those rapes . . .'

'Like the other man in Emily's case?'

'Yes, but only one of the two is ever tracked down. Somebody, *somebody*, is behind it all. What we have here are the first — Emily — and the most recent — Ishbel Simm — of a series of incidents.'

'What we *might* have here, you mean. We need to wait to hear what the surgical team has to say about Itsy's injuries.' Anderson glanced at Costello, who was pondering something, her eyes on the board.

She shrugged slightly. 'Well, I'm not happy about walking away from this. Colin?'

Lambie sensed an advantage. 'One thing that Emily was firm about is the use of a gun. We need to know if Itsy was threatened with a gun as well; maybe that's why she didn't scream. But the more important thing for me is that Stephen Whyte's been out of the country. So it wasn't him carrying out the other attacks. Is the other man the link?'

'Playing devil's advocate, David, are you sure, absolutely sure, that this testimony of Emily's can be relied upon?' Costello suggested. 'Information obtained from a victim still drugged and traumatized, brain-damaged? It would fall down in front of any half-decent defence counsel. And the so-called supporting evidence is no more than a hearsay statement from a drunken money-grubbing slapper.'

'Emily wasn't wrong,' said Lambie. His tone allowed for no argument.

'And it is a very unusual MO,' said Anderson, 'that penetrating wound to the mouth.'

'I thought Itsy's case might help me pinpoint any further activity by the other man. It could give us a reason to interview all those other women again. Marita being who she is, surely the force would want a result. We'll never get a better opportunity, or the money, to reopen Emily's case, and maybe investigate all the others as well.'

'While you were in with Quinn, Lambie, the phone's been busy,' Anderson said. 'The hospital say Itsy wasn't raped. The SOCOs can find only a few size-four boot prints out on the Moss, apart from some from the guy who found Itsy. The stone has some hair on it – a couple of human strands – and some fibres that look like green wool stuck in the blood. But the stone was in the hole, where it has been for ages.'

Costello turned to glance at the board. 'So you're saying she just hit her head? I'm pretty sure O'Hare said there was more than one blow. And I'm certain somebody else was there!' she insisted. 'That scarf was carefully folded.'

'Look, Costello, how many times have we seen it? Somebody comes across a body, they put them in recovery, they pull a jacket over them, close their eyes, put their head on something soft. It's an automatic reaction. They never stop to think that they're buggering things up for us. I'll ask English if he did it.'

'Somebody still drove her out there.' Costello's finger jabbed the desk.

'Which is not a crime,' Anderson shot back.

Lambie said in a conspiratorial whisper, 'We need to keep these cases together as long as possible. Itsy is Marita's sister, so everybody's sitting up and paying attention. Emily's case has only been reopened as a vehicle for solving Whyte's murder. But if someone walks through that door right now and confesses to killing Whyte, then Emily goes right back to the bottom of the pile. If Itsy's assault is treated and charged as a separate crime, Emily still gets nothing. Those other poor women get nothing. We need Itsy to be part of this for as long as possible.'

'We're too small a team to pull that off. It's a thirty-, forty-detective job. With a canteen,' added Costello.

'Think of the kudos if Partickhill pulls it off,' said Anderson.

'Trouble,' Littlewood said loudly, as footsteps stamping along the corridor heralded the arrival of somebody in a foul mood. Nesbitt got to his feet.

The door behind them banged against the wall, making Lambie jump. His glasses tumbled to the floor.

Mulholland was right in Anderson's face. 'Look, DS Lambie and I have background knowledge of each and every one of these cases. We've read and reread the interviews, and we know it all like the backs of our hands. So we *respectfully* request that *we* should be allowed to work on it.'

'You are part of this investigating team. So why are you feeling left out, Vik?' asked Anderson, as if he was speaking to a child.

'I'm going straight to Marita Kennedy with this, Donald Corbett too. If this —'

'Oh, sit down and be quiet, Vik,' said Anderson kindly. 'Don't throw your career away by being stupid.' He placed both hands on the desk, pressing them down, watching the skin blanch. 'I agree with both of you, but first things first. Vik, you are going to run me to the Moss where, with the help of Mr English, we shall try and solve the mystery of the lack of footprints, and clarify that he didn't fold Itsy's scarf and stick it under her head.'

Costello remembered what Browne had told her about the woman in Ninewells Hospital in Dundee, a patient in her care who was too scared of the dark to sleep, a woman who had been raped at gunpoint. She had to get Anderson on board with that and she had to get him on his own, soon. As she looked down at the photocopied reports Mulholland had flung down on the desk, her gaze resting on the buff files with tabs, her brain registered the University of Liverpool logo, the words *Psych Report*. Lambie was still talking. Costello slid her finger into the file and examined the letterhead, noticing a name she knew. She subtly placed her finger on it, an eyebrow raised interrogatively, and waited for Anderson to notice. He nodded imperceptibly. Noted.

'We'll wait and see what DCI Yorke has to say . . .' he

said, getting up and patting Lambie on the shoulder. On his way out, he whispered to Costello, 'Nice one.'

He was pulling on his coat at the door, ready to follow Mulholland out, when Costello blocked his way.

'Can it wait, Costello? I'm pleased Mick Batten is involved in this but I'm running late.'

Costello wasn't taking no for an answer. 'It's not about Batten. Two minutes.'

'Can we really not do it later? The bird man of Ailsa Craig will be waiting for his lift to the Moss.'

Costello ignored him. 'As you and Lambie know, location is important. It's one of the database's search criteria. Lambie's been working on a clustering theory, a small number of rapes in one area, then the activity moves. It needs one incident to kick each new cluster off, doesn't it? But we might have another victim in a location that has not been searched for. And for completeness we need to cover them all.'

Anderson sighed and looked pointedly at his watch.

Costello pulled out a chair and almost sat Anderson down next to her in front of the computer keyboard. 'Better to check than to miss one.'

'Yes, of course,' he said resignedly. 'Name?'

'Can't tell you that. Although we know where she was and what happened to her.'

'Costello, that doesn't even make sense. Not that that is so unusual with you. Why can't you tell me her name?'

'I had a good chat with Gillian last night. Amazing what fatigue does for the brains of the righteous and ethically aware, but listen . . .' she leaned in closer, '. . . what if she knew about a case from where she worked before, but she can't say? Confidentiality and all that.'

'And you wheedled it out of her? Don't tell me. Look, if a crime was committed it would have been reported. And we would have every right to look at it.' Anderson was suddenly aware of Browne looking over, listening keenly to the conversation. Light dawned. 'Ah, do I remember somebody saying Gillian Browne was a nurse . . .'

'So you do pay attention sometimes.'

'If somebody came in with those injuries then it's unethical for her, as a nurse, to talk about it, as you just said – patient confidentiality and all that.'

'It was a reported rape. Gillian is quite clear on that. But if we didn't know about it because it was in Dundee, then the Strathclyde search engine wouldn't pick it up. It wouldn't hurt to check.' Anderson leaned forward, and Costello sensed acquiescence. She pressed home her advantage. 'And you're the only one with enough clearance to go poking around in the database.'

'Quinn's trusted me with that clearance. It's not for you to –'

'Once you find Gillian's rape victim, you might find another link that would make the database spill it out to you anyway. And that's what you tell Quinn.' Costello sat back. 'All you'd have to do is ask the right question.'

'Fishing expeditions are not allowed, Costello. That's why you do not have full access. Do you want me on a disciplinary?'

'Not at the moment,' she answered sweetly, but still refusing to move.

'You need to give me a specific start point. Anything.'

'OK. Without fishing then. Go back to 2002, 2003. The victim said she was threatened with a gun. What was the worst date in Scottish history?'

'Seventeen forty-five?'

'Worse than that.'

'Nineteen sixty-six? The day England won the World Cup. The goal that never was.'

Costello gazed at the ceiling. 'Right. Minus nine hundred.' She yawned to no one in particular.

'Ten sixty-six?'

'Well, it would have been really unethical of her to *name* the victim, wouldn't it?'

Anderson's fingers tapped away.

Costello leaned over the computer.

Anderson tilted the screen away, blocking her view. 'Hastings?' he enquired. 'Corinne Hastings?'

Costello gave a slight thumbs-up to Browne behind her back.

Anderson sighed and typed some more. After a few minutes he scrolled, and then stopped dead. 'Fuck!'

'What?' asked Costello, spinning the screen so she could see.

'The case was solved. Reported rape, March 2003. Highlighted: *use of firearm to control victim*. There's a name — Edward Pfeffer. DNA found at the scene.'

'Is he in jail?'

'No, he's in the ground. Found dead, on 10th November 2003. Head battered in, left side. He'd been dead a good long while.'

'Shit! A dead rapist? Like a dead Stephen Whyte? I'm not getting any of this. Is somebody out there cleaning up for us?'

Anderson's fingers danced over the keyboard, with a flourish on each Enter. The printer wheezed into life. 'Browne? Come here.'

Browne trotted over from her seat in front of the board, where she had been pretending she was not listening.

'Costello's just told me about something – someone – you mentioned.'

Browne's eyes flicked to Costello.

'Just tell me, did this patient of yours have an injury to her mouth? A penetrating injury?'

'Well, she'd already had maxillofacial surgery by the time she came to the Psych ward, and I think she was due to have more.'

'OK, Browne, that's really helpful, thanks. Costello, keep quiet about this. Just dig up what you can on Pfeffer, but speak to no one apart from me. I don't want Quinn hearing about it until I've paved the way with her a bit. Now I'm really late. I'd better join Vik.'

'There'll be a chilly atmosphere in his car. Better have your thermals ready.'

'Wait until he finds out he's taking me to Strathearn to pick up my own car first,' Anderson muttered, as Costello walked away, clutching Pfeffer's details to her chest.

DCI Quinn replaced the receiver. DCI Yorke had been helpful. And after Quinn offered to take him for a drink sometime, the conversation had become even more fruitful.

Both his officers had jumped at the chance to come over to Partickhill, Yorke told her. He thought Mulholland was a good cop, though off the record he thought Mulholland was getting a bit too confident, trying a little too hard. Yorke was going to stick his neck out and make Mulholland's next appraisal a little less than glowing. As for Lambie, Yorke had no time for Lambie at all, and was pleased Quinn had taken him off his hands for a while. Exactly why Yorke was so against Lambie, Quinn couldn't quite grasp – and Yorke wouldn't say, no matter how many times she rephrased the same question. There was something he wasn't telling her. Lambie had a fixation on the Corbett case, granted, and was always badgering them to investigate further. But it had been done to death. They'd always known who did it. They just hadn't been able to find him.

'And now we have found him,' Yorke said jokingly, 'I bet Lambie's trying to get you to reopen the case in search of the driver of the Isuzu.'

'You're right. Why shouldn't we?' Quinn asked.

'I turned over every stone, but there's nothing to find. Nothing.'

'Why did he take such a special interest, do you think?'

'No idea. He had no exceptional involvement with the original investigation, nothing out of the ordinary.'

Quinn thanked him and hung up. There was more to this; there had to be. She picked up the phone again and asked for HR. Three phone calls later, she was waiting for access to DS Lambie's service record.

She pieced it together in her mind. Stephen Whyte had been found dead, so that would trigger an interest in the old case. It would really boost Mulholland's career if he could answer all the unanswered questions that hung around Emily Corbett's case. It was the kind of investigation that an aggressively ambitious cop like Mulholland would steal from a team player like Lambie. In fact, with Emily being the daughter of a top lawyer, he could build his entire career on it. And then Itsy was found brutally beaten, with similar injuries, right in K Division territory. Mulholland must have been wetting his D&G boxers over that one.

Quinn opened Lambie's personnel file on screen. He hadn't been promoted beyond sergeant in ten years, though before that he was considered a potential high-flyer. There were no major career glitches, so there had to be something lurking in the subtext, something that Yorke knew about and wasn't saying. Was it the obsession with Emily? Or was it deeper than that? Something more sinister? Quinn thought about that unreadable emotion in Lambie's eyes when she mentioned going to DCI Yorke for advice. Anger? Resentment? Disappointment? Lambie was an unknown but, as the saying goes, my enemy's enemy is my friend. So she was going to go on a charm offensive with DS David Lambie.

And as for DS Vik Mulholland, DCI Yorke could have him back any time.

Quinn came out of her office and sniffed. The air was ripe with canine flatulence. 'Can you get that bloody dog out of here?'

'Yes, ma'am. Can I have a word, please?'

'Indeed, Costello.'

'Ma'am, how good is the budget we have? This case could be a budget wrecker, so we need to be economical.'

'But the catch is . . . ?'

'I think you need psychological help. Not you, ma'am – with the case, I mean. These cases are not simply rapes; we need to know the thinking behind them. Like Lambie said, there is a malevolent intelligence at work here. We need a profiler, a criminal psychologist. Might point us in the direction of whom and what we are looking for.'

'Good thinking, Costello. We'll get that girl – Dr McGregor – in. She's good.'

'Can we not get Batten?'

'Batten?'

'Mick Batten. The *effing bloody profiler*, as the old DCI called him. Ponytail, chain-smokes, wears rude T-shirts. He's helped us before. We need him; he's the best.'

Quinn shot a glance to left and right. 'You do know what happened, Costello? In Birmingham? Kim Thompson? For God's sake, he made a huge error in his profile. The cops passed over the real murderer three times – *three times* – in interview to pursue a suspect that fitted Batten's profile. And while the suspect was being grilled in custody, the killer went out and stabbed a young mother called Kim Thompson twelve times on her own doorstep. Every national paper, every national news programme, pilloried the poor bugger. The BBC did a whole bloody documentary about it only last year. And you think we should ask him to come in on this? That suggestion would go down like a fart in a spacesuit at HQ. No way. Anyway, why do we need him when we have a perfectly good one in our pocket?'

'Because she's pretty and aged about twelve. Mulholland is very charming, and manipulative with pretty young women. We'd get a skewed profile, I know it. We need somebody who can walk all over Mulholland, and if anybody can do that Batten can. Mulholland does respect him, as much as he respects anybody. And another thing; he'll be cheap because he has, as you say, been discredited.'

'He has indeed, so this conversation stops here.'

Costello didn't move. 'I saw that documentary. It wasn't a huge error. I think he said – and not only him – that he was right about ninety-five per cent of the profile. The cops gave too much weight to certain aspects of his report without looking at who else it might fit. The word scapegoat was used more than once. Agreed, at the moment he's untouchable, so we'd never get it authorized. But he might do it for free as a research project. And there's a good bit.'

'Oh, there is a good bit? Please enlighten me.'

'I happen to know he's already been contacted by the sex crime unit in Edinburgh, about an unsolved rape . . . involving a gun.'

Quinn went very quiet. 'And how do you happen to know that he's been contacted?'

'Batten signed off on the report; it's in the file. I saw the university logo. And I know Vik Mulholland. He'd have read the gist of the report, but not who wrote it. He never reads the small print.'

'Well, we're not the only force in Scotland, are we? Maybe Lothian and Borders are just one step ahead. Edinburgh is their territory, after all.' But Quinn, even as she said it, knew it could not be so. There were no electronic footprints from the other force anywhere else. L & B were looking at their rape case as a separate incident. She allowed herself a complicit little smile. Possibly, just possibly, a link had been made. Another force might also have found what they too suspected. Dr Mick Batten, the criminal psychologist, had been contacted for a reason. 'I'll get on to Batten straight away. Good work, Costello.'

At quarter to ten Anderson got out of Mulholland's car, leaned on the bonnet and took a deep breath of the cold, clean air. The morning sun was doing its best to burn off the fog, and the field that ran down from the road to the Barochan Moss was green and picture-perfect. The road, barely more than a single track, ran across it, winding its way past the farm and round the bend. A narrow lane, bordered by bare hedgerow which blended into a drystane dyke, forked off from it and followed the edge of the field where Itsy had been found. He couldn't see the copse at all for the fog. The smaller lane, two tracks with weedy growth in between, was closed off with tape, and a uniform was kicking his heels, walking back and forth across the two-stride width of it.

Anderson began to get his bearings. Of course, their car had turned down that lane last night. The grass verges had been chewed up by track after track of nearside tyre prints that all merged in a single frozen rut before disappearing back on to the tarmac. If Itsy had been brought down here by car ... he looked up and down ... the driver would surely have got the car as close to the copse as he could. Unless Itsy had been dropped off innocently, and ran into her attacker purely by chance. But who would drive her out here, miles from the main road, down a single-track road that went nowhere? Whoever gave her a lift would surely come forward, once the circumstances of the case got out. Unless he had something else to hide. Maybe he'd thought Itsy was up for it then realized in conversation that she was not the full shilling. How simple did Itsy actually appear? Anderson wondered. 'Crafty as a box of monkeys,' Diane the PA had said.

The birdwatcher had been picked up at his B & B in Kilmacolm and driven out to the Moss in Mulholland's glossy Audi, his little bobble hat incongruous with the sporty *GQ* car. Ernie English was older than Anderson had expected, a hard little man with a hard little face, weather-beaten and worn, a face that could survive anywhere. On first seeing him, Anderson had given a sigh of relief; if Ernie English had any inclination to go about attacking women, then surely to God he was too old. But he was right on the spot at the time, looking for a sight of the albatross. What if he was about to realize his lifelong ambition, when some silly bint came blundering through the undergrowth, scared the bird, and knackered his plans? Would he strike her, hard enough to fracture her skull? There had to be one scenario that fitted all the seemingly incongruous facts. Was this it? If Itsy had shrieked with delight on seeing the bird, or had maybe got a fright and screamed – Anderson could see how someone might have hit her, once, not realizing she was simple. Or maybe realizing and hitting her even so. Then, the damage done, composing himself, carefully putting back the rock he had picked up, and calling the police. And then feeling remorseful, folding the scarf and putting it under her poor broken head. In the fog nobody would have seen anything, and any footprints would have been made by him 'discovering' the victim. Which was exactly what they'd found.

But it told them nothing about the injury to her mouth. So how did that happen?

English was already relating his story as they walked down the lane, his nylon cagoule rustling as he gesticulated. Anderson did not interrupt the monologue; he fell into step alongside him.

'I'd been sitting on the dyke over there, near that tree.' English gestured with his hand. 'I think I must have been sitting there for about an hour.'

'In this weather?' asked Anderson. 'Fifteen minutes was enough for me.'

Ernie English fixed him with a beady birdlike glare of disapproval. 'I am a birdwatcher and photographer. I am well used to sitting still for long periods in all weathers. Thermal underwear and a flask of hot lemon tea is all it takes to keep warm. No such thing as inclement weather, just inappropriate clothing.'

'So why did you come out here, Mr English?' asked Anderson, noting that Mulholland was more interested in keeping his wellies clean than paying any attention to what English had to say.

'I worry about that bird, Inspector. We thought he would have flown off by now, and the fact that he hasn't makes us wonder if he's OK. The lack of wind will not help, neither does the flat land. And I'm in two minds about our feeding rota. We want him to fly out to sea, out to Ailsa Craig, up to the Hebrides, the Shetlands. Some-where where there are gannets; they eat the same way, eat the same things.'

'And what time did you get here?'

'About eight, I reckon. It was pitch dark, and the fog was still rolling in.'

'And you saw no other vehicle parked here?'

English thought for a minute, intelligent red-rimmed eyes screwed up in a lined, parchment face the colour of old tobacco. He shook his head. 'There were some – there have been cars every night that I've been down here – but nothing out of the ordinary. Some of them were up nearer the road, others much further down. This is the easy point of access, the lowest part of the dyke; other bits still have barbed wire to keep the cows from pushing it over. How-ever, it was difficult to see anything parked more than ten yards away.'

'But did you see anything odd last night?'

'A posh car, like that one . . .' he nodded towards Mul-holland's Audi glistening in the sun, '. . . a real plonker's car; it would have stuck in my mind. Anything run-of-the-mill wouldn't have registered at all.'

They both looked at Mulholland slipping and sliding on the frozen ground in his designer wellies, and shared a scarcely perceptible smile.

'Would you like to show us where you found her?'

'Yes, of course. Bearing in mind I was coming from the other direction.' He circled widely with his arm. 'I was looking for broken twigs, droppings. And I was checking the feeding stations. We've been leaving raw fish out for the bird. That's what I was doing when I heard a scuffling sound, not very loud but I heard it . . .'

'Exactly that? A scuffle, no muted screams, no gasping?'

'No, it was the sound of movement in the undergrowth. Nothing . . .' he paused, looking for the right word, '. . . vocal.'

'And you didn't run, didn't try to find out what it was?'

English replied patiently, as though explaining to a slow-witted child, 'No. I thought it might be the albatross, you see. You don't make any sudden movement around birds.' He hopped over the dyke, with a lightness of foot and a litheness that belied his years.

'I hear Harry Castiglia is working with you guys at the moment,' English flung over his shoulder as he stumped off across the field.

'How did you hear that?' said Anderson, wishing the little man would slow down.

'Professional photography is a small world. I heard his name mentioned last night.' He stopped and took a register of the hill and the land, and changed course slightly. 'Good guy, Harry; he's been out to Ailsa Craig to photograph the gannets a few times. We have twenty thousand pairs, you know. And he also came up to do a piece on the puffin revival. We were down to –'

'And how did you find Mr Castiglia? To work with?'

'Oh, an interesting man. Very talented. Very patient.'
English said it in a considered way that made Anderson
think he did not give praise often.

'I've not met him properly yet, just said hello in passing,' said Anderson vaguely. 'I met Ronnie Gillespie,
though. Do you know him?'

English stopped walking; they had reached the side of
the copse. 'Oh yes, I know him.' He pulled a face, as if it
troubled him.

At the bottom end of the field, the grass gave way to
rough, newly cleared ground bristling with sawn-off sapling stumps. 'Watch yourself. I've come a cropper a few
times,' warned English. He pulled back some bare branches
on the fringe of the copse, and showed them to Anderson. 'These twigs had already been broken. Much of this
is caused by the bird – these lower breakages for certain.
One downstroke of those massive, powerful wings will
do damage. Unfortunately, it doesn't give an albatross
enough lift to take off. And some of this higher damage is
from your guys coming the other way last night.'

'Or some earlier struggle maybe. So you walked round
to here . . .'

'I think I stood still for a while, maybe back there . . .'

'Can you just point?'

'Of course. That was when I heard scuffling. Well, I
came in about here – yes, I had to hold that branch out of
my face – and I stood, waiting. I didn't see her at first. I
was looking up into the trees. I almost tripped over her.
She was lying – well, as you saw. Right here.'

They stood looking down at the patch of bare earth.

The lab boys had taken away the top layer of soil and grass; it was being examined in microscopic detail even as they stood there.

'She was lying curled over on her side. I thought at first – silly of me – that she was asleep. I knelt down and put my hand on her neck. I think I said something to her, something like, "What are you doing out here?" She was cold, very cold. I think I put my hand on her wrist, under her cuff slightly, but that was cold as well. I could see blood. She was dead. Well, I thought she was.'

'Did you recognize her?'

'Not at all. I wouldn't know Marita if I found her in my soup. I don't watch that kind of TV programme, full of talentless idiots famous for being famous. Give me Bill Oddie any day.'

'You didn't touch any part of her clothing?'

English thought again. 'I felt for a pulse in her neck and at her wrist, as I said. Apart from that, no.'

'Nothing else?'

'No.' He turned to walk on. 'Then I walked back up here – well, jogged really. I kept trying to phone 999, but I had to go almost to the farm before I could get a signal.'

'Did you walk out the way you came in?'

'No, I went straight back by the path.' English began striding ahead.

Anderson followed him, single file on the narrow path. Looking up towards the lane, the slight rise in the land, trying to get his bearings, he tripped on an arc of bramble root that was making a bid for daylight. White with frost, against frost, he hadn't seen it, and it had caught his toe perfectly.

English dusted his gloves together. 'Right, come on, you should be timing me now as I walk back up by the direct path. That's why we're here, after all.' He turned to look at the sorry figure of DS Mulholland, slithering and sliding around a long way behind them. 'Your colleague,' he said drily, 'might get on better if he invested in some decent footwear.'

'Indeed,' said Anderson, setting his watch. 'So what about Mr Gillespie then?'

'Come on, Quinn wants somebody to go down and speak to the Prof. We'll have to walk it, seeing as neither of us have a car,' said Costello. 'We'll stick together,' she added, seeing Browne's stricken expression.

'Right, is that another dead body I have to look at?' Browne asked.

'Pictures of the same dead body probably, but it will be a bit cleaner. And we'll have live commentary. We need to know about the injuries to both faces, particularly the mouths. And any deposits left.'

'Both faces?' Browne picked up her jacket, swinging it over her shoulder.

'Whyte's and Itsy's. It might confirm they were attacked by the same person, or that they weren't.'

'Will you be OK?'

'Dead bodies don't bother me,' said Costello, then realized Browne was not talking to her. She looked to see who was on the receiving end of such concern and saw

Nesbitt the Staffie curled up under the radiator, all comfy on a new cellular blanket. He stretched out his front legs, yawned and went back to sleep, gnashing his teeth like an old man snoozing on a deck chair.

'You fancy a muffin on the way?' asked Costello.

'Don't think I do. Well, I do, but I'm trying to lose weight. You know, I think that Castiglia chap has the hots for you.'

Costello smiled. 'Oh, I'm far too old and cynical to be taken in by his good looks and immense personal charm.'

'And nice bum.'

'Hadn't noticed.'

'First thing I bloody noticed!'

Out on the street, the temperature was well below freezing, and the air stung their lungs, silencing all chit-chat. Costello stopped at the kerb, putting her arm out to stop Browne stepping out, as a white van slid out of the fog like a basking shark, missing them by inches.

'I didn't even hear that,' Browne puffed, breaking into a run to keep up as Costello dashed across. 'Ouch,' she said, putting her glove to the side of her face. 'Any sudden movement and my eyeballs rattle.'

'How is it today?' They relaxed on the far side, the gauntlet of traffic in fog having been jointly defeated.

'A bit better. Costello, can I ask you something? It's about Donna McVeigh, Stephen Whyte's girlfriend at the time.'

'What about her?'

'I can't find her. It's the first thing I've been given to do on my own, and I can't bloody find her. I've done every-thing I thought was obvious but I don't know what more to do.' Her face was strained. 'And I followed procedure, to the letter. She's just vanished.'

'Since when? Recently?' Costello kept walking, more to keep herself warm than with any great desire to get to the hospital quickly. 'What have you got so far?'

'Well, everybody says she's not there, but nobody knows where she is. Her mum, her husband, her sister. I think I'm getting the runaround.'

'Well, keep at it. She must know what we want to talk to her about; it was all over the papers this morning. Just tell them she's not in any trouble, you only want a chat. If that doesn't work, maybe ask David Lambie. He's spoken to her in the past often enough. I'll go out with you for the interview if you think she's going to be sticky.'

'Her husband told me to fuck off.'

'Such is the state of holy matrimony.'

'She works as a barmaid, but she's not been there for four days. The day before that was her day off. Her moby's been switched off the whole time.'

Costello stopped in her tracks. 'So when was she last seen?'

'Saturday. Well, Saturday's all anybody will admit to. She hasn't even been around to look after her kids.'

'Bloody hell. You'd better check that out. If that's the case, I know the next place I'd look for her.'

'Oh, right. Where?' Browne's voice was hopeful.

'The mortuary,' Costello answered bluntly.

*

'Come in,' said Quinn in response to Anderson's tap on her open door. 'Can you close that behind you? Where is Castiglia at the moment?' she asked.

'Down at the Moss, I think, or maybe being charmed by the lovely but distraught Marita. Have you had anything from Tayside? Dundee in particular?' Anderson sidled over to the radiator and warmed his hands on it.

'No. Why? Are we waiting for something?'

'Not really. Look – do you want a word? Because I'd like a word with you.' Anderson reiterated the conversation he had had with Ernie English, including the bit about Ronnie Gillespie. 'I tried to clarify what he meant but he wasn't telling.'

'Seems a strange thing to say,' said Quinn.

'It was more the way he said it. I don't want anything to splash back in our faces, the way things are with HQ at the moment. Better to be squeaky clean. Have you checked out Harry?'

'I'll look into Gillespie, but Castiglia *is* squeaky clean, impeccable. Loath though I am to say it, the commissioner made a good choice. Well, the PR folk did.' She wrote something on her pad. 'But the timeline – is it any clearer?'

'Not much. I'll put it on the board. Do you want to put Browne on the Strathearn end of that? She's supposed to be tracking down Donna McVeigh so she's not exactly stretched. Costello can go to the hospital and sort out that end. They're on their way there at the moment to talk to the Prof but I want Costello to be a presence at Itsy's bedside later.'

'Whatever you think best. And I've contacted Batten in Edinburgh. I only had to mention you and he said he'd be on the next available Glasgow train. At least, he's coming over to have a look. Are you best buddies or something?'

'Just auld acquaintance, that's all. We get a pint in if he's up here. Will you let me know when he arrives? I'd better get on with this,' he said, and turned to pin a piece of paper on the board.

'DI Anderson?'

'Ma'am?'

'Has Costello asked you to use my password to look at anything on the restricted database?'

'Not . . . exactly, ma'am . . .'

'Want to try for *exactly*? Tayside *exactly*?'

'Yes, I did look up something for them, ma'am. Costello and Browne.'

'Why didn't they ask me?'

'You were otherwise engaged, ma'am.'

'And the truth?'

'We didn't want Mulholland finding out first. But it was fruitful, and it is connected with this case.' Quinn did not react, forcing him to continue. 'As you gave me your access code I thought it pertinent to check the lead first. Nobody was looking over my shoulder while I was doing it. I believe there will be a formal request on your desk within the hour.'

'And am I pleased about this?'

'Ma'am, I think you'll be giving us a commendation. Mick Batten could be kissing our arses. We might have found another victim. By the name of Corinne Hastings.'

A quizzical look crossed Quinn's face. 'I don't recall that name. Why did it not come up in Lambie's report?'

'Whole load of reasons. Solved, closed, different police force, different databases, access restrictions.'

'If it is that important, can I see it first – on my desk within thirty minutes rather than the hour? And that wasn't a question, DI Anderson. That was an order. And tell Wyngate I want these lists on the wall, everything cross-checked and referenced. Now.'

'Hello, ladies,' said O'Hare, as Costello knocked on the open door of his office. 'Glad you made it before lunch. I presume DCI Quinn told you that I have news for you?'

'Answers to some simple questions, please, Prof,' said Costello, closing the door behind her to keep the heat in. She noted the sign that said *All mobiles to be turned off*, and complied. 'We need to know about the head injuries of Stephen Whyte and Itsy Simm. Similarities and differences.'

'I went one better than that. I can do three. Stephen, Itsy and Emily Corbett. I thought it might be useful for comparison. Here.'

He put three films up on the X-ray box. The first film was creased and marked slightly, the other two pristine. O'Hare stabbed at each one with his finger. 'Emily, Itsy, Whyte, in that order. They all share this fracture, here, on the zygomatic arch. Not an uncommon finding; the cheekbone is a prominent bone and not a strong one.'

'So maybe we shouldn't read too much into the fact that they all present with the same injury. It's not necessarily a clue that they were attacked by the same person,' reasoned Costello.

'Not really, but look at this. All the zygoma fractures are associated with these parietal and temporal fractures. Which means they were all whacked up here . . .' he indicated the area of the skull above the ear, rolling his hand on to the top of the skull, '. . . maybe once, maybe more than once. Itsy was hit with something broad and heavy enough to cause those three bones to depress – two or three blows. But Emily and Whyte were hit repeatedly with something long and narrow, like a small-bore pipe.' O'Hare put a different kind of film on the box, removing Stephen Whyte's X-ray to make room. 'This is Itsy's CT scan. Computed tomography. It was taken on admission as she had a serious head injury. This type of scan is good at picking up bleeding from head trauma, blood clots and internal bleeding, as well as the site of any skull fracture. The interesting bits to look at are here, and here.' He pointed at the scan with his pen, then moved the pen from one scan to the other. 'See that there, and there?'

'No,' said Costello honestly.

'Can you not see that?' The nib of O'Hare's pen kept moving from one to the other.

Costello shrugged.

'Now the interesting injury is here, the penetrating injury. Just run your tongue across the roof of your mouth. It's like two arcs joined in the middle. Now look – can't you see how that bit there is a complete arch, and that one isn't?'

'Honestly? No. You know those Spot the Difference

pictures where you have to see six and you can only find five? Well, it's a bit like that: different, but I can't see why.'

'And,' O'Hare continued very quietly indeed, 'this CT scan of Itsy, and this X-ray of Emily, taken ten years apart, both show a pattern of injury which is not common in physical assault. It happens when something is rammed through the roof of the mouth. In Emily's case, it was thought to be a gun barrel. It certainly wasn't pointed. Same with Itsy. However, in her case the damage is less defined. Don't ask; I have no idea what would cause that.' He put another plate up on the screen. 'Now look at Whyte's. This is a post-mortem X-ray. You'll notice the wound is further back, on the soft palate. We found oily residue in Whyte's mouth injury, which on initial exam could be Silicolube.'

'Which is what Emily had?' clarified Costello.

'Indeed, and we're looking for something similar in what we got from Itsy in the ambulance. But looking at that with the naked eye, it's not the same stuff; her deposit was more fibrous –'

He was interrupted by the ring tone of Browne's phone.

Costello whipped round and indicated in no uncertain terms that Browne should leave now. Browne scuttled out.

'Is that woman an idiot?' asked O'Hare, more loudly than necessary.

'Not got her properly house-trained yet,' said Costello. 'So all three were belted with something on the left side of the head by a right-handed person. All three had a small round thing rammed in their mouths – two accurately, one not.'

'But one of the accurate ones is not as defined as the other.' He pointed at Itsy's scan. 'I would not stand up in court and swear that was made by the same thing that made those.' He tapped Whyte's and Emily's plates. 'But there's one other difference.'

'Oh, Christ, I was following you up till now.'

'Emily and Itsy both had severe contre-coup injuries.'

'That's when someone's hit on the upper left side of the head, the brain gets rattled against the skull and bruising appears on the lower right side of the brain, right?'

'Basically, yes.'

Costello pulled a face. 'Could Itsy have fallen and hit her head on a stone?'

'That particular blow was on the upper left side of her head, so unlikely to have been caused by a fall. I can't think of anything that would cause this combination of injuries,' said the pathologist.

'You're no help, Prof.' Costello tried again. 'What about running into a branch and being knocked badly backwards to strike a stone that was lying on the ground?' Costello hit herself on the head with the palm of her hand to demonstrate.

'She'd have to be running slightly sideways, then fall backwards, then forward and then impale herself on something through the mouth. Not likely, is it? However,' O'Hare went on in his usual dry, didactic style, 'in Emily's case, the pathologist at the time noted that while the blow was savage, her attacker stopped. The ability to stop is unusual. And it suggested to the pathologist that he'd done enough damage to achieve the control he wanted.'

'You mean he hit Emily just enough to render her unconscious?' There was no levity in their conversation now. 'I think her statement says she was lying down, on her back, when she was struck.'

'That would be right. And Itsy – one blow, and I would say she was also lying down when she was struck.' O'Hare turned his attention to the last film. 'Stephen Whyte had a hard tube-like structure, like the muzzle of a gun, rammed hard in his mouth. But I think he was hanging at the time so the angle is slightly back. Then he had his lips super-glued shut – nice for bleeding down your throat – then he was struck about five or six times; his face and skull were a mess. He would have been bleeding into the nasopharyngeal cavity, so he was also suffocating while they set about him.' For once even the normally imperturbable O'Hare seemed shaken.

'But was it the same person?'

'Your guess is as good as mine. But I think any impartial psychologist would agree with me: if, and I repeat if, it was the same attacker, they were full of rage for Whyte, a bit pissed off at Emily, and Itsy got off lightly. Well, in their strange scale of relative brutality, I mean.' He pulled the films from the X-ray box. 'Might be interesting to get a psychological opinion on that one.'

Costello shrugged. 'It would be helpful if we could keep them officially connected as long as possible.'

'You can't take on the world, Costello.'

'Maybe not. But the world has never experienced the Browne-Costello dream team before, has it?'

'I bet they're quaking in their boots.'

O'Hare was interrupted by Browne, who slipped back through the door, her phone in her hand. 'That was DI Anderson. He has a question.'

'Then why didn't he phone me?' asked Costello.

'Your phone is off,' said Browne simply. 'He wants to know if there's any injury to Itsy's face, on her skin, around here.' She drew a gloved finger down her own cheek.

'I'll take DS Costello up and she can look for herself,' said O'Hare with a not-so-subtle look at his watch.

'Hang on. Boots . . .' said Costello.

'Boots . . . ?'

'Boots. The only thing that makes us think Itsy was there on her own. Apart from the guy who found her, there was only one set of small boot prints at the scene.'

'If I were you I'd ask those SOCOs, or whatever the hell they're called these days, to consider the evidential value of what they lifted from the ground. The earth's been frozen for days now.'

'It took Itsy's prints well, though,' argued Costello.

'But if the attacker knew what he was doing, he might have left no prints for us to find. That doesn't mean he doesn't exist. You'd be amazed how forensically aware some people are nowadays.'

O'Hare was echoing exactly what Lambie had said of the other cases. 'So he knew what he was doing, Itsy's attacker?' she asked.

'Of course. So get down there, test a few theories.'

Costello scribbled in her notebook.

'And while you have your notebook out, can I have a

private word with you?' O'Hare swung his jacket over his shoulder.

But Browne made no move to leave the room.

'Browne, you go and phone the station,' Costello told her. 'Find out if we're needed back there, or if we can grab a bite to eat. I'll go upstairs with the Prof and have a look at Itsy.'

In the long blue corridor leading to the high dependency unit, the cleaner was now wiping down the glass panels. The pathologist spoke to a nurse who told him to go ahead, but not before she had eyed up the small, spiky-haired blonde at his side. Along the corridor, they gazed through a window into the stark white room where Itsy lay, her face half covered in gauze, in the middle of a jungle of wires and technology, a monitor sine wave scribing her breath in and out. Wires protruded from her cheek, two tiny titanium wing nuts pierced her skin where her scalp had been shaved, and scalpel tracks ran across her skull like motorways on a map.

'Jesus.'

'Anderson wants to know if there was any injury to the skin on Itsy's face. Not the mouth injury, but the skin. I thought there was.'

'See for yourself — a bad laceration, deep too, on the left side.'

They were very close now, and she could smell that faint clean odour of surgical alcohol and soap. 'Could she have fallen and got that?'

'Are *you* thinking that she fell out there? That she got those wounds by a terrible coincidence?'

'Is it possible?'

'The mouth injury, yes. I've seen it in kids. Running with a pencil, running with a stick, they fall, mouth open, it's easily done. But never in an adult. And it doesn't explain the contre-coup injury, or the two blows to the head. That's for you to sort out.' O'Hare's voice was very quiet, as if Itsy might hear and waken. He thought for a bit. 'What do you remember about her mouth, while you were holding her head in the ambulance?'

'I remember it looked as if it had no edges, no lips on the left side. No . . . shape.' She sighed. 'I'll look at the photos when they come back.'

'I'll see if they took any before surgery. Sometimes they take some if they expect they might have to do reconstructive stuff. At least her skin will be clean, so you might get a better idea.'

'Thanks, Prof. I know that's above and beyond for a victim who's not . . .'

'Dead?' O'Hare nodded at the two figures hunched in chairs beside Itsy's bed. 'Iain was a good friend.'

She looked at him, noting the past tense. O'Hare was tired; this was taking it out of him. 'Do you know Marita as well as you know him?'

'No. Iain and I were at school together. We're Chamberlain's old boys.'

Costello wondered why O'Hare was making no effort to alert Marita and Iain to their presence. She felt she was spying on their grief.

'Actually, it's Iain I want to talk to you about,' O'Hare went on.

Costello stepped back from the window. 'Off the record, I presume?'

'Your female intuition will get there anyway. You know the samples we took from Itsy in the ambulance, in the operating theatre? Well, there were signs of recent sexual activity in her vagina and on her thighs. We have a pubic hair that is not hers. There was some staining on her underwear – we're waiting for that to come back. But no sign of force, and absolutely no sign of rape. The evidence suggests she had consensual sex, then got up and walked about afterwards. So I've advised Iain to . . . ahem, another time. There might be more,' he added quietly, and subtly nodded at Iain.

Costello jumped as a hand tapped her on the shoulder. It was a uniform. 'You DS Costello? DC Browne wants you. She's out at the lifts.'

'Oh Christ, what's she done now?'

'Your phone's off. The station is looking for you.'

Forty minutes later, Costello was crouching at the top of a ravine known as Sergeant's Gully, looking across the bleak fogbound Gleniffer Braes. This was where Emily Corbett had been left for dead ten years ago, thrown from a moving vehicle on the last steep bend O'Hare's powerful black Shogun had negotiated before they got to the viewpoint car park. The bitter cold gnawed at Costello's ears, and she felt as if her forehead was in a vice. Thirty feet below, at the bottom of the ravine, Donna McVeigh was lying on a bed of brown bracken. From her vantage point, Costello could see that Donna, now a blue-tinged tangle of limbs, had been dressed in something skimpy and pink, ready for a grand night out.

A SOCO was knocking in a wooden upright to make a rope handrail for a common access path which would go down the ravine. DS Lambie was talking to a woman in a green waxed jacket, who was hanging on to a harnessed Weimaraner, no doubt the dog that had found the body. The powerful animal was standing stock still, sniffing the air, his perfect pose making him look ghostly in the grey air. The Hound of the Baskervilles, thought Costello. She raised a hand in greeting to Lambie, trying mentally not to tar him with the same brush as Vik the Prick Mulholland – who of course was down with the body, right in the thick of it.

She jumped at a movement behind her. 'God, it's you!' she said, as she heard a shutter snap.

Harry Castiglia crouched down beside her. 'Am I OK here? If the delightful DS Mulholland sees me, he'll insist on showing me things.'

'You're OK here,' she confirmed. 'You're not interfering with anything.'

He put one camera away and pulled out another. 'I'm going to fire off a few shots up here at ground level. No way I'm going to get the body in by accident and offend people. Any idea what happened here?'

'Not yet,' Costello answered.

'Well, she's wrapped in a tarp, she's been dead a few days, and she's had her lips glued together. And she has ID in the names of Donna Campbell and Donna McVeigh on her,' Harry told her. 'And I gather she also had on her a scrap of paper with the numbers of journalists on the *Star* and the *Sun*. I know those names: sensationalist hacks. I'd bet my bottom dollar Donna was trying to sell her story.'

'Who needs *CSI Miami* when we have you?' Costello muttered.

'The uniforms forget I'm here, and talk. Don't worry, it won't go any further. Oh, and her mobile phone is missing, so it's going to be a bit iffy, tracking the records of who she was speaking to.'

Costello looked over his shoulder, trying to ignore the very nearness of him, the scent of him. So different from O'Hare. 'Indeed,' was all she could say.

'How's your wee pal?'

'Gillian? Fine,' said Costello. 'Where's your sidekick?'

'Ronnie's developing and doing some computer stuff this morning. I want to be on this 24/7. I want to live this life, you know. You're knackered, I'm knackered; it gives real sense to what I'm looking for. I've been to the mortuary, central records, the forensic lab, the DNA testing suite at Strathclyde Uni. I've seen all the technology of the modern police service. But this is so much better.'

'Really?'

'My feet haven't been dry for a whole day now; I've never eaten so little, or so badly; and you learn never to need to pee.'

They both got up from their crouching positions as O'Hare walked past, ready to climb down the side of the gully that was slippy with dew and shrouded in a rising fog that seemed to bloom from the ground. What started as a dignified climb down ended in an inelegant scramble.

'This reminds me of those pictures of the Yorkshire moors during the Brady and Hindley trial.' Castiglia was gazing at the landscape again with all the passion of a true artist. 'I was thinking about going down to the Moss tonight,' he said. 'The forecast is for dense fog and ice. I'm going to spend half an hour scouting about, getting a few shoots, looking for Ally. You can join me if you want; I'll bring a flask of soup. You could give me a guided tour.'

'I'll be working; we're in the middle of something big here.'

'We're both in the middle of it, numpty. Anyway, you will be working,' said Harry with mock authority. 'You'll be showing me around the scene of a crime, the PR function of the modern police service. I've cleared it with DCI Quinn.' He winked at her as he walked away. Costello was stunned into silence. In fact, all she could hear was her heart beating.

A shouted conversation was going on between O'Hare at the bottom of the gully and the SOCO at the top. Donna McVeigh was lying across a stream, and evidence was being washed away; there was a debate as to how much effective photography Bob MacKellar could still do. Could they get the body out now?

The tarpaulin had been moved slightly and Costello could make out more details. Donna was lying on her back, slightly overweight, fake-tanned, wearing a short pink vest top that didn't cover her bulging stomach. Costello couldn't make out her arms and legs among the brittle fronds of bracken, but could see that she had long mid-brown hair with a blonde streak at the front, and something like a dark red scarf or shawl flowing across her body. O'Hare deftly put both of Donna's hands into sealable plastic bags, moved her head slightly and shouted something up to the SOCO, but Costello was too far away to catch it. Then she realized what the dark red streak was.

Blood.

8

Quinn had a quick look at the lists on the wall. Wyngate's attempt to trace everybody who had had the keys to Clarence Avenue was just a mass of phone numbers and left messages. But he was making a good job of collating the reports on the rape victims in other jurisdictions, and the search references were starting to appear, ticked, crossed or question-marked.

'Right,' Quinn started briskly. 'I am going to be brief, so pay attention. Our investigation into the death of Stephen Whyte has thrown up a great many parallels to other investigations – some solved, some not – across Scotland.' There was a brief flutter of approval but Quinn just grimaced; she had a lot to do and was impatient to get on with it. 'First, note this: this briefing is going to continue as it was planned. There is more information to come on Donna McVeigh, so we'll leave her till last.' As if to emphasize her point, the fax chattered into life. 'Meanwhile, we have a growing body of evidence that points to the same rapist, or at least the same MO, in some if not all of these other rape cases. We need to find the link. I would like to start with Corinne Hastings.' She pointed to the last name on the wall. 'Corinne was the victim of a rape and vicious assault, March 2003, in Dundee. She was twenty-eight, she was out running, a vehicle pulled in behind her. She was blindfolded, pushed to the ground and quote *the cold muzzle of a gun* unquote, was held to her head, and somebody tried to force her mouth open. She put up a fight and was struck on the head. She suffered a fractured skull, which required major surgery. But in comparison to the others she got off lightly, with no mouth injury; she did not lose consciousness and she struggled all the time. Her assailants hit her again, then they ran off, and she heard a vehicle pull away. She thought there were two sets of footsteps, and that she heard two doors close on the vehicle. I've requested the full file but it might take a while.' Quinn avoided looking at Browne. 'One thing she recalled was that the attacker spoke; he told her to *keep still, bitch.*'

Anderson automatically flicked to Emily's points of interest listed on the board, the words . . . *Stay still, bitch.*

'Corinne identified his accent as Geordie. A used Elastoplast was found at the scene. In November 2003, Edward Pfeffer was found dead in a disused part of the old sewage works in Dundee. He had been dead six months or more. He was from Tyneside, and had lived in Dundee for two years. His DNA matched that of the pus on the plaster. Anybody want to guess what his injuries were?'

'Fracture of left parietal, superglued lips? Hard palate shattered?' asked Costello.

Quinn nodded. 'Wyngate has before and after pictures of Corinne for us. And one of Pfeffer. Familiarize yourself with her case, OK? She was a librarian at the time, but had also had a little success in publishing two kiddies' books, about a squirrel with superpowers.'

Wyngate finally found the picture and placed it on the wall, using his elbow to hold it in position while he fumbled with a drawing pin. Corinne Hastings was a round-faced woman with short brown hair, and an expression of studious seriousness. She looked like a librarian.

'All these victims, not surprisingly, suffered psychological trauma after being attacked, so let's go through the files with a fine toothcomb, and prepare very definite questions to put to them. Remember, whatever part of the investigation you are scheduled to work on, you will report to DI Colin Anderson. He is the senior investigating officer. I want DS Costello to liaise with the Kennedy family and do all background checks there. And I want that timeline precise. So, since DC Browne and DS Costello still have no viable form of transport, Professor O'Hare has kindly agreed to drive them to Strathearn. Costello will pick up some clothes for Marita to wear for the televised appeal, and the Prof will then take her to Marita at the hospital. Where he works,' Quinn added, her forehead wrinkling as though the thought had only just occurred to her. 'Then when Littlewood is through here, he will join Browne at Strathearn, and they will interview the two gardeners Anthony Abbott and Robert McGurk. We are particularly interested in McGurk – he knows Itsy well, he's young, strong and of limited mental ability. So Littlewood and Browne, do the initial interview, and ask for a voluntary DNA sample. But if you feel he could be a vulnerable suspect or that he doesn't understand – then pull out and we'll get a specialist in, OK? Now, I do not, repeat not, want any female officers wandering about in the fog on their own. Do you all understand that?'

There was a murmur of consent, edged with nervousness.

'I want Mulholland to liaise on Marita's TV appeal, since he is the most experienced among us at media manipulation – apart from Marita Kennedy herself, that is. In addition to Costello and Browne working on Itsy Simm's case, I want DS Mulholland and DS Lambie to work on the McVeigh-Corbett-Whyte angle; something might connect to Emily's case. Wyngate is gathering the files on the victims on Lambie's list. They will all appear on the wall, so please familiarize yourself with them. Then hopefully by nine tomorrow morning we will have found an area of common ground between the victims, because there has to be one. Their job? Their hobby? Their age? Their education? We're still waiting for some evidence from all three recent crime scenes, so watch the board for that. We need to know who talked to Stephen Whyte and Donna McVeigh in the twenty-four hours before they died, so that is where we start.'

'Donna's phone is missing. It'll take time to obtain the records,' said Anderson. 'We've asked for a trace on numbers that called her number. It'll doubtless go back to a pay-as-you-go cheapie. Any news on Whyte's mobile?'

'His mum had a mobile phone which a niece took. Archie has asked for it back, so once we get hold of the SIM card, it'll be straight to the IT guys,' said Costello.

'So we might get a trace if Moira Whyte stayed in touch with her son and phoned somebody here to tell them he was coming back. Don't hold your breath, though. As Lambie rightly said, this man is intelligent. So, DS Mulholland, find out who Donna had been talking to, and what about – particularly the media. You can do that and the appeal, can't you?' Without waiting for his agreement, she continued, 'Costello, what news from the Prof?'

'Basically, he confirmed what we know about the injuries.' She pulled out her notebook and repeated what O'Hare had said. 'But the inconsistency is Itsy herself. She simply can't have struck her head on the stone as the evidence suggests, and ended up injured the way she was.'

'So, if she was attacked, was she attacked in error, by somebody thinking she was her sister? Right! Let's have the results of the investigations into Marita's Stalking Hell up on the board in ten minutes.' Quinn looked at her watch. 'Dr Mick Batten is arriving from Edinburgh by train any time now. As you may remember, despite the appalling Kim Thompson business, he has an excellent record with this division. So the more information we can give him tomorrow, the more ammunition he will have and the better armed we will be. I want you to give him all the support you can.'

Quinn sighed with exasperation, and continued. 'It's beginning to look as if we are indeed touching the tip of a much bigger case. We might have a few more victims that fit the MO. And a few others will be dropped. However, we are not trying to clear up every unsolved rape that has occurred in Scotland over the last ten years – do I make myself clear?'

'Oh, and who's going to decide?' scoffed Mulholland. 'We've hardly started any investigation at all. Any categorization of the crimes must be pure conjecture at this stage. We're going to need a bigger team. And an expert who knows what he's talking about.'

'Don't worry, DS Mulholland, we have an expert. We have Mick Batten. Like I said, if you can give him enough evidence, he will support your theory. And if you can't, he won't. I will remind you, if you need reminding, that we have a vicious killer, or killers, on the loose, so any personal agenda goes out the window – or you can walk out now. Do you understand?' Although her eyes panned around the room they settled on Lambie, who nodded briefly, then on Mulholland, who looked through Quinn as though she wasn't there. 'And if anybody doubts that . . .' she held up a fax, '. . . here's a brief report from O'Hare. Donna McVeigh, née Campbell, aged twenty-eight, had been dead for seventy-two hours at least. The side of the head is almost completely crushed. Lips sealed with superglue, and tearing and bruising around the area as if she'd been trying to scream, which indicates that it was done pre-mortem. There was also a savage rape, while she was alive and while she was struggling. It also looks as though somebody tried to ram something hard down her throat, something oily and dirty, before the superglueing. The Prof's asked for a rush on the swab analysis of the roof of the mouth.' Quinn then reached for three separate faxes. 'Donna was last seen by her husband on Saturday night, about half seven or eight, when she walked out of their home in Greenock and got a cab to Paisley. The hubby, as far as we know, is in the clear. His opinion is that she was with "some bloody ex-boyfriend".'

'Whyte?' asked Costello.

'According to this report, he doesn't think so. He knew Whyte and says if it had been him, Donna would have said. And anyway Whyte was dead by the time Donna was getting phone calls from the vague stranger on her missing mobile. Donna lives in Greenock, so we've got K Division tracking down the cab driver and looking at some CCTV in Paisley. The crime scene guys also, strangely enough, found a white feather at the scene.'

'Same as Whyte?' asked Costello.

'The feathers are a common finding so I've asked for them to be examined by an ornithologist at the Natural History Museum, but that might take some time. And can somebody check whether feathers were mentioned at any of the other scenes – and if so, whether they match those at the Whyte and Campbell scenes? We have various combinations of gun, superglue, and a penetrating injury to the roof of the mouth. But it seems certain that somebody did not want us to know whatever it was Donna had to say. So we seem to be on the right track. I thank you for your attention.'

'Can I go now, ma'am, for the teas?' said Browne. 'I need to eat before I can take my next set of painkillers, and it has been some time. And Professor O'Hare . . .' She looked at the clock.

Quinn glanced at her watch. 'As long as you're quick. But be careful out there. Don't fall over anything.'

Browne went out, clicking her tongue at Nesbitt, who trotted out behind her.

Quinn closed the door of her office, not asking Castiglia to sit down. 'It's been brought to my attention that your assistant, Ronald Gillespie, has a rather chequered past.'

Castiglia narrowed his eyes slightly. 'I'd hardly call it that.'

'I gather he's been involved in rather dubious photographic activities. Under-age nude girls, to be exact.'

'Where did you get that nugget from?' Castiglia casually leaned against the door; he seemed vaguely amused. 'Oh, yeah, Ernie English. He's a right old woman.'

'He sends his regards to you too,' Quinn said sardonically.

'Ronnie was set up.'

'But you being so hot on ethics, surely his association with you could be rather damaging to your career if it got out?'

'There's no *if it got out* about it; it's never been kept in.' Harry Castiglia gave a smile that almost melted Quinn's heart. Almost. 'It's no secret. He was set up by the girl's father. The girl asked Ronnie to take some photographs of her, they went into the woods to shoot them, and she gradually took off more and more clothes. Maybe a more experienced photographer would have said: *Enough*. I've seen the shots and I'd have said she was well over twenty. Turns out she was fifteen.' Castiglia pulled a wry face. 'Her dad pretended to go berserk and demanded money from Ronnie, who contacted me for advice. I told him to call

220

the cops in; that sort of thing can ruin your career. Anyway, the father soon backed off. If Ronnie had pursued him, the man would have been facing charges.'

'So it was the dad's idea all along?'

'Of course. The cops had a word with them, end of story. But it left Ronnie a bit bitter. And wary. He was young at the time, and he's worked with me on a few projects in Scotland. We met about five years ago when he was doing a feature on classic cars. We've both had old Jaguars ever since.'

'I can do without the *All Our Yesterdays*,' said Quinn.

'If he was in any way unreliable, I'd know. But please check him out, check me out as well,' he offered. 'Ronnie keeps well away from that kind of work now. Ask around if you don't believe me. He does landscapes and factories, industrial stuff. Any portrait work, there's always another person present. You even have some of his pictures on the wall out there. That flat with the attic conversion – that was one of his.' He leaned forward, and Quinn recognized the lawyer's trick of drawing in a jury. 'Look, I don't expect you to trust me. I'm going out on my own with Costello tonight, but I cleared it with you first so you'd know where we were going and why.'

'Yes, yes, that's fine. But Ronnie Gillespie – you say he photographed the loft conversion on Clarence Avenue?'

'Yes, for some design magazine. He mentioned it when I said I was coming up to Glasgow to do this commission.'

Quinn nodded, her analytical mind digesting the information. They were waiting for a call back from Towerhill

Magazines. 'OK, Mr Castiglia, I think we understand each other. I think you can be trusted with DS Costello. But I doubt she will be taking her clothes off out on the Moss tonight; it's too bloody cold.'

She let a smile linger on her lips as Harry Castiglia slipped out the door, leaving a waft of good aftershave in her office.

Donald Corbett was a small dapper man who believed in getting straight to the point. 'I asked to see DCI Quinn. Where is she?' he demanded.

Quinn herself was nowhere to be found, and Anderson had no idea what she had wanted to say – and no idea what Corbett was to know and not to know. While he was inwardly cursing the man for appearing unannounced and Quinn for buggering off, his face showed nothing but professional concern.

'Yes, you did, sir, but we didn't know in advance that you were coming. I am the most senior investigating officer available, so can I be of help?'

'You know who I am; you know *what* I am.'

It was not a question, it was a statement, so Anderson nodded, willing Quinn to walk in through the door. 'Indeed I know, sir. But this is just an unofficial chat,' said Anderson soothingly. 'Boss's office, no tape. Coffee?'

He ushered Corbett through to Quinn's office, where the walls immediately seemed to shrink round them, such was the force of Corbett's personality.

'It will be official if I want to make it official,' Corbett said, hitching his immaculate trouser legs over his knees to avoid them bagging as he sat down. 'You know how badly the previous investigation was . . .'

'Misjudged?' offered Anderson. 'Mr Corbett, you're a distinguished lawyer. You know as well as I do that any criminal lawyer straight out of uni would have got the case thrown out. I understand that the horror of the attack on your daughter demanded results, but there was simply no hard physical evidence.'

Corbett said aggressively, 'You have no idea, no idea at all, how that has affected my family.'

Anderson sat down in Quinn's chair, weary. He sensed Corbett sizing him up, the suit with the bagged elbows, the loose tie, the red-rimmed eyes. He knew he looked as if he had not eaten or slept for a week.

'You're right, sir, there's no way I can know.' He picked up Quinn's fountain pen, 'But I do have a daughter, only a few years younger now than Emily was then. Investigating brutality to young women is part of my job.'

Corbett obviously decided that anger would get him nowhere. But his tone was still fairly crisp. 'I'm a busy man –'

'I know, sir, so am I,' Anderson said appeasingly, and placed the pen back on the desk, as if creating a small barrier between them. 'The reason I'd like this chat to be off the record will become clear. I think we both want a speedy resolution to this.'

Corbett placed his folded overcoat carefully over the arm of the chair, the collar falling almost to the floor. A small tumbleweed of Nesbitt's hair, rolling slightly in the draught that wafted under the door, drifted towards the soft cashmere as if drawn by a magnet.

'Agreed, K Division didn't cover themselves in glory the first time . . .' said Anderson.

'You don't need to tell me that,' Corbett spat.

'. . . so we think a new team, a smaller close-knit team, will get better results. We are used to working that way.'

'DI *Colin* Anderson?' Corbett fired the question suddenly.

'Yes.'

'You worked with Alan McAlpine?'

'I did, for many years.'

'I felt DCI Yorke was too . . . *soft*, for want of a better word. It takes a bastard to catch one. McAlpine was a bastard. And a good detective. Fond of his malt.'

Anderson smiled wryly. 'All three statements are correct. But I don't think you need worry about DCI Quinn not being equal to it. She'll fight tooth and nail to get the bastard that attacked Emily. As I said, we are a small team, we all know what the others get up to. We don't go tripping over each other. But let's say we are confident that finding Stephen Whyte's body means a big break, and leave it at that. We will need to talk to Emily. And maybe your other daughter – what's her name?'

'Jenny, Jennifer.'

'And what does she do?'

'She looks after Emily,' said Corbett. 'Emily's condition has deteriorated over the years, so if the whole thing is to be stirred up yet again I want her kept out of it as much as possible. Jennifer too. I need to protect both my daughters.'

'But you agree that we can chat to Emily?'

'If you think it will help, of course you can.' A sad smile crossed Corbett's face. 'Chat isn't the word. You say you have a daughter – please, just treat mine as you would wish yours to be treated.'

'Of course, we'll keep it brief, take it at her pace.' Anderson picked up Quinn's pen again. 'Just one thing, Mr Corbett? You usually work in London during the week, and fly home every weekend? Where were you the weekend of 30th January?'

Corbett said, 'I was here in Glasgow. But if you do find the man who murdered that bastard, tell him I'd like to take him out for a drink.'

Browne pulled back the curtain of the hall at Strathearn a little and looked out into the fog. 'I'm not going out there on my own. It's getting darker than the Earl of Hell's waistcoat.'

'John Littlewood will be here in a minute,' Costello said impatiently.

'Why can't we two go?'

'Look, all you have to do is walk out there, have a chat and come back. We need two cops there, because it's an interview. But I have to go with O'Hare back to the hospital with clothes for Marita for this bloody appeal. And Littlewood needs to run you back. Gillian, you'll be fine.'

'Just don't get lost,' said O'Hare. 'The greenhouse is way over beyond the pond. So take the path from the drive, and bear right. Go down the left side, you'll end up in the pond, which is unfenced and deep. It's lethal in any weather and twice as bad in this fog. So just take the right-hand path and stay on it.'

'Stay right and I'll be right,' Browne muttered as a mantra.

The ever-present Diane had heard the buzz from the entry system at the gate and had already opened the door for them when they arrived. Costello had phoned ahead to explain that the black Shogun belonged to the pathologist and that they needed to pick up a list of clothing for Marita to wear for her televised appeal.

'How is Marita?' she asked, looking past Costello at Browne's bruised face but not commenting, her dazzling smile firmly in place.

'She's bearing up,' said Costello. 'And Itsy seems to be holding her own for the moment,' she added, although Diane hadn't asked. There was obviously another question on Diane's lips but Costello forestalled her. 'Do you have any videos or DVDs made of the family together, something to give us an idea of them?'

Diane's eyes flitted to Browne, who was content to look out the window, watching for Littlewood, but her smile did not waver. 'Of course, please come down here.' Costello followed her down the corridor to what looked like an office, a nice office but a workplace all the same. A coffee percolator in the adjoining kitchen was hissing slightly and Costello, a confirmed tea drinker, immediately felt sick. There was a range of Marita videos here – her fitness DVD, her TV appearances. Diane ran her finger along the shelf, almost a caress. 'Take anything you think might be helpful.' That smile again.

'Thanks,' said Costello.

Diane saw her eyeing another three or four in an untidy pile on the bottom shelf. 'Oh, those are Itsy's. Filmed here.'

'Just what we need. I'll give you a receipt.' Diane looked nonplussed but before she could argue Costello was on her way back down the hall, the DVDs in her bag. 'Have you any idea where we'd find Anthony Abbott? Robert McGurk?'

Diane shrugged. 'They could be anywhere. I'd try the greenhouse first.'

'We will. Do you have Marita's clothes ready?'

'Oh yes, all laid out ready to pack. I know she was hoping to come home and get ready here, but I think she's having a shower at the hospital.' She shook her head as if there were just too many things to do in the day and went upstairs, leaving Costello and O'Hare to join Browne back at her vigil by the window.

'It's OK,' said Costello, sarcastically. 'We don't really want to have a seat or a nice hot cup of tea while we wait. What does she actually do, that woman?'

'Anything her employer requires. I'd imagine Marita is fairly high-maintenance,' said O'Hare caustically.

'So Marita pays *another woman* to get her car its MOT?' Costello said in mock wonderment.

'I admit, if I could afford it,' said the pathologist wistfully, 'I'd quite like to have women running around after me.'

His comment was met by a glare stonier than the accompanying silence.

The buzzer sounded. Costello looked out to see Little-wood, pacing up and down on the cobbled yard outside. She thumbed the green button, the door slid open, and Browne walked out into the fog. Both cops immediately turned up their collars against the biting cold as they faded from view. Costello noticed Littlewood's arm on Browne's elbow, correcting her as she attempted to head in the wrong direction across the drive.

'I hope Rebecca knows what she's doing, sending John out on a night like this,' said O'Hare. 'He doesn't look well.'

'That's a medic's opinion. But he nearly smiled when he knew he was getting out again. The frustration of sitting back and watching us girls doing it because he can't is worse for him than his angina,' said Costello, looking up at the huge staircase, trying – and failing – to imagine herself sweeping down it in a swanky frock.

'Look at this. I remember Iain talking about it at the Rotary.' O'Hare was looking at a display arranged on a length of board covered in green felt and mounted on the wall of the corridor which led to a side wing. It was a chronological collage of local social history, photocopied documents and newspaper cuttings, and dozens of old photographs, some of them sepia-tinted, going right back to the nineteenth century. 'It's for the Open Doors day and the visual art festival.'

'When scruffs like me get to mooch round posh houses?'

'Houses of historical interest, Costello. I know there was a piece in the paper a while back; Iain was asking for old pictures of the place. I think Hillhead Library donated a few.' He pulled his glasses from their case and peered more closely.

Costello strolled down the display, whistling 'Yesterday' under her breath.

'Good God,' said O'Hare over her shoulder. 'There's the old hospital; that's going back a bit.' He bent over for a closer look. 'No traffic. Those were the days. There's another huge photo of the Western down here. Look here, Costello, recognize that?' He pointed to a black and white picture of a magnificent sandstone tenement. 'Hyndland Road, before it was bombed. That is where you work.' He stabbed at the picture with a short, very clean fingernail.

'Really? Wouldn't have recognized it.'

O'Hare moved along the display, curiously interested. But Costello was bored, wanting to get up to the hospital with Marita's stuff. She looked at her watch; Batten would be arriving any minute and she had questions for him. Plus there was the prospect of her evening stroll through the fog on the Moss with Harry Castiglia. She looked out the window. O'Hare's car was shrouded in fog. She shivered; she was getting as nervous as Browne. She knew that what Quinn had said about the women not going out alone was only for Browne's benefit, but Costello did feel as if somebody was out there. She pushed the thought to the back of her mind, wondering if she had time to get home and grab a shower before the jaunt out to the Moss. But how could she get home in the fog with no car? Shit, she'd meant to phone the garage about the MOT, but it would be closed by now. Oh well, she'd just have to fling herself on the mercy of the oh-so-charming Mr Castiglia. She turned to the next set of pictures. Marita and Iain were standing on the steps at the front of the house, Diane in her navy-blue twinset a few steps down. A wheelbarrow was parked in front of an old man, his face shaded by a hat, and a tall young man stood at his side. They had borrowed a wolfhound from somewhere to complete the picture. Costello looked more closely at the younger man – Bobby? Powerfully built, but a blank face, totally blank. Itsy was nowhere to be seen. Costello's eyes moved to the window of the great drawing room; the curtain was pulled back slightly, and she hoped she could imagine a wee face peeping out.

The next set of pictures looked like Polaroid shots from the seventies. One caught her eye: a man, and a woman in shorts and a T-shirt, standing next to a pond.

Costello pulled it from its drawing pin, ripping the corner.

The woman held in her hand a small broken fishing rod, and a jam jar half filled with dirty water. Behind the figures were trees and more trees, a park perhaps. Off to one side was an old boathouse crumbling into the water. The couple were not standing together but slightly apart, as if awkward with each other. Between them, resting on the man's hip, was a kid, not yet a year old, her face turned away from the camera in a tantrum refusal to cooperate. The breeze had brushed the child's blonde wispy hair across the face of the man who held her. She was dressed up for her outing in a blue sailor suit, and the white hat that belonged to it was bobbing in the water at their feet. The shadow of the photographer was cast in the water, as if he was standing in the shallows.

Costello peered at the little floating hat, trying to make out ... Was it a sewn-on badge from the safari park at Blair Drummond? Had it been a dolphin, a fish, *the little fish*? She struggled to remember. She looked again at the woman's face. She would know her anywhere.

'What have you got there?' O'Hare put his glasses on and took the picture from her. 'Good Lord, that's the pond out there. I used to come and mess around here as a kid, you know; the public were allowed in then.'

'So that was taken here?'

'If you go out there you can still see where that boat-house used to be. Did you never come here as a kid? In my day we treated it as a public park; it was *our* pond.'

Costello felt something crawl over her skin, a chilly memory that numbed her brain. 'Seemingly I did come here.' She pointed at the figure in the little sailor suit. 'That's me. Don't remember that suit but I remember the hat, funnily enough.' She looked at the photograph for a minute longer, looking at the three blurred faces. Then she put the photograph down and turned away abruptly. 'How long is that bloody Diane going to be? How long can it take to stick a few clothes in a bag? And tell me another thing, Prof. Why did she ask after Marita when we came in? It's poor Itsy who's in –'

'Shhh, I can hear her coming down the stairs now.' O'Hare unzipped his anorak and put the photograph carefully in his wallet.

9

Rain.

Water.

Streaming down her face.

She raised her head, letting her face take the jet from the shower. She heard only the streaming of the water past her ears, deafening her. She could hear nothing else; her life was a world away.

She reached her hands above her head, stretching as far as she could, right up to the head of the shower. The jets of water hammering into her eyelids, so hard it hurt. She saw stars, the midnight sky on the back of her eyelids, and beyond that the eternal beauty of dark nothingness. And silence.

She slowly breathed out and kept breathing out until every last breath had gone; out and out, out . . . out . . .

She felt herself surrender.

Tears streaming down her face.

Costello gently knocked on the door marked Staff Toilet. She had been told Marita was in there getting ready to film her appeal. As she opened the door, she could see a sink top covered with make-up brushes, sponges, eyeshadows and powder stretching the width of the room. The air was heavy with perfume and hairspray.

Marita immediately started talking without looking up. 'Thank you for bringing the clothes. I feel much better now that I've had a shower and put my professional face on, and got something nice to wear.' Marita smoothed out non-existent creases in her cream jacket, and stepped over a pile of damp towels on the floor. 'I've had a long chat with Vik over the phone – he's rather lovely, isn't he? – and we've worked out some kind of provisional script for the appeal. Vik says I need to persuade anybody who was in the vicinity and might have seen Itsy to come forward. That's all. That's what I have to remember.'

Either the nursing station was quiet or the staff had been warned that Marita was in here and to use other facilities. Costello looked wistfully at her watch, then at the clock on the staff-toilet wall. It was just after 6.30 p.m. now, and time was slipping away from her. She really wanted a shower and a change of clothes herself, before she went out to the Moss with Harry; she still had on the clothes she had been wearing the day before, and she was stale and grubby. And Marita, with her classic figure, wearing brown linen trousers, a matching brown silk top and the cream jacket which went perfectly with her titian hair, was doing little to help the situation. She looked like a tiramisu, thought Costello cattily. Every bit as sickly, but less sweet.

'How do I look?' asked Marita with the confidence of someone who already knew they looked a million dollars.

'Well, you're looking much better than I think I would in these circumstances.'

Marita Kennedy gave Costello a look that said she

would look better than her in any circumstances, but what she said was, 'Thank you. Everybody is being so kind and so supportive.'

'Has there been any change?' Costello asked.

'Change?' Marita asked vaguely, using her powder-compact mirror to check the back of her hair in the big mirror.

'In Itsy?'

'Oh – no, she's just the same. I don't think they can stop the bleeding into her brain, something about a clot growing like a bruise that's causing pressure. They measure it on some kind of scale, and apparently she's getting worse, not better.' She said it impatiently, as if an incompetent plumber was having difficulty fixing a leak.

But then, Costello reminded herself, grief took different people in different ways. She still thought Mulholland should have advised Marita to look at least slightly upset and dishevelled for the camera. Appeals were much more effective if the relatives were out of their minds with worry, deranged with grief. And Marita Kennedy appeared to be neither.

'Are you going to sit with her while I'm away doing the filming?' Marita asked, her voice plaintive.

For a moment Costello was tempted to say, 'Yes, of course,' but then remembered Harry and the trip to the Moss. This would be her one chance to nip home. 'I'm afraid I can't,' she said. 'I'm going down to the Moss for another look around.'

That made Marita turn. 'Are you not finished down there? Surely you've found all that you're going to find?'

'Not really. We have no real idea how she got there, or what caused her injuries.'

'*Who* caused her injuries,' corrected Marita.

Costello made a non-committal noise. 'And the time-line is still incomplete. Two officers are up at Strathearn now talking to your PA, and McGurk and your gardener, Anthony Abbott.'

'I wish your colleagues luck with their timeline. I know when I first spoke to Diane they were both at the gatehouse. Then when I spoke to Iain about an hour later, Tony went out to look for her for a while. Then after that I went out with Bobby.'

They'd want a more definite statement than that sometime soon, Costello thought. But now wasn't the moment. 'What had you been doing all evening?' she enquired.

'I was going through my clothes, deciding what to keep and what to give to charity. I do it every few months. You'd be amazed how long it takes.'

Thinking of her own meagre wardrobe, Costello thought she would indeed be amazed.

'You don't notice time passing when you're busy.' Marita fluffed her hair one last time so it fell in a perfect curtain of copper and auburn against the cream linen of her jacket. Then turned to Costello. 'Can I ask you something? Do you think Itsy really was the intended victim? Or could it have been me?'

Costello didn't answer directly. 'We are looking into that possibility. Now can I ask you something? Did Itsy ever borrow your clothes, you know, the way sisters do? That peach-coloured top? And that lovely scarf?'

'Iain bought that for me, in Italy.' Marita was gazing at herself in the mirror.

Costello moved closer so her face appeared beside Marita's in the mirror. *She's only three or four years older than me*, Costello thought, *but I look about ten years older than she does*. 'Did she often nick your clothes? Ones she liked specifically, or things Iain bought for you?' Costello was staring right at the face in the mirror and caught the reaction, the open mouth, the slow blink. The tourmaline-green gaze met hers in the mirror, a study in bemused innocence.

'I never really thought of it. But yes, now you say that, I think the ones she takes are always things Iain's given me. But Iain buys me a lot of clothes. Men tend to buy me what I want.' She smirked wickedly to herself.

'I don't know why you had to join the police. If you'd left nursing to be a teacher, do the same hours as the kids, that would have made sense . . .'

Browne sighed, holding her mobile from her ear while she waited for her mother to take a breath.

'Now, your sister's friend . . . you know the one –'

Browne took her chance and butted in. 'Mum, Irene's having the kids tonight. They'll be fine. And she'll take them to school in the morning.' A recurring vision of Donna lying battered and dead in the gully flashed through her mind, and she said firmly, 'Mum, I really do have to go,' and cut off her mother in mid-rant. She shut her eyes, breathing in the moist earthy warmth of the great Victorian hothouse.

The darkness was lit only dimly by the security lights over on the far side of the pond. Browne switched on her torch and adjusted the beam to give a diffuse light that would illuminate everything, but not too much. Overhead she could see wrought-iron beams, their ornate moulding obliterated by layer upon layer of gloss paint over the years. A couple of bare light bulbs were strung loosely over them.

She removed her glove to stroke a tiny fern with the pad of her finger – so delicate, so beautiful. She began to relax in the warm air, savouring the lovely smell of paraffin and clean moist soil. It was so comforting, the scent of mother earth, she could almost fall asleep in here. Indeed, it looked as though somebody else had exactly the same idea and did so, frequently. At the end of the central concrete path stood an old armchair, its seat and back moulded to the shape of a body, with an old golden cushion with tangled tassels jammed down the back. Somebody habitually sat there, falling asleep and snoring, somebody who might slip their wellies off and warm their socks on the paraffin heater. She slipped her other glove off and stuck the pair in her pocket. The darkness lay heavy above the glass roof. She could see light bulbs overhead, but she could find no switches. Maybe by the door, she thought. The greenhouse had two doors – one for people to walk in from the gardens, the other a big double door, more like a garage door. Tyre marks and the odd patch of oil stained the concrete, suggesting that something was regularly parked there. She wondered if it was the wee white van that was sitting at the side of the path. Littlewood had stopped to examine it. Well, he'd stopped for a cigarette and a breather, leaning against the roof of the vehicle. Browne had decided not to hang about in the cold and had come into the warmth of the greenhouse.

She shone her torch up into the roof, trying to act like a detective, searching for CCTV cameras or security lights. Nothing. She wiped the glass with her sleeve and peered out at a driveway, unkempt and with a grassy midline. Not the well-kept main driveway they'd come in by; this was another one, a sort of back drive, that probably came out on to one of the mews lanes behind. Could the van come and go unseen from here? Unrecorded? Browne made a note in her notebook.

There was a workbench halfway along the glass wall, with two spotlights poised to light it. It was covered with trays full of tiny seedlings, not more than two inches high, small, fragile, vulnerable. *Vulnerable* – why had that word floated into her mind? She shivered, and gave herself a shake. She kicked something with her foot. It was Littlewood's Coro-Nitro spray, the one for his heart. He must have come through the greenhouse on his way up to Strathearn. She picked up the spray, and slipped it into her pocket.

Then she heard a noise, a faint rustle, that stopped as soon as it started.

She halted and turned.

Marita put her saintly face on again. 'If I'm in any way responsible for the state she is in now . . .' Her voice had a theatrical strength behind it. 'I must do everything I can to find out who is responsible, for her sake as well as my own. He failed once, but he might be luckier next time. I'm terrified to go out in that fog, you know. I keep thinking somebody is watching me. I'm sure somebody's out there. You know I was sent horrible mutilated photographs of myself? But I'm not going to let it stop me. I can get my TV appeal into every national paper, and on to every news bulletin. My face will keep Itsy in the national press; she won't be forgotten. Did you know lots of journalists have been in touch with my agent? One of them wants to do a big feature article. My Anguish for My Beloved Sister.' Marita turned back to the mirror, putting the finishing touches to her face. She knew how to look her best for the camera – though in the brittle light of the high dependency unit's staff toilet, her make-up looked like a bad paint job on old leather.

The more she knew of Marita, the more Costello wondered about the location of the attack. Following Marita Kennedy to Harvey Nicks she could understand, but following her to the Moss? Why would anyone think Marita would ever go there anyway? No, she couldn't swallow that. Marita was absorbed in her own appearance, so Costello took her chance. 'Why do you think she only borrowed the clothes Iain bought for you?'

Marita paused, but only for a moment. 'What people don't understand is that Itsy might act like a child, but she wanted nice things, things she saw in magazines. This was her first chance to have all that. Anything I had, she wanted. If I got a leather coat, she wanted one. I got Ugg boots, she wanted them. Her idea of men, her entire experience of men, is my husband. She hangs on his every word. She'll play me up, but she does as he says. It's like having a manipulative teenager in the house.' She turned to Costello, her face earnest. 'It wasn't easy, you know. On the one hand, I wanted her to be happy, to look pretty, to live as normal a life as possible; on the other, she . . . well, she's a little girl of eight, but she had feelings that she didn't know what to do with. She was vegetating in that home. Iain and I talked about it and he agreed she could come and live with us. He was so supportive. And I wanted to change her name; she's Ishbel, not Itsy. She shouldn't be treated like a child any more. It's time she grew up.'

Costello smiled, nice and friendly. 'Did Itsy settle at Strathearn?'

'Quite honestly, Itsy was happy anywhere she had company she could rebel against.'

'And did she form any romantic attachment, that you know of?'

'Maybe she and Bobby were a little too friendly at times,' Marita said blandly. 'You might want to look a bit further into that. He seems like a great silent hunk of rough, but there's something very strange there.'

Costello made a mental note to get that statement up on the board. 'Is that a photo of him, with the wheelbarrow on the step? You have it on the wall at home.'

Marita looked confused for a minute. 'Oh, that. That's Iain's project, local history and all that crap. People can send in pictures to go on that wall, then come in and ogle at them for a few days over the summer. I'll be in New York. But yes, that's Bobby – all muscle, no brains. I think

240

he's a bit simple. And Itsy is — well, what you need to understand is that Itsy was cunning. She always wanted her own way, and she usually got it. I bet I know exactly how she got to the Moss — she hitched a lift. DS Mulholland told me there's a farm near where she was found. She probably just told somebody she lived there, said she had no money, and needed to get home. If you were driving out there and saw a woman hitching a lift, and the moment she spoke you realized she didn't sound quite right in the head, a wee bit backward — you'd make sure she got home safely, wouldn't you? And Itsy could play the helpless little girl when she wanted to. She wanted to see that bloody albatross and nothing was going to stop her. The more we warned her that it wasn't safe out there, the more determined she was.'

'Do you think maybe she knew about the farm from her visit before? Would she make that connection — that that was the place to go to see the bird?'

'I don't doubt it for a minute. People like Itsy can hold on to the most trivial piece of information and keep harping back to it, but it'll be something important to them, not what is appropriate for life. But she must have remembered, otherwise she would never have got there. You should phone your colleagues, the ones who are at the house now, get them to ask the boys if they took her there when they visited. I bet they did.' Marita went back to the mirror, wiping a slick of glistening colour on her lips, then drawing her lips back to ensure none had got on her teeth. She had snaggle-teeth, Costello noticed. 'I really don't want to leave her alone. Can you not stay until I get back? I won't be long.'

'Your husband will be staying with her.' Costello noticed a slight pause of the lipstick wand on its second pass over the lips. 'He's coming in for a chat with us, but not until you get back. We planned it that way.'

Marita recovered herself, with a flick of the hair and a smile. She snapped her make-up bag closed and flung it in the huge Chanel sack she called a handbag. 'Well, that's me ready.' Then her mood changed again; she closed her eyes as if praying, and then opened them. 'It's just that Iain has been through so much, I don't want him here alone if anything happens while I'm away. That's all. You'll stay, won't you? Please?'

'Yeah, why not?' sighed Costello. *Nothing better to do, after all.* 'You'd better watch the time.'

She opened the door for her, and Marita gave her arm a slight squeeze in passing. Costello smirked to herself behind Marita's back, knowing that every single inch of her televised appeal would be analysed, frame by frame. Marita had the feeling somebody was watching her every move now. That was nothing to what Mick Batten was going to do.

In the warmth of the hothouse Browne started to relax and decided to have a good look around. She was a detective on a murder squad now and was starting to feel like one.

Under the bench she saw a cardboard box, a bit bigger than a shoebox, the top punched with holes. Something inside it was making a noise like a baby mumping to itself. She bent down and gently pulled the box out. Her heart pounding in her chest, she eased the lid off, and directed the beam of the torch away. In the straw cowered a bird, a beautiful mouse-brown bird with a fine collar of black feathers across the back of its neck. It regarded her with dark unblinking eyes like drops of black ink. An ice-lolly stick had been tied with meticulous care along the length of its outspread wing.

Vulnerable.

She closed the box, carefully put it back under the workbench, and heard the heavy footfall of a man approaching. She stood up, sure it was John Littlewood, but glancing through the greenery she couldn't see him. She hoped he was OK. She patted the spray in her pocket, glad she had found it for him. She stayed still, listening, running her eyes over the old rickety table, a Thermos flask, and a pile of gardening magazines, old and tattered, one folded open at an article about how to keep koi carp safe outside during the winter.

She took a step backwards, into the shelter of a large cheese plant, her mind starting to run riot. Did Itsy creep down here, to be with the two men who worked here? She was certainly an attractive woman; at least, that was how men would see her. And with the mind of a child. Had something sinister been going on among the plants in this greenhouse at the bottom of the garden, away from prying eyes? Had Itsy been too innocent to realize, too innocent to know she wasn't supposed to talk about it? Had she become dangerous to them? Browne tried to remember what she had learned during her training, about selection, grooming, control, how sexual predators preferred to keep it all close to home. Had the two men feigned an interest in birds to attract the childlike Itsy? Such an innocent would trust without question anyone who helped an injured creature.

Browne's heart was thumping again. Evidence, she told herself. She needed evidence.

Her eyes scanned the shelves, noting the selection of fertilizers and weedkillers placed high up, set back so that even she would need a ladder to get them down. That same degree of care, keeping poison out of a child's reach. There was an array of small trowels and forks and other things – she had no idea of their right names – all lined up on nails in the wall like instruments for surgery. She thought about the wounds the victims had to the roofs of their mouths, and she squinted her eyes to focus. She was about to step out to lift up a chisel when she heard the noise again, more definite this time. The garden door had closed. She heard a step on the path inside.

She switched off her torch. Somebody was in here with her. And she didn't think it was Littlewood.

Every instinct told her to keep quiet, and she tried to hold her breath. She crept along towards the door, keeping close to the bigger plants, moving leaves from her face as she brushed past. She could hear him breathing, getting closer. She kept her eyes fixed ahead of her, struggling to see in the gloom. She had only the length of one bench to go before she'd be at the big door.

Had he known she was in here? He could have been following her, out there in that fog, and she wouldn't have known. She tried to keep her breathing calm, tried to still her heart from beating. He had stopped moving. She looked round. The figure was standing behind the armchair, his hands grasping the back of it. This could not be Wee Tony. This man was younger, powerfully built, with a scruffy jacket and dirty-blond hair. He looked up, directly at her. She had made no sound, but he had known she was there. Browne screamed at the top of her voice and ran for the door – three strides, two strides, one stride . . .

She yanked on the handle, praying it would open.

It held firm.

She stepped back and pulled again. He was bounding towards her. She was easy prey, trapped. She could see a figure in the dark outside, and banged on the glass as hard as she could, the sound of the blows muffled by the fog.

The glass became a mirror. She could see him coming up behind her, his huge filthy hands reaching for her throat. She closed her eyes.

Iain Kennedy had given Costello a strange look when she'd asked to nip out for a cuppa. Now she was sitting on the internal stairwell of the hospital that was used by those who couldn't be bothered waiting for the lifts, a place that stank of curry and illicit cigarettes, thinking about what to say to Harry. She couldn't even drive out and meet him later without her own wheels. It was seven o'clock, way too late to do anything now, so she decided to sit here and be miserable.

How long would it take to get back to the flat? Taxi out, taxi back? Not long at this time of the evening. She needed to get her keys from her neighbours – that would be OK; they never went out – but she couldn't wash her hair and dry it, not in the time she had, and to go out in this weather with wet hair would be suicidal. She didn't know if there was such a thing as triple pneumonia but if there was then this was the weather for it. She had a strange vision of herself lying on O'Hare's cold stainless-steel table, his forefinger on her collarbone, ready to cut.

She was asking, 'Why are you doing this, I'm not dead?'

And he was saying, 'Of course you're dead, Costello, you just haven't stopped talking yet.'

And then the first cut, but she couldn't feel it, and he said –

'Penny for them?'

She jerked into wakefulness.

Harry Castiglia slid on to the step above her, giving her a playful shove with his knee. 'You were miles away.'

'Why are you here?' She said it in a way that suggested she was next in line for experimental surgery for haemorrhoids.

'Most women are glad to see me.' Harry twisted a lens on to the body of his camera. 'I'm following Marita as she films the appeal. Honestly, the words drama and queen were made for that woman. She'd go to the opening of an abattoir if she thought it was a good photo opportunity. She's spent her life manipulating people like me into making her look more attractive. But as far as I'm concerned, those snaggle-teeth make her look like a bloody vampire.'

'Yes, I noticed. Is that why you never see her laughing?'

'That presupposes she has a sense of humour. She can be a bloody nightmare.'

'Do you know her then?'

'Oh yes, I did a photo shoot for her once, just after I came back from North Africa. I'd won a few awards and I was the "in" thing. I did her in black and white, hard and dangerous.'

'Is she?'

Harry nodded. 'The camera never lies.'

The door on to the landing opened, a nurse looked down, saw who it was and turned away, closing the door. The metallic slam echoed down the chilly stairwell.

Costello persisted. 'Did you ever photograph Itsy?'

'No, not Itsy, but I'd seen shots of her in magazines, her and Marita together. Interesting how they look so much alike now, wouldn't you say? I'd like to capture that in a picture – two women who look the same, but one as hard as nails, the other as hard as soufflé.'

'So would you say Itsy is an attractive woman?'

'From the photographs, yes. But what's with the questions, Costello?'

'I was wondering how a man might feel about a woman with the mind of a child?'

'Someone like Itsy would give you unconditional love, like a puppy,' Harry said thoughtfully. 'Such people need protecting. I'd kill any bastard that hurt her.'

Costello was glad she was not looking at Castiglia, glad she could not see the expression on his face. Something had hit a raw nerve there.

She was about to change the subject on to albatrosses, but he suddenly said, 'Think of the great shots of Audrey Hepburn, Marilyn, Piaf. Black and white – all showing the woman behind the beauty. That's every photographer's dream. But Marita Kennedy has no woman behind that beauty; Marita is what you see. Makes my job bloody difficult. Anyway, you set for tonight? We'll try for a great picture of Ally, while pretending to document the raw nature of the scene now the search team has packed up. All bleak and ravaged, but deserted.'

'Yeah. I'd hoped to get home and get some warmer clothes, but I haven't got any wheels and I'm not allowed out in the fog on my own – Quinn's orders. Anyway, I've been told to stay here until you've finished the appeal.'

'So we're both kiboshed.' He spread his arms in a very Gallic gesture. 'We can go with the flow. I don't suppose the crime scene or Ally are going to go anywhere soon. What about nine tonight, vaguely, approximately? You're just along the expressway, aren't you?' He looked at his watch. 'When Marita or Iain get back, just text me and I'll run you home, leave you for half an hour. I could go down and see what mood the Clyde is in. Then I can collect you.'

'That would be great,' said Costello, trying to ignore the excitement that was rising in her stomach.

She heard the camera shutter snap a few times and he was gone, bounding down the stairs. He stopped briefly on the flight below her, and she heard it again, a few more times. He was snapping her through the banisters. He had a good eye for a picture, she could see that. Maybe he had a good heart too.

He hadn't invited himself in, so clearly he had some degree of sensitivity – Quinn had used the word integrity.

'Oi!' she called after him. 'How do you know where I live?'

But he had gone. Maybe he'd asked at the station. She wondered what else he had asked about her.

Browne felt firm hands on shoulders pulling her away from the glass, and she collapsed into the arms of DS John Littlewood. Bobby McGurk was shaking alarmingly, grunting incomprehensibly. A small grey-haired man stood in front of him, his hand on the young man's chest, calming him. It was Wee Tony. He was glaring at Gillian Browne.

'For God's sake, he frightened her!' Littlewood shouted furiously.

'He didn't know there was anybody in here; why should he?' Wee Tony was as furious as Littlewood. 'Look, let me speak to her. What's her name?'

'DC Browne,' said Littlewood aggressively.

Wee Tony addressed her rather formally. 'I'm sorry, DC Browne, if you got a fright, but Bobby didn't know you were in here,' he said, his lined grey eyes looking deep into hers as he pleaded. 'How could he? The thing is, if Bobby sees somebody upset he goes up and tries to put his arms around them. He didn't mean to frighten you.'

Browne dissolved into tears.

'I bet he crept up behind the armchair without making a noise,' Tony went on, his voice calm and friendly. 'He knows I like to have a wee kip there in the afternoon and I've given him a row often enough for banging the door, waking me up. So instead he likes to creep up behind me.

Sometimes he has a cup of tea for me, but occasionally he puts worms down the back of my neck, or a slug . . .' He seemed to run out of steam, and turned to Littlewood. 'I'm sorry if the young woman got a fright. But you have to know how to treat Bobby. He wouldn't hurt a fly, but he's not —'

'Normal?'

'No, I guess not, but I'm not having this conversation in front of him. Believe me, miss, he meant you no harm. He scared you, and you scared him. It's all been a misunderstanding.'

'Browne? Are you happy with this?' asked Littlewood, a cough catching in his throat.

'That's just what he did. He crept up behind the chair, and he seemed confused when he found it empty.' Browne was going to start crying again. 'I'm sorry; I'm so sorry. I just got a fright.'

'So why didn't he put the bloody light on? Why didn't you, for that matter?' growled Littlewood.

'I couldn't find the switch,' answered Browne simply.

'Well, no harm done,' said Tony, cradling Bobby's shoulder with the palm of his hand. 'Right, I'm going to put the kettle on. Anybody want a cuppa?'

Anderson knocked gently on Quinn's door, hearing a muffled, 'Hang on a minute,' before he was told to come in.

Quinn had put down the phone. 'I've just been speaking to O'Hare. He's invited us all round for a takeaway curry tonight, though it'll be more of a midnight feast by the time we get there. It's gone seven and I've a pile of work to do yet. Us, by the way, does not include Lambie or Mulholland.'

'Tonight. Batten too?'

'Oh yes, he's invited. Going to be the star of the show, I should think.' Her smile was weak, unconvincing. 'What can I do for you?'

'I have the list from Wyngate about the keys. I think we can disregard the power companies and the council, but this magazine company, based in London – they commissioned a local agency, who picked up the keys, and they commissioned a local photographer . . .'

'Gillespie.'

'And yes, he had the keys for a 24-hour period.'

'Long enough to get them copied. These magazines have months of run-in time, so when was that?'

'Eighth of January. Bannon had early proofs sent to him just for interest. That's them on the wall.'

'Background?'

'There's nothing we can find, ma'am. Gillespie seems clean.'

'Too much of a coincidence, surely?'

'And K Division have traced the taxi driver. He dropped Donna McVeigh at Gilmour Street Station in Paisley, but she didn't go in. She walked under the bridge, out of sight. CCTV picked up nothing in the fog.'

Quinn tapped her desk with her finger, as if she was having difficulty concentrating. 'What's that?' She pointed to the file under Anderson's arm.

He hesitated.

'Sit down if you want.'

'I have a few interesting facts. Might mean nothing, of course. Strathearn House was bought by the Kennedys three years ago. It had been lying empty for three years before that.'

'I know. The previous owner was trying to get planning permission to turn it into flats and was turned down. Problems with access on to the main road. Traffic Division was asked about it.'

'It was sold to the Kennedys in 2007 by our friend Stuart Bannon. They signed the deal on 13th January and they got married on 14th February.'

'And . . . ?'

'My point is that Marita is now entitled to half the value of the house if anything went wrong. She'd be quids in.'

'So she has nothing to lose and half his fortune to gain if the marriage breaks up. Interesting. But probably not relevant to the case. What else?'

'Anthony Abbott came to work for them in May that same year, and Bobby McGurk a month later, in June. And another thing . . . we found this.' He handed over a picture of a bevy of bikini-clad beauties, a recognizable Marita at the front holding a cheap crown to her head.

'The lovely Marita being crowned Miss Caledonia, twenty years ago. And you and Wyngate call looking at this work?'

'Look again, ma'am.'

'Well, it's definitely her. She looks exactly the same.'

'Take a look at Miss East Kilbride.'

Quinn narrowed her eyes. 'Diane the housekeeper, PA, whatever she calls herself? Yes, definitely her. That explains her constant grin. I thought she was simple.' She handed the photograph back. 'So they've been friends for years? So what?'

'Wyngate's been reading the reports of the so-called stalking, and going through the magazine articles. Most of the evidence for it seems to stem from "sources close to the TV star".'

'Diane? Naughty, but no crime, though.'

'But incidents were reported in the press before being reported to the police.'

'Still no crime, Colin.'

'Can Wyngate do a bit more digging, ma'am? I have an uneasy feeling.'

'About what?'

He shrugged. 'Just an uneasy feeling.'

Iain Kennedy was alone at the high dependency unit, standing up at the glass, leaning his forehead on it. 'So she's doing the appeal. Are you sure that's wise?' he said without moving. 'I'm not sure that it's the right decision, putting her in the front line like this. We've had problems in the past . . .'

'Mrs Kennedy is keen to do it. I think it gives her a feeling she's doing something useful.' Costello sat down, flinging one leg over the other, leaving the ankle resting on top of the opposite knee, and took a surreptitious look at her watch. She had to stay here until the uniform came up from downstairs, and he was taking his time about it.

Kennedy saw that the sole of her scuffed boot was almost worn through. This detective looked knackered and grubby, and he wondered where the older, smarter one was. DCI Quinn. That was a woman who looked as though she knew what she was about. He had his doubts about this one.

'It's the worst thing in the world, that feeling of being powerless,' he agreed.

'You have to reassure yourself that they know what they're doing. These guys can twist the media any way they want. And anything might help Itsy.'

It was now Kennedy's turn to sit down. The sheer weariness of the scruffy blonde woman in front of him was reinforcing his own tiredness, and he felt himself succumb. He also felt he was safe in admitting that he was not coping with this. 'And nobody is better at manipulating the media than my wife, I can tell you.' There was a slight bitterness in his voice.

'It takes all sorts,' said Costello blandly. 'And, like I say, it's that skill that we need right now. I'd like to ask you something, off the record. I've heard about the stalking business, read about it. Do you have any idea who was threatening your wife?' She kept the question deliberately vague, seeing if Iain Kennedy came up with something that had not been formally reported.

'I know her first husband had been nasty, making a few threats. Probably thought he could get money out of her since she'd married a rich man. We heard from the cops at Partick Central that he was in Aberdeen when the incident happened but Marita thinks he put somebody up to it, and that they put superglue in the keyhole of a vintage Mercedes I bought her for her birthday. That did worry me, as it was parked at the house and it meant there'd been a breach of security. Somebody sent dog faeces to her in the post, and she got pictures, then photographs of herself with lines cut across her throat, that type of thing.'

'That must have upset her. Did she report it immediately?'

There was a pause before he answered, as if he was tempted to turn and look over his shoulder, making sure Marita wasn't about to walk through the door. 'No, so I did. She was very angry with me for that. She thought it would show whoever was doing it that they had got to her. My wife doesn't like to show weakness.'

Costello nodded. 'I can understand that. So what about Anthony Abbott and Bobby McGurk? How do they get on with Itsy? And how do you come to know them all anyway? You seem rather an oddly assorted bunch, if you don't mind me saying so.'

'Tony and Bobby.' Iain stuck his hands in his trouser pockets, and smiled reflectively, his mind going back to happier times. 'Well, Tony was a bit of a lost soul when he came to us. He has a prison record . . .'

'Yes, I know,' Costello lied.

'But that's all far behind him. He came back to Glasgow when we were starting the refurbishing work at Strathearn – when was that? – nearly three years ago now. We heard about him through the Rotary; he'd been helping out with some garden planning somewhere and had proved himself a bit of a star. He started as our odd-job man and ended up almost being project manager. Well, he was looking for somewhere to live, and the gatehouse was empty. It was a wreck, but he's a hard grafter and worked on it in his own time. Then he started on the gardens, the woods, the pond. We were going to get contractors in, and professional landscapers, but there was no need. He'd do it 24/7 if we let him. His interest in wildlife was a bonus; parts of the gardens are breeding habitats now, for dragonflies, nightjars, kingfishers – they were never there before.'

'The gardens are certainly very beautiful, from what I've seen. Do you know what he was in prison for?'

'I thought you knew.' Iain dropped his gaze to look at her directly.

She felt like a difficult pupil being caught out by the headmaster. 'I asked whether you knew,' she replied, her tone reminding him who he was talking to.

'From what I heard, his barber shop became a haven for stolen goods.'

Costello smiled. 'I think that was common in those days. My dad used to work in a barber's, and that place was exactly the same.'

'Well, I think Abbott got in a bit too deep. He did a bit of time, then he went off to London to make a fresh start.'

'Did he say why he came back?'

Kennedy pursed his lips and shook his head. 'I've never asked. He keeps himself to himself. And who knows what brings people home? I never heard him speak of any family or anything up here. Actually, he's always treated Itsy like a daughter and Bobby like a son.' Kennedy smiled at a happy memory. 'They're always fooling around; one day Bobby was giving Itsy a ride on the big wheelbarrow, and she toppled off, and all the cuttings were spilled all over the lawn. Tony was trying to get them to clear up the mess, but he was laughing too much. Or they'll be down at the pond trying to sail this model boat Bobby made, but it always sinks. Itsy told me Tony had to tie a long string to it so they could pull it out again. She's scared of water, always scared of water; she won't even go close to the edge of the pond. But she hooted with laughter when they were playing with the boat. I think that's what I miss most, the laughter – I can't bear the silence. I'd rather be here.' His eyes drifted down the hospital corridor.

'Did Bobby McGurk know Abbott before? Was there any connection between them?'

'None that I'm aware of. We realized it was all getting too much for Tony; he looks tough, but he's in his sixties, and his health isn't too great. Bobby came to us the same way as Tony did, through the Rotary, a few weeks later. He arrived as a general labourer; now he's our maintenance man, does a bit of painting, clears the gutters. And heavy stuff in the garden. As a team they're spot on. Brains and brawn. Tony knows what needs doing, and Bobby's as strong as an ox. Couldn't ask for better.'

'And where does McGurk live?'

'Tony simply took him to live at the gatehouse, and that was that. Tony's devoted to Bobby and Itsy. Two damaged creatures. And they're devoted to him. And to each other.' Kennedy's voice sounded rather wistful.

Something was telling Costello that he was talking for a

reason, and she was happy to let him talk. 'Damaged? Is McGurk not quite the full shilling?'

'Some people think he's a bit lacking up here.' Iain tapped his own forehead. 'But he's no fool. Monosyllabic, yes, and he's very nervous – well, nervous of strangers. I think life has been difficult for him. But he's not stupid; it's just that he's never had a proper education. There's something of the little boy about him, something of the innocent. But he needs Tony to keep him at it, otherwise he'd be off checking the nesting boxes, picking up wee creatures that have got hurt. He's very good with them.'

'Do you mind if I ask you – what was it exactly that was wrong with Itsy?'

Kennedy looked at her for a long moment, as if weighing up what he should tell her, if anything. Then he relaxed. 'I'd always believed that she'd had been brain-damaged when she was born. It's hypoxic brain injury she has. It's usually caused by lack of oxygen to the brain at birth.'

Costello nodded. She knew Mick Batten's daughter had had a blue face when she was born. 'The worst moment of my life,' he'd said. 'But she was lucky.'

Kennedy went on, 'I never questioned it. And Marita never put me right on the matter. But something Itsy said once made me wonder. I mean, she fantasizes about things but she can blurt out the truth like nobody I know. She told me she could remember her mum shouting at Marita, them both shouting at each other. Their mother telling Marita it was all her fault. Marita shouting back that she should never have been left alone with a three-year-old.

Maybe I'm wrong, but I put two and two together. Itsy is terrified even of bathwater; she won't get her face wet. Two little girls, left alone in the bath together – who knows what happened? And Marita would never tell me – not that I'd ask her.'

Costello asked carefully. 'What do you think happened?'

'Itsy couldn't quite remember. All she said was it was a game. She liked it. Putting her head under. But she's terrified of it now . . .'

'So Itsy might have slipped under the water. Or Marita might have . . . pushed her . . . ?'

'No,' Iain said sharply. 'Well, maybe – but if Itsy was three, then Marita could only have been five. I'd never have left my boys unattended in the bath at that age. How would she know what to do? How would she even know anything was wrong? Though there's something else. . .' He twisted his fingers, his eyes fixed on the floor, then looked up, a man in great pain. 'I also get the feeling that Itsy is a little bit scared of Marita; not just in awe of her big sister, but actually scared. Itsy tries so hard to please her.'

'And how does Marita respond?' asked Costello neutrally.

Kennedy shut his eyes for a moment, as though voicing such disloyalty to his wife was a great effort for him. 'She just . . . ignores her. Unless they're both in front of the cameras, she always has.'

Yes, we'd cottoned on to that, Costello thought. 'How is Itsy doing?' she asked gently.

'She's sinking deeper into her coma.' It was a simple statement, quietly spoken.

259

'Is there nothing else that can be done?' Costello stood up, looking through the glass window at the bed and the inert figure at the heart of the mass of tubes and machines.

Kennedy sighed wretchedly. 'I think they've done all they can.' Then he looked up at Costello, eyes full of raw pain. 'I don't know what to do. I really don't know what to do.'

'Would they allow you to go in and speak to her, talk to her? Does she have music or anything? What kind of stuff does she like?'

'I think we're waiting for some CDs to arrive from up the road. *The Sound of Music* is her favourite.'

'I could have picked them up – it's no distance. You should have said.'

Kennedy managed a weak smile. 'That's a kind thought, thank you.'

'And what about her wee Snoopy dog?'

'Yes, I'm sure she'd like him with her. That's a good idea.'

'So why are you not in there, talking to her?' Costello deliberately made the question sharp but kept her voice kind.

Kennedy ran a hand through his thinning hair. 'Because I have no idea what to say to her, no idea at all.'

'Why does that matter? Just talk to her, tell her anything – the weather, how bad the coffee is in here. That should keep you going for a while.'

Kennedy nodded, re-evaluating the woman. She had a valuable ability to make you forget she was a cop. And now that she was standing up, and he could see her properly, there was something about her that seemed familiar.

'Why don't we both go in and talk to her?' Costello asked.

'What, now?'

'If we gown up, why not? Do you not think she would be glad to speak to somebody?'

Kennedy glanced round, as if looking for Marita to tell him what to do.

'We need to wash our hands and faces – they'll have some antibacterial stuff somewhere . . .' Costello disappeared off, and came back a few minutes later with shoe covers, head covers, and two blue aprons. 'Here.'

'Is this wise?'

'If I was lying there, sinking ever deeper into some kind of darkness, I'd want to know that you were there.' Costello smiled at him, and he was touched that she'd said 'you'.

They gowned up in silence, adjusting each other's hats, tying each other's bows.

Costello hung back, leaving Iain and Itsy alone. He stood by the head of the bed, as if wanting to place his hand somewhere to comfort her, to communicate with her, but he hesitated. There was hardly an inch of flesh that wasn't covered by a dressing, a wire, or a tube.

They stood still for a minute in comforting silence. The ventilator sighed gently.

Costello studied the left side of Itsy's face. A jagged tear ran up from the side of the mouth like the smile on the face of the Joker. The wound was held together with some kind of reinforced tape but at the corner of her lips it was being pulled apart by the brace that was supporting the palate injury in case the surgeons had to go in again. Itsy's teeth had been loosened and badly damaged.

Iain Kennedy seemed rooted to the spot. Costello was aware of something more than hesitation – a strong emotion – emanating from him like an electrical charge. This, she realized, was not a man comforting his sister-in-law. This was a man about to lose the woman he loved.

She found a small patch of forearm, covered in fine downy hair, and gently placed her fingers on it. She could feel warmth through the latex of her glove, and remembered O'Hare's hand covering hers in the same way. She hoped Itsy could feel it and gain some comfort. For a minute she forgot Iain was there. 'I never realized you were so small, Itsy; you look so much bigger in your pictures.'

'She takes a nice picture,' Iain said.

Costello nodded at the prone figure. *Don't tell me, tell her.* 'How are the koi? Surviving in the fog, Iain? Must be cold out there.'

'They're doing fine . . .' He laid his hand on the pillow above Itsy's head, and the one-way conversation started. 'Tony is still feeding them, but they should really be asleep at the bottom of the pond, sleeping their way through the cold winter. Are you going to do that too, Itsy? Sleep through the winter?'

Kennedy's words made Costello think of the photograph that had been taken at the lake.

Her mother. Herself as a baby. And the man who held her . . .

Littlewood was glad to be indoors, in the warmth. The smell of the hothouse was making him feel rather mellow and nostalgic for his youth, so he was content to sit there and wait for the kettle to boil. At the tap in the corner, Gillian was having a good go at the old stained mugs with a Brillo pad, as though the activity would calm her after the fright she had had. He relaxed in the saggy old armchair, letting the heat seep through to his bones. He was waiting for it to reach the chill in his chest, for the dull crushing pain to ease off a little. He didn't want to use his spray in front of these people, not that they would have noticed, but his hand was in his pocket, feeling the small cylinder, knowing it was there if he needed it.

'Had Itsy been down at the Moss before?' he asked.

'Oh aye,' said Wee Tony, running his hand through the thinning grey hair that grew untrimmed down the back of his neck. 'Last time we were there the two of them were playing King of the Castle on that drystane dyke.'

'And you?'

'No, the last time I played it I did my knee in.'

'I mean, are you familiar with the land round there?'

'I know where to park the car to get easy access, if that's what you mean.'

'When was the last time you were down there?'

'Early Friday, about teatime. That was the last clear night before the fog, wasn't it?'

Littlewood was listening to Tony, but looking at Bobby,

263

hiding slightly in the shadow of some broad-leaved tropical plant, sitting on an upturned bucket to give Littlewood the chair. The fright he had given Gillian seemed to have left him as shaken as it had her. The idiot boy, as Littlewood thought of him, was not a boy of course, but a powerfully built man in his thirties with muscles chiselled from hard physical work, and not an ounce of fat on him. And it was hard to tell how much of an idiot he was. He had a coarse-featured face that was not unpleasant, and an air of gaucheness. But the bond between him and Wee Tony was more like father and son than any father and son Littlewood knew nowadays. Father and son? Wee Tony, thin, grey-haired, grey-eyed, was five foot four in his socks at most. He had the look of somebody familiar about him, but Littlewood couldn't place who. Bobby was big-boned, taciturn and slow, but not clumsy. He moved economically, and handled things with care.

Another thing was obvious: the real concern of both men for Itsy. Bobby looked up at every mention of her name, and twice in the few minutes Littlewood had been in their company, he had tugged at Tony's jacket and asked if Itsy was OK.

Gillian brought the tea over on a battered tin tray and put it down on top of the bird books.

'Do you remember the night Itsy disappeared, Bobby?'

McGurk folded himself back into his hiding place, and nodded, looking intently at Littlewood, as if translating what the old policeman was saying. Littlewood kept an eye on Tony, making sure he did not prompt an answer, but Tony was standing back, distancing himself from the younger man. Littlewood nodded slightly to Browne, signalling her to get involved. If Bobby was in any way emotionally vulnerable, he wanted Gillian's evidence that they had taken the softly-softly approach.

'Bobby, can you tell me what happened that night?' asked Gillian. She crouched down beside him with her notebook on her knee, and began trying to prise the events of the night from him bit by bit, with infinite patience, but to no avail.

Bobby seemed confused by the questions, he just shrugged and shook his head, looking at Tony as if the old man would give him the right answer.

Browne persisted. 'Did Itsy come down to the gate-house while you were eating your tea?'

Bobby looked up at Tony, who said, 'Well, tell the lassie, don't ask me.'

Bobby shook his head.

'Before we had our soup, Bobby?' Tony prompted him. 'He can be like this with folk he disnae know,' he said quietly to Browne.

'So, Bobby, what happened before you had your soup?'

'Itsy came,' Bobby said, as if a light had gone on some-where in his head.

'She knew a dove was in trouble out there, and she wanted Bobby to get to it before the fox did,' Tony took over. 'She was dressed for it, wrapped up nice and warm. She likes to go out in the grounds at all hours, and – well, you can't imprison someone, can you? We chased her back to the big house. Diane phoned later to ask was she with us. Then much later, I'd nodded off. The phone woke me.

That was Marita saying Itsy was missing. So I went out to look for her, round the far side of the lake. After I came back, Marita came down to get Bobby.'

Bobby looked up, thinking hard. 'The dove broke her wing,' he said. 'I heard her in the long grass and we brought her back here. Fixed it.' He gazed at Browne and recited carefully: '*In the Spring a livelier iris changes on the burnish'd dove.*'

'*In the Spring a young man's fancy lightly turns to thoughts of love,*' Browne completed the couplet, smiling back at him.

Abbott rolled his eyes. 'He's a great lad for the poems.' He smiled, and took a sip of his tea.

'Can you remember what time it was when Marita came out to talk to Bobby? Even roughly?'

Tony looked up at the glass roof; the fog was like a blanket pulled down over the greenhouse. He automatically reached into the pocket of his old jacket and pulled out a packet of Silk Cut. He handed one to Littlewood without offering it, and Littlewood took it without acknowledgement. 'Eight, or just before,' he said.

Browne nodded. 'That would fit. By the time she'd got dressed and come over here, Iain had phoned Partick Station.' She pulled two plastic bags from her pocket, each with a long scraper and two tiny plastic cones inside. She started opening one of the bags. 'It would really help if we could have a DNA sample. Just a scrape along inside of your cheek, it doesn't hurt.' She smiled encouragingly at Bobby, who looked at Tony, and Tony shook his head.

'No way, sorry.'

Browne looked at Littlewood.

266

'Your choice, mate. But if you're innocent . . .' said the old cop nonchalantly. 'What about you, Bobby? Are you going to give DC Browne a sample?'

Bobby looked at Tony, then shook his head.

Tony pulled a deep breath of nicotine into his lungs, then blew the smoke out, letting it curl into the air. 'You just get the bastard who hurt Itsy and I'll kill him with my own bare hands. Then you'll have my DNA.'

'From what I hear, there'll be a queue ahead of you,' said Littlewood.

10

Anderson was listening to Costello's voicemail, wondering if the charismatic presence of Castiglia had got to her and she was seeing romance everywhere. But she was an intuitive cop, he reminded himself. She might be right. Kennedy and his sister-in-law? He deleted the message and eased himself through the narrow door in search of Mick. The room was far too small to be used as a formal interview room without catching an infectious disease. He had to clamber over a holdall with a jacket and laptop lying on it, and move the homburg hat from the desk.

'Mick, how are you?'

Batten got up and the two men embraced each other, a warm genuine hug.

'I never saw you come in.'

'You were busy, and I had things to do. I've been here for a couple of hours and I've made a nuisance of myself already. No canteen these days?'

'Long story.'

'So how's life been abusing you?'

'Usual police life. I'm overworked and tired out, the wife's permanently boot-faced, I never see the kids . . .'

'Blood pressure through the roof? Don't sleep? Eat too much crap?'

'That's about it.'

'Ditto,' Batten sighed, 'with knobs on. Life's been a bit tough, it has to be said.'

'I know, Mick, and I'm sorry. These things happen.' Anderson looked around. 'So tell me, why were you sitting in here with a huge pile of files and video tapes?'

'Victim profile. Basically, these women were all self-confident achievers. Our killer is not. Any idea where Lambie and Mulholland have got to? I'd be a lot happier speaking out if I knew those two weren't around,' Batten said quietly.

'Why?' asked Anderson, then added, 'Lambie?'

'Just a precaution.'

'Later we're going round for a midnight speakeasy, curry and some booze, to O'Hare's flat. Well, he knows about the curry, maybe not about the booze, but there's a rumour that he keeps a nice malt. Can it wait until then?'

'Some of it can, but some of it I want you to see here and now.'

'Is this your bag? Have they not even put you in a hotel yet?'

'No time. I've been reading up on a guy called Adrian Wood. Mean anything to you?'

Anderson shook his head.

Batten smiled quietly to himself and rustled around in the pockets of his leather jacket, found a packet of fags and an old silver lighter. Then he put them on the desk, looking for something else.

Anderson caught a glimpse of Batten's T-shirt: *Kiss me, I'm drunk enough to find you attractive.*

'You know . . .' Batten said, sticking a ballpoint between his teeth so it waggled as he talked, his hands busy making the pile of files and paperwork more chaotic, '. . . I remember talking to Alan McAlpine once – it was bloody cold night that night too – and somewhere along the line we were talking about converging lines, killers and cops slowly coming together. I have that feeling now. What you are working on and what I am working on, and what *he* . . .' Batten flicked his forefinger at the whiteboard outside, '. . . is working on, are all on converging paths. But my impression is that we are not getting closer to him.'

'The rapist?'

'No, the other man, as you call him. We should never forget about the other man. However, I think he's come closer to you. Geographically, if nothing else.'

Anderson said nothing. His expression said simply: *Convince me.*

'OK, follow this. My career went down the shithole. No fault of mine but Kim Thompson died and I got made a scapegoat. Shit happens. So I'm back at the university, talking to students who watch too much television, interviewing cons, doing reports and boring my arse off. I've always been interested in NPD, some funding came up, and I decided maybe I'd do a research paper.'

'NPD?'

'Narcissistic pathological disorder. Do you remember the Blackwell case?'

Anderson had a quick think. 'About five years ago? Killed his parents with a hammer or something? Then went on a spending spree? That was in your part of the world.'

'Brian Blackwell admitted manslaughter with diminished responsibility due to NPD. That sparked off a lot of interest. Yet he was only one type of narcissist. He was what people believe a narcissist to be.' Batten indicated Anderson should sit down. 'No one will ever know what really drove Blackwell to murder his parents but NPD can now be argued in court as a serious mitigating circumstance in British law. But we know bugger all about it. Psychiatrists don't know what causes it, and have no idea how to treat it. Most can't even diagnose it.' Batten reached out and lazily lifted up a plastic evidence folder with the brown label *My Name Is Stephen Whyte* inside, and said, very quietly, 'What does this mean to you?'

'That Mr Whyte was delivered. But to who?'

'Good question. And if you sit and listen, you'll have a lot more questions.'

'Like, who are we after, exactly?' asked Anderson, trying to keep up. 'And what are all these?' He picked up a single file from a stack of them at least three feet high.

Batten had been busy; the files were tagged and Post-it notes visible. On the other chair was an open shorthand notebook; on the top sheet was scribbled *Wyngate List 4*.

Anderson reached out to read it. 'You've been bloody busy if you got through all these.'

'Oh, I knew what I was looking for. *Exactly* what I was looking for. Don't touch, I have them in a specific order. And I'm making a To Do list for Gordon Wyngate. I want files, reports and evidence tracked down. He's going to be busy. Right, those ones there are the files of all the rape victims that Mulholland and Lambie think are the victims of our serial attacker – well, all the ones from Strathclyde, Lothian and Borders, and one from Tayside. I'm waiting for the rest to come through. Emily is on that pile because we know her rapist is in the mortuary and he isn't going anywhere else.'

'Do we *know* that?' asked Anderson.

'Yes we do, because he's dead. We also know who raped Corinne Hastings, the librarian with the squirrel books. We know that Pfeffer raped her, because he's dead too.'

'And why does being dead make them the rapist in each case?'

'Because they would be alive if they weren't, obviously,' said Batten in the annoying way he had. He settled down on the other chair in front of the video screen, remote control in one hand, notebook in the other. 'Look, you're totally convinced you have the person responsible for Emily Corbett's rape. Note my use of the word responsible.'

'As opposed to the guy who actually carried it out?' Anderson sighed heavily. 'OK, I get it. In each case we only have the accomplice, but we want the man of big intelligence. Mr Forensically Aware.'

'Well done. But what I have up my sleeve is a rapist who is alive but not talking. I was asked up here to Scotland to talk to Adrian Wood. An interesting case. He's in Saughton, serving a recommended fifteen on a life tariff for the rape of a bright young furniture design student called Iris Everitt. She was subjected to a brutal attack while walking home from uni on a warm summer night. The Lothian and Borders police charged Adrian Wood, and brought him to court, but he said nothing in his own defence. Not one word. Now there's an earlier unsolved attack they're looking at, nice middle-class Edinburgh girl called Abigail McGee. She gave some friends a lift home from some posh wedding at the castle, then set off for her parents' farm. Never got there. Both assaults indicate a very similar MO to the pattern you have identified, with a penetrating injury to the mouth, victim blindfolded, et cetera. Both women said they were attacked by two people. The only slight difference is that Abigail was knocked out by the initial blow, but it left a smear of Silicolube on her temple.'

'And you think this Wood is . . . ?'

'Somebody you might want to observe me interviewing.' Batten was off again, flicking through papers and generally acting like a caricature of an academic.

Anderson thought that maybe he had been away from police work for too long.

'What we need to know is why Mr Wood has kept silent. Fear? Love? Responsibility? What would make you take a secret to your grave, Colin?' It was a throwaway question. Batten was now rummaging in his case.

'Can't think of anything.'

'Everybody has their push point. For instance, I reckon you'd keep schtum if somebody threatened to kill your kids.'

Anderson shifted uncomfortably. 'Quinn said something about profiling these victims.' He looked along the row of women on the wall.

Batten looked up as if he hadn't followed Anderson's chain of thought. 'In time, yes. But first we need to profile *these* victims: Whyte, Pfeffer and Wood. I'm waiting for their files, but from what I know of Wood, I deduce that Whyte and Pfeffer would both be early twenties, tall thin men, from unhappy and slightly criminal backgrounds, and definitely no father around. Each probably thought of as a bit of an arse and an underachiever . . .'

'True so far of Whyte, but I know nothing about Pfeffer. He's dead.'

'Humour me while I ask you some apparently pointless questions. How far a walk is Clarence Avenue? From here?'

'Just round the back of the station and down the lane.' Anderson picked up the pile of reports lying nearest his feet. Rejects from the other pile? There were no Post-it notes.

'And how far is Strathearn?'

'Five minutes by car.'

Batten was suddenly enthusiastic. 'And do you agree with that list Lambie compiled? Interesting guy, Lambie; he's been on the trail of this for a long time, and with no official support, so I'd rather he didn't hear a word of this until I know why he's so emotionally involved.'

'Agree? I'd say his list makes logical sense,' Anderson said. 'Now I've got something for you – want to help me profile a 55-year-old man who might be in love with a woman with the mind of an eight-year-old?'

'Interesting,' said Batten.

'Who happens to be his sister-in-law.'

'Very interesting.'

'OK. You, me and Quinn, Interview Room Five, half past.'

*

Batten spent the next few minutes sitting in front of the board, making yet more notes, and still coming to the same conclusion.

And that was making him uneasy. No profiler should be one hundred per cent sure – he knew that better than anyone – but he was. And it terrified him.

He looked up at the clock: 8.15 p.m. He'd wander down to the interview room in a minute or so. God knows how much longer they'd all be stuck here.

He dropped his head into his hands, trying to ignore the deep gnawing in his stomach. God, he needed a fag, a drink, anything. He breathed out a long slow breath, as if to expel the yearning from his body. If only Anderson hadn't uttered those words, *a nice malt*. He didn't know if he would be strong enough to resist when temptation was put in front of him. In fact, he didn't know if he could function without it. These days it was the only thing that drove away the image of Kim Thompson, the young mother who was killed because of him. He'd never expected that in his career – the burden of someone else's life or death. Mistakes had been made all over that case, and the press coverage had been intense. As far as the tabloids were concerned it was the death knell for criminal profiling. And for Mick Batten's career.

He took a deep breath. DI Colin Anderson had faith in him, the whole team had faith in him. They knew to treat a profile as another tool in the box, no more.

But he had heard the rumours. If they messed this up, Partickhill Station would be closed, the team disbanded. If they succeeded – if he, Mick Batten, succeeded – all would be well. It was hard not to feel that absolutely everything depended on him.

All his insecurity was fuelled on his certainty. The minute he had started researching the earlier rape case in Edinburgh for L & B, he had known what they were after. The SIO had already tipped Adrian Wood as the main suspect, and they had been keen to take the profiler on board.

Batten looked up. Emily Corbett was smiling down at him, enchantment in those huge brown eyes. It was quiet in the incident room now. Anderson was away phoning his children. Quinn was in her office. He looked back at Emily, who radiated quiet confidence. Then over to Stephen Whyte with his spiky mullet haircut and pockmarked face. Lastly, the picture of the Isuzu, with a red question mark over the driver's seat.

The map with the locations pinned on it clearly showed geographical clusters across Scotland. With the dates added, a temporal pattern also emerged. Which meant that if the other man who attacked Emily had also killed his accomplice Stephen Whyte, and had been responsible for other attacks on young women since, then he was gradually moving back closer to where he had started, on millennium night ten years ago.

He was coming home.

Promptly at 8.30 p.m., a tray of tea was carried into Interview Room Five. The moment the door closed again, Iain Kennedy's lawyer said, 'My client is here to make a voluntary statement,' then sat back. Quinn and Anderson did likewise, leaving Kennedy the only one leaning on the table.

Anderson wished they'd get on with it. He had told Quinn of Costello's suspicions and the DCI now seemed content to let Kennedy stew for a while. He was only here because Iain Kennedy was important; he was anxious to get back to what Batten had been working on.

Kennedy looked from one to the other and wished it was the scruffy blonde one sitting opposite him now rather than the well-dressed, rather severe DCI and the tall fair-haired man who had on the same shirt he'd been wearing when they last met. Then he noticed the slim, balding man in a battered leather jacket, his remaining hair pulled back into an apology for a ponytail, sitting in the corner.

'If you don't mind, Mr Kennedy, we would like Dr Batten to sit in on this interview. He is a psychologist.' As Batten handed over his business card, Anderson addressed the lawyer. 'We need to know, informally, about Ishbel Simm's state of mind, about her general well-being. So we would like to hear anything your client has to say.'

Kennedy looked at his lawyer, who simply shrugged back: *It's up to you.*

'It's . . . it's just that the relationship between myself and my sister-in-law . . .'

'By sister-in-law, do you mean Ishbel Simm, usually known as Itsy?' snapped Quinn.

'Yes, Itsy. My relationship with her had developed into something else. We were – are – very close.'

'And what form does this closeness take, Mr Kennedy?' asked Anderson, his voice deliberately non-confrontational.

Kennedy looked sideways at his solicitor, who nodded slightly, but no words came forth.

Now it was Anderson's turn to glance at Quinn, who gave an equally subtle nod. 'Mr Kennedy,' he said gently, 'your sister-in-law was admitted to the Western after a savage attack which may, or may not, have included an attempt at rape.'

Kennedy looked up.

'It's very clear that Itsy had had recent intercourse, possibly consensual. The evidence suggests that the sex took place only a few hours before she was found. Can you suggest who she might have had sex with?' Anderson added, 'Bearing in mind that we can test the DNA.'

'Me,' said Kennedy. He sighed, as if with relief. 'We did have sex. Consensual.'

'And you would be willing to give us a DNA sample for exclusion purposes?' asked Anderson.

Kennedy glanced at his lawyer. Another subtle nod. 'Yes, of course.'

'My client is happy to do that, and wishes to assist in every aspect of the investigation that he can,' said the lawyer. 'He also asks that the nature of his relationship with his sister-in-law should remain the knowledge of as few people as possible.'

'We can't guarantee that,' said Quinn. 'But I agree, it's not the type of thing I would want broadcast.' She folded her arms, biting the corner of her lip.

Anderson went on, 'Do you have anything to add, anything you know that might help? Where were you last night, for instance?'

Iain Kennedy went through his story again. He was tired, worn out, beaten almost. But he was trying to get the details right. He was doing paperwork, Marita was upstairs, Itsy was about before six, then she disappeared. Marita had phoned to ask him where Itsy was.

'Phoned? But I thought you were in the same house.'

'It's a big place. We phone each other quite often. I said I hadn't seen her but would wait in the garden room in case she came back or in case anybody phoned on the landline. I think I phoned the police about eight . . .'

'It was 7.59 p.m.'

'If you say so. Then Bobby and Marita went out looking for her. Tony had already been to the pond. When she came back in, Marita was very cold – chilled through – so she had a lie-down, and Diane ran her a good hot bath.'

'What about earlier – when did the incident in question happen?' asked Quinn.

'The incident . . . ?'

'The sex,' said Quinn, brutally. 'Between you and your sister-in-law. While your wife wasn't around, I would imagine.'

Kennedy looked at the ground, swallowing a few times, before he answered, his voice totally reticent. 'That was earlier, much earlier. I'd been sitting at the computer all day and I went out for a run, before it got dark. I was upstairs having a shower and she came into my bedroom.'

'Did she?' asked Quinn dryly.

'She was there when I came out the shower. I have an en-suite bathroom. My wife and I . . .' he coughed slightly,

'. . . we no longer share a bedroom. The answer to your question is about four or four thirty.'

Anderson could hardly bear the man's discomfiture and the intense waves of disapproval emanating from Quinn.

'Was that the first time you had had sex with your sister-in-law?'

'No.' Kennedy put his hands up, palms out. 'I don't mean it to sound so . . . so clinical, so thoughtless. It's been going on for quite a while. I really do love Itsy. I know you won't believe that, and to tell you the truth I really don't care if you do or don't. Just ask me anything you want to know. Itsy is fighting for her life and I know it has nothing to do with me, so the sooner we're over with this the better. I last saw her about five fifteen on the Tuesday night when she was asking me to take her to the Moss to see Ally.'

Anderson could imagine the separate bedrooms, the separate lives. He could empathize totally. He felt almost traitorous as he asked the next question. 'Mr Kennedy, was the sexual relationship totally consensual?'

'Yes, totally. What kind of man do you think I am?'

Quinn raised one finely plucked eyebrow.

'Mr Kennedy has broken no law,' said the lawyer quickly.

'But you can rest assured we will try to find one,' said Quinn.

'You can try,' said the lawyer caustically.

'Mr Kennedy, did you know Itsy was pregnant?'

Anderson and Kennedy both turned to stare at Quinn.

Anderson recovered first and caught the look on Kennedy's face. Total and utter shock. If Kennedy had had any idea, he was one of the best actors Anderson had ever seen – and in his day he had seen a few, mostly in the interview room.

Kennedy sat like a statue, as if paralysed by the news. Then he took a deep breath that silenced the room. 'No, I did not know that,' he said quietly. 'I didn't know. I don't see how . . . oh, yes, I do.'

At that point the lawyer breathed out, a long slow breath. Kennedy was fighting back tears.

'Do you want a drink of water?' asked Anderson.

'No, I'm fine. That was a bit of a shock. A few weeks ago, a condom split, that's all I can . . .'

Anderson continued slowly, 'Do you think she knew? Was there any change in her behaviour that might lead you to suspect that?'

'No, nothing. But I can't really think . . . I mean, she didn't say anything to me.'

'Might she have said something to your wife?'

Kennedy collapsed completely. 'I hope to God she didn't. Marita . . . she can't have children.' A tear ran down his face.

Anderson tried not to catch Batten's eye, but he saw the movement of the pen on the notebook.

'I remember now; Itsy had been vomiting. I thought she had a virus or had eaten something that disagreed with her.'

'And you the father of three sons,' Quinn said dryly.

Anderson couldn't bear the humiliation that burned on

Kennedy's face. 'Did anybody else in the house know about her vomiting?' he asked.

'Everybody, I suppose. Oh my God . . .' Kennedy buried his face in his hands.

Anderson saw Batten relax. Kennedy was presumed innocent. Of murder, at any rate.

His mobile vibrated suddenly. 'It's Costello,' he said, getting to his feet. 'This won't take a moment, ma'am. Please carry on without me.'

Quinn answered, not taking her eyes off Kennedy, 'That's all right. We'll wait.'

It had taken Harry Castiglia less than seven minutes to drive the E-type along the expressway from Hyndland Road. Costello had then spent five minutes getting away from Ethel the neighbour as she picked up her spare keys, refusing invites for bowls of soup 'to keep warm in this terrible weather'. She had spent a more glorious five minutes in a steaming hot shower, and then blasted her hair with the hair dryer, giving her what she hoped was a slightly spiky casual *supposed to look like this* style. She looked in the mirror, recalling Marita's intense colour and sharp beauty, thinking that she herself looked like a hedgehog with anaemia and no hope of recovery. She put on clean black jeans, three jumpers and two pairs of woollen socks. Her clothes had been lying about, not put away from the last time she had washed them. That had become a habit over the years, and more so since Tulliallan; putting things away properly was a waste of time. Costello went to her jewellery box to get out a different pair of earrings, otherwise she would be wearing the same ones in every bloody photograph Harry took. She found her small gold studs instantly, paired up next to each other in the padded tray. She didn't remember tidying it, but then she couldn't really recall the last time she had looked in there.

She glanced at the time, then sloshed on some moisturizer that was supposed to protect the skin from everything except an all-out nuclear attack, and swiped her lips with Vaseline. She put the tub into her handbag, then decided the handbag was a bit ridiculous for the Moss, and shoved it into her rucksack.

She checked her face in the mirror and pulled her scarf around her neck. She'd do. Then she remembered the two text messages that had come through from Colin. One about a curry, one about Marita. She rang him for a quick update. From the sound of it he was in an interview with somebody.

'Look, I'm busy. Do you fancy a curry later? Much later? We're getting a takeaway at O'Hare's place.'

'Oh, you poor sad people!' she scorned. 'I've far more interesting men to have a curry with than my colleagues.'

'You might be more interested in Harry Castiglia than in us, but I bet you're even more interested in the conversation we're having just now with Mr Kennedy.'

'Something to do with why Marita was so reluctant for Itsy and Iain to be left alone together?' asked Costello. 'I knew it – the way he looked at her, Colin. You should have seen him at the hospital. He was a broken man.'

'So would I be in his position . . . you know that –'

Then Anderson recalled how Quinn and O'Hare had kept the information about the pregnancy out of common knowledge. 'Anyway, enough of the Mills and Boon. There's a change of plan, Costello. Go back up to the hospital and sit with Itsy until somebody relieves you. We want a higher authority than a uniformed officer in case the high and mighty of Strathearn start flinging their weight about.'

'But I'm going . . .'

'Yeah, out to the Moss with lover boy. Get him to run you back to the hospital instead. Twenty minutes max, I promise. We don't want any of the staff at Strathearn nipping up to the hospital on the pretext of visiting Itsy and conferring about the timeline. Just in case there's any collusion . . .'

She heard a car horn outside.

'And stay close to Castiglia, Costello; for your own safety, I mean. We're still not sure what we're dealing with here. We'll hook back up around . . . midnight? Sorry we can't include the boyfriend, but it's going to be business. Don't you eat anything – there'll be plenty of curry.'

Costello rang off, picking up her rucksack and slinging her jacket around her shoulders as she bounced across the hall, stopping at the sight of her mail jammed up against the wall when she had opened the front door. But surely she never opened the door wide enough to push the mail that far back? Maybe, in her hurry on the way in, she'd opened the door further than usual. She checked she had her spare set of keys safely in a zipped pocket, and ran down the stairs.

*

284

'You're looking at me as if I were some kind of monster.'

'I'm trying to find another word,' said Quinn. 'A word to describe a 55-year-old man who has sex with a woman with a mental age of eight. But I can't. Not a polite one anyway. It hardly makes you Husband of the Year, does it?'

'I'm afraid we were hardly Couple of the Year, but I can see how it looks.'

'Would you like to explain how it could look any other way?' Quinn's tone was not pleasant.

At that moment Anderson came back in.

Quinn raised a questioning eyebrow.

'I've told Costello to go back to the hospital for a bit before she goes down to the Moss with Castiglia,' Anderson told her. 'I don't like the idea of Itsy being left alone.'

'Quite,' said Quinn. 'Mr Kennedy was about to explain his relationship with her.'

Kennedy sat back in his seat. 'Well, I met Marita while I was still married to Sarah, my first wife. We'd been married for twenty-five years . . .' Every word seemed steeped in regret for those twenty-five years. 'Marita and I bought Strathearn – well, I bought it as a home for us; I think Marita thought of it more as a venue for her parties. She still wants her face out there. Even now, the press cover everything she does. We get a new kitchen; it's in a colour supplement. We attend a friend's wedding; it's in a gossip column. The nightjars come and nest in our wood; it's in a magazine. Even this tragedy – Itsy's tragedy – is being turned to a PR advantage.' He sounded disgusted.

It was time to steer him back on track. 'Did you know Itsy before you married Marita?' Anderson asked.

'Marita never really spoke about her at all. So I didn't meet Itsy until after the wedding. Their mother had died a couple of years earlier, and – oh, perhaps I'm being too hard on Marita – but Itsy had been in a home since then, and she wasn't happy there. She wasn't being well looked after, and it didn't look good. Marita's agent suggested that as she hadn't been in the papers for a while, the situation could be used to boost her profile. I can see now how it worked. I was invited to meet my wife's sister, who I thought would be some kind of gibbering idiot. But she was nice, if a bit childlike. The home had done nothing to stimulate her. The staff were great, but they didn't have the time to give Itsy the attention she needed. I said of course I was happy to have her come and stay with me – I mean, us. Gradually she blossomed, and I found her enchanting. She was a sort of fairy foundling, like Marita but starting from scratch.'

Iain smiled, tears forming at the memory. 'All her life she'd been told she was backward and she'd been treated that way. But I didn't treat her like that. She became interested in all sorts of things, and asked questions – so many questions. But I never found it tedious. It was so nice, in this day and age, to find a woman who needed me, looked up to me.' Kennedy risked a look at Quinn then put his head down again. 'It – well, it was as if her whole mind had opened up and wanted to absorb everything that was going on. Marita was out all the time, so more often than not it was just Itsy and me in the house at night.' Kennedy addressed Anderson directly. 'You know how, when you've had a hard day, all you want is somebody to pour you a wee whisky and listen to how bad your day was?'

'Sounds like domestic bliss,' said Quinn with more than a hint of sarcasm.

Anderson had to admit, to him it did.

'Marita was never there to do that. Her life was more important, more high-octane, than mine. Nothing squares with some useless celebrity signing up for some new event. Does it?'

'I'm the wrong one to ask,' said Anderson.

Quinn asked, 'How long had she been at Strathearn before your relationship became sexual?'

'Over eighteen months, but she had changed so much in that time. Then she started borrowing Marita's clothes, and . . .' he faltered, '. . . that's when the trouble started. I began treating them both the same. I even bought them the same boots for Christmas . . .'

'Ugg boots?' asked Quinn.

'Yes.'

Batten spoke, his voice quiet and considered. For the first time the atmosphere in the room was empathetic. 'Would you say Itsy imitated your wife? Marita must have been a role model for her?' He looked straight at Kennedy. 'Did she deliberately make herself look like your wife, do you think?'

Iain laughed harshly. 'It was the other way round, if anything. A few months ago Marita was in hospital, having a minor facelift or something, and she showed the surgeon a picture of Itsy. She said, this is what I want to look like. Marita's always liked a drink, and smoked in her youth – still does occasionally – and her face was starting to show it. Whereas Itsy didn't worry about anything, and was as fresh-faced as a daisy.'

'Did your wife know about your affair with her?'

'I don't think so. But if she did, it wouldn't have been the fact that I was having an affair that would bother her, but because it was Itsy.'

'Why do you say she wouldn't be bothered, Mr Kennedy?'

'Because Marita has never . . . you know . . . been faithful. To any of her husbands. That seems to be fairly generally known,' he finished miserably. 'That was another thing I only found out after we were married.'

'Mr Kennedy?' asked Batten. 'Did Itsy have a special friend? Somebody she really trusted?'

'Me, I think. Bobby. Wee Tony Abbott. Nobody outside our circle.'

'Thanks.'

The simplicity of the question and the satisfaction the answer gave Batten took them all by surprise. The lawyer was the first to recover.

'Well, if you don't need us any longer,' said the lawyer, putting the cap back on his pen and breathing a deep sigh of relief. 'Come on, Iain, I'll drive you home.'

'I have to ask you not to leave the country. In fact, don't go anywhere without telling us,' said Anderson conversationally.

'I think I'll be spending most of my time at the hospital,' Kennedy said. 'With Itsy.'

*

I see her walking, the fog swarming at her feet as she crosses the street in front of me. I am sitting with the engine off; she doesn't even look my way. Not as prudent as she should be, my little Prudenza. She could easily come to harm, and who would know? I need to be here, I need to make sure she is OK. She is walking along, and I see she's limping slightly as if she has a bad knee or as if her boot is hurting her, but she seems warm in her big padded jacket. I can see the outline of the rucksack as it bobs around on her back, moving with her stride as she walks.

I know that she is hurrying. She is not easy in this fog, and she keeps up a good pace, into the entrance of the hospital car park where she stops and fumbles in her pocket for her mobile phone. She is distracted, not paying attention to her surroundings, and that is not good. Have these women not been warned? She seems to be having a casual conversation, then I see her look up at a window. She cuts the conversation and is gone, in through the back door of the Western. I look at my watch; it's leaving five past nine, and the car park will get darker once visiting hour is finished and only the security lights are left on. Cars are already streaming out the gate, so it's easy for me to sneak in and find a space. I get out as they emerge from the door, Prudenza and Mrs Kennedy. Mrs Kennedy is wearing an ankle-length black coat or cloak swirled around her body. I walk in front of them, keeping to the shadows that fall against the wall, and they walk past me; they do not recognize me. I overhear some of their conversation as they pass; they're on their way over to the University Café. Marita 'just had to get out of that place'. Prudenza doesn't say anything as she passes me. Old habits die hard, instinct does not leave you; I know she is going to turn round a second before she does. I step sideways into the car-park exit, and I hear them walk on.

'Whatever Batten is on to, is here.' Mulholland was tapping away at the database. 'And we are going to be cut out the loop.'

'Why aren't you doing the background checks on Abbott and McGurk like you were told?' said Lambie, who was holding the line while tracking the numbers Donna's mobile phone company had supplied, both dialled and received.

'Abbott doesn't exist – not that name or date of birth – and McGurk has either been in a home or has drifted all his life. Strathearn is the first permanent address I can find for either of them.'

Lambie seemed to consider this while Mulholland looked at the small room where Batten had been working. 'Do you know what Batten has been looking at, Wingnut? You were there – tell us.'

'I'm not your spy,' said Wyngate. 'He entrusted me to gather documents for him and that's what I am doing.' Gordon Wyngate looked at the list from the psychologist and nodded, in his element as king of document retrieval.

Lambie said, 'Why don't we just speak to Batten? He's not in charge, he's here on an advisory level, but his expertise might be valuable.' His voice was weary but resigned. 'DCI Quinn is right. We need him to tell us which of these cases are connected and which are not. He's an expert at that.' He looked up at the rearrangement of the photographs on the wall, noting that Emily's was still in the middle.

'I wouldn't like to tell Kim Thompson's family that Batten is an expert,' said Mulholland acidly. 'Anyway, Batten's part of the gang, and we are not. Are you part of the gang, eh, Wingnut?'

Wyngate ignored him, and went about his business.

'We need to go straight back to the horse's mouth and interview all the original sources. We need to make the connection ourselves, by old-fashioned police work,' said Mulholland.

'Alternatively, what we need is the link,' said Lambie. 'There must be something here that would seriously tease a criminal profiler. Some link that we're missing. Jobs? Religion? Hobbies? Sports? There must be something. And it'll already be here, or a vestige of the pattern. That's what we need to identify, and present to him. Has Itsy's case told us anything else?'

'Batten's not going to rock the boat; his confidence and professional reputation are at rock bottom.' Mulholland tapped his pen on the veneers on his top teeth, 'I don't think he's going to do us any favours; he'll sideline the Itsy Simm case by saying it isn't connected. We need to be ready to point out the connections with so many others. That's why we need to get one step ahead. We need to know more about that second man because that is the connection. Emily's our best hope. She might have seen his face. We need to show her another photograph of Whyte, see if it sparks any memory of the other one.'

'We are not going anywhere near Emily Corbett,' said Lambie firmly.

'Why not?'

'Because we're not. Anything she knows, we know. Anyway, we've no authority.'

'There's nobody here to stop us. It's a legitimate line of enquiry. Stephen Whyte's recent demise gives us a reason to talk to her. We don't have that reason for any of the other victims. Quinn's not around, so we can go out, do the interview, and get Batten on our side first thing tomorrow.'

'No point.'

'OK, but when Batten asks, "Why has nobody spoken to her in all this time? Are you all scared of her dad?" we should be the ones with the answer.'

Lambie kept tapping away at his keyboard. 'More likely he'd bollock you for causing her more psychological trauma for no gain whatsoever. And I'd agree with him. So you are going nowhere near her,' he said quietly, blew his nose and stuffed the hanky back in his pocket, suddenly animated as a voice spoke on the other end of the phone.

Mulholland looked over at Lambie scribbling down numbers, a slightly overweight redhead with bad skin, his glasses dotted with little flecks of dandruff that fell from his scaly eyebrows. Mulholland knew the answer was on that board, something that they were missing. He smiled to himself.

Anderson had twenty minutes to spend on his own, and a pile of reports in the boot of his car to take somewhere and read. So he made a formal request to look at the medical records of Ishbel Mary Simm, and slipped out of the station.

Batten had wanted to spend time examining some film; he had an idea in mind after the interview with Kennedy. So Anderson left him to it. He could have been phoning Brenda, making arrangements for her to put the kids' Valentine cards from him under their pillows at the weekend. He could have been sorting out where he'd be sleeping that night. He could simply not drink, and drive home after the curry. Home. Home. He preferred the thought of a good dram.

And he wanted a few things clear in his own mind about Iain Kennedy. Which was why he was sitting outside Helena Farrell's house at ten past nine on a Wednesday night. He lifted his mobile and called her number.

She answered quickly. 'Hello?' Her voice sounded distracted.

'Helena?'

'Colin!'

'Are you doing anything right this minute?'

'Yes.'

'OK, sorry to bother you at this time of night. I was –'

'I didn't say I was doing anything I couldn't stop right now. Is that you sitting outside my house? I think I can see exhaust fumes through the fog.'

'Like a stalker? Yeah, that's me.'

'Kettle's on. I'll buzz you in. Come in, and come downstairs. I'm in the kitchen pretending to do some accounts.'

He had snapped the phone closed when it rang again.

'Do you think I could be being stalked?' a voice demanded.

It took Anderson a moment to realize who it was.

'I mean, have you got that feeling as well? Like there's somebody watching you? Like somebody is walking over your grave?'

'If it was your grave, I'd be jumping up and down on it. Matter of fact, instead of a headstone I'd put down a bloody dance floor. What do you want, Costello? Where are you?'

'I'm at the University Café, with Marita. I think Harry's on his way to pick me up. But listen . . . somebody definitely left the hospital before me. *Just* before, I mean. They got into their car, just as I was on my way out of the car park on foot. I heard the car start up but it didn't move until they saw which way I went. Even in the fog, he would have seen which way I was going; so I hid in a doorway until he went past.'

Anderson sighed slowly, thinking about Helena and good hot coffee and a comfy warm sofa. 'It's a hospital, Costello. People come and go, any time of the day or night.'

'So why didn't they drive away immediately?'

'Because they were defrosting the windscreen? Setting their sat nav? Checking their texts? Being careful in the fog? A hundred reasons. They might even have waited until you were out the car park and on the pavement in case they ran you over. Tempting though the idea might be.'

Costello suddenly changed the subject. 'Do you know

what Lambie and Mulholland are up to? Are they at the station?'

'Don't know to both. I'm going back to the station in a wee while.'

'But where are you now?'

He hated it when Costello did this; the bloody woman could sniff an evasion a mile away. 'No business of yours,' he said lamely.

'So you're not at home in bedsit land? And you're not at home with the kids because you'd say so, wouldn't you? But you're not saying anything . . .'

'Give it a rest, will you!'

'. . . and I don't hear anybody else there. In fact, all I can hear is traffic. But you can't be driving, or you would never have answered the phone. So, sitting near traffic, holding your mobile phone . . . ?'

Anderson felt sorry for Harry Castiglia. He'd need a strong constitution to put up with this every time he had a lame excuse for being late.

'You're going to see Helena McAlpine, aren't you? You're going to see if she can dish the dirt on Marita and Iain Kennedy. Well, that's as good an excuse as any. Enjoy.' She rang off.

Nothing in the kitchen had changed very much, and he was glad. The tiles hadn't changed, the Aga was the same, and the huge old worn pine table was still there. And there was the same glorious smell of fresh bread and coffee that he always associated with this house. It was the first time he had felt warm all week.

Helena, looking maybe a bit more lined, with a little more grey softening her auburn hair, was standing at the Aga, her hand hovering over a copper kettle which was thinking about whistling. 'Shift all that paperwork out the way, and have a seat,' she invited him.

He moved some papers to one side, noting it was the same set of documents repeated in different languages. He couldn't help but notice the names of the directors of the Gallery Cynae – Helena Farrell and Terence Gilfillan.

Helena observed him noticing. 'I do know that cop's trick of reading bits of paper upside down, you know, Colin. Terry's been a director for a while now.'

'Sorry, none of my business.'

'You did know he was a partner, didn't you?'

Anderson nodded. 'Yes, you told me.' He wondered whether *a partner* meant *my partner* – it was one of those words that had changed meaning recently – but he didn't want to ask. Well, he did but he wasn't going to.

A mug of hot coffee landed in front of him, with a jug of milk, a bowl of raw sugar, a silver spoon, and a plate of shortbread, still warm. The heat of the Aga radiated out towards him like welcoming arms, and he felt his feet begin to thaw and the circulation returning to his fingertips. He always felt at home here, but always at the back of his mind was that night on the step outside. He had almost kissed her – and if things had turned out differently, where would they be now? But time had moved on; three years of it. Yet now she was here, he was here, and it seemed time had stood still. He looked at her fingers as they reached for a piece of shortbread. He could recall the feel of them, soft and warm on the skin of his neck . . .

'You can even take your jacket off if you want. If you're staying more than two minutes, that is.'

'Sorry, the station's freezing these days. I don't think this is a jacket any more, it's more of a skin graft.'

'There's a rumour that Partickhill is up for closure; any truth in that?'

'You know as much as me. Quinn's due for retirement, but we've just landed a big case, so who knows what's going on?'

'And that's why you're here?'

'It's not the only reason I'm here. I mean, I don't just call in here when I want something.'

'Oh yes, you do. At least, you usually wait for some other excuse to come here.'

Helena had her back to him. He could hear her stir her coffee, tap the spoon twice on the side of the mug, and he wished he had Costello whispering in some discreet microphone earpiece, to tell him exactly what Helena had meant by that.

But Helena sat down, and smiled at him as she bit into a piece of warm shortbread, her hand cupped underneath to catch crumbs, and his heart melted. But he forced himself to stick to business. 'One name. Well, two names – Marita Kennedy and Iain Kennedy.'

'So this is about poor little Itsy Simm. That sounded very nasty. How is she doing?'

'Touch and go.'

'That's so sad. What do you want to know?'

'I was looking through a magazine. You and Marita were at the same function recently. Do you know the Kennedys, either of them, at all well? Can you give me some background?'

'Gossip, you mean?'

'That's exactly what I mean.'

Helena lifted her cup in both hands, cradling it in her long fingers, breathing in the aroma of the coffee for a moment, as if thinking about what to say. Which meant she had something to say. Anderson stayed quiet, studying her face in profile, noticing that she still wore Alan's rings, the wedding ring and the engagement ring, on the fourth finger of her left hand. Their eyes met; she knew where he had been looking. It was an uncomfortable moment and it was he who looked away first.

'I know Marita, and I think she's a pain in the bum. She's a publicity seeker, and I mean a real self-promoter, which is a bit bizarre when you've nothing to actually promote apart from yourself. Maybe that's why she does it. She pushes the rules of networking way too far; in fact, she's pushy full stop. Does she have *any* discernible talent? Or is she just a FART?'

'Beg your pardon?' asked Anderson, thinking he had misheard.

She giggled wickedly. 'Famous after reality television.'

He laughed. He couldn't remember the last time he'd laughed.

'The only talent I can see she has is for marrying rich men; she's good at that. Each one richer than the last.'

'Makes me glad I'm skint.'

'And married.' Helena's voice was slightly pointed, and Anderson shuffled uncomfortably in his seat. 'Not that that would stop our Marita. I've heard it said – well, whispered – that when she first started doing that moronic reality TV show, she actually had herself sterilized. No inconvenient pregnancies to keep her off our screens, no messy abortions for the tabloids to write about, no screaming kids who might actually want a bit of love and attention. OK, I'm going to sound snobby, but she's a media celebrity who thinks she's somebody, whereas all she's ever done is look pretty and steal husbands. I was friends with Iain's wife, Sarah; well, not good friends, but I knew her. God knows how Iain got entangled with Marita. It was all rather awkward.' She gave a little laugh, twisting her coffee mug in her hand. 'There are women other women can leave their husbands alone with, and women they can't. Marita Kennedy is one I would not, simple as that. At charity functions, I always wonder: is she there for the greater good or for herself? I've heard it said that she refuses to attend unless she's guaranteed a certain amount of coverage in the right magazines and papers. Iain would do anything for anybody, but he likes to put in an appearance and then retire to the bar and sip whisky with a few old friends; that's more his thing. I have a lot of time for Iain.'

'Do you think he and Sarah are in touch?'

'I don't think they ever stopped being in touch, though I know the boys don't have much to do with their dad. I think Sarah knows perfectly well Iain's marriage to Marita will fall apart on its own.'

'Do you think Iain Kennedy is a pervert?'

'*What?*' Helena's head shot up.

'You heard.'

She had been a cop's wife for twenty years or so, and considered the question carefully. 'No, I don't. Not Iain. I'd bet my last cent on that.'

'There's no evidence that he is, so don't worry.'

'I'd watch her, though. That poor sister's always being dressed up and stuck in front of a camera, so Marita can gush about "my tragic secret sister and how marvellous I am being" and all that crap. Colin, you're looking at my rings again. I don't take them off, you know. Why are you so fascinated by them?'

'I thought I'd read that you and Gilfillan were engaged. I thought I might see another ring there.' It came out quite casually. Too casually.

'His name's Terry.' She sounded only slightly exasperated. 'Colin, we run a business together, so we see each other every day; that's what business partners do. I know the piece you mean; I was furious about it. You shouldn't believe everything you read. We are not having a relationship.'

'None of my business if you are.'

'Shame,' she said, smiling, and sipped her coffee.

'You were a long time in the toilet.' Marita's voice was accusatory.

'You were the one who wanted an Americano and some fresh air,' Costello retorted, refusing to be cowed. It would be hell to be married to a woman like that, she thought, unless she could be fitted with a mute button. Her head was starting to feel like a bagatelle; all she wanted to do was stay in one place for ten minutes and put her feet up. Her heart had sunk when Marita said she wanted a walk. The duty uniform was having a break so, since Marita always got what Marita wanted, Costello had to go with her. She had the feeling of eyes boring into them with every step of the five-minute walk from the Western to the University Café, which they did in double-quick time.

'Have you finished your coffee?'

'Yes.' Marita dabbed her lips with a paper napkin before inching herself out of the corner bench seat. Costello watched and waited as Marita made sure she had the other customers' attention, then flicked her hair and smoothed her black velvet coat down over her slender thighs, waiting for looks of appreciation.

'I'll wait outside,' said Costello.

She walked towards the door, and heard one of the students whisper, 'There's that bird off the telly.' She couldn't be sure that the reply was 'overblown tart'; it might have been her own wishful thinking.

Outside, she waited for longer than she'd expected. The bill had been paid but Marita was obviously getting cigarettes or something. The huge building of the Western Infirmary was just across the road and they were less than two hundred yards from the car-park entrance. All she had to do was get Marita across the road, into the lift and up to High Dependency, then she and Harry Castiglia could get away out to the Moss. Suddenly she was aware of a group of people standing a few yards away. She groaned as she saw the cameras.

'Go away, all of you, please,' said Costello, but it was too late. Marita came down the steps at the wrong moment, and automatically turned on her film-star smile in a barrage of flashbulbs.

'Marita, how do you think the police are handling this . . . ?'

'Can you tell us how badly Itsy was hurt? Was she raped?'

'Not now!' Costello hissed at Marita, who was about to strike up a conversation. 'You really shouldn't talk to the press unless it's been cleared by the press office.' She seized Marita's elbow and hustled her unwillingly across the road, the paps keeping pace with them.

'Of course, this is a very difficult time for us . . . Everyone's being very kind. The hospital . . .'

'But what about the police? Are you happy with the way . . . ?'

'Look, Marita,' Costello hissed, 'you don't want to jeopardize the investigation, do you . . . ?' *So why don't you shut the fuck up, before I bloody lamp you?*

But Marita wouldn't be stopped. She turned placatingly to the importunate shouting gaggle. 'Maybe we could talk another time. Tomorrow, perhaps? Why don't you call my agent?'

Suddenly Costello felt Marita's long coat flapping around her boot, and she tripped on the kerb and slammed right into a photographer, who was doing the journalist's trick of walking backwards in front of their subject.

'Out my way!' Costello snarled, right in his face. '*Now!*' And he too tripped, and fell backwards.

She charged over him, and frogmarched Marita through the doors of the hospital where Harry Castiglia was waiting, stamping his feet in an effort to keep warm.

He looked up to see a furious Costello, yanking on Marita's arm as if she was pulling a two-year-old out of a sweetie shop. And he roared with laughter.

Costello told him she needed to find the loo, even though she didn't, and would meet him outside in five minutes. She came out the toilet having put on a smidgen of lipstick, and walked right into O'Hare. She felt her heart sink. Had they a bloody conspiracy between them to keep her away from the delectable Harry?

'Costello,' the pathologist greeted her. 'We're meeting for a curry at my house later, but it's not going to include Castiglia. So tell him it'll be way past his bedtime, and get him to drop you at the station. Anderson and Batten are going to stay there until you appear. Just make sure you're not hanging around anywhere on your own for any length of time.'

Costello shivered involuntarily. 'I did think earlier there was somebody out there.'

'You think you were being followed? Please be careful.'

Costello did her jacket up and started to walk back towards the lifts, O'Hare falling into an easy stride beside her. 'It was probably nothing. Fog does strange things to your mind, and I'm bound to be safe with all those bastard reporters about,' she grumbled. At the lifts, she pressed the Down button.

'Enjoy yourself tonight.'

'It's only for an hour, and it's work.' She ignored his eyebrow raised in disbelief. 'I'm now doing PR for Strathclyde Police Service. It's a great job; you work a sixteen-hour day for a curry and no chance of a sh–' She remembered who she was talking to. 'We're going to revisit the crime scene, that's all.'

'Such dedication does you credit.' O'Hare stood back to look up at the digits flicking round. The lift was on its way.

'Oh, all right, he's a handsome bit of distraction from all this.' She grinned at him, pulling her scarf tight around her neck. 'See you later, Prof.' As the lift door opened, she stood to one side to let an old man out. He turned away to lift a bouquet of flowers clear of her, and the doors closed on Costello.

O'Hare let the man pass, then followed him, pausing on the corner as he saw him walk to the high dependency unit. The old man checked the names, found who he was looking for, and had a word with one of the nurses. Iain Kennedy came out, saw the older man and smiled; they embraced awkwardly, and a quiet conversation followed. Their comfort and sorrow seemed mutual.

Kennedy looked up and saw O'Hare watching from the other end of the corridor; neither reacted, both mindful of their recent conversation. The visitor turned and walked away, obviously going to see Itsy. Kennedy made his way slowly up the corridor towards O'Hare.

'There's no need to stay away, Jack. It's OK. I just didn't know Itsy was pregnant.' He had tears in his eyes. 'The thought of her being a mother, and me a dad again – it's all gone now. But I don't regret a minute of it. These few months with Itsy have been the best of my life.'

O'Hare smiled understandingly. 'Did they give you a rough time?'

'Like you said, Anderson was fine. The DCI, she's a bit . . .'

'Sharp?'

'They have their jobs to do. But in some ways it's a relief that it's all going to be out in the open. I have bigger things to worry about now.'

'Have things taken a turn for the worse with Itsy?'

'It's not looking good.'

'I'm so sorry, Iain; they're doing all they can. And – well, if there's anything I can do . . .'

'Thanks.'

'Can I ask you – who was that? The old guy with the flowers?'

'That's Wee Tony – Tony Abbott. He's our gardener, odd-job man.'

'He looked familiar, that's all.'

'I thought only the dead looked familiar to you.'

'That's my point,' agreed O'Hare.

'This is fog at its worst. Visibility must be down to twenty yards along here,' Costello said, getting out of Castiglia's E-type and pulling up the zip of her jacket. She was glad she had put on an extra layer of clothes.

Castiglia tipped the front seat forward and did some rummaging in the back, pulling out a heavier jacket from under a pile of car tools, and a bag with his digital camera. He handed her a surprisingly light tripod. 'If I get lucky here tonight . . . sorry, I'll rephrase that . . . if we find the bird, if I get a good shot, I'll treat you to a pizza.'

'Tonight? I can't do tonight.'

Castiglia looked up sharply. 'Why not? It's not ten yet. Does Glasgow close early or something?'

'I'm working later. Maybe some other time.' She was pleased to see that he looked quite put out. She dug her hands deep into her pockets, and started to walk down the lane to the drystane dyke.

They climbed over the wall, Castiglia giving her a steadying hand. He gestured to her to keep silent as they walked across the Moss, down the slight slope to the copse. 'We now have to keep quiet. Very quiet,' he said, kneeling down and pulling her down with him. 'Because we won't see it in this fog; but we will hear it waddling around in the undergrowth. Then we'll see if we can get close to it. A ghostly outline in the fog would make a great picture. As long as we don't frighten it.'

'I thought they were supposed to be scared of nothing.'

'In their natural habitat, yeah. But this is Scotland. Bandit country.' Harry's face was very close to Costello's. He turned and looked right into her eyes, his expression unreadable, and for a minute she thought he was going to kiss her. In that instant she forgot the cold that was nibbling at every part of her. But he pulled away, patted her on the head, and tugged her hat down a bit further. He stood up and walked on. 'According to this morning's report, it was down here somewhere, guzzling half a ton of raw fish.'

'How do you know all this?' Costello followed him; she tripped on a two-inch sapling stump and stumbled, her rucksack propelling her forward.

Harry stopped and put his arm out, cradling her elbow in his cupped hand as she wriggled her heel back into her boot. 'Be careful. This is a new path, and it's still a bit rough. So don't break a bloody leg.'

She looked at the scatter of recently sawn-off stumps, most of them less than two inches in diameter, and involuntarily rubbed her face. If Itsy had been running, carefree, but clumsy, like a child, she might have tripped and fallen face first on one of those. Might have. It was feasible, just.

The path was like a black ribbon with a fine white border. Harry's footsteps had crushed the glistening rime, so the dark grass showed through. She remembered the old dance books her granny had had, the black feet making slow-slow-quick-quick-slow patterns on the white page. Her own boots on the hard path left no such marks. Was that how he had done it? Itsy running around in her size-four boots, but her attacker keeping to the hard-packed path, leaving no discernible trace to be found after another couple of hours in the big freeze?

She heard Harry come up beside her, a gloved hand on her shoulder. 'Don't think about it,' he said quietly, mis-reading her silence. 'Come on.'

The path widened, and he moved to let her walk along-side him, as if sensing her disquiet, thinking she was scared. They went carefully along the clearer, older path.

'We'd better take care not to stumble into the crime scene – the tape must be around here somewhere,' said Costello, glad to have something to say.

'Why are they taking so long to clear the scene?'

'This fog slows the whole thing down. You don't realize the difference it makes, not being able to see what's there.'

'You were right; there's the tape.'

They both stood stock-still, and she was aware of Harry leaning in towards her, aware of his breath warm on her neck. 'Listen,' she whispered. 'I can hear something. I think it came from over there.'

Costello was aware that she was holding her breath. She was sure she could hear a large animal moving some-where behind them. She shivered involuntarily.

'Don't worry, it's only a cow,' said Harry, taking the chance to put his arm around Costello's shoulder and giving it a squeeze.

'Oh no, it's not,' she whispered, gazing over his shoulder. 'Just turn round, Harry. Very slowly.'

Harry turned very slowly indeed, his eyes unblinking.

Perched on a tussock, no more than twenty feet away, was the albatross, his snowy breast opaline and luminous in the hazy dark.

'Look at the size of it!' Costello was almost breathless with delight.

'It must be a metre long. More. Jesus!'

They both stood perfectly still, regarding the bird. The bird looked back at them from his grassy plinth with regal disdain. The downturn of his black eyebrows gave him a stern expression, as if he had been watching them for some while, and had not approved.

'Don't you think you should take a picture or something? You are supposed to be a photographer,' Costello whispered, holding on to the tripod tightly, terrified she would drop it.

Castiglia gently pressed her to her knees, his hand on her shoulder. He sank as well, resting one elbow on his knee as he lined up shot after shot with speed and accuracy. The camera softly whirred; the noise seemed deafening in the silence. Costello watched the bird intently, just as it watched her, but after a few seconds a swirl of fog blew across the Moss, and when it cleared the bird was gone.

'Did it fly away?' Costello asked, sounding like a disappointed child.

'Numpty. It needs a high place and a strong wind for that. It would just have waddled off. Not dignified at all.'

'I can't believe we actually saw it.'

'Well, I've proof we did,' Castiglia said. Then he smiled and whispered, 'I knew you were a lucky charm.'

He turned to face her, looking deeply into her eyes for what seemed like an eternity. She could see small flakes of grey hair in his stubble, the tiniest of lines starting to gather at the corner of his eyes. At the corner of his nose a broad but faint scar drifted into the stubble, an imperfection that made him a little more human.

His eyes narrowed, as if sensitive that she might have noticed the blemish. From the corner of her eye she saw his arm reach for the tripod, and she instinctively pulled back.

He smiled and tipped the end of her nose with his gloved finger before plonking the tripod in her lap. 'Once a cop, always a cop. Never quite off your guard, are you?' He fired off another couple of shots. 'Race you back to the car.'

Quick as a flash she tipped the tripod back on to his knee, got on her feet and was off.

He didn't stand a chance.

'Who is it?' asked Anderson, opening the door of the cupboard-like room Batten had claimed as his own and peering out.

'Let me in,' said Costello. She came in and put a frozen cold hand down the back of Batten's neck, but he didn't even move. 'Welcome to sunny Glasgow, Mick.'

'Wish it was in better circumstances,' replied Batten. 'You well, Costello?'

'Fine, thanks. Just broken the Winter Olympics 100-metre record.' She noticed that Mick's hair was a little thinner, the ponytail a little limper, than when she had last seen him, but the face was the same. Only his eyes were . . . more nervous, somehow. 'Guess what we saw – Ally. Like, this close.' She held up a hand in front of her face. 'Harry got some great shots of him.'

'Hope that was all he got,' Anderson muttered.

Costello peered closely at him. 'You have lipstick on your face.' Instinctively he put his fingers up to wipe it. 'Ha, got you! You were seeing Helena, weren't you? I knew it.'

'The penalty for strangling a colleague isn't so bad when you plead provocation, DI Anderson. I'll be a witness,' said Batten, his eyes not leaving the screen. His arms were folded in front of him, fists locked.

The silent video screen showed a woman's face, tears running down her cheeks. Periodically she would wipe a tear with a paper handkerchief. She would blow her nose, look attentive, nod, then start talking again.

Anderson closed the door behind Costello, and placed his hand gently on Batten's shoulder. The psychologist still did not react; his eyes never strayed. Then he reached out to press Rewind, and the face yanked and jerked, then stilled, the mouth moving, the tears flowing, as the victim silently began her story again.

Batten pressed Pause, then sat up and removed his headphones. 'Have you two seen this?' he asked.

'Only now.'

'It's the interview tape of a woman called Lucy McCallum. Wyngate dug it up for me.'

'She was on Lambie's list. She's the chemistry graduate.'

'A real achiever,' Batten agreed.

Anderson's brain decided it was refusing to work without a promise of sustenance. 'We need to phone the order in for the curry now, so it'll be ready when we get to O'Hare's.' His stomach rumbled at the thought of some decent food. Decent *hot* food.

Batten looked up, preoccupied. 'Chicken korma for me, rice, whatever. I want you to watch this first. I mean, watch it and pay attention. Lucy McCallum is on both Lambie's list and Mulholland's, and she fits all the MO criteria. This was recorded two days after she was raped, on . . .'

'Seventh of November 2008, in Edinburgh,' said Anderson. 'She seems remarkably focused.'

Batten turned off the light and pressed Rewind again, then Play. A sallow-skinned woman with well-cut short dark hair started talking. She was upset but she was also angry. She was dressed in some kind of tracksuit with a towel wrapped around her neck, probably just after examination by the doctor. The film was from the rape suite.

'She was a chemistry graduate, and a rising star in the Territorial Army. She'd recently run up Ben Nevis, beating a whole lot of men to the top. One super-fit young woman. Like Corinne Hastings, she was out running when she was attacked.'

They watched one face, listened to two voices.

The off-screen voice asked, 'And what happened then?'

'I can't really remember clearly; all I remember was my back on the gravel and thinking that my knee was sore.'

'What could you see?'

'Oh, I couldn't see anything. I was blindfolded, with terrible pressure on my eyes, as if he was trying to force my eyeballs out the back of my head. And then I felt him sit on top of me.' A handkerchief was handed to her from off-camera. 'I could hardly breathe. I felt something . . . something small and hard . . . poking at the side of my head. Then I heard a noise, right in my ear.' She tapped the side of her head with a tanned forefinger.

'You heard a gun being cocked?'

Lucy McCallum shook her head tearfully. 'I heard a noise, but it wasn't a gun. And then he . . .'

Batten pressed Pause, Rewind and Play.

The tanned forefinger rose to the side of Lucy's head. *I heard a noise, but it wasn't a gun. And then he* . . . Pause. The screen froze, a tear about to fall from the victim's eye.

Batten stood up and walked behind Costello, his hand on her shoulder.

Costello's eyes were fixed on the screen, fixed on that frozen tear. Then she heard a faint click right behind her head and she jumped out of her seat. 'Jesus fucking Christ! What was that?'

Batten turned the light on. 'My cigarette lighter.' He showed her his old silver lighter, flicked it open and clicked the ignition. 'What we hear depends very much on what we expect to hear.'

She was glaring at Batten over her right shoulder. Anderson saw him move his left hand behind her, there was another click, and she jumped again.

'And what was that?' Batten demanded.

'The bloody lighter again?'

'No, an empty stapler.' Batten sat on the desk in front of them and picked up the headphones. 'Have you ever heard a gun being cocked, DS Costello? In real life, I mean, not in the movies.'

'Not that I can recall.'

'I can't say that I have either. I've heard plenty of knives go through Kevlar, though,' said Anderson, feeling he ought to contribute to the conversation. 'Less than two per cent of the Scottish police service are firearms-trained. We've no need to be; it's you bloody English who go about shooting people.'

'That's 'cause you lot are so pissed you can't shoot straight and you have to chib them instead,' said Batten. 'Yet listen to how Lucy confidently corrects the interviewer and moves on, very matter-of-fact.'

'The interviewer should have asked what she did think it was,' Costello said. 'If she was in the TA, she'd have had some degree of weapons training. She'd know what a gun sounds like.'

'She's certainly totally dismissive of the suggestion that it was a gun she heard,' Batten agreed.

'But Emily said that she had a gun held to her head. Right from the start she said that.'

'And Emily is an intelligent young woman. Her brain told her: *I am in danger, something cold and round and metal is being pressed to my temple, therefore the noise I hear is a gun being cocked.* She's probably never actually heard that noise in her life but her brain made the connection for her. So we need to identify which of the victims said there was a gun, and whether it was subconsciously suggested to them. Some of them were interviewed formally by DS Lambie, after their initial interview. I want the three of us to go through all the transcripts, and all the tapes. All of them – not just the formal sanitized statements. If anything, we pay more attention to the early ones before they have time to think. I suggest that we'll find very few of the victims actually said they'd had a gun at their heads, until they were more or less told, in the form of an indirect question, that they had. I think we'd be better concentrating on the blindfold; that's a constant in the files Wyngate has found for me so far.'

He scrolled the tape back . . . *pressure on my eyes, as if he was trying to force my eyeballs out the back of my head . . . Then I heard a noise, right in my ear.*

You heard a gun being cocked?

'I want to know *exactly* what was said, by every one of them. Lucy McCallum's statement is the most consistent. She doesn't change it the way some of the others do. We need to apply to L & B to speak to her. I'll try and pull some strings.'

'But the others were scared shitless, confused,' argued Costello. 'And DS Lambie is not an inexperienced officer. Could he not have been clarifying what the victims said? It's not easy getting a clear statement from a victim in shock.'

Anderson stepped in, recalling how many times he had wanted a victim to say something only to be disappointed. 'Listen to him, Costello. These women were misled. And so were we. Lambie might have his own reasons for doing this. He has some personal agenda to do with Emily, and we can't blame him for that. That's why we're sitting talking about this in a bloody cupboard.'

'But that stuff they found in Emily's mouth and Whyte's – Silico something – is that not used on guns?' asked Costello.

'Not exclusively. Wheels, motorbikes, anything that might seize up. Sure, it's an avenue to follow. But why the blindfold? Why the pressure on the eyes? And what is making that noise? There are important pieces missing in this puzzle.' Batten's eyes were fixed on the photograph of Lucy's face. 'These attacks are planned, highly organized, and daring. And another thing . . .' he leaned back, '. . . we've all known each other for some years now, you and I. But say I suggested to Colin that we go on a raping spree – how long would it take for enough trust to build up between us before I could even ask that question? Months? Years? Which says to me that there is a close connection between the two attackers. They work as a team.'

'OK, so there has to be time for a degree of trust to build up between these guys. Or these *people*. I suppose one could be female. So how many victims are we talking about, Mick?'

'I think nine. The names on Lambie's original list. We've added Shelly Lewis and Shannon McCullough; both raped, outdoors, skull fracture, vehicle involved, et cetera.' Batten waved his hand as though he was reciting a shopping list. 'Shelly did sustain a penetrating injury to the mouth, Shannon got off lightly with smashed teeth and soft tissue damage. Three of Mulholland's list don't fit. The important

316

components of the MO are missing, so I'm discounting any victims who were picked up in a bar, raped indoors or were drunk. But the final number of victims could be more than nine, could be fewer. We need to go through them again. And look again at the databases outwith Strathclyde.' He sighed. 'Who knows how many more are out there, Colin.'

'And Itsy's not one of them?'

'No, and I don't think she ever was. She doesn't fit, she never did. Everything leading up to the attack is wrong – the location, the pick-up . . . *She's* wrong as a victim; she's not an achiever. Far too easy a target. It's all wrong.' Batten rubbed his eyes. 'But tomorrow we're going to interview Adrian Wood. He's on a life tariff, so maybe we could use that to negotiate with him. If he shows remorse, helps us out, we might suggest his life tariff could be cut. It won't be, of course, as he did brutally rape and injure Iris Everitt. But by the time I'm finished we'll have him for the attack on Abigail McGee as well.' He got up stiffly. 'Did someone mention a curry?' He yawned. 'Talk's good, but food's better.'

Costello did not move. 'I know I'm being thick, but just backtrack a moment. Why the pressure on the eyes?'

'Their eyes were covered, and then they felt pressure. Intense pressure,' Batten replied.

'But why?' Costello pressed her palms to her own eyes.

'I've no idea.' As he walked behind her, he snapped his fingers right in her ear, and she jumped.

'Bastard,' she snarled.

*

317

O'Hare was sitting at home, thinking about Abbott, the Kennedys' gardener who he had seen at the Western. Where had he seen that face before? But he couldn't quite place it. Tony Abbott. Anthony Abbott. The name meant nothing that he could remember. But it would come to him if he left it long enough.

He looked around his living room, ready for the invasion. He had put out a tray of cutlery, put the oven on low, and looked out some dishes that were dusty from lack of use. When was the last time he had had guests? It was far too long ago, and he was looking forward to having all his colleagues round.

He went into the living room, put on the flame gas fire, plumped up the cushions on the big chesterfields, and moved everything of value off the big oak coffee table. He tidied his professional magazines, making sure nothing gory was visible that might upset a sensitive stomach – although where Quinn, Anderson, Batten and Costello were concerned, the word sensitive didn't come immediately to mind.

He poured himself a finger of malt. Then he sat down in front of the fire in his big chair, the one he usually fell asleep in, and thought some more about Tony Abbott and Iain, the warm greeting, the mutual concern for Itsy. And, fleetingly, he thought of Sarah Kennedy. It was a long time since they had spoken – how was she coping with all this?

He sipped away, trying to relax, but a small doubt at the back of his mind began to gnaw. *Wee Tony* – he knew that face, maybe as part of a case in the distant past . . . He sent his brain rifling through his mental filing cabinet; it might take him a while, but he would reach it, it *was* there. How long ago had it been . . . ?

He jerked awake as his front doorbell went. He got up and opened the door; it was Quinn, wrapped up in her big cashmere coat, carrying her laptop and a huge briefcase.

'You look knackered, Rebecca,' he said jovially.

'Thanks.' She handed him her briefcase. 'Is this for me?' She lifted the malt from his hand. 'I need it.'

It has been a difficult night. The fog is bad and the little fish was here, there and everywhere. I now know why she has achieved so much in her little pond. She swims hard, she works hard. She played bodyguard to Marita and I lost her for a couple of hours. I sat outside the station, reading the newspapers that now lie scattered on the floor of the van; the very public private hell that Marita is going through, speculation over the identity of the body hanging in Clarence Avenue, that terrible picture of the poor girl that was raped on millennium night. Back when it all started.

And now we are full circle.

I saw her return, emerging from the fog as she walked up the lane that runs down the side of the station, looking cold but happy. I wondered where she had been. I waited; surely she must go home soon. But when she emerges from the station again, she's with Anderson and a thin man who seems to have a scarf or a ponytail. He wears a homburg. The three of them walk down the lane into the fog, quickly, purposefully, and I conclude that they are still 'at work'.

I drive to the top of Hyndland Road and pick them up again in the maze of narrow one-way streets behind the station. They are easy to follow; I can almost predict their path. After a ten-minute walk they turn into the long driveway of a big conversion. Posh, moneyed. I park on the corner and watch through the fog, waiting for a glare of light to tell me the door has been opened. I see them disappear into the warmth.

For the moment, Prudenza, my little fish, is in safe hands and I can rest easy.

O'Hare's flat was a quarter-villa conversion deep in the West End, at the front of a house with a huge sweeping drive that at one time would have been only a slightly poorer relation to Strathearn. The big front room had been the library in the house's previous incarnation, and with its old parquet floor and huge oak table it still looked like a library, much as Costello had expected. But the rest of the furniture in the high-ceilinged living room showed all the signs of having been chosen for emotional reasons on the break-up of a family home. O'Hare, such a practical man, did not live in a practical home, and Costello liked him for it. She would bet her bottom dollar that the radio was welded to Radio Four. Photographs filled the mantelpiece. Centre stage was a formal wedding photograph, of a young dark-haired Jack O'Hare with a young woman in her bridal veil, standing on the steps at Glasgow University chapel. Costello knew Mrs O'Hare had been a successful lawyer, but couldn't recall ever meeting her.

There were pictures of a daughter too – a daughter who was never mentioned. Her life seemed to have ended with a family photograph taken when she was about fifteen. Costello estimated they would have been the same age if she had lived. Then she wondered why she assumed the girl was deceased. The case was getting to her; O'Hare's daughter was more likely to be a very efficient GP in somewhere cosy like Chipping Sodbury.

Costello leaned back on the settee, staring up at the cornice, feeling tiredness seep into her. Quinn was doing something bossy and clattery in the kitchen, and Anderson was sinking into a big chair as though he was thinking of taking root in it. Both he and his shirt looked as though they needed a good ironing.

'So how did you get on out there in the ghostly fog with Heathcliff?' O'Hare enquired.

'He's quite a nice bloke really. And we saw Ally.'

O'Hare raised a quizzical eyebrow, and for a moment looked not unlike the albatross himself.

Anderson could feel himself drifting off. Tiredness was taking over, and he felt himself sink deeper into the leather chair, glad of its age and the comfort of its worn seat, relishing the heat from the fire and the warmth of the twelve-year-old malt in his veins.

O'Hare had offered his flat for a meeting, and the offer had evolved into a bed for the night. Anderson couldn't refuse. He had no desire to go back to his igloo of a bedsit.

The offer had then been extended to Batten, who had not yet found his hotel and, sitting on the arm of the sofa, in quiet conversation with Costello, looked as though he had no intention of doing so. Anderson wondered how Costello was going to get home. Then he realized his glass was getting a refill. O'Hare patted him on the shoulder, an acknowledgement that he was too exhausted to stand up.

He closed his eyes. The chatter eased off, until there was silence apart from the gentle purr of the gas fire, the deep tick of a clock somewhere else in the flat, and the noise of Quinn stacking plates in the kitchen. Anderson was vaguely aware of a car pulling up outside.

O'Hare drew back the curtain and looked out the window. A squad car was turning before driving off, and a female figure was walking up his path. He looked up the street; he knew every car out there, except the wee white van sitting on the nearest corner, the flume from the exhaust pipe showing the engine was running. O'Hare let the curtain close and went to open the front door.

Anderson heard him say a rather formal hello to somebody he knew less well than the rest of them, and Gillian Browne walked in. She shot a look at Costello, a panicked indication that she had no idea what was going on.

'Have a seat, Gillian,' said Costello. 'We're waiting for the DCI to serve us our dinner. Have you two met?' She indicated Batten.

'Yes, we spent a hour in the station earlier; Mick gave me and Wyngate a shopping list of files and photocopies, all to be done without DS Lambie or DS Mulholland seeing anything.'

'And did you?' asked Batten.

'Of course. And I've got it all with me. DS Mulholland's

far too wrapped up in his computer to pay any attention to what I'm up to. Sometimes it pays to be daft.'

'Not harmed your career, has it, Costello?' said Anderson, his eyes half closed.

Quinn appeared, wearing a pinny over her designer suit and carrying a tray loaded with popadoms, spiced onions, pakoras, samosas and multi-coloured sauces.

Costello noticed that Browne was hovering, still in her anorak, uncertain whether to stay or go.

'Sit down, join in,' said O'Hare.

'Oh, I thought this was for the team only. I was just going to deliver the stuff . . .'

'You're part of the team,' said O'Hare. 'So sit.'

For a few moments, friendly chaos reigned as they filled their plates, passing spoons back and forth, ripping naan bread apart and dropping rice on the carpet.

'Can I say something intelligent?' asked Costello.

'That'll be a first.'

'Seriously, down at the Moss, I noticed that footprints on the path leave almost no trace. Everything just freezes over again. But they show up, and stay showed up, on the frosty grass. I think the guy kept right to the path – he didn't cut across, he didn't run around. So I think those boot prints are Itsy's, all of them.'

'And there's another place where prints don't show up so well,' said Anderson thoughtfully. 'That newly cleared area close to the copse, with the wee stumps. The frost doesn't lie so well on all the twigs and bark and stuff.'

'I'll get the lab boys on to that tomorrow, see if they can test in similar conditions. Just to see if it's possible another person could have been there and left no obvious prints. Right, Dr Batten, what do you have for us?' Quinn opened the proceedings.

Batten waved a bit of chicken around on the end of his fork. Browne hastily handed him a paper napkin. 'Thanks. Overview – an unsolved case I'm working on, the rape of Abigail McGee. The L & B think that a night porter called Adrian Wood is responsible. He's in Saughton for another very similar rape. Both attacks have the same MO, the noise like a gun, the blindfold, the mouth wound, the head wound. In academic circles you can let it be known that you have a special interest in certain psychiatric conditions, and the psychologist in charge of Adrian Wood suggested I might like to have a word with him.' Batten paused to shovel down a few mouthfuls. 'The minute he was caught, a sequence of rapes in Edinburgh, with our signature MO, stopped. Now, let's move to Dundee. Tayside's turf . . .' Batten speared another piece of chicken, caught it between his teeth, and munched as he reached down beside the sofa and hoisted up his battered old leather satchel. He pulled out four photographs.

Browne was sitting on the very edge of her chair, as if she knew what was coming.

'Four names, but let's concentrate on the one you know: Corinne Hastings.'

'The squirrel-book lady?'

'The very same, aged twenty-eight.' He threw a quick glance of acknowledgement to Browne and passed around Corinne's photograph. 'We also have Linda Michie, Lisa Arbuckle and Margaret Bowman, all raped between

October 2002 and January 2003.' Those three names are on Lambie's and also Mulholland's list. We know that a taxi driver called Edward Pfeffer, who raped Corinne Hastings in March 2003, was found dead much later that year. By which time that particular cluster had stopped. So basically, we have a series of clusters of attacks, in different areas of Scotland. They stop for a while, for – as far as I can ascertain – as little as seven months. But it could be anything up to two years before they start again, somewhere else. This pattern is repeated four times over a ten-year period.'

'So you're saying that, despite the fact that some rapists are accounted for, the rapes continue, showing that distinctive MO?' asked O'Hare.

'Which is why this is all such a mess.' Batten took a huge bite of pakora, and continued, 'I need to put all this through my computer programme and I need two of you sitting there opening old files and answering my questions.'

'Count me in,' said Browne.

'Me too,' said Costello.

'You can have Littlewood,' snapped Quinn.

'And please be clear that Donna McVeigh wasn't killed as an escalation of the rape sequence. I think she was killed as part of the "keep quiet" sequence of Pfeffer and Whyte. Which is why she got the superglue. And if I am right, we should also anticipate that somebody left their DNA under her nails. So should we expect to be handed another rapist that the Other Man, the intelligence, is finished with?' Batten sat forward, elbows on knees, and flicked the catch on his retractable pen, the mechanism snicking loudly in the silence. 'If I am right, the DNA of the next guy we find dead will match that under Donna's fingernails.'

'The DNA may be back tomorrow, or more likely Friday. I expect he's very alive and very dangerous,' said Quinn, dismissing the theory. She licked some sauce from her finger. 'If you say there's a pattern of clustering, does that mean there's a definite link between all the other victims? There has to be something that we haven't found yet.'

'These women are intelligent, educated, they have good jobs, they're under thirty. Achievers, if you like. I believe they were all chosen. Lain in wait for, so to speak,' said Batten quietly. 'But the important thing is that we shouldn't think just in terms of looking for the rapist. What we need is the intelligence behind the rapist.'

'The second man,' Browne interrupted. 'So Emily was right all along.'

Batten nodded. 'I think that the rapist is expendable,' he went on. 'Once he's past his sell-by date, he's killed. There may be other murders of young men over the past ten years that can be explained by that. Of course, if he's lucky, he's hauled into custody before he can be killed, and I'd say that's the only reason why Adrian Wood is alive. So does the intelligence find a new partner, and start to "groom" him, as we would say?' Batten took a drink of water. 'There's something else that's been confusing the picture – the gun. I don't think it is a gun.' And he told them about his theory, watching Quinn's face go white as he voiced his doubts.

'Oh, for fuck's sake,' she said quietly. 'The Chief is really going to love this.'

'Can I just go back a stage?' O'Hare asked. 'Looking at it diagnostically, are you saying that in each cluster, only the last victim retains some evidence of the identity of the rapist? But that there is never, ever, any physical evidence that might lead to the identity of the intelligence?'

Batten nodded again. 'That's my working theory. Basically, there's an intelligent one telling a stupid one what to do.'

'So might the intelligent one be sexually incapable, and using the other as a surrogate rapist? Then once he's finished using him, he leaves a trace of evidence that points to him and kills him? Or do you think that the rapist is killed as punishment for accidentally providing some evidence to link victim and assailants?'

'I don't know, at the moment,' Batten said, looking slightly shell-shocked. 'Both those scenarios have certain traits that are consistent with a narcissist. But at the moment that's a step too far. Once I speak to Adrian Wood, I'll be on firmer ground tackling the other victims face to face. Tomorrow we'll start examining the clusters, taking the last victim of each cluster and running them through my computer.'

There was a murmur of assent.

'OK, I have a question,' said Quinn. 'DS Lambie. Why is he not here? What do you think he's up to?'

Batten said, 'He troubles me. He's always been after the person who attacked Emily – he makes no secret of it. He was in the original enquiry team. He could have struck up some kind of relationship with Whyte's mother over the years. He might have known Whyte was coming back.'

'But Mum would have to keep quiet about that. In that family, I mean,' Costello observed.

The room was silent.

Batten then said, 'Lambie is a small cog in a large machine that was getting nowhere. So maybe he took the law into his own hands. Wouldn't be the first time.'

'I was rather hoping you'd shoot that down in flames,' Quinn said. 'I don't wholly trust Lambie. Neither did DCI Yorke. Do you think he killed Whyte? Really?'

Browne and Costello both stopped eating.

'No! David's a . . . nice bloke,' Costello muttered, then said defiantly, 'How did he get the keys to Clarence Avenue?'

'Not difficult, Costello. He's a cop; he'd know how to think like a con man. He'd send somebody round for a viewing, then later send them back for the keys, just to nip round for ten minutes to measure something. Bannon has loads of properties on his hands with the credit crunch – he probably wouldn't remember, even if we asked him. So Lambie could take the keys and copy them.'

'But once we found Stephen Whyte hanging he should have been happy. Emily's rapist was dead, honour should have been satisfied.'

'But he isn't satisfied, is he?' said Batten.

Quinn suggested, 'No, he's now on our squad, keeping an eye on us, waiting for us to get close to the real killer.'

'Lambie has a highly personal agenda,' Batten said. 'He

328

thinks he has a personal involvement that he does not in fact have. Or not one we know about.'

'Wyngate is digging, but all he's discovered is that Lambie was a junior officer who worked on Emily's case, that's all,' said Quinn.

'Tell Wyngate to keep digging. Lambie needs to be seen as the incessant pursuer of the truth. He needs to be seen as the great hero – *they will appreciate me, they will!*' Batten stabbed the air with his fork.

'Or the right-minded citizen removing scum like Whyte from the face of the planet?' agreed Anderson.

'You have been wrong before, Dr Batten,' warned O'Hare quietly.

'But just in case I'm not wrong this time, I think Lambie should be watched. Just watched, nothing else.'

'You're saying we should spy on a colleague?' Anderson looked at Quinn.

'For the sake of the integrity of this investigation, I agree,' Quinn said. 'Leave it with me.'

'And where does wee Itsy come into all this?' asked Costello.

'Into all this?' Batten leaned back in his chair. 'Nowhere. Absolutely nowhere.' He released the nib of his ballpoint. Click . . .

Costello stepped on the pedal of the bin and tipped in a plate full of leftovers. She then gently kicked the door behind her closed. 'It's a terrible thought, that it might be one of us that killed Whyte, isn't it?'

'Actually,' O'Hare said, 'no. I'm surprised it doesn't

happen more often. And I confess I've no compunction at all about feeling that justice has been done.'

Costello stacked the plates up on the worktop, noting it was a man's kitchen. Tidy. Functional. Nothing homely. 'Prof?' she asked. 'Could Itsy have been brain-damaged as a child by being suffocated or held under water for a period of time? Could that account for the way she is?'

'Oh yes,' said O'Hare, his brain too hazy for lengthy thought.

'And this "intelligence" – could that be a woman, do you think?'

O'Hare turned off the tap and slipped some plates into the sink to soak. 'Could a woman have done that – stood by and watched somebody else commit such violence? Yes. Could a woman commit that amount of violence if the victim was subdued? Yes.'

'Could a woman have attacked Itsy?'

'Didn't Mick just say that they weren't connected?'

'Oh, forget what he said,' Costello said tetchily.

She was leaning against the worktop, a dishcloth over her shoulder, and O'Hare thought she looked totally shattered.

'Could a woman have attacked Itsy?' she repeated.

'I don't see why not,' he said. 'Why do you ask?'

'I have a theory. Which falls at the first hurdle if nobody can get out of Strathearn in a car without being seen.'

'Not much of a theory then. Because you can't get out of Strathearn without being seen. Or at least recorded in some way.'

'The entry system that monitors everything that goes in and out – can it be turned off?'

'I would imagine it would record the fact that it had been turned off. And probably by whom. I bet you'd need to put in a code of some sort. There's a computerized keypad, in the hall I think, which controls the gate. You will have checked that.'

Costello pulled the dishcloth from her shoulder and wiped the worktop with it. 'Hmmmm. We do know no vehicle got in or out those gates.'

'Well, that answers your question then. Your theory is rubbish.' He was too tired to have this conversation any more.

'Shit,' Costello muttered. 'Prof, wouldn't it be easier if you put all those dishes into that dishwasher?'

'Never found out how to use it. That's women's work.'

12

Iain Kennedy had made a decision to sleep in the guest room, not wanting to remember the last time he and Itsy had been in his room. He hadn't slept well; he had had twisted dreams about Itsy and Marita. The sisters had morphed into each other, so that Marita – or was it Itsy? – had smiled and kissed him, and Itsy – or was it Marita? – had spat at him like a cat. He rubbed his gritty eyes; his subconscious wasn't telling him anything he couldn't have worked out for himself.

He had stayed late at the hospital, drained by his visit to the police station. He and Marita had agreed that one of them should stay, and the other should go home and get some sleep. Yet Wee Tony had found out that the minute he'd left, Marita had swanned off to be photographed again.

He was going back to the hospital now, and would take the tattered little Snoopy dog with him. Wee Tony had gone down there early, combining his visit with his morning constitutional for his heart. Marita would already be having coffee and a chat with the photographer while she was getting her hair done. He understood now, all too well, that she was getting her own photo shoot out of the way early so she could appear to turn up at the hospital at

8 a.m., ready to run the gauntlet of the waiting media with smiling and heartfelt thanks for their concern, despite her own personal tragedy.

The crowd of journalists never moved from the gate at Strathearn; they were outside in their cars, drinking take-away coffee in the freezing cold, but they obviously thought it worth their time. He wondered who had fed them that idea.

The fog still hugged the ground, as it had since Itsy had been attacked. What he could see of the lawn was perfect apart from gouges where Itsy and Bobby had overturned the wheelbarrow. Wee Tony had replaced the divots and put down grass seed, but nothing had grown yet.

Tony and Bobby had come over to the house in the wee small hours. They had shared a silent pot of tea with Iain, and a few rounds of toast that had stuck in his throat. Bobby had just sat in the corner like a big miserable kid, knowing that the others were under strain but unable to say anything to help. Bobby had formed a strong fraternal attachment to Itsy, so that she and Tony were in a sense the family he had never had. It was hard to know exactly what he felt, as he scarcely spoke. His emotion had nowhere to go.

If Marita was being photographed, Iain suddenly realized, and he was here, that meant Itsy was on her own. He felt tears prickle behind his eyelids, and a shudder of grief passed through him. He couldn't bear the thought of losing Itsy.

He sighed and reached for the car keys.

*

Gordon Wyngate took a deep breath and knocked on Quinn's door. He never knew how the DCI was going to take bad news; she had been known to shoot the messenger. In fact, the whole team were behaving very strangely this morning; quiet, secretive, no banter, no teasing. Something was going on and he was happy he knew nothing about it.

'Yes!' Quinn growled.

Wyngate entered, his speech ready. 'I thought you might want to know this before we go into the main room, ma'am – Harry and Ronnie are out there. We've got further instructions from HQ about allowing them greater access . . .'

Quinn groaned.

'And Towerhill Magazines in London got back to me. They . . .'

'. . . subcontracted the job through the journalist to a local photographer, Ronnie Gillespie. Yes, I know.'

'Yes, but we know the team from the magazine had keys off Mr Bannon, ma'am. Ronnie might have had an opportunity to get them copied.'

'Ronnie Gillespie's on my To Do list for you today, Wyngate. Look into his background. Where has he been? Girlfriends? Family? I know he has no convictions on record but sniff about. And keep it to yourself for now.' She stood up and smoothed her navy-blue skirt down. 'Right, come on.'

Wyngate followed her out into the main incident room. It wasn't his imagination – the entire squad almost stood to attention politely and waited for her to speak.

'Right, first things first. We are treating the case of Ishbel Simm as an attack, though whether it ultimately proves to be one, we shall have to wait and see. The samples taken from her in the ambulance have been tested and we're waiting on the results, which should be in any minute.' Quinn ticked them off on her fingers. 'Also the blood on the scarf that Costello took from under Itsy's head. The scarf has also proved positive for semen and we are waiting on the DNA profile of that. It's not Kennedy's – we know that from an initial comparison – but whose it is, we do not know. The pre-op swabs taken from Itsy's mouth wound apparently contain some fibrous substance, which is away for further analysis. Nail scrapings are mostly soil, and skin cells from her brother-in-law. The blood and hair on the stone are hers. We are waiting for the analysis of the wool fibres also found on the stone. The DNA test results from Donna McVeigh's fingernail scrapings will be back later today if we're lucky. Tomorrow for sure. The lab is checking for signs of Silicolube or anything similar.'

Quinn dropped her notes and folded her arms. 'Second thing: we're having trouble with the press up at Strathearn.' Her brisk manner had changed swiftly to cold fury. 'And they've been up at Kelvin Avenue, at the Corbetts' house. Emily's father is not pleased, to say the least. Turns out somebody claiming to be a police officer went there, and they were followed by a lady or gentleman of the press. So the media are now camped out there in force. I am having to eat so much humble pie with Donald Corbett I'll need liposuction, and I also have his friends in high places to appease, the Chief Constable for one.

When Mr Corbett has calmed down, I will approach him to find out who it was who went to his house. And they will have drawn their last breath.' Quinn glared at them all.

'But it's a legitimate line of enquiry for a member of the team,' said Mulholland. 'And our information and actions should be treated in confidence. Privileged information should be kept from those who might abuse it. Like a photographer, for instance.' He glanced pointedly at Gillespie and Castiglia.

'I've been nowhere near that house,' said Harry, standing like a dark prince in the corner of the room, casually leaning on a pile of his equipment. 'I asked for permission, it was refused, and I left it at that. If I pursued it, I'd be prosecuted. There are laws about that sort of thing.'

'Well, Mr Castiglia,' said Quinn, 'I've found you rather more respectful and ethical than some of the officers working on this case. But it's your living, so you have to be squeaky clean. And if you stepped out of line, I'd have your balls. But I do draw a line over Itsy Simm. Iain Kennedy can put up with all the media nonsense that's encouraged by his wife, but if anyone infringes Itsy's privacy, then I will step in. So if you hear of anything, let me know asap.'

'We might suggest to Iain that he keeps a low profile, comes and goes in a friend's car, not his big BMW,' volunteered Anderson.

'Or he could use the back way,' said Browne. 'Well, it's a bit of a trek round the pond and down the overgrown track at the far side, and he'd get his car scratched to pieces, but it'd be better than being papped every time he goes in and out . . .' She became aware that Anderson, Costello and Quinn were all staring at her, and faltered into silence.

Batten dropped his forehead on to the desk.

'You stupid cow,' said Mulholland.

'Shut up, Vik,' snapped Anderson. He turned to DC Browne and spoke very slowly. 'Gillian, are you telling us that a vehicle can actually go in and out from Strathearn without using the front gate?'

'Yes. You can only see the back gate from the greenhouse and even then there's another old dilapidated greenhouse and a whole lot of trees in the way. Why?'

'Why did you not tell us this before?'

'Nobody asked me.'

'Who was with you when you found that out?' Quinn demanded crisply.

'Well, nobody. I went up there with . . .' She pointed hesitantly at John Littlewood.

'First I've heard of this,' he said, shrugging.

'We shouldn't have such an inexperienced officer on a squad like this,' Mulholland objected. 'She could be jeopardizing the whole case, for Christ's sake. She's a fucking liability!'

Costello jumped to her feet. 'And you aren't? Just be quiet, will you!'

Mulholland was red in the face with rage. 'You going to make me shut up? You and whose fucking army?'

They eyeballed each other. Harry moved to intervene and was stopped by Anderson's outstretched arm.

'I don't need a fucking army!' Costello hissed. 'My knee in the happy sacks and you'll be singing soprano, pal.'

Mulholland took a step back. Browne started to cry.

Quinn had had enough. 'Right. It's my fault for not clarifying the purpose of all the officers detailed to work at the back of the house. Not just Browne. Not *just* her.'

'Don't let Vik get to you; he's being an arse,' Costello told Browne. 'He's not usually as bad as that, though.' In the shelter of Quinn's office, Costello put her arm around the tearful junior officer.

'I think he's under a lot of pressure,' said Browne. 'He tries so hard to do the right thing, but he just makes himself unpopular.'

Anderson mimed to Costello to zip it. 'If he was the one who went up to Kelvin Avenue, Quinn will have his guts,' Anderson said. 'You OK now, Gillian?'

Browne sniffled, and nodded. A mug of hot coffee from Hazbeanz was making her feel better. 'There's another thing – my mum isn't keen to have the kids after school today, so I really need to get home by three.'

'You've put the hours in, no reason why you shouldn't get away,' Anderson said. 'In fact, I should check in sometime today too; no doubt some hopeful young boy is after my daughter.'

'But I did enjoy last night. I'm glad I stayed,' said Browne, giving Anderson a beaming smile, which made her look a little less like a sleep-deprived panda.

Anderson saw Costello smirk. 'Well, I had a blissful four hours' sleep with a belly full of biryani and good malt, and an earful of Mick's snoring,' he said. 'And if it's any consolation, the road map doesn't show the back way out from Strathearn. We might have clicked otherwise. We've sent a squad car to do a recce.' He walked over to the much-written-on board. 'The timeline's a bit blown apart now that we know Itsy could have been driven away from Strathearn that night. Anybody in the house – Marita, Iain and Diane – would all notice the BMW or the Jag was gone, or the old Merc, but probably not the wee white van. There's no point in doing a forensic overhaul, because Itsy was in it all the time. And they'd already been down at the Moss in it, so no point in checking the tyres for soil.'

'But Abbott was there, in the greenhouse. He would have seen.'

Anderson shook his head. 'Not necessarily; he was at the gatehouse, then out looking for Itsy. He wouldn't notice the van wasn't there unless he went to get it.'

'OK, redeem yourself, Browne,' Costello said. 'Phone him right now, and ask if he noticed anything different about the van next time he used it – seat position, fuel gauge, anything. Oh, and find out whether Bobby can drive.' Costello turned to Anderson. 'What's this Bobby like?'

'From all reports, he's rough and a bit scary. He scared the crap out of Browne. Why?'

'Just something Marita said; she called him a "hunk of rough".' Costello thought for a moment.

'We know Itsy had consensual sex with Kennedy a few hours before she was attacked,' Anderson continued. 'But if it wasn't Iain's semen on Itsy's scarf – Marita's scarf, to be exact – it takes us back to asking whether there was a sexual predator hanging around. We need that DNA!'

'We'll have to get on without it for now. What's Mick Batten doing out there?' asked Costello.

'Oh, the nerds are in their element. Batten and Wyngate are moving things around on the board and thinking.'

'What the fuck did you think you were doing?'

They heard a table crashing over, the sound of a fist connecting and somebody falling heavily to the floor. Anderson rushed out of the office, Browne and Costello hard on his heels. Quinn and Batten arrived only seconds behind them.

Lambie had Mulholland by the neck. He cracked his head soundly against the wall, and held him there by the throat. Then he drew his fist back and rammed it into Mulholland's stomach and Mulholland doubled over. 'What the fuck did you think you were doing?' Lambie screamed again.

Anderson and Littlewood were on Lambie like a shot. Although only a small man, he shook them off, his face red with fury.

'Lambie!' shouted Quinn at the top of her voice. 'You will stop this now!'

Anderson then got an elbow in the ribs and he doubled up.

Browne shrieked, and scrambled backwards to avoid the melee. She banged into the desk, and Nesbitt, brutally woken from his peaceful slumber, jumped up and tugged his lead free as the leg of the desk left the ground for a second. The little brown Staffie squared up to Lambie, snarling at him, teeth on display, his hackles up and his one ear back. He meant business.

Everybody fell silent.

'Good boy,' said Anderson soothingly, standing well back in case the dog decided to have a go at him. But Nesbitt just snorted and went back to his bed under the desk, circled twice and lay down.

'Right,' said Quinn, taking a deep breath and smoothing down her jacket. 'DS Lambie, I'd like to see you in my office. DI Anderson, can you join us please? DS Littlewood, please make sure DS Mulholland is OK; take him to hospital if necessary. DC Browne, can you clean the place up? DS Costello will help you. And someone buy that dog a steak for his tea.' Quinn strode back to her office, risking a sidelong glance at Batten.

Both of them were wondering exactly the same thing – just what was the extent of Lambie's emotional involvement in the case?

Lambie was not asked to sit down. He stood in front of Quinn's desk, chewing at the corner of his mouth, his face redder than ever.

Quinn slid into her chair and put some files to one side, giving herself time to think. Anderson leaned against the filing cabinet.

'This is unofficial at the moment, DS Lambie. You have an excellent service record and I can only presume that something has happened which has upset you greatly. I want to hear your side of the story. No crap, please. My life is quite complicated enough.' The phone rang. Quinn closed her eyes in frustration. 'And is probably about to get worse.' She lifted the phone. 'Yes, sir.' She then held the phone from her ear as whoever was at the other end screamed at her. After a minute she said, 'Yes, I have been made aware of the situation ... No, he is outside; DS Mulholland is outside my office right now and I'm interviewing his colleague to ascertain the precise facts. Yes, indeed, sir.' She put the phone down and let out a long sigh.

'That was the ACC Crime. We are in deep trouble. Let me guess, DS Lambie. You found out that it was DS Mulholland who went to see Emily Corbett last night. Her father is flying back up from London tonight and wants us all dead by the time he gets here. His best friend in the world is the ACC. And the case is to be handed over to Partick Central.'

Lambie ruffled slightly.

'What are you so upset about, Lambie?'

'I'm just a conscientious officer doing my job,' he said. 'That family shouldn't suffer any more harassment.'

'I'll try and calm Corbett down, don't worry,' said Quinn.

Anderson knew his boss was in trouble. 'I'll go up to their house, ma'am,' he said. 'I've time before Mick and I go to Saughton. If we explain to the other daughter how close we are to solving the case and drawing a line under it, she'll understand. I'll tell her Vik is an overenthusiastic wanker. It'll be OK. Ma'am, if the phone rings, don't answer it. They can't sack you if they can't find you.'

Quinn sighed. 'Thanks, Colin. But you, Lambie? Explain yourself.'

Lambie hesitated. 'I don't think the Corbetts should have been disturbed.'

'Neither do I. It was in contravention of my express orders.'

'Ma'am, I'd no idea he was going to go charging off to the Corbetts' house, or I'd have stopped him.'

'And within five minutes, the press had turned up mob-handed. I'd given my word they wouldn't.' Quinn rubbed her face with the palms of her hands. 'I'm sorry, David,' she said. 'Truly sorry.'

'About what?'

'About stopping you after only two punches. If I'd known, I'd have let you get a few more in.'

13

Anderson was in dire need of caffeine. Trying to pin down Itsy's timeline was like trying to pin down jelly. Costello said she'd timed the drive out to the Moss the night before at twenty-one minutes. Another ten or so until they saw the albatross, and after that she forgot to look at her watch. That pretty much fitted with Ernie English's timing. Nobody had hung about out there; it was too bloody cold. But the main problem was, nobody knew exactly when Itsy had left Strathearn.

'OK, say a half-hour there, a half-hour hanging around, and a half-hour back – has anybody got a ninety-minute gap?' asked Quinn, sitting with her eyes closed, trying to concentrate.

'Between the last sighting of Itsy, and her being found? They all have.'

'Are you sure? Who saw her last?'

'Tony and Bobby, a bit after six when she left the gatehouse to go back up to the house. Marita, sometime before six, she said. Before that, Iain Kennedy at around four thirty, and Diane who saw her on her way out at about five thirty. And we have to remember that all calls in that time were made on mobiles. They could have been made from anywhere. Kennedy was in the house to answer the landline phone but the records show a good hour and a half with no incoming calls.'

Anderson sighed. 'OK, has anybody made a corroborated statement that they were with someone else?'

'McGurk and Marita, Kennedy and Marita. Abbott and McGurk. Diane and all of them.'

'Well, keep trying to firm it up. See if a mobile used out at the Moss would use a different transmitter. This re-interview of Bobby McGurk and Tony Abbott – has somebody been assigned for that?'

'Yes. You.'

'But I'm going to Edinburgh, to Saughton, with Mick.' Anderson sat down, lack of sleep catching up with him. He caught sight of the photographs Castiglia and Gillespie had pinned on the wall earlier. The images were remarkable. Anderson's eyes were drawn to one of Quinn sitting at her desk, pencil in mouth, and him leaning over her shoulder, both concentrating on a file. A single light bulb hung from a wire and four coffee mugs were neatly lined up on the desk.

Behind them, the window framed them exactly. Outside, the fog seemed to seal them in a private universe.

Mick Batten stood in front of the whiteboard as the squad terminated conversations, hung up phones and wandered in. To Quinn's relief, Castiglia and Gillespie said goodbye and went in search of coffee. Nesbitt trotted over to the radiator and lay down like a frog with his legs stretched out behind him, nose down on his front paws.

The room was silent for a few moments. Then Batten

introduced himself formally before indicating the board. 'There are three strands here. First, we have Donna, Whyte and Pfeffer, all killed because they had either slipped up in some way, or had outlived their usefulness. Donna was going to speak to the press. Whyte had already blabbed, ten years ago. And Pfeffer, I presume, was stupid enough to leave a pus-stained Elastoplast at the scene. The current rapist has recently left his DNA on Donna. If the other man,' he flicked his forefingers as quote marks, 'finds out about it, he will execute the current rapist. So don't release that to the press. The second thing is the victims' profile: all under thirty, all attractive, all achievers, all with tertiary education, all outdoors at the time of assault. Lastly, the geographical clustering. Check the exact locations of attacks. Near universities? Near a well-known pub? These guys *knew* that Emily would drive over that road, they *knew* Iris walked home round the uni playing fields. They were so sure, in both cases they stole a car and waited, then followed them.' Batten's hands reached deep into his jeans pockets and he stepped aside from the board.

So far the photographs of seven women – Emily Corbett, Lucy McCallum, Margaret Bowman, Linda Michie, Iris Everitt, Abigail McGee and Corinne Hastings – had been placed in a row, with a date and a location above each one, the cluster pattern emerging. Glasgow, Glenrothes, Kirkcaldy, Dundee, Edinburgh. Batten tapped the photograph of Corinne, then Lucy, then Emily. 'Look at them all, and look hard. We're missing something, a piece of information common to them all, and we don't have it.'

'We should speak to all the victims again,' Costello suggested. 'Try to find a connection. Find out who they all chat to? Their hairdressers? Did they take a car to a garage?'

'Did they rent property from the same company? Did they use the same travel agent? We could use the misinformation about the gun as our reason to open a dialogue.'

'Could we start off with that girl Lucy, the TA girl? She stayed conscious and alert. And she's easy to locate. Corinne Hastings stayed conscious as well.'

'But she's in Dundee. And Emily is up the road,' said Mulholland with quiet defiance. 'That's the logical line of enquiry. But you're all so shit-scared of her father.'

Browne stunned everybody, Mulholland especially, by saying in an authoritative voice, 'Vik, think like a human being for once, please! We haven't been able to go and talk to her before because we haven't had anything new to ask about. Now behave yourself.'

Anderson looked at her, thinking that Browne's kids would probably be very well behaved.

'Browne, I want you to ring Lucy McCallum and tell her we want to talk to her as soon as. Maybe letting her talk freely might bring something else to light,' said Quinn. 'And Colin, rather than interviewing Abbott and McGurk, I think it's probably more important that you go and talk to Emily.'

'When someone does talk to the men at Strathearn, be alert for any sniff of a sexual relationship between Bobby and Itsy,' said Costello. 'Even though Marita's the only one so far who's suggested it.'

'Thank you, DS Costello,' said Quinn. 'And you can go with DI Anderson to talk to Emily.'

'Later on today, Colin and I are away to talk to a surviving rapist who would rather serve a life sentence than give up the name of the other man,' Batten said. 'However, the thing you should all be worried about is that the geographic cluster has changed again. It has returned to Glasgow. And not just to Glasgow.' He rapped the board with his knuckle. 'You shouldn't be surprised that when there's another attack, you find it's on your very doorstep.'

A dull-haired woman in jeans and a knee-length jumper opened the door tentatively, her arms folded across her chest as if already cold. Anderson showed his warrant card. The door started to close again.

'We're here to talk to Emily, and to apologize to you,' Anderson said, his voice at its most tender.

The door stayed half open. 'She has nothing to say.' The woman smiled slightly, and Anderson realized she was much younger than she had first appeared.

'Well, we have plenty to say,' said Costello. 'And most of it is apology. We realize that one of our colleagues was out of line and we want to assure you that –'

'It won't happen again? Until the next time?'

Anderson took a step back. 'There won't be a next time.'

'But somebody stuck one on him on your behalf,' Costello said. 'In fact, there was a queue. Even the station dog went in for a nip. Look, it's cold out here and five minutes picking your brains would make us happy. Just five minutes, no more. And we have two questions for Emily, just two.' Costello smiled that nice-girl smile that never failed when she made the effort.

Jennifer Corbett relented and opened the door. They followed her into the house. Tracks made by a wheelchair were clearly visible on the brown carpet. As they followed her, Costello couldn't help noticing the mule slippers, and the cracked, flaking skin of her heels.

There was a noise from somewhere inside the house, a subhuman screech.

'OK, Emily, it's OK.' Jennifer turned to them. 'Sorry, but she's very wary of anybody coming to the door.'

They were led into a living room, with a large leather three-piece suite and walls covered with small prints and paintings. On every spare surface of the dark wooden furniture was a piece of Japanese porcelain, and larger specimens stood on the floor. The place could have been a museum. On the mantelpiece, in a silver frame, stood the photograph that gazed at them from the incident board. They all sat down. Emily's sister was probably only in her mid-thirties, but she had the hands of a much older woman, hands that looked as if they were never out of water. There was another screech from the back. She simply got up and closed the door, looking apologetic, and sat down again.

'Coffee . . . ?'

'No, we're fine, thank you. About yesterday . . .'

'I didn't mean to get that young man into trouble but he did upset her. Then all those press people came, with cameras. When Dad phoned – well, he's very protective of us, and he went berserk.'

'What we want to know is: in what way did DS Mulholland upset Emily? Was he pressuring her, or threatening her or . . .'

'He came to the door, showed his card. He was such a nice-looking guy, with nice manners. He said that things were moving along in Emily's case, and I thought it was true as somebody had already been in contact with my dad – was that you?'

'No, that would be DCI Quinn. I had a chat with your dad yesterday.'

'He's determined to fly back up today but I put him off. Emily I can manage, but I can't cope with him stamping around as well.' She gave a little glance at the grandfather clock in the corner, then turned her attention back to them. 'It was all my fault,' she said, and smiled, a pretty smile that transformed her tired face. 'Emily was having a good day, she was quite calm. We all hold on to the hope that someone will be brought to justice – sometimes it's the only thing to hang on to – so I let him in. Well, he started talking to her, and it was going well, then the next thing I know, she's screaming the place down. He'd shown her that photograph of Stephen Whyte, the same one she saw before. It happened so fast . . .'

Costello swore softly. 'I am so sorry.'

'When he left, Emily was in such a state, and she's been upset ever since.' Jennifer began nervously playing with her hair. 'Anyway, I hear you're after the other man who was in the car the night she was attacked.'

'How do you know that?' snapped Costello, more sharply than she meant to.

Jennifer wasn't offended; in fact, she seemed quite pleased. 'Do you know Lucy? Lucy McCallum? She comes and sits with Emily sometimes. She's just rung.'

'How do you know each other?' asked Costello.

'It's a strange bond, being a victim of rape. Some of the other girls keep in touch. By email, mostly . . .' They were interrupted by another weird sound, a cawing like a crow. 'That's Emily again,' Jennifer said. 'She wants to know what's going on. Do you mind coming through? She'll know you're OK if I'm calm.'

Anderson and Costello followed Jennifer into a large garden room that had been built on to accommodate Emily. All the windows were closed, the heating was on, and there was an unbearable and all-pervading smell of urine, disinfectant and air freshener.

The figure on the bed was not recognizable from the photograph in the living room. Emily looked skeletal and old; one eye was taped closed, her head half bald, her teeth chipped at one side. Her whole face looked as though it had collapsed. She raised her right hand.

'She wants to shake hands with you.'

Anderson stepped forward and formally picked up the lifeless hand. Costello did likewise. Emily's eye drifted sideways slightly, then back to Costello, then off to the side again.

'Can I ask her a question?'

Emily's head rolled. 'She means yes.' Jenny picked up a huge flat touchpad, the letters arranged alphabetically, and slid it under Emily's hand. Then she reached over and flicked a switch, and a monitor on a table at the end of the bed flashed to life. Jenny adjusted her sister's pillows, 'They want to ask you . . .'

The finger jabbed at W, and a W appeared on the screen. WHO R U

'I'm DI Colin Anderson and this is DS Costello.'

HELLO WOT DO U WANT

'First question. Did your attacker have a Geordie accent, Emily?'

NO GLASGOW

'I mean, he only said . . .'

The hand batted on the keyboard. I NO WOT HE SAID I WAS THERE

Anderson was aware of the single brown eye staring at him, like that of a caged monkey, with a depth of sadness, and of intelligence. He felt sick.

'This is an important question, Emily.' He took a deep breath. 'Did you see a gun? Actually see one?'

Hesitation. NO

Anderson and Costello looked at each other. 'But you were sure.'

HEARD IT FELT IT SMELLED IT DID NOT SEE IT

'You heard a click?'

YES FELT IT AGAINST HEAD IT SMELLED OF – the hand hesitated – OILY

'And it *was* Stephen Whyte you saw?'

MILLION TIMES YES

Costello asked, 'Can you just look over there for a minute, Emily?'

Jenny leaned forward and helped turn Emily's head.

Costello clicked her ballpoint pen beside Emily's good ear, and she yelped and writhed away instantly, terrified.

'Ssssh, it was a pen, Emily, that's all,' said Jenny, running her fingers through her sister's lank hair, and glaring furiously at Costello. 'Has she been wrong all these years?' she asked.

'I'm really sorry about that, Emily. But are you still sure what you heard?' asked Costello.

A long pause. NO IM SORRY

'Don't be. You've helped us a lot.'

Emily writhed a little, then hit her fist on the keyboard. Her finger began to type. FIND HIM FIND MR CLICK

A few minutes later they were back in Anderson's car.

'Can you drop me off at the hospital?' she asked.

'Just about,' he said. 'I've to pick up Mick and take him to Saughton, and we can't be late. But at least we've got somewhere this morning. Something concrete we can re-interview on. There was no gun.'

'They're the way sisters should be, those two,' said Costello thoughtfully.

'Giving up her whole life and career to look after her sister? When their father can afford the very best care for her?' Anderson wasn't convinced. 'Certainly nothing like Marita and Itsy, though.'

'Christ, I feel like shit about pulling that bloody ballpoint stunt,' said Costello.

'We had to know.'

*

353

Costello got out of Anderson's car and walked across to the back door of the hospital. She had not been here in daylight for a long time. She walked past O'Hare's office, its frosted windows obscured from the inside by books and papers and on the outside by twenty years' worth of Byres Road grime.

She jumped as somebody stepped out from behind a wall and grabbed her. 'Jesus, Harry, you scared the shit out of me!'

'Where have you been?' he demanded.

'What do you mean, where have I been? What are you doing here? And let go of my arm, you're hurting me.'

'Sorry.' He let her go. 'But where have you been?'

'I'll explain later. Why are you here?'

'I'm supposed to be taking photographs, remember?' He was angry.

She continued on her way to the door. 'No, I meant why are you out here, in the car park in the freezing cold? Why are you not in there?'

'Some arsewipe of an official threw me out. The dickhead had no idea who I was!'

'You don't have any ID on, Harry; that's against the rules.'

'I don't need any fucking ID! They should know who I am!' He kicked the tyre of a car on the way past, setting off its alarm.

'Oh, the old "Don't you know who I am?" speech,' she teased him.

But he stopped walking, his face like thunder. 'I am a fucking international award-winning photographer, and I do not have to put up with shit like that. That waste of sperm even threatened to call Security! To me! Me!' He sounded mad enough to hit somebody.

Costello nipped a smile. 'Harry, I'd seen your work before I met you, but I'd never seen your face. I wouldn't have been able to pick you out in an ID parade. So come on, let's get this sorted.'

She turned to walk into the hospital. Again she felt his strong fingers around her upper arm.

'And another thing – why did you not tell me what was going on last night?'

She turned on him. 'It wasn't any of your business, Harry. I do have to obey orders, you know!'

'You lied to me.'

'Don't be an arse. I didn't lie to you. Can you let go my arm, please? We were all round at the Prof's; it was work. So pardon me for doing my fucking job!'

He blinked, and let go her arm. 'Sorry, Costello; but I thought I was one of the team.'

'Of course you're one of the team. So are you having a sulk? Poor diddums! I don't have a berky every time you talk to Gillespie without telling me, do I?'

Harry flicked his hair behind his ear. His stubble was a bit longer, more not-had-time-to-shave than a fashion statement now. He looked like a rather fanciable Jesus. 'Are we having a row?'

'I don't row. I just get even. Anyway, you missed nothing much. But you might not want to leave the station this afternoon. Things might break.'

'Thanks. And I have a snippet for you.'

'Oh yes?'

'DS Pretty Boy is sniffing around the lovely Marita.'

'Let's hope he gets more than he bargained for. Like genital herpes. Any idea why?'

'I overheard two names. Itsy. And Bobby McGurk.'

'Well, thanks. But in itself that's not much to go on.'

'And he saw your request for a report on Itsy's brain damage in that file. He was on the phone chasing it up. Are you on to something?'

'Back off, Harry. That's police business.'

'I thought if Itsy trusted Bobby, she might have been more likely to go out to the Moss with him.'

'Are you trying to change career?'

Harry was standing very close to her now, and she could feel his breath ruffle her eyelashes as he spoke. 'So tell me, what does it take to become a member of the dream team, DS Costello? The wee clique that is you and DI Anderson?'

'A lifetime of working together, and the knowledge that if I ever had a gun at my head, he wouldn't hesitate to take the man down. That kind of thing.'

'So, a little more than a shared love of curry then?' he asked ruefully.

'Just a tad, yes.'

The interview room in Saughton was as depressing a place as anywhere could be. Even though it was still only early afternoon, it looked and felt as though dusk had fallen. Adrian Wood, chewing gum, regarded the other two men with suspicion disguised as superiority. Anderson was mentally describing Wood as a skinny acne-ridden waste of space. And that was the best he could say about him. If he was being totally honest, he might have added moronically stupid. Then he noticed the slight thickening and puckering of Wood's upper lip, evidence of some trauma to his face, and decided to be less uncharitable. Clearly the boy had had a hard life.

Even though the attack on Abigail McGee had occurred outside Strathclyde's jurisdiction, Lothian and Borders police had granted Batten's request that Anderson be allowed to sit in on his talk with their suspect. Batten sat down and introduced himself to Wood, only vaguely hinting at any reason for Anderson's presence. Anderson had been warned in the car: *No matter what happens, just go with it.*

Batten smiled at Wood, but the smile fell flat on the table between them. 'I grabbed some food; hope you don't mind — time is short.' He unwrapped the greaseproof paper from a ciabatta roll filled with fresh salad and tuna, then popped the top off his coffee and took a deep drink.

Wood moved in his seat.

'Oh, would you like one? I did buy two. One's for DI Anderson here, but we can always stop and get him one on the way home. He won't mind.' Batten took a bite of his roll, letting the salad crunch at the corner of his mouth, whetting Wood's appetite. 'This is really good.'

He pushed the other roll towards Wood, who opened the top, and sniffed at the contents.

'It's Italian. There's a good deli near here.'

'Whit ye here fur?' Wood fastidiously picked out a piece

of tomato and left it on the greaseproof paper. He ripped a bite out of the ciabatta, saliva dripping down his chin. 'Ah'm dooin ma time.'

'You're doing life, sunshine. No chance that you'd want to be out sooner? We might be able to do something for you, if you do something for us.'

'Nuh.' Wood said it without hesitating.

'Why – you got nothing to go out to? Nobody to go out to?'

The slightest smile flickered across Wood's face.

'The problem we have is that you are in here, but somebody is still out there committing rape and mayhem.'

'So whit?'

'So. Two things can happen. The best thing would be that you stay in here. The worst thing would be that you get out.'

'Oh aye?'

'Your friend? The man who drove the car?'

'Ah drove masel.'

'Big mistake, to keep on being so loyal. You owe him nothing. He's out there, grooming another to replace the one he groomed after you.'

A shrug.

'You see, Adrian, Aidey? You meant nothing to him; you were just an experiment.'

Wood gave a brief toothless smile, the scar on his lip suddenly obvious.

'So it interests me that you sit here and say nothing about him. I have no idea who your friend is, but I do know what he is.'

Wood smiled again, a strange ugly smile that puckered the scar under his nose.

Anderson noticed that Batten hesitated before he continued.

'I think he knows something about you he ought to hate you for. But he doesn't, does he? He liked you for it, praised you for it. In fact, I bet he was the only person who ever took you seriously in all your life. Because, Adrian, let's face it, you are a bit thick, aren't you? Unfortunately for you, your friend knows that and he knows how to use it. After all, you're prepared to sit here and rot for him. How long has it been – coming up five years? And if I report back that you could have helped prevent further rapes but decided to withhold information, you can watch any early release go down the Swanee.' Batten took another bite. 'But, as I say, that might be the best thing for you, to stay in here. While he is out there.' Batten sat back and let Wood digest that.

Anderson watched the small cogs in Wood's brain move slowly, while a stupid expression crossed his face, a happy memory of something.

'And when you do get out, this is what he will do to you.' Batten put the photograph of Stephen Whyte's bloated face right in front of Wood. 'Look at the mouth, lips superglued shut. We both know what that means: *Don't say a word.* So when you get out he'll superglue your mouth shut and batter you to a jelly with a baseball bat. And you'll scream so much the skin around your mouth will come apart. By the time death comes, you'll welcome it. Some reward for your loyalty, Aidey. And the person who'll help him do that to you is the one who's replaced you in his affections, because you're nothing to him now.' Batten pressed the plastic lid on to his coffee cup, and it snapped home.

A sliver of mayonnaise trickled from the corner of Wood's mouth.

'I know you're going to say you were on your own,' Batten went on. 'But call me at three in the morning and let me know how your dreams are. We're your only chance to escape this.' He jabbed a finger at the photograph.

Wood lifted the back of his hand to wipe the trail of mayonnaise, and vomited all over Stephen Whyte.

The door to Partickhill's incident room flew open, and a young woman in a black tracksuit and matching anorak strode in. Wyngate appeared in the doorway behind her.

'Sorry, guv, ma'am, sergeant; I couldn't stop her.'

'Who's the senior investigating officer here?' the woman demanded, pulling her hat from her head, letting her short dark hair fall into a smart bob.

For a moment Costello thought that Mulholland would actually have the nerve to stand up, but he simply rose slightly out of his chair and settled again.

'And I don't mean that arsehole.' The woman indicated Mulholland.

'I'm DCI Quinn. Can I help you?'

'No, but I think I can help you. Can we talk somewhere?'

Quinn opened the door to her office, gesturing that they should go through; she beckoned to Browne as well.

In Quinn's office, once they were all seated, Costello recognized the woman from the video. 'Lucy? Lucy McCallum?'

'Yeah.'

'Well, thank you for coming in so promptly.'

Lucy sniffed, and crossed her tracksuited legs. She had very clean trainers on. 'I want you to listen to me.'

Costello leaned back slightly. 'We're all ears. Can I call you Lucy?'

'You can call me anything, as long as you listen to what I have to say.' Lucy's aggression had subsided a little. She looked through the window wall at Mulholland, and her eyes narrowed. 'So you're reinvestigating Emily's case. I've spoken to Jenny.'

'We were only handed this investigation yesterday, officially.'

'Yes, and that's why I want to talk to you right away, not wait till you make an appointment. You've a pair of fresh eyes. I want to make a statement. Now.'

'We've seen the videoed interview . . .' Costello began.

'Yes, but what's in my head is not what is on that DVD. They asked questions in such a way that they led me to answer the way they wanted. They were trying to make something fit. I want my guy caught; I don't want to be lumped in with a whole load of prosecutions against somebody else just to help your clear-up rate. I want *my* rapist arrested and brought to trial. I'd bet my bottom dollar that you're looking for a rapist who used a gun.'

Costello's face remained non-committal.

'I kept saying it wasn't a gun, and I'm sure it wasn't.

There was something . . .' Lucy gestured to the side of her head, '. . . there, but it wasn't a gun. I didn't think so then and I don't now.'

Costello kept quiet. If she said nothing, Lucy would go on talking.

'I knew what was going to happen to me. I tried to stay calm. I *was* calm. I tried to remember things that would help later. I tried to notice things. The smell of him. The smell of the other one.'

'Definitely two?'

'No doubt at all. But one was . . . involved. I still remember the feel of his hands, the sound of his voice, the pressure on my eyes . . . I tried to get him not to hurt me, tried not to let him get to me. I really did my best.' She shut her eyes, hands gripping each other tightly to steady herself. 'The other one kind of stood back. I could sense him a little way away, hear him moving around, as if he was trying to get the best view of me being . . .' She started to cry, and she did not look like a woman who cried easily.

Costello looked around for help.

Browne came up trumps. She said, 'Lucy, why don't we get you a nice cup of tea?' and went off to find one.

'Lucy, just from the little you've said, I have questions. Can we go ahead now?'

'The blindfold,' Lucy said firmly.

'What about the blindfold?'

'Last year, I was at a surprise party. We were all hiding and my cousin was brought into the room with a blindfold on. Her husband put his hand over her face, over the blindfold, as she came in so she really couldn't see at all. It brought it all back. I had to run out into the kitchen, I was shaking so much. But it kicked off something in my head when I saw him do that. I understood what my rapist was doing – he was taking away my peripheral vision, making sure I saw absolutely nothing.'

'And this was before . . . ?'

Lucy nodded sharply. 'For a moment, a few seconds only, it felt like he was trying to push my eyeballs into my brain.'

'You said that in your recorded interview,' said Costello. 'I remember.'

Lucy flashed a wry smile of gratitude.

Carefully Costello got up, and stood in front of Lucy. 'What if I do this?' She put her hand up sideways, her thumb down, to cover both Lucy's eyes.

Lucy pulled her head away violently, her hand snatching at Costello's wrist. She was breathing heavily and sweating.

'I'm really sorry, Lucy. But was that more like it?' Costello asked.

Lucy nodded, struggling for breath. 'You're right. That was what it was like. Only harder. Much harder.'

At that moment Browne came back with the promised mug of tea, which Lucy gulped as though it were neat gin.

After a few minutes Costello asked, 'Do you mind if I ask you some more questions? I realize this is going to be hard.'

'I'm OK. Go ahead,' Lucy told her, putting down the mug.

'I'd like to ask about guns. You know about guns, don't you? What kind of gun do you think could batter a skull in, and leave just a narrow impact site?' asked Costello. 'It would need to have a long barrel.'

Lucy frowned. 'If you want to hit someone with a handgun, you grasp the barrel and clout them with the handgrip. It's heavier; it'd do more damage.'

'Can you tell us what Silicolube is used for?'

'Guns, to prevent them jamming. But I keep saying – it wasn't a gun,' answered Lucy defiantly.

At that moment the door opened, nudged by Nesbitt, dragging his frayed rope behind him, hopeful of a biscuit.

Lucy gave a quick tearful laugh. 'God, what a sight! I suppose there is somebody with a worse life than mine.'

Ten miles from Glasgow, they caught the first of the fog warnings. Until then they'd had a clear run from Edinburgh, but now the traffic was slowing badly. A few minutes later, they were stuck in a jam which looked unlikely to move any time soon.

Batten, who had been submerged in some deep thought of his own, drawing symbols and faces on the passenger window, suddenly said, 'Once upon a time, there was a beautiful young man called Narcissus.'

'Story time?' Anderson grunted.

'That's right. Well, one day, young Narcissus came to a pool of water and saw his own reflection. The nymph Echo, who was in love with him, tried her best to catch his attention, but he took no notice. He'd fallen in love with the image of his own face in the water. He may have drowned when he plunged into the water to get at the object of his affection or maybe he just starved to death, unable to take his eyes off his own face long enough to catch a square meal. Anyway, he died. And the narcissus flower grew up where he died, and poor little Echo pined away from grief until only the last sounds of her voice remained.' Batten fell silent.

'So they didn't all live happily ever after.'

'The thing is, people think narcissists love to be adored and admired. But they don't love it; they *need* it. They can only exist in the adoration and attention of others, otherwise they disappear.'

The traffic to their right started to inch forward. Anderson glanced in the rear-view mirror and swiftly changed lane. 'And what has that got to do with anything?'

'Only a narcissist would demand – no, *command* – the sort of loyalty we have just witnessed from Adrian Wood. The narcissist chooses for his associates people he can dazzle and dominate, and feeds on their awe of him, their eagerness to obey him, to please him. That's what validates him. I've had my suspicions that the other man – the intelligence – is narcissistic, and that half-hour with Wood pretty much confirmed it.'

'Bit of a stretch, surely?' Anderson said.

'OK, take Marita Kennedy then. Her only excuse to be on the face of the planet is her adoring public. Can you see how fragile that ego must be? Never to be content with yourself, never comfortable in your own skin?'

'My heart bleeds,' Anderson muttered.

'I daresay you think I'm starting to see narcissists every-where,' Batten said. 'Marita is a classic narcissist, but is she a pathological one?' he mused.

Anderson made a non-committal noise, watching for a break in the crawling traffic.

Batten suddenly changed tack. 'Wood told us so much,' he said. 'The only time he registered anything like fear was when I told him he might not have his friend to turn to. It was pathetic, in the true sense of the word.' He picked up his mobile to ask for the background reports on Wood, Whyte and Pfeffer to be ready when they got back, and Anderson mentally ran through what they already knew. So far there was no trace of Whyte having had a job, and Pfeffer and Wood had done menial low-paid jobs. The connection between them and the victims, and between them and the 'intelligent, forensically aware' other man, eluded Anderson completely.

He tried to think logically about Adrian Wood's victims. Abigail McGee had been at a society wedding; Iris Everitt, the one Wood was actually serving time for, had won an award for her design show at the university where she'd been attacked. She had no idea if she had ever met her attacker; she lived in Edinburgh and had never needed to stay in a hotel there, never mind the one where Adrian Wood worked as a night porter. Anderson tried to think how else a man like Adrian would know a woman like Iris, and he couldn't.

Once on the M8 he plugged in his hands-free and lis-tened to his messages. Quinn: Lambie was up to some-thing, she was sure of it; he was taking tonight off, strange behaviour for one so dedicated. The subtext was clear, but it was Batten who voiced it.

'Strange, for one so committed to the case.'

Quinn's message went on to say that the CCTV at the Corbetts' house had produced a few grainy images of somebody, but whether male or female, fat or wearing a thick warm jacket, it was impossible to tell. Littlewood was keeping an eye on Lambie. But Anderson could tell by Quinn's voice she was worried.

Brenda: Claire was thinking of becoming a vegetarian, and she'd asked for a second piercing in her ear. Could he come round and tell her 'no' to both?

Costello: Lucy was a good witness, and they were getting somewhere.

Anderson dialled on the hands-free phone and asked Wyngate for the background check on Lambie to be on his desk when he got back. Then he phoned Claire's mobile twice and left messages, phoned Brenda at home and on her mobile, and then gave up.

The phone rang immediately.

Anderson let Batten listen; it was Quinn. 'Wyngate's just told me that Lambie does indeed have a very personal connection with the Corbetts. His mum used to be their cleaner. He and the Corbett girls played together as kids. In fact, he knew them well, kept in touch as they got older.'

'Interesting,' Batten chipped in. 'Two girls, beautiful, intelligent, rich, privileged. But look at Lambie. Not the sort of lad to take home to Dad, eh?'

'That's horrible,' said Anderson.

'No, just the way things are. Imagine – he's grown up wanting their approval. Look, this is something I can do for you; I can bring you the head of Emily's rapist on a plate. It's a motive for him to kill Whyte.'

'So he's a narcissist now as well, is he?' Anderson tried to joke, but Batten was talking to Quinn.

'Think about it. The problem is that *we* are now pushing the investigation further,' he said. 'Which has pushed Lambie off the Corbett sisters' appreciation list. So Lambie's not happy.'

'Will you both be back by six?' Quinn demanded. 'I'm going to call a briefing. I want Mick Batten there.'

'Don't know about that . . .' Anderson began. 'We're stuck on the . . . hang on, traffic's moving up ahead . . . it's looking hopeful . . .'

'Use the blue light, drive on the hard shoulder,' Quinn snapped. 'Be there.'

'Twenty minutes, ma'am,' Anderson said, and closed the call.

'An unhappy narcissist is a dangerous narcissist,' Batten observed.

'A pissed off DCI ain't so safe either,' Anderson muttered.

By the time Anderson walked back into the office, trying to ignore his incipient headache, somebody had found another board and Browne and Wyngate were reorganizing the entire wall, following instructions from Quinn. Donna McVeigh, Stephen Whyte and Edward Pfeffer's photographs were all together, a blue circle around them.

They had one person in common, the person who had killed them. Four phone numbers had appeared, two from Stephen Whyte's mother's phone and two from Donna's. All four numbers were listed with pay-as-you-go mobiles, none could be identified by anyone connected with the owners, and all remained unanswered when called. The numbers meant nothing to Anderson but he did note that one ended 666. Beside them was a note of when the calls had been made and received. The 666 looked tasty – an increasing number of calls up to 30th January, then nothing.

Stuck on the wall was a tube of the superglue identified on Pfeffer, Whyte and McVeigh and a small bottle of Sili-colube, nozzle intact, and a list of its uses as a non-greasy clean lubricant – guns, wheel nuts, light engines, medical equipment, working models. The word 'gun' had been changed to 'unidentified implement', with two arrows pointing to photographs of the shaved skulls of Donna and Whyte. Long, narrow, heavy, dangerous – a crowbar?

The word 'noise' was boxed and subtitled . . . Click, snap, crack.

And in the middle, Emily's beautiful face shone out, like an angel helping them on their way.

More photographs of victims were going up as details were clarified. They formed a frightening, linear pattern . . . Anderson's eyes passed back and forth, naturally stopping at the ones he knew.

Emily, Corinne, Abigail, Iris. Then Shelly, Margaret, Linda, Shannon and Lisa. An arrow pointed down to Lucy, their star witness.

Another uniform came in, with further details about two of the girls. Browne wrote them up. Anderson was too tired to go up and read it; anyway, he was sure the answer was in the big picture.

Batten sank into the chair next to him, wearing depression like an overcoat. 'Look at them, all bright women,' he sighed. 'How have these guys got away with it for so long?'

'You said yourself – he's clever, very clever, the other man.'

'That's what gets to me, you know. If we – I – get this wrong, that line of photographs will just go on and on getting longer.'

'Don't get it wrong then.'

14

Costello and Browne settled into the comfortable hired van Anderson had eventually authorized, which was parked in the driveway of the bungalow directly across from the Corbetts. It had proved difficult to stop Mrs Morrison, owner of the bungalow, coming out every half-hour with cups of coffee and scones 'to keep those nice girls warm', thus alerting all and sundry that there was a police presence in the van.

But for their purposes it was as good as they could have wished for. The Corbetts' house opposite had a beech hedge on three sides, a pedestrian gate and a vehicle gate, both locked. Beyond that was a driveway, and a clipped privet hedge, staggered like a maze, gave total privacy from prying eyes. It was the house of somebody who was scared of something, scared of everything.

The Morrisons' bungalow was in stark contrast. Only a knee-high fence separated the front lawn from the pavement, and the entire garden was open plan. Two small conifers stood as sentinels at the garage door, and Costello had parked the van between them to gain some cover while also commanding a view of the entire street.

DC Wyngate and DS Littlewood were parked on the upper corner. If Lambie approached on foot from

Great Western Road, they would see him before the women did.

'So did that briefing get us anywhere?' asked Browne. 'I know Dr Batten's very clever but I was getting a bit lost. All I got was there's a clever person bossing stupid people about and the stupid ones get killed by the clever one.'

'That's about it. I was kind of keeping up until he got really technical about pathological narcissists. That was when Anderson fell asleep,' said Costello.

'He's so tired.' Browne sighed. 'You know, people don't haven't much time for David Lambie, but I rather like him.'

'But we don't trust him, which is why we are sitting in a van in the middle of the night doing a surveillance job on him,' said Costello. 'He's still a damn sight nicer than bloody Vik Mulholland, who really has become an arsehole.' She twisted the top of her flask closed as though she wished it were Mulholland's throat. 'Apparently Lambie was definite he was leaving at ten tonight, and he's never said or done that before, which means he's up to something.'

Browne leaned forward to peer up and down the street. 'All the journalists seem to have gone.'

'Amazing what a hotshot lawyer who knows everybody can achieve.' Costello checked her radio. It was on point-to-point to Littlewood, so if Lambie came with his radio, he couldn't listen in.

If he came.

'I really don't understand what we're doing here,' said Browne. 'What do we suspect him of?'

'We don't quite suspect him of killing Stephen Whyte – if we did, Quinn would have him by the balls in an interview room somewhere – but we suspect him of some involvement with Whyte's death.' Costello moved in her seat. 'Don't you think it's a bit odd, Lambie spending ten years on a case, just because his mum used to clean for the victim's parents? Ten years he's been living alone and spending every off-duty minute looking into one case? That's obsessional.'

Brown looked up quickly, her gaze sharp and intense. 'If I had the slightest piece of evidence against my husband's killer, even after ten years,' she said fiercely, 'I'd go after him, you know, no questions asked.'

'No, you wouldn't. Your kids – what would happen to them? Dad gone and Mum serving a life sentence? You have a life, Gillian. Lambie doesn't. He works as a cop. He plays at being a cop. The thing that gets him out of his bed in the morning is something to do with the Corbett family. I think that was the point Dr Batten was trying to make. Oh, hello . . . do you see what I see?' Costello ducked down, making sure the outline of her head was blocked by the headrest. She grabbed Browne to stop her leaning forward for a better look. 'Just look down to the right, on this side of the road,' she hissed. 'That's Lambie, isn't it? Dead of night, freezing fog, and he's walking the streets.'

At that moment, Lambie walked across the driveway right in front of them, hands in pockets, shoulders hunched against the cold. The rotund short-legged silhouette, with its slightly effeminate gait, was unmistakable.

'So is he casing the joint with a view to getting in? Or

doing his rounds to make sure the place is secure?' Costello reached for her radio. 'Littlewood?'

'Yip. No sight of him yet.'

'He's on his way down our side of the road. Two minutes max.'

Radio silence. Costello watched a minute tick over on the dashboard clock.

'No sign of him?'

'Confirmed – no sign.'

It would take Lambie a lot less than a minute to walk the length of the Corbetts' garden wall.

'I'm not happy. I'm going to have a look.'

'I'm coming with you,' said Browne.

They got out the van, closing the doors as quietly as they could, and crossed the road into the cover of the Corbetts' beech hedge. Costello flicked her torch on. A quick flash up and down the street. No sign of anybody. She walked on, Browne falling in behind her. She wished she had Anderson behind her. If they did come across a murderous Lambie, she couldn't be sure that Browne would have her back covered. She walked the length of the hedge, looking for a gap. Lambie obviously had not gone through the gate.

'Aha, I bet he went through here.'

The coppiced beeches had divided near the roots and a sort of tunnel, not noticeable from the street, ran for a few yards along the middle of the hedge. 'Come on.'

'What are we doing?' asked Browne apprehensively.

'We're only having a look. Investigating a prowler. You stay behind me.'

'I'm scared,' said Browne.

'Stop saying that. So am I. But the boys are listening. They know where we are.'

Costello slipped through the gap, and Browne struggled through after her. Costello had to pull her out at the other side.

Lambie had already crossed the lawn, and was on the patio, creeping the length of the house and staying close to the wall. Browne breathed in sharply, and Costello put a hand on her arm. Lambie was now up by the sliding doors; the automatic lights had come on but he was too close to the door to be caught in them. He knew the place.

Costello heard the patio doors slide open.

Whatever Lambie was about to do would take time. She waited for the lights to go off, a full two minutes which seemed like an eternity. She could hear her heart thumping. Littlewood could probably hear it over the radio.

As soon as the lights went out Costello sidled round the lawn, and Browne followed her.

They waited at the patio doors. Costello put her finger to her lips. They heard a subhuman grunt, the sound of somebody fighting for breath. It went on, a noise of soft struggle, of suffocation, of somebody being punched, having the wind taken out of them. Then a faint cry, the sounds of struggle. Costello paused, trying to remember the layout of the garden room. Inside, beyond a closed door, somebody was moaning in pain. She moved quickly, her torch out ready to use as a weapon, pointed to the bedroom door, made sure Browne was ready, and kicked the door open, shouting, 'Lambie! Stop!'

On the bed lay the naked figure of Jennifer Corbett with the half-naked figure of DS Lambie on top of her. His bare buttocks had paused mid-thrust, and the gold hairs on his bum twinkled in the light of the torch.

They both froze.

Costello dropped the beam of her torch and looked round. Browne was holding a garden gnome, ready to use it as a weapon.

Then Costello started to laugh.

'You think I'm stupid, don't you?' Jennifer Corbett offered Colin Anderson a slice of toast before buttering her own with very precise strokes of her knife.

Anderson shook his head at the toast; he'd already had his breakfast. 'No, I don't. Not at all. I just popped in to smooth things over after last night. I have to get back to the station.'

'What will happen to Dave?'

'More like what are you going to do to us? I think we might have invaded your privacy somewhat. Oh, David is in trouble, all right. He has not declared a personal interest in a case. And that's not on.'

Fresh-faced and wide-eyed, Jennifer looked like a lovesick teenager in her big checked shirt and jeans, her hair clipped up into a ponytail. Her hand reached out to his across the table. 'But do you know why he never said he knew us? It was for me. We want to get whoever did that to Emily.' She looked deep into Anderson's eyes.

He could see in there a lower-voltage version of her sister.

'You know, I remember the first time I saw him – as a cop, I mean. We were all at the hospital, and we weren't sure if Emily was going to make it. Mum and Dad were beside themselves. But they had each other. Emily's my sister, and we were very close. All these police were coming and going, going through Emily's life, taking her apart, and it was horrible. And then Dave turned up. He just asked me how I was coping. Me. He made me a cup of tea, and we talked about me. Even now, everybody who comes to the house asks about Emily. Or asks about Dad. I don't mind, but Dave was my secret. Was.'

'I understand, I think.' Anderson sipped his tea. 'So it's been going on for ten years?'

'Yes. And we've both been totally focused on finding out who . . . that man . . .'

'I have to ask, did he share any sensitive information with you? After all, you know Lucy McCallum, and you shouldn't.'

'I was studying law, same as Emily. I took a year off when it happened, and I never went back. So I put my brain to use. I have a better brain than that bloody database you used to use. I had nothing else to think about all day but catching the bastards.'

'So what happened last night?'

'We'd arranged to meet. I gave him a precise time, when I knew Emily would be fast asleep. He texted me from the bottom of Queen Margaret Drive, and I unlocked the French windows. I knew he'd be there in a matter of minutes and . . . well . . .' She opened her arms. 'Well, sometimes I rip my clothes off and get into bed and just let him climb in.' She looked Anderson in the eye challengingly. 'Ten years of that. Do I have a sad life?'

Anderson sighed, feeling very old. 'I wouldn't say so, Jennifer. Not at all.'

Back at the station, Anderson realized he had no idea what the DCI would want to do now. What they needed was the one thing they didn't yet have – the results of the DNA tests. So Anderson had arranged the briefing for ten, giving the others a little time to sleep in, not that he expected any of them would. There was no point in starting any earlier. Before going to see Jennifer Corbett, he'd had breakfast with Brenda and the kids, and had run Claire to school, enjoying twenty minutes of animated chit-chat, with him trying not to play the heavy father and saying she could have a piercing when she was sixteen and he'd think about the vegetarian thing. In her own considerate way, she sulked and said she'd do what the hell she wanted and Anderson consoled himself that that was probably the talk of a healthy teenager. Then as she left the car she'd popped her head back in at the driver's window and given him a kiss while her pals weren't looking.

Peter had sat through breakfast in silence, eating cornflakes one at a time, locked into his own wee world, not allowing anybody else in.

Anderson didn't have any answers to that one.

Costello and Browne had taken advantage of having hired a van and gone home for a few hours' sleep, appearing in good time for the briefing. Now Costello was on the phone – listening to Harry, no doubt. She laughed, her face animated, almost pretty. She looked ten years younger, Anderson thought.

Suddenly she noticed Anderson watching her. 'Thanks for telling me . . . yeah, we need to talk to him as soon as poss. I'm getting dirty looks from the Boss, so I'd better get going . . . have to go . . .' She hung up, and glared at Anderson. Then she sighed. 'I thought he was going to ask me out on Sunday.'

'Sunday?'

'Valentine's Day. But all he wanted was to say he's been leaving messages for Ronnie, but Ronnie hasn't called back, so he's probably sleeping off a hangover.'

'That was a long phone call just to tell you that.'

There was no punchy retort, just the tip-tap of her pen on her desk. 'Can I ask you something?'

'If it's a man–woman thing, don't. There's no point.'

'Do you think I'm . . . you know . . . ?'

'Sorry, that didn't translate to man-speak.' He turned back to his monitor, sensing a conversation he did not want to get into.

'Would you sleep with me?'

'Is that an offer?' he asked dryly.

'No, what I mean is . . . Harry – apparently – never, ever even thinks about it.'

Anderson looked at the clock; it was ten to ten. No escape. He chose his words carefully. 'Costello, there are two kinds of attractive women in the world: the kind you instantly want to . . .'

'Shag?'

'Indeed, though not the word I'd choose. But you never

379

marry those. The other kind are women you can have a laugh with, the kind you might not object to waking up with for the next forty years. Harry might see you as the latter rather than the former.'

'But what if I'm in the category you haven't mentioned – too awful to contemplate?'

'Then he wouldn't be finding ridiculous excuses to phone you up, would he?' Anderson took the chance to change the subject. 'How's DS Lambie this morning? I've just had a coffee with Jenny. She's a nice girl. Not going to run to the complaints committee.'

'He seems OK. Corbett found out, of course, and is making sure no journalists hear about it. We really don't want that in the papers. You know they'll print anything.'

Suddenly, Anderson swivelled round to look at the pictures of the women on the wall. 'Maybe we really have been looking at this the wrong way round. Can you check if all these women did something to get into a newspaper?'

'They all did. They were raped,' Costello said acidly.

'Before that, I mean,' Anderson said, his gaze never wavering. 'Women of achievement, somebody – was it Batten? – said. Emily was Young Scot of the Year, Lucy had just run up Ben Nevis.'

'Corinne had published the kiddies' book . . .' Costello felt a chill in her heart. 'Batten did say he – or they – seemed to know what the victims were doing, where they would be. Do you really think that's the connection?' She stood up, walked up to the board and started pointing. 'Iris had won a prize at her degree show. Abigail McGee was at a society wedding. Linda Michie: doctorate? Maybe something there? Lisa Arbuckle works for the council? But they're not remarkable, nothing that would get into the national papers.'

'But they had all been in a newspaper, and even local papers go on the net,' Anderson pointed out.

'What if it's the photographs that are important?' Costello whispered. 'What if it's Gillespie we should be looking at? Was he involved with the photographs in some way? We know he's based up here. Colin, we need to talk to him, just to ask him about the keys to Clarence Avenue if nothing else. He never told us about that job.' Costello swung round on the chair. 'And that photograph was up on our wall, so he must have seen it. But he said nothing. It was Harry that told us. Maybe we should lean on Gillespie a bit.'

'Maybe.' Anderson rubbed his chin.

'Or do you want me to have a conversation with Harry, off the record? Find out where Gillespie was, what he did, before he came here? And find out if he asked to come to this station to do this job? But then how would he know this job would bring him right here?'

'Don't be thick, Costello. If he got Harry to sign him up as his assistant for the next big case, then all he had to do was kill Stephen Whyte, and that would be our next big case, wouldn't it? It would explain why Stephen was dumped where he was dumped. But yes – make that call. Be careful, tell him as little as you can get away with. Harry and Gillespie are friends, so don't push his loyalty. If you get the feeling you are, just back off.'

Costello tapped her mobile phone on her chin. 'OK, I won't push it. Well, not so that he'll notice.' She wandered off to a quiet corner.

Nesbitt, who was keeping a low profile and hoping nobody would notice he was still there, followed her hopefully.

The door to the incident room opened, and Quinn walked in, pale and hollow-eyed. O'Hare was two steps behind her, holding car keys. Anderson got the impression he had driven her in; but why shouldn't he? They were old friends.

'Right, DI Anderson.' She pulled her gloves off. 'Storm clouds are gathering at HQ but I'm refusing to have this case taken from me. DS Mulholland and DS Lambie will be working directly with me. And O'Hare has news for us.'

'And I have some for you,' said Anderson and quickly filled his DCI in on the events of the morning so far.

'Thank God! We are getting there.'

The pathologist said, 'And I have the report from Itsy's surgical team.' He scanned a sheet of A4. 'Basically, there were tiny splinters – fibre, dirt and cellulose, plant material – of wood in the palate injury, which have gone off to a botanist for further identification. The wound to the side of the face is ragged, which, while it is consistent with a penetrating wound, is not the same thing. The semen on the scarf is being tested against the samples we got yesterday and the results will be phoned through any minute.'

'No refusals?'

'We'll talk about that later,' said Quinn evasively.

'Well, we might be on the trail of something good as well,' said Costello, and went back to her phone call.

Costello snapped her phone shut and bit her lip. 'You were right. Ronnie had worked with Harry before on a few things but when he found out he was coming to Glasgow to work on this, he jumped at the chance. Willing to work for basic wage. But Harry didn't think there was anything significant in that.'

'It does prove the point – he asked Harry if he could work on this case, not vice versa. Harry also says that Ronnie does some portrait work to keep his hand in, but doesn't ever work on his own. So I'm thinking, what if he was part of the team that took those newspaper pictures, that photographed the graduates, that were at the squirrel-book launch, at the charity event, whatever? That might be how he keeps under the radar.'

'How did we miss that?'

'We didn't. The files were checked for the company name, and their employees, and I bet these companies subcontract loads of work.' Costello slapped her forehead with the palm of her hand. 'How many people turn up to take photographs at those events? Look at Emily, the press, her family, the university, the students' mag. All you need is a good camera, the gear and an ID badge.'

Anderson scowled in thought. 'Let's work backwards. Let's get Wyngate to phone round each station involved, ask if they have any record of the other victims having been at an event that might have been photographed. We can work back from there. Better than simply asking for any connection with Gillespie. There are many reasons why they might not have clocked his name – not officially anyway.'

Costello grinned at him. 'We're on to him, aren't we?'

Quinn had issued stern instructions to Mulholland and Lambie; they were to behave. Lambie seemed uncharacteristically relaxed. According to Jennifer Corbett's official statement, he had been with her when Stephen Whyte was attacked. The call had come through on his mobile, and he still had the Paisley Station number stored as an incoming call. Jennifer added that her dad had been with Emily so she was at the Pond Hotel with Lambie the Saturday Stephen Whyte went missing. Lambie was in the clear. He had not killed Whyte. Quinn was almost disappointed in him.

After Costello's update about Gillespie, Quinn said briskly, 'Well, we still have the separate matter of Itsy to solve. Come on, a free-for-all – what really happened out there that night? Let's start with how she got there.'

There was a knock at the door; it was O'Hare, mobile in hand, Anderson two inches behind him. 'The lab called just this minute. The blood and hair on the stone are Itsy's. The wool fibres are – and I quote – olive-green dyed vicuna. However, the DNA on the scarf belongs to Robert McGurk. You'd better get your skates on, Rebecca.'

'*Bobby?*' Quinn clarified, hoisting her handbag on to her shoulder. 'Jack, thanks. But you'd all better know, he refused a DNA sample, so that was an illegal sample

Browne got for us. No use in court but who gives a stuff? She's not as stupid as she looks, thank God. She lifted a swab from his mug in the greenhouse when she volunteered to rinse the cups, and it matches. Just don't make it official, because it isn't, though it will be when we drag his sorry arse in here and get a sample that way.'

'My God, wonders will never cease. What gave her that idea?' asked O'Hare.

'He scared her out of her mind, quite simply.'

'And it gets better – we have a match for the DNA of the skin under Donna's fingernails. Gillespie.'

'Time to move on this. Come on.'

They went, leaving Mulholland sitting at Anderson's desk, thinking. He had listened to Batten talking about narcissism at the six o'clock briefing the previous night. It had struck a chord with him. He had spent time with Marita, going through the TV appeal. But he wasn't convinced about Bobby. Itsy's attack had shown an intelligence, a sense of timing, that Bobby simply did not possess. But he could see Bobby doing it for the admiration of a woman like Marita; she'd have that hunk of a guy hanging on her little finger. And Itsy pregnant – no way would Marita allow that. Costello had noted it in the file, and Anderson had noted comments about Itsy and Bobby, Bobby and Itsy. Yet what was Itsy but a shadow of her sister?

He decided to go and have a word with Marita. Shower, shave, good suit and charm. He was the best detective in this squad, and he wanted a murder squad of his own. This was his case now. Narcissism worked both ways.

*

385

'Thank God he's gone,' said Costello as Mulholland left the investigation room. 'He's too quiet for my liking.'

'But Ronnie Gillespie, the photographer? So why did he volunteer a sample?' Wyngate asked.

'Because he thought he'd been careful. He was wearing gloves and a condom, didn't think she'd get a scratch at him. Uniform are bringing him in for routine questioning. Batten will sit in on the interview.'

Wyngate sidled over to sit down beside Costello.

'This is all kicking off now, Gordon. What do you want?'

'About this stalking, well, non-stalking of Marita . . .'

'Do we have to talk about it now?' Her hand paused over the phone in mid-dial.

Batten came over as well, took her hand off the phone, and sat down. 'What do you have, Gordon? Anything that illuminates Marita's real personality is of interest to me and my studies.'

'Should you not be reading up on your notes, ready to interview Mr Gillespie?'

'I doubt Mr Gillespie will be in a state to be interviewed,' Batten said cryptically. 'What is it, Gordon?' he asked again.

'It's just that, if you map Marita's working career, there are gaps when she was doing nothing.'

'Which is when she gets married for the publicity or, in Iain's case, the money,' muttered Costello, writing down another number, trying to track down the newspapers, magazines and freelancers who had attended the society wedding along with Abigail McGee.

'Or she has an "incident".' Wyngate mimed quotes with his fingers. 'Which is reported to the media, but not to the police. When the police try to investigate, Marita withdraws the complaint and says it's all too much fuss about nothing. And it's never Marita who reports it. Plenty of coverage in the gossip mags, though. Always a "source close to the star" or a "source close to the family".'

'Indeed, all this stuff could be done by Marita and her husband, or by somebody they trusted,' Costello said. 'It doesn't seem to matter how secure the place is, somebody walks in and superglues the car. The mail is always opened by Diane but on the day the dog shite arrives, Marita opens it. Oh, horror!'

'Is that a type of Munchausen's syndrome?' Batten asked himself. 'Or the narcissist pleading for adoration?'

'Just fucking attention seeking,' muttered Costello. 'She manipulates men. Men buy her things, men do things for her. Like she says, men always do.' She was a cruel mimic.

'Well, one doesn't obviously.'

'And the home Itsy was in was a private one, paid for by Marita, after the mum died. It wasn't the social services who made that decision.'

'You mean she was just dumped there?'

'I can't find any further record of her being tested or assessed, but I've not got to the bottom of it yet. Another thing . . .' Wyngate was on a roll now. 'Marita's PR people conveniently forget the first husband she married when she was sixteen. He doesn't merit a mention, having a criminal record for petty housebreaking. She gave her status as single when she entered beauty competitions, so hubby number one was dropped like the proverbial hot potato.'

'Too much of a reminder of where she really came from?'

'Her second husband is now a car mechanic, and he had a fair bit to say, which I'll type up. He said she'd had a sterilization – considered it a career move. I thought I'd mention it, because of the . . .' Wyngate patted his stomach.

'Pregnancy?' offered Costello.

'The thing is, husbands come and go. But there's one person who's constant in her life.' Wyngate produced the picture of Miss Caledonia 1990 surrounded by bathing-suited beauties. He tapped the toothpaste grin of Miss East Kilbride.

'Diane,' said Costello. 'Of course. The "source close to the star".'

Costello, Browne and Wyngate had sneaked out for a pub lunch at the Three Judges for an hour while uniform were out looking for the suddenly elusive Mr Gillespie. Anderson had subtly asked Harry to come in to help with enquiries, mostly to stop him talking to Gillespie. It was three o'clock by the time Costello reached the hospital and Harry was already there, edgy and upset. He had spent an hour in an interview room with Littlewood and Anderson, telling them what he knew about his colleague.

'I know you have your reasons but he's a good bloke. What you have on him must apply to loads of other guys.'

Good guy or not, uniform couldn't find Ronnie Gillespie.

In the hospital car park Costello decided to be indiscreet and describe the incident with Lambie and Jennifer to Harry in great detail.

'A police officer caught shagging? That's not funny,' said Castiglia with mock propriety. 'It's bloody hilarious.'

They were still laughing as they went round the corner of the hospital corridor, towards the high dependency unit.

A nurse was standing in the corridor holding a clipboard, and a young doctor, looking stressed, was leaning against the glass window of Itsy's room.

Costello pulled her ID from her pocket.

'Family?' asked the doctor, obviously hoping they were.

'Police. Is Marita Kennedy here?'

'No, no, we've not seen her since early this morning,' the nurse said.

'What about Iain, Mr Kennedy – is he here?'

'No.' She looked at the clock. 'She left shortly after he did.'

'Is there a problem?' asked Costello, all her good mood gone. Something was very wrong.

'Marita said not to let anybody in. And Itsy is . . . well, she's slipping away. Just a matter of time really.'

Costello actually took a step back. 'Oh, I didn't expect that.'

'I'm sorry,' said the doctor. 'We were actually about to switch her oxygen off. We thought you might be family wanting to say a last goodbye.'

389

'Have you phoned Marita?'

'No, she left specific instructions,' said the nurse, looking increasingly uncomfortable.

'To switch off her sister's life support? But you have phoned Iain?'

'Marita said her husband must not be contacted. She was very specific – family only. And she is the next of kin.'

'So you can't phone him?'

'Not without her permission.'

'Harry,' said Costello, getting her phone out. 'Can you call Iain? Just tell him to get himself down here.'

'Are you allowed to do this?'

'No, but you bloody are. Get on with it.'

Harry looked at her screen and punched the number into his own phone, then jogged back down the corridor, towards the lifts.

'How long does she have?' Costello asked the nurse.

'She's not breathing on her own at all, there's no sign of brainstem activity and with Marita giving permission to turn the oxygen off, it's really down to us.'

'Can you keep her going? Please? Just for a wee while.'

The nurse leaned in to Costello's ear. 'Just out of interest, who is closer to Itsy – him or her?'

'Him, definitely.'

'That's what we thought,' the nurse said. 'He seemed the more distressed of the two. But there's no reasoning with that Marita.' She looked at her watch. 'I'm running late, and so is Doctor Wylie, so we couldn't do much about it for a while anyway.' And they both wandered away into the nursing station.

Costello slipped into a protective gown and went into the room. There was already less technology in there, as if Itsy was being unplugged stage by stage. Costello picked up her hand – a tiny hand that felt colder now. She held it between her own, rubbing gently, holding the chilly knuckles to her own lips in a vain effort to warm them. 'Hold on, Itsy, just hold on. Iain's on his way.'

Ronnie Gillespie's last known address was a rented flat in St Andrew's Square, an old Georgian terrace around a manicured garden, right in the middle of the Merchant City.

The uniform branch had not been able to gain entry. That made Anderson uneasy. He was even more uneasy that still nobody knew where Ronnie Gillespie was.

The button for flat 3/2 had *R. Gillespie* typed in italics on a label stuck over the previous occupant's name. Anderson pressed four different bells until he got a response. He simply said, 'Police,' and asked for access. The door buzzed loudly, and they found themselves in a sterile light blue hall, which still smelled of fresh paint and new carpet.

They heard a door open somewhere up the concrete stairs at the end of the hall. Anderson pulled his ID from his pocket.

From elsewhere in the building, echoing off the bare concrete walls, came the noise of Wii Guitar Hero, somebody having a go at 'St Elmo's Fire'.

'Much more of that, and we'll do them for breach of the peace,' said Anderson as he climbed the stairs.

A figure met them halfway up, a young man who looked as though he had come home early from the office.

Anderson showed his warrant card before he reached the landing. 'DI Anderson, Partickhill,' he said. 'And you are . . . ?'

'David Brady,' the man answered.

'We're looking for a Ronald Gillespie. Do you know him?'

'Lives in the flat upstairs. Right above me,' Brady added with an edge to his voice.

'Oh, is that a problem?' asked Anderson, on the one hand reluctant to delay their search of the premises, on the other keen to find out what Brady had to say.

It turned out it wasn't much; Gillespie had been there for eight months, and the flat was one of only two in the entire block that were rented.

'It's not that he's noisy. But they cut corners when they did the underfloor sound insulation, and he's got cheap laminate flooring up there. You can hear every footstep, and it gets annoying.'

'But if you're out at work all day . . .'

'Gillespie comes and goes at all hours of the day and night. I never know when he'll be in or out.'

'Do you talk to him much?'

Brady shrugged. 'Not really. We've shared the occasional pint, but he doesn't talk about himself. So, really, I know nothing about him.'

Iain Kennedy looked like a man whose heart was breaking. He looked as if he hadn't slept, hadn't washed, hadn't eaten, as though he had spent the last twenty-four hours in a gutter somewhere. And behind the desolation lurked a furious anger.

Castiglia had jumped into his Jag and driven the half-mile to fetch him. He had dropped Kennedy at the hospital gate and gone off to park. Kennedy was allowed into Itsy's room without any protective clothing. After all, what was the point of protecting a lost cause? Costello simply let go Itsy's hand and stood up, leaving Iain the seat.

Outside, Castiglia was walking swiftly towards her. He didn't say anything, just rubbed her shoulders, then sat in silence.

The doctor appeared. 'Shall I go in and have a word with him?'

Costello looked at her watch. 'It's only been a few minutes.'

The doctor nodded, and walked away in the other direction.

She looked up to find Harry proffering some mints. 'Did he say anything?' she asked, ripping the packet open. 'What happened between him and Marita? Have they had a fight or something?'

'No idea, but he's bloody furious. She'd broken her part of the deal. They agreed that one of them would always be here, and he thought she was. He wanted to know why the hospital hadn't phoned him. I just told him what they told us. Then he was really furious.'

'Poor guy, what a bitch she is. Imagine denying somebody the chance to say goodbye to somebody they loved.'

Castiglia placed his hand over hers and gave it a slow squeeze. 'Mulholland's car is at Strathearn. Quinn's car is outside the gate.'

Costello shook her head. 'I don't know what that's about.' She stood up, uncomfortable with his concern. She walked to the glass partition and leaned her forehead against it. Itsy was still lying there; the sine wave on the screen of the cardiac monitor was snaking left to right, left to right, like a vivid green sidewinder.

She watched as Iain reached over, lifting the dressing from Itsy's forehead. A single wisp of titian hair had escaped the pre-op shaving, and it curled like a copper-beech leaf on her pale skin. He wound it around his finger and stroked it. Then he leaned over and kissed her. 'Goodbye, my Itsy Bitsy,' he murmured. Behind him, the sine wave lost strength. It gradually dropped to a sinuous curve. Then it flatlined.

Iain sat still beside Itsy for a full minute, then he got up and came out to join Costello.

'She's gone,' he said. 'She was waiting for me. Waiting for me to say goodbye.'

Then he dropped his head on to Costello's shoulder and cried like a baby.

The room was very dark. Anderson paused at the door, letting his eyes adjust. The venetian blinds were closed, the heating was on full blast, and the room smelled of sex and blood and violence. He slipped a pair of shoe covers over his feet, then walked over to open the blind with gloved hands. He and Browne stood gazing round at the white leather suite, the laminate floor, the cream walls, the coffee table. The search team followed them in from the landing.

'You have a good look around the bedroom and bathroom,' he told her. 'Look for any sign that Gillespie's done a runner.'

Browne set about methodically opening cupboard doors, and checking under the bed. She briefly opened the bathroom door and looked inside.

'No gaps in his wardrobe,' she reported. 'Cases and gym bag still here, toothbrush present.'

Then she suddenly shrieked, making Anderson jump out of his skin. Her hand covered her mouth, and a wavering finger was pointing at a bloodied mess in a cage in the corner.

White feathers.

'There are some feathers here,' called Anderson to the search team, trying to prise Browne's clamplike grip from his arm. At first he could not make out what the mess was, but his eyes gradually began to make sense of it. It was the remains of a bird, and it had been stuck through with a knife.

Littlewood went over to investigate. 'It's a bloody cockatoo,' he announced.

'OK, someone needs to run the word cockatoo past Quinn's ornithologist. I bet the white feathers found at the scene came from that.'

Littlewood was still gazing at the dead bird. 'Oh my God, somebody's cut its wings off.'

'They used to do that in medieval times,' said Batten

from the door. 'If you were a rapist they'd cut the wings from your falcons, the head from your horse.'

'Why not just chop the balls off the rapist?' said Browne, her head now buried in Anderson's shoulder. 'Or is that too bloody simple?'

Mulholland pressed the entryphone at Strathearn and was told to 'come on up'.

'Straight up the main stairs, turn left, and it's the second door,' Marita's voice said.

If he had first thought Marita Kennedy a physically attractive woman, he found her even more so now. She wasn't quite as perfect as the day they had filmed the appeal, and somehow that made her more enchanting. She was dressed in a black high-necked dress that was a little too tight, a little too short, to be mourning. Her freshly washed hair was not quite dry, still slightly fluffy around the edges.

'Hello,' she said casually on opening the door he had gently knocked with his knuckle. Then, as if she had just realized who it was, 'Oh, hello.' There was an automatic attraction of one beautiful person to another. With a hint of intent in her voice, she invited him in.

He thought he was going to walk into some kind of private living room, but he entered a series of rooms that all ran into each other, divided by a huge arch where the wall had been knocked through. It looked like a film set. This room was obviously a dressing room, the next one was her bedroom, and beyond that was another, but all he could see was the back of a settee. Everything was carpeted in cream, with beige and gold everywhere. There was a huge dressing table, its mirror surrounded by electric bulbs. There was a rack full of make-up, and an entire wall of mirrors, two of which swung out to give a 360-degree view. Mulholland was enough of a new man to admit that he himself was vain, but this was something else.

'Do come in, and make yourself at home.' Her taloned fingers clutched his forearm, and he was pulled into the boudoir. 'Maybe you can tell me what's happening? I don't know what to think any more. I can't help wondering if somebody out there is after me. Is this all to do with me, do you think?'

Mulholland gave a little cough. 'Have you heard about your sister?'

'I left instructions for them to switch off her oxygen when they thought the time was right.' Marita choked a little and held a fingertip under her eyes, stopping a tear from damaging her make-up. 'In any real sense, she died sometime yesterday; she just floated away. I wouldn't have her kept like a vegetable, she wouldn't have wanted that. I know, I'm her sister. I did what was best.' She put her hands on her chest, her fingers spanned, ten perfect nails. 'I'm afraid I'm going to have to go.' She smiled charmingly. 'Was there something in particular you wanted?'

'I don't think you should be going anywhere.'

'That Quinn woman won't give me any protection. Of course *anybody* could be waiting for me in that fog, but I have to live my life.' Her fingers were on his chest now.

Vik smiled his most beguiling smile, and lifted her hand

from the front of his coat, curling her fingers around his own. 'It must be terrible, what you're going through, but you must bear with us,' he said gravely. 'We're very close to the person who attacked – killed – your sister. Are you sure you should be going out? It really might not be safe out there.'

'But I can't live my life cooped up like this.' She gave him a dazzling smile.

'Where are you going?'

'Out to see a friend. Don't worry, I'll be quite safe. I'm not going anywhere on my own.' She looked over her shoulder at a sound in the other part of the suite, a soft noise like somebody getting up off a chair.

Diane appeared through the archway, dressed in a cotton tracksuit, her short blonde hair damp from the shower. She pulled a towel from her neck.

'A quiet word please.' Mulholland leaned over to Marita, so Diane couldn't hear. 'Twice I've seen notes of what you've said about your sister and Bobby McGurk. Is it true? Were they in a sexual relationship?'

Marita smiled like a naughty little girl trying to charm her way out of trouble. 'Oh, I can't remember if I said exactly that. Not in so many words.'

'But is it true?' he repeated.

Marita sighed impatiently. 'Well, they were close. Maybe too close.'

'And which of you normally wore that red scarf?'

'I did. But Itsy loved it. She liked anything Iain bought me.'

'Do you ever drive the white van?'

'Don't be stupid. That's my BMW out there.'

'Have you ever driven the van?'

'If you've searched it for DNA or whatever you do, then yes, I have been in the van in the past. I've driven it when I wanted to go out without attracting attention. Should I get a lawyer? You policemen are far too clever for me.'

Really? 'Well, take care,' said Mulholland.

Marita smiled at him, enjoying his discomfiture as he looked uncertainly at Diane. She leaned seductively on the door frame. 'Oh, I will.'

He left, and Marita closed the door after him.

Mick Batten sat alone in the incident room at the station, sipping cold coffee and thinking. Then he went and stood in front of the board, placing his finger first on the photograph of Itsy, then Marita, then back to Itsy. He needed to know more about these two sisters, and he needed to stop thinking about Emily and Mr Click. He needed a bit of space in his head.

On Costello's desk was a list of files and DVD titles, all Marita's television programmes and celebrity appearances. Then he noticed among the papers a DVD Costello had picked up from Strathearn. He took it into the small room, and slotted it into the machine.

There was a soundtrack of gentle jazz, chatter. Stiletto shoes appeared first on the screen, coming down a splendid flight of stairs, and a slender leg could be glimpsed through a slit in the skirt of a long, deep-turquoise dress.

'Hello, Mrs Iain Kennedy 2010,' said Batten. 'Once a beauty queen, always a beauty queen.'

The camera panned up slowly, as Marita made her grand entrance, lingering on the nipped-in waist, the low neckline, the piled-up titian hair and the perfect smile. Marita took a glass of champagne from a tray that magically appeared, her little finger sticking out. The camera caught Itsy sliding in behind her, her own pinkie sticking out in mischievous imitation.

Batten pressed Pause, Rewind, then Play.

Not imitation, he corrected himself. *Mockery.*

'So Marita makes her big entrance,' he whispered to himself. 'Then . . .' On cue Iain Kennedy appeared, his hand out to welcome his beautiful wife. He put his arm around her and they embraced, cheek to cheek, in a salvo of camera flashes. Itsy sashayed across to join them, and Iain put his other arm around her and kissed her as well. Batten froze the picture. Iain and Itsy's faces were close, so close, and they were laughing. But Marita was looking away, posing with a brittle smile for the cameras.

A cold, brittle, frozen smile.

Batten placed his finger on Marita's face.

'You knew, didn't you?' he whispered. 'Oh yes, you knew.'

Mulholland's heart was thumping as Marita's door closed behind him. Nothing in the drugs unit at Paisley was as good as this. Marita was another bloody narcissist, he knew that; he had just seen and heard it with his own eyes and ears.

He wondered if she was also one of those sex addicts? It seemed to be her way of communicating with people.

There had been a subtle invitation in the air. He was sure if he'd hung around he'd have been asked to join a three-some. The glamorous redhead, the blonde fresh from the shower, the young policeman at the door – it was a scenario for a bad porn film.

Mulholland went down the main stairway, across the hall and out to the driveway where his Audi was parked.

His mind racing, he slipped into the driver's seat and pulled out his mobile. Batten answered quickly.

'Listen, have you found Gillespie?'

'No.' Batten sounded distracted.

'As a psychiatrist –'

'Psychologist,' corrected Batten. 'What do you want, Vik? I'm busy.'

'Tell me, could someone like Marita have wound up Bobby enough to get him to kill Itsy? Does she have the strength of personality to do that?'

'To manipulate men? Of course she does.'

'And Bobby? Could he be set on Itsy, like a dog?'

'I don't know. I've never spoken to him, but I know he's vulnerable, insecure. He could look to her as a matriarchal figure, and she is a bloody narcissist, of course.'

'Bobby and Marita gave each other alibis, didn't they?'

'How should I know?'

'Can you put Wyngate on?'

'Phone him yourself.' And the phone was cut off.

But Mulholland smiled. His promotion was in sight.

Suddenly a black Shogun came up the drive in a blast of Wagner, narrowly missing the Audi as it swung round to park. O'Hare silenced Bryn Terfel, and took a call on his mobile before jumping out and walking to the front door. He didn't press the buzzer; he just waited. Mulholland watched as the door opened and O'Hare went in, spoke briefly to somebody, then came out again and strode off across the lawn and into the shrubbery. It was great, this fog, Mulholland thought; nobody could see a thing unless they knew where to look.

And Mulholland was looking for Bobby McGurk.

He speed-dialled Wyngate; he needed to know if anybody else had alibied Marita. Or was it just Bobby?

He fiddled with the heater as he listened to Wyngate tapping at a keyboard. And he failed to notice the front door to Strathearn open slightly, then close again.

15

O'Hare surveyed the pots and pots of small seedlings, too weak to survive outside, carefully positioned to get the best of the weak wintry sun during the short daylight hours. A smelly paraffin heater kept the chill of winter at bay.

'Am I disturbing you?' he asked politely.

'Would it make any difference if I said yes?' Wee Tony Abbott kept working away, stubby fingers nimble and sensitive as they pressed the clean earth down around the stalk of the seedling. Then he picked up the next in line, delicately, almost lovingly. 'You cops have been all over here in the last two days, I expect to get huckled any minute.'

'I think they're pursuing leads, as they say. Any idea where Bobby McGurk is at the moment?'

'That bloody Marita's just rung asking for him, so bugger knows where he is. He's supposed to be helping me with this. No way I'm going to get all this done on my own, is there?' He picked up another seedling and shook it gently. 'Why? Do you want to talk to him?'

'No. I want to talk to you. And I'm not a cop.'

'So who are you then?' Wee Tony drew a grimy hand under his nose.

403

O'Hare made his way down the central concrete pathway. He looked up at the vines twining overhead. 'Must be difficult to keep these alive in this weather.'

'OK if you know what you're doing,' Wee Tony said guardedly.

O'Hare pulled the gloves from his hands, placed them in the pockets of his jacket. 'I'm a pathologist.'

'I'm not dead yet.'

'Forensic pathologist. I do a lot of work in court, suspicious deaths, that sort of thing.'

'Weird life, working with the dead. I prefer the living.' Wee Tony held up the potted seedling to prove a point.

'Indeed, but I do notice things about people.'

There was the briefest sliver of a reaction to that.

'I can always place a face, you know, a likeness. I never forget a face.'

'I can forget my own name these days,' said Wee Tony.

'I bet you wish you could.'

Wee Tony went back to his seedlings, with slightly more concentration than before. 'What does that mean?'

'I think you know exactly what it means. If people give themselves a new name, sometimes they don't quite let go of the name they had.'

'Oh, believe me, I let it go, son, I let it go.'

'They're a good murder squad at Partickhill. Particularly DI Anderson and DS Costello. They have a bit of a reputation.'

'Good for them. I just hope they find out who's responsible for hurting wee Itsy. Poor wee Itsy Bitsy.'

O'Hare caught the slightest rasp in the older man's

voice. 'Well, they'll be talking to you soon. Don't lie to them, just let things take their course. Please.'

'I'm busy, son. I've to get all these done.' Wee Tony turned and gave O'Hare the briefest of smiles that didn't quite reach his guarded grey eyes. Then he went back to his task, picking up the next seedling, examining it before placing it in a finger-sized hole, and pressing it in.

O'Hare went outside. He had been prepared for Tony Abbott to have no idea what he was talking about, but he did know. O'Hare hoped he had done the right thing. He looked up into the fog, along the overgrown path that had got Browne into so much trouble. He walked a few paces along it, remembering it from forty years ago. It had been a proper back drive then. A vehicle had been along here recently; tyre marks showed in the frost, and the frozen puddles were cracked. But the tracks disappeared into the bushes.

O'Hare followed the wheelmarks, pushing his way through, noting the recently – very recently – snapped twigs. He nearly walked into a wooden upright hidden by undergrowth, part of an older building almost obscured by trees and shrubs. It was derelict, its broken glass thick with moss.

And in it, hanging, a darker shape among the shadows, was a body.

Mulholland had driven the Audi down to the gatehouse and was just parking it close to the wall, when his mobile sounded. Batten's number. He thought about ignoring it, but then answered. Was he with Marita? No. Did he know where she was? Up at Strathearn. No she wasn't, not now, and they really needed to speak to her. Mulholland smiled and closed his phone. Something had rattled Marita right enough – something he, Mulholland, had said.

And now for Bobby.

He knocked on the door.

He had been expecting Bobby to be a simpleton, easy to interview, easy to control. He was wrong. Bobby McGurk was way over six feet tall and moved with the graceful strength of a tiger, and the same controlled power. But he was jumpy; his muscles tensed, and his eyes darted towards sounds and sights he didn't recognize. Littlewood had said how well Abbott had calmed Bobby down just with a pat on the shoulder and a gentle word, and Vik Mulholland wished that Wee Tony was here now. Bobby was in his own home, within his comfort zone, yet he was pacing the small front room of the gatehouse, blond fringe flopping across nervous eyes, refusing to sit, refusing to be calm.

Yes, he had seen Marita on Tuesday night, and they had gone out looking for Itsy. He just shook his head and grunted 'dunno' to every question after that.

Mulholland had to find a way in. 'We're asking Tony the same questions. He's helping us. Don't you want to help us too?'

A grunt.

'Do you remember the night Itsy went away?'

A nod. 'I was looking for her. I said.'

'And you met Marita?'

There was a slight change there, that feral look in the eyes again. Bobby was wary, uncertain.

'Tony says you have to tell us the truth.'

'I found the collared dove, the one Itsy was worried about. I took it back to the greenhouse, splinted its wing. Then I went out again. I caught up with Tony at the pond.'

'So Marita was with you when you found the dove?'

The feral eyes darted sideways, as if looking for a way out.

'Funny she forgot to mention it,' Mulholland went on. 'I don't think she was there. Well, not until a bit later. So, Bobby, what really happened?'

Bobby bit his lip and muttered: '*At last I knew / Porphyria worshipped me: surprise / Made my heart swell, and still it grew / While I debated what to do.*'

'Pardon?'

'*While I debated what to do,*' Bobby said again. 'It's from "Porphyria's Lover". It's a poem.'

'Who was your lover, Bobby?'

'Marita.'

'Don't you mean Itsy? Marita said it was Itsy.'

Bobby walked up to Mulholland. 'Marita, Marita, Marita,' he growled, stabbing Mulholland three times in the chest with his finger, so powerfully Mulholland was forced to take a step back.

Where the fuck was Batten when you needed him?

But Bobby was talking. 'It was after dinner she came, a long time after. Tony was asleep.'

Mulholland took a deep breath. 'Did Marita tell you to keep that a secret?'

'Yes, a secret. Nobody's business, is it?'

'Good. Well done. And do you always do what Marita tells you?'

407

'No, I do what Tony tells me. He's the main man.'

'Bobby, has Marita ever asked you to hurt anybody?'

A shake of the head. Bobby was standing very close to Mulholland. 'How's my Itsy?' he asked. His breath was hot in Mulholland's face.

Mulholland pulled his head back slightly. He had to think fast. He was dealing with a wild card. Bobby's mind did not work the way the minds of other men worked. 'You like birds, Bobby. You saved the dove. I hear you've a nightjar down beyond the pond.'

Bobby eyes narrowed slightly.

'Terrible the way the weak can get hurt, isn't it? I'm sorry, Bobby, but Itsy's dead.'

Bobby's eyes flared, and Mulholland sensed danger.

Instinct told him to keep his voice soft, to keep talking. 'We think Marita killed her, Bobby. We think Marita hit her on the head with a stone. That wasn't a nice thing to do to Itsy, was it? Leave her out there in the cold, to die? I mean, you didn't let the dove die, did you, Bobby? So you have to tell me where Marita is now. Itsy would want you to do that – Tony too. Tony's helping us. He's talking to Gillian – you know Gillian. So will you help us out? Where is Marita? Do you meet her at a special place?'

But Bobby seemed to have drifted off somewhere else.

Mulholland tried to get his attention back. He took a risk and said, 'I know you and Marita have a special place to go to, and what you do there. When you and Marita were together, did she tell you she had killed Itsy?'

Mulholland recognized some emotional instinctive intelligence kicking in. Bobby leaned forward as if to whisper quietly in Mulholland's ear, and Mulholland leaned forward to listen.

Then Bobby punched Mulholland so hard that he flew over the back of the sofa.

'It looks like we've found Ronnie,' said Anderson. 'Well, O'Hare found him.'

Costello stepped off the mossy old slabs that formed the central aisle of the derelict old greenhouse, crouched down and put on a pair of plastic covers over her boots.

'Is there any doubt now that this is being brought home to us?'

'Or to Strathearn, surely?' said Costello, looking up at Gillespie's distorted face. 'Did Abbott never come down here? I see Uniform have taken him away.'

'Well, obviously somebody was here. But this place is bloody isolated. Did *you* know there was a disused greenhouse down here till Browne mentioned it?'

The body hung, swinging infinitesimally, the only noise a slight grating from the cord on the rusted crossbeam. Vines were still growing across the wrought-iron rafters, but nature was slowly winning the battle to reclaim the place for her own. Gillespie's shoes were level with Costello's face, and she could see the pattern on the sole of his trainers, a wad of chewing gum stuck on one heel. He was wearing socks, both black but not matching.

She looked up at the swollen goggle eyes, the tongue protruding from a rip in the cheek, the lips puckered like a half-closed rose.

'He didn't get up there by himself, did he?' asked

Anderson. 'It would take a man of some strength to hoist him that high. And it looks as though his mouth was superglued.'

'So Batten was right. The minute that DNA was found, he'd signed his own death warrant.'

'But who knew?'

Gillian Browne knew she was going to have to admit that she really wasn't any good at this. Anthony Abbott had been picked up from Strathearn the minute Gillespie's body had been found, and she and Wyngate were supposed to be interviewing him. Anderson had quickly discussed with her what she was supposed to ask, what she was to find out. She would try out what she had learned about interview techniques during her training at Tulliallan. Gillian was to ascertain how Tony saw the relationship between Marita and Bobby, whether he thought it was sexual. Dr Batten had said that was important; there would be an element of 'love', of sheer adoration, directed from the subordinate to the superior. It was the way these things worked. She then had to find out how much he knew about the old greenhouse, and if he had seen any vehicles going in or out the back way. She had her pad and pen ready, and the tape machine was on standby.

But here she was sitting in the fridge that was Interview Room Two faced with an old man with trembling hands, far removed from the kindly and authoritative figure with whom she had drunk a cup of tea in the hothouse. Wee Tony had a worn and lined face. He reminded her of someone she knew, someone she liked. But it was obvious he did not want to be here, and she wished she could allow him to have the fag he so desperately wanted.

She couldn't even do anything at the moment, as Wyngate had been called away. No doubt something else about Marita had come to light. At that point Abbott had leaned over and pointed out that a formal interview could not now go ahead. Even before that, he had stonewalled her attempts to ascertain whether or not he had a criminal record, as there was nobody of his name and of the right age in the system. Abbott had shrugged and said, 'Well, there you go then.' Not a denial, not an admission.

He looked out of the grimy window of the interview room and commented on how bad the fog was. He asked her what they were doing up at Strathearn.

'Searching,' she said.

'Are you stuck here because you're female? Not allowed out in the fog?'

'No. DS Costello's up at Strathearn and she's a female officer,' said Browne, proudly. 'They'll be up there all night.'

Abbott nodded at this. Then he put his hand on his chest. 'I've mislaid my spray. I'm sure I left it in the greenhouse. I really need to take a tablet now. Can I have a glass of water?' He reached into his pocket and pulled out a foil blister pack, placing it on the table.

She recognized the pills as the ones her dad used to take before his fourth and final heart attack. 'Of course,' she said, her own heart softening.

He looked drawn, almost grey, and very tired.

She was away for all of two minutes, getting a plastic

cup of water from the toilet downstairs. She stopped to give wee Nesbitt a pat on the way past.

She opened the door of Interview Room Two. 'Here you are,' she said brightly.

Then she realized she was talking to an empty room.

Batten answered his mobile in the ghost room that was Partickhill main incident room. Everybody else had gone up to Strathearn, the focus now of both investigations.

'We found Gillespie,' said Anderson.

'Dead.' It wasn't a question. 'Hanging? Superglue?'

'Yes.'

'Colin, does he have the keys on him? We think he got the keys to the Clarence Avenue flat and made a copy. Are they on the body?'

'What?'

'You heard – just look! If our man is following a plan, he'll have left us something.'

Batten heard Anderson talk to somebody, probably O'Hare. There were a few muffled sounds. He heard both Anderson and Costello swear loudly, and O'Hare's deep voice saying, 'Well, well, well.'

Then Anderson's voice. 'They were in his mouth.'

'And the lips were superglued?'

'Yes. Mick, do us a favour and just tell us who is doing this?'

'Just let me think.'

Batten snapped his phone shut and looked at the wall. He had that old tingling feeling, which felt strange to him now. It had left him the minute he had heard about Kim

Thompson. He had failed to do his job then. But now, he wasn't making the killer fit the profile; his profile fitted this killer. The prison psychologist had seen it as soon as he had first interviewed Adrian Wood, which was why he had called in Batten.

Wood was an insignificance of a man, who had met a beguiling and very dangerous other.

'Iain, I'm so sorry about Itsy.'

Iain Kennedy just nodded. 'I know.' He was sitting on the chesterfield at Strathearn, a photograph of Itsy beside him. The room was both cold and dimly lit, isolated from the outside world. 'They don't mess around, your boys, do they? What was that man doing hanging in the Old Vinery?'

'I think that's what they're trying to find out,' O'Hare replied.

'I can't go out or do anything. There's a cop on every door. I've been given the third degree about stuff I know bugger all about and Itsy's lying dead up in the . . .' He ran out of steam. 'Nobody seems to be doing anything about Itsy.'

'Do you want a whisky?'

'Another one? Yes, please.'

'Is anybody coming to stay with you? Family? Friend? One of your sons? I'm sure they'd come if you asked.'

'I'm afraid I've well and truly burned my boats there. God, who would want to walk into this nightmare, Jack? Do you know where Marita is? Nobody will tell me a thing.'

413

'I don't know. I think they might be talking to her about . . .' he searched for the right words, '. . . recent events.'

'Do you know what they're doing out there?'

'Not really. I'm waiting for Gillespie's body to be picked up.'

Kennedy had to be content with that. 'I want to thank you for what you did for Itsy. I know you saved her life out on the Moss, gave her another couple of days. Time to say goodbye . . .'

'Just doing my job. You mind if I . . . ? Just a mouthful – I'm driving.' O'Hare lifted up the bottle of Laphroaig ten-year-old cask strength.

'I will always be grateful to you that she died in a warm bed, with me holding her hand, rather than alone out there in the freezing cold.' He registered that Jack was still holding the bottle and an empty glass. 'Oh, please, help yourself.'

'Mind if I put the fire on?'

'You're trying to look after me, Jack.'

'Trying to look after myself. I'm feeling my age and it's minus ten out there. It's warmer in the mortuary.'

The two friends sat in silence, as the hum of the gas fire came through, the living flame getting stronger and brighter, offering an imagined warmth rather than any real rise in temperature.

'Do you know why they were asking me about Diane? How long she'd known Marita? They didn't seem to believe me when I said she just applied for the job. I never knew Diane before then. What was that about?'

'I don't really know.'

414

'You do, but you can't say.'

'I really don't, but they're trying to establish a link with your wife, I think.'

There was silence again, broken only by the occasional squeak of leather as O'Hare got comfy, and the friendly hissing of the fire. 'If you don't want to stay here, you can come and stay with me if you like. This is a big house. You might not want to be on your own.'

'So Marita isn't coming back?'

'I don't think so.'

'Right, boys and girls,' said Anderson. 'The dogs won't be here for a while yet, but you know the search areas we're looking at and you know who we're looking for. Marita's out there somewhere – probably inappropriately dressed, as she left the house pretty sharpish. We don't know what mental condition she is in, so we approach with caution; we don't want to spook her. She's a slightly built female so should be easily overpowered, unless she decides to set McGurk on you. Uniform are doing a direct outward search from this spot. Browne, you come with me; Little-wood, go with Costello; Mulholland . . .' Anderson saw the DS wince a little, no doubt suffering the effects of Bobby's punch, '. . . and Lambie, stick together and stay out of trouble. Everyone, stay with your partner, and on no account get split up; the fog is very dense. Stick to the paths unless you hear something.'

There was a shuffle of papers as they looked at their little maps.

'Check your torches. Make sure you have them with

you at all times. They'll give you about four feet of visibility in this fog at best. Good luck.'

Anderson's phone vibrated against his leg, and he fished it out, his fingers clumsy in his heavyweight gloves. It was Brenda. He switched his phone off. For the next few hours, anybody who really needed him would use the radio.

Costello and Littlewood moved off first. They walked in single file down the path to the pond, their footsteps clacking hollowly on the crazy paving. Littlewood went first, and Costello just followed the fluorescent strips on the back of his padded jacket.

There was total silence down here, and a threatening stillness in the murky air. Mature rhododendrons flanked the path, and behind them loomed great park trees, all part of the older garden, from Strathearn's glory days as a grand manor.

As they neared the water Costello could swear the air was getting colder. Her nose started running with the icy nip in the air, and her sinuses hurt. Her breath puffed out in billows as she kept up with Littlewood, who was coughing every few seconds. It was easy going along the path, which was flat and well maintained, though starting to ice over. Then they came to a small group of high conifers, planted to mark where the path divided to go round either side of the pond, one to the left and one to the right.

'There's a small bench along here somewhere, I think,' said Costello.

'I could do wi' a sit-down and a smoke.' Littlewood delved into his side pocket and came up with a packet of cigarettes.

'Is the smoke an excuse for a rest, or vice versa?' Costello asked.

'Just gie's a wee spell.'

She knew better than to try and persuade him not to, so she stood and stamped her feet to keep warm and to signal her impatience.

'So you think he could be dangerous, this McGurk?' she asked.

'Oh, I'd say that Marita is much worse. Bloody women.'

'We'll get this done a lot quicker if I go right and you go left round the pond, and I'll meet you at the other end. But this fog is so bad we'd lose sight of each other.'

'Not one of your better ideas. I'll wait.'

Littlewood drew long and hard on his fag, letting the smoke warm his lungs. He blew out a birl of smoke that Costello watched twirl and drift in the night air before it melted into the fog. She knew Littlewood would not be rushed.

Her colleagues could only be a hundred yards away, maybe less, but the fog muffled everything. She and Littlewood seemed to be the only people on the face of the planet, stilled to silence by a blanket of icy cold air.

She rubbed her gloves together and smiled quizzically at Littlewood, but he was looking out over the pond, listening, thinking. She took a couple of steps down to the water's edge, where the bare spindly fronds of the willow hung over the water, the needles of frozen reeds bristled through the ice, and the stark uprights were all that was left of an old boathouse stuck up like accusing fingers. This was Ice Queen country, she mused, and she shivered, but not from the cold. She walked a little way up the edge of the lake, and shone her torch over the frosted surface of the water; it glittered like countless millions of diamonds.

'You should come and see this, John,' she called softly. 'It's so beautiful.'

Batten forced his mind not to race, to consider everything with care. He was thinking like a detective now. Harry Castiglia was the one closest to Gillespie. Had he seen details of the DNA found on Donna Campbell? He would certainly have seen the information about the keys to the flat on Clarence Avenue. In fact, it was Harry who had alerted Quinn to the fact that Gillespie had taken the magazine photos. Batten's gaze passed over the board, caught by the lovely picture of Emily. In the intense clarity of black and white, he could see the shades of grey in the iris of her eyes . . . How extraordinary, how astonishing, that a single movement of a shutter could capture an image in such marvellous detail.

With a click. In a flash.

A flash . . .

Fuck!

The victims had described 'pressure' on their eyes . . . was that the blindfold being jammed down so they could not see a flash? Yet not one of them had mentioned the distinctive sound of a camera being wound on. That would have made the *click* recognizable. So – one photograph, one flash. One chance. One chance to catch the face of a woman who thought she was about to die. A lifetime's fear distilled into a single moment.

If he was right, then the violent damage to the mouth wasn't pseudo-rape at all. *But what the fuck was it?*

Batten reached for his phone, and speed-dialled Anderson, his mind racing.

Costello shone her torch over the sugar-coated pine trees, taking a childish pleasure in the way the frost sparkled and glinted in the beam. But she couldn't waste any more time like this. 'You ready to move yet, John?'

Littlewood ignored her.

Her radio bleeped, crackled, then fell silent. She heard Littlewood's radio crackle in unison. She stood for a moment, scanning her torch round the edge of the pond as far as she could see, illuminating poplar, spruce and deciduous trees. Tony Abbott did a good job of keeping the old and combining it with the new. The right-hand path was the less used, more overgrown. Would that be the one that Bobby would take? Bobby and Marita would be meeting somewhere, close by. But where? All vehicles were accounted for and it was heading down to minus ten.

The fog was growing denser; it seemed to crawl up from the water, as if climbing up her body and pulling her in. She wedged her torch between her knees and pulled the collar of her jumper around her neck, her hat down, and the collar of her jacket up. She picked up her torch, looking for any sign that somebody had passed this way recently.

She could see nothing. They needed the search dogs.

She called loudly, 'You finished your fag yet? If the cold doesn't get you, lung cancer will.'

419

No answer.

'Oh, for fuck's sake!' she swore.

'I beg your pardon?' A voice came through the fog, quiet, friendly. 'Such language from a lady.'

'Oh, Harry. God, you gave me a fright! I didn't know anyone else was down here.'

He placed his gloved hand on hers. 'What are you doing?'

'Looking for someone, and I need a partner. I'm not allowed to do it on my own.'

'I'll come with you.'

'No, I need a proper partner. That's why John's here.'

'Oh, him. He's happy with his fag.' Harry slapped his hands together, trying to keep warm. 'Look, I'm here to photograph the pond and the search.'

'Isn't it too cold for you?' Costello looked back to the shady bulk of Littlewood hunched on the bench, a single stream of smoke curling into the air before being killed by the fog.

'Look, I *need* to work,' Harry said, almost in a fit of temper. 'Since Ronnie . . . My home is five hundred miles from here, and I really have nowhere else to go.' He back-handed something from his eye. 'I really don't want to be on my own right now. So you do your search thing, and I'll make sure the bogeymen don't get you.'

'I should radio in.'

'I spoke to Colin, so he knows I was heading down here; it'll be fine. Does this path take us round the pond? I've been down here before but, good God, it's spooky and deathly now, isn't it? Look at the ice baubles hanging on that willow just above the water. Jesus . . .' Harry lifted his camera from his bag, his creative mind focused. 'I need you in it so I get paid, but try not to spoil it, OK? Can you kneel down and shine your torch towards those branches?'

'I'll try,' she said sarcastically. She was rewarded with his torchlight smile, and was suddenly glad he was there.

He slung his bag down, and pulled out another camera, an old one. The kind that used proper film. He pushed her towards the edge of the frozen pond with a firm hand on her shoulders. 'You stand over there. Can you hold the torch low so the light catches on the ice and reflects back a bit?'

She did as she was told, risking another look at her watch.

'Don't bother about the time. Quinn and the Chief Constable will just be thrilled that you're out here getting your arse frozen off in the line of duty.'

'Hurry up, can't you? I'm freezing to death, waiting for you to get organized.'

'This will be a beautiful picture, on the front of every newspaper,' he said, and flicked a small lever on the camera.

She heard the film wind on.

'You're kind of beautiful too, in a Glaswegian no-sleep-for-four-days kind of way.' He smiled at her and tipped the end of her nose with his finger.

'I'm supposed to be on a manhunt,' she protested, but her heart started thumping. What if he tried to kiss her now? She couldn't think of a more beautiful place to be kissed, or a more beautiful man to be kissed by . . .

'If you get into trouble, I'll take the blame. But you get weather like this once in a lifetime.' He smiled that smile again, and she could see the length of his eyelashes, the deep, deep pond of those eyes. He had not shaved for ages, and he looked tired too.

He was standing very close to her.

She turned her face up to be kissed.

And felt something cold and hard at the side of her head.

Click.

It was Anderson who saw them first. Lying entwined in the fog, they could have been sleeping children, happy and protected in each other's arms.

The blond head moved a little.

'Bobby?' called Anderson softly. 'Is Marita OK?'

Bobby didn't answer. He wound his arms protectively around Marita's neck, pulling her towards him. Her head lolled alarmingly, her hair and her scarf coiled down her neck, just like in her portrait over the living-room fire.

'Bobby, can you hear me?'

'She's dead, isn't she?' whispered Browne in his ear.

'It would look like it. Take your hat off, slowly, so he can see who you are.' Anderson did the same. 'Bobby?' he said softly. 'Can we have a look at Marita? See if we can help? Gillian here is a nurse. Do you remember her from before?'

All the time he was inching slowly towards them, Gillian following close behind.

'You know Gillian; she made you a cup of tea in the greenhouse. So could Gillian have a look at Marita?'

Bobby muttered, '*I propped her head up as before, / Only, this time my shoulder bore / Her head, which droops upon it still . . .*'

'Oh Christ, he's lost the plot,' Anderson muttered. He was very close now; he could see the gaping wound in Marita's head. Not so much the wound, but the blood soaking her hair and blackening the side of her face. The injury was a parody of Itsy's.

Bobby raised a hand wet with blood, idly feeling the weight of the stone in his palm. '*No pain felt she; / I am quite sure she felt no pain.*'

'Let me speak to him.' Browne inched forward beside Anderson. 'I know that poem, Bobby. It's by Browning, isn't it? "Porphyria's Lover"? Is that your poem? Who was your lover, Bobby?'

Bobby drew the back of his hand under his nose and sniffed loudly, refusing to meet Anderson's eyes. It was a gesture that Peter made when unsure; but this was not a boy, this was a strong powerful man. A man lying with the woman he had murdered in his arms.

'Itsy,' he said dreamily. 'Bobby and Itsy. Always Bobby and Itsy.'

'Oh, you love Itsy too?' said Browne. 'I like Itsy.' She crawled up a little further. 'I saw all those drawings she did, of the birds. The nightjar. She was very good.'

Bobby looked up. Browne had his attention. 'How's your face?' he asked with real concern.

'It's still sore, Bobby. And I think Marita has a sore face too. Can I come over and see?' Browne edged closer. 'You wouldn't want to hurt her, would you?'

'Yes,' he mumbled. Then a glint came into his eyes. 'I would. She hurt Itsy.'

Batten couldn't raise Anderson or Costello. He tried Quinn, but she was on her phone. He looked out into the night and thought about going to Strathearn himself. He phoned the switchboard and asked them to get calls through, requesting DI Anderson, DS Costello and DC Browne to phone him back immediately, urgently.

Beyond urgent.

He reached over and opened an envelope that was lying on the desk. Harry had left it for Costello a while ago. It was a photograph. Costello sitting on some stairs somewhere.

Why her? Was something going on between them? He had not seen them together enough to make any assumption. He checked his phone again, checked the control room. They were trying but it was busy up at Strathearn, said the snotty female. They would try the radio.

Batten looked around and saw the pile of Castiglia's and Gillespie's equipment, the padded camera bags, other bags, and an aluminium case. A long plastic case, about eighteen inches long, was propped up against the wall in the corner. Batten opened it. The collapsed legs of a tripod slid out, heavy, cylindrical, long. He undid the clasp, letting the inner extendable leg slide out, bent his head and sniffed. There was something . . .

He strode over to the board and pulled down the package of Silicolube, ripped off the rigid plastic and cardboard, and unscrewed the plastic cap. He shut his eyes, and sniffed.

Then he seized the phone again, and pressed a speed-dial number. It rang immediately.

'Browne? Gillian! Thank fuck – now listen . . .'

It would make a great photograph, Costello thought confusedly. Harry was holding her face firmly in his grasp as if he was going to kiss her. Then she heard her radio go off, deep in her coat pocket. 'I have to respond to that.'

He smiled. 'They can wait.'

'You know I'm not allowed to wait.'

'There are plenty of them, but only one of you. Turn it off.'

'I can't do that.'

'I'm not asking.' He released his grip, pulled the radio from her pocket, and threw it skidding across the ice.

Then his grip on her face resumed, his lips touching her forehead. 'You grew up around here, didn't you?'

'No, I grew up on the south side.'

'But you were born here.'

Christ, what was this about? 'I was born on the south side.'

'No, you were born over here. I was there. I remember.'

'Well, I was there when I was born too, but I was kind of young to remember.' She pulled her head back to smile at him, humouring him.

Harry's eyes were full of pain. 'Why did you never come looking for me?' he whispered, like a child.

'Looking for you . . . ?'

'You must have known; you must have had some idea.' His voice was racked with hurt.

'Known? About you?' She looked around her, at the water, the remains of the boathouse. Yes, it had made a good photograph. Herself in her little sailor suit. And she remembered the way O'Hare had looked at it, and him saying, 'Did you never come here as a kid? In my day we treated it as a public park; it was *our* pond.' And she remembered that feeling of being followed. *Who had taken that photograph?*

'Did we know each other as kids?' she asked, playing for time. 'Did we play here?'

'Prudenza,' he whispered.

Costello felt a chill around her heart that had nothing to do with the coldness of the night. 'Only my dad ever called me that.'

'*Our* dad called you that.'

Costello shook her head, the icy chill melting a little. He'd got it wrong. Then a faint memory ... A splash, her mum screaming, her dad running. She'd been left alone, crying. But reason told her to reject the memory. 'Harry, I don't have a brother. I've never had a brother. I'm the classic example of the only child of a single mother.'

Even as she said it, she knew in her heart it was not true. Memories started thudding through her head, ghosts of a hideous face kissing her, frightening her, memories that should have been left sleeping.

'No, no, Prudenza. You were one half of the family, and I was the other. You were the favourite, so you were kept. But I was taken away. Do you know why?'

'Know ... ? None of it is true. I'm an only child.'

'Don't lie to me,' his voice punched back at her.

'I'm not lying, Harry. But you're wrong. My mother was a drunken alcoholic bitch; she had no time for me . . .'

'She named you after Granny Winnie and Granny Prudence,' Harry said, almost as if he was telling her a bedtime story. 'She called you Winnie-Prue. But dad always called you Prudenza, pretty Prudenza, the clever little fish. All those years ago.'

He turned her to face the pond. Then she heard a click, just behind her ear. A flash. Her photograph had been taken again.

'It was OK till you came along, the sweet little girl they really wanted.'

A single click. And it all became clear. *But I haven't been blindfolded,* she thought.

No, because she wasn't going to live to tell the tale.

'You really don't remember me jumping in?'

'I've no memory of you at all, Harry.'

'I'd caught a minnow and put it in a jar. I was trying to show it to them. But all they wanted to do was photograph you, taking your first little baby steps. So I jumped in. Right here.' He was talking now as if she wasn't there at all. 'But Dad just hauled me out, slapped me around and dumped me soaking on the ground, and went to calm little Prudenza, who was crying. Dear perfect little Prudenza was upset, and I was nothing but a nuisance.' The grip tightened on her neck, and she could feel her pulse starting to weaken. 'No matter that I couldn't swim, that I might have drowned . . . ?'

Thinking fast, she threw herself forward, intending to

run for it. But he caught her and threw her down, turning her on her back.

'Why are you doing this?' she asked.

He grasped her head and brutally rammed it back on to the ice-hard ground.

She felt blood running down the back of her throat; she had bitten her tongue. 'Harry? Harry?' she repeated.

'Who are *you*?' he asked, and she felt his weight shift. She saw the fist coming too late, felt bone crunch, a tooth come loose, blood in her mouth . . . She opened her eyes, but could not see.

Then the blood cleared. She turned her head, agonizingly, and saw him raise his fist once more, felt his body weight shift again. She took her chance and writhed away. But Harry was on his feet, and his foot caught her in the stomach. She lay winded, unable to move.

He kicked her again, hard, and suddenly she was sliding, sliding face down across the ice, arms and legs splayed. Absurdly, she thought of Bambi.

Then she felt the ice judder and realized with horror that this was how she was going to die. Under the ice. She saw Harry's feet, then his knees as he knelt down beside her, and his hand caressed the side of her face, a cold fingertip down the outline of her cheek. The finger stopped around her mouth. It was a soft touch, a lover's touch.

'Harry, Harry,' she said through blood.

'Yes, Harry,' he repeated.

Then he grasped at her hair, jerking her head backwards until she thought her neck would snap. Above her, she saw his face full in hers, the tiny telltale scar. Then he rammed her face down on to the ice, and she heard it crack . . . Or was it her skull? Had he snapped her neck like a frozen twig?

Her cheek was resting in her own blood, comforting and warm.

She tried to breathe but it was getting so hard, so hard to get the breath in and out through the blood pouring from her lips. She felt a resounding blow to her head, then another. And she could hear the cracking and groaning of the ice, feel the lapping of the icy water beneath, waiting for her, ready to suck her down.

Then Harry was gone. Something, someone – an angel? – had taken him.

The blood was pooling around her face now, and it felt as though the ice was warming beneath her. She could hear the water lapping under it, so close, so very, very close, licking at her. And her blood was melting the frost so she could see through the ice to the black, the deepest black she had ever seen. She heard muffled noises behind her, and the ice juddered again; somebody called her name, but it was only the water . . . An angel didn't have Harry. An angel had her by the hand. The whole world was cracking; she could feel her arms and legs drifting this way and that in warm water. Through the blood, in the indigo-clear sky beneath the ice, she saw her own face, old and lined, a halo of grey hair around her head. She was dying, floating past herself. *Goodbye*, she said to herself as she died.

And then she was going down, down into the black depths, into the dark water.

*

There was a massive jagged hole in the middle of the pond where the ice had given way, and something – someone – was lying right beside it. Browne's torch caught the short blonde hair, the familiar jacket; it was Costello.

'Stop!' she shouted, as loudly as she could, but Costello was still being punched like a rag doll. Browne screamed again. The man lifted his arm high, some kind of stick in his hand, and the blows rained down, the black map of blood on the ice spreading. Browne yelled down her radio, then screamed with fright as something shot past her, through the beam of her torch, out on to the ice. She watched in horror as the smaller figure rugby-tackled the other. She heard fists go in, heard bones crack, and then the ice itself gave way. In terrible slow motion the gaping blackness of the water opened up and took them both under.

Browne couldn't see Costello at all now. She swung her torch frantically, and there she was, her outline distorted by the lapping water. It was devouring her. The slab of ice she was lying on suddenly cantilevered, one way then the other, and Costello too slid slowly into the dark water.

Under the ice.

Browne did not hesitate. She screamed, a primeval cry that sent the night birds flying out of the trees. She ran down the sloping lawn, took one leap and jumped.

Anderson picked up a discarded radio, looked at his own and pressed the alarm. Suddenly the night echoed to a deep resonant crack – the ice had shifted. He shone his torch out on to the surface of the pond. He had heard a scream but now it was quiet, too quiet. Then his ears caught a faint whimper coming across the ice.

'Oh, fuck.' Browne was out there. He shouted at her, 'What are you doing, woman?'

An answer came, like a weak echo. 'I've got her, I've got her.'

He saw Costello's body move as if gently lifted and dropped by an unseen hand, and Browne struggling to move through the water, trying to keep Costello's head up. But there was a thick ledge of unbroken ice between them and the bank.

Anderson hit the alarm again, then threw the radio down, stripped off his jacket, and lay down to roll on to the ice. Flat out, he tried to slither towards them, uneasily aware of the ice yielding beneath him. Closer now, he could hear Browne talking, talking to Costello. *Hold on, just hold on.* And he could hear the panic in her voice – *Oh my God, she's bleeding so much, her face is missing.*

'Put your left arm around her neck, Gillian,' he panted. 'Grab on to me with your right hand. I'm right behind you, Gillian.'

Browne tried, missing his fingers by inches. Briefly she and Costello went down, but a few air bubbles and they were up again.

'Just reach back, you silly cow! I'm right here – come on, Gillian!'

Another alarming crack, and they sank again. Gillian bobbed up seconds later, gasping. Costello's head remained under water, completely under. One more crack and they'd be under the water for good. And if they went under the ice, they would never survive, not in this cold.

Anderson slithered inch by inch across the ice, willing Browne to try once more. Grunting, almost weeping with the effort, she strained to touch her hand to his. Just as their fingers touched, there was a massive crunch. He grabbed her, let go, reached further, and grabbed her sleeve. But Browne slipped from sight.

Anderson felt the icy water slap his face, he tried to hold on, but his eyes were staring into the deep water. Just as he went under he saw a light, and heard a voice, somebody shouting his name.

He just hoped it wasn't God.

16

2.00 p.m., Saturday 13 February 2010

'Why the hell did nobody think to ask where Harry Castiglia actually lived?' Quinn demanded.

'He didn't mention it and we didn't ask. He was just a guy we worked with,' said Batten. 'I don't even know where you live.'

'But the close next to where Stephen Whyte was left hanging? Did the search team and the door to door never follow it up?'

'It's listed as a rented flat. They called twice and never got in,' said Lambie.

'I suppose they were too interested in that flat on the other side, the one with the party wall, the flat that might have heard something.'

Lambie opened the living-room door and all three went in. Quinn walked over to the window and looked out. 'Four flights up. And high on the hill.'

'Just where a narcissist would like to be. Lord of all he surveyed. Or so he imagined. I bet he used to sit up here in his own wee world, headphones on, lights off, watching what was going on. Creepy.'

'What's even more creepy is that he seemed such a genuine guy, really likeable,' said Quinn.

'The mark of the narcissist,' Batten reminded her, and

his stomach lurched. He had really fouled up this time. The 'other man' had been walking about right under his nose, and another death could be laid at his door. He just couldn't do this job any more.

'Well, if the only people we can really trust are those who appear to be out and out psychopaths, then I'm glad I'm retiring. I can't wait to be out of it,' Quinn sighed.

Batten opened another door. 'You might want to come and see this,' he called.

'Nobody ever says that when it's good news,' said Quinn, pulling herself away from the window.

Castiglia's bed was a wrought-iron affair in the middle of the room, the duvet and pillowcases pristine white, as smooth as snow. It looked as though it had never been slept in. There was no other furniture in the room – no wardrobe, no clothes, no shoes, no bedside cabinet, no books.

The walls were painted dark brown, the carpet was brown, and the curtains hanging over the small window matched. It was a dark, dark room, the only bright spot the huge white bed.

On the wall facing the bed were four huge canvases, each three feet square. Each one with a blown-up black and white photograph. Quinn recognized Castiglia's own publicity photograph; with his black turtleneck and a shy smile for the camera, he looked like a French film star. She recognized Tony Abbott, standing outside Hazbeanz, arms folded, leaning against the wall, a half-smoked cigarette hanging from his mouth, waiting for his little Prudenza to walk past and never ever acknowledge his presence. The face showed the lines of a lifetime of worry, and Quinn now knew what he had spent his entire life worrying about.

The third photograph was of a female. The image was less defined, but she could tell the picture was older than the other three; the hairstyle, the jewellery said 1970s. Was it the mother? The background was not clear but there were trees, a stretch of water. The fourth she knew without looking twice; the blonde spiky hair and pointed face were those of a hobgoblin, a changeling sitting caged in a concrete stairwell with her knees up to her chin, a cup of tea in her hand.

Quinn sighed. 'Poor Costello's going to have a lot to come to terms with. I'd prefer to let her head mend before she tries to get it round any of this. Christ knows what else is going to come out.'

'She'll have to know it all sooner or later. She's a tough one.'

'Even so,' said Quinn. 'Harry had a long history of killing for pleasure, of grooming his accomplices. We're slowly piecing it together, but it goes back years. You can imagine him staying in the same hotel every time he went to Edinburgh for a job, and chatting to Wood the night porter – "I'm a stranger here, fancy a drink?" – charming and grooming him. And before that in Dundee, with the taxi driver, Pfeffer. Every time he came up to Dundee . . . "Just give me a hand with my equipment at this location; I could do with an assistant at that swanky function." Think how impressed those two no-hopers would be by an alpha male like Castiglia. He'd have them hypnotized like rabbits. And others like them, all over Scotland. But all the time working his way back to his wee sister. And the last few killings were done to – in some perverted way – impress Costello. Not easy for anyone to understand.'

'He was a killer; she's a cop,' said Batten. 'And the best praise he could get from Costello, his sister who had achieved so much, was for her to admit that he'd beaten her at her own game, that he was too clever for her to catch.'

'Well, he wasn't, was he?'

'Oh, I think he was,' said Batten, and shut the bedroom door as they went through to Harry Castiglia's living room. Almost a whole wall was taken up with shelving, and row upon row of immaculately matching grey box files, all neatly labelled. Only one black box file was unlabelled. Batten prised it from the shelf, and opened it. It was full of large glossy black and white photographs, which Batten wordlessly laid out on the desk. Quinn raised her hands to her mouth as if she was going to be sick.

'Oh – my – God,' she whispered.

There was a tentative knock at the door of the examination room. Colin Anderson stood up cautiously to open it. A brand-new pair of jeans, a sweatshirt and a jacket had already appeared from somewhere. All he needed was a pair of shoes and he was good to go. His right hand felt totally numb as he tried to grip the door handle. The doctor had told him to be glad it was numb – when he got the feeling back it would hurt like hell.

It was Brenda, holding a carrier bag with his shoes.

'How are you?' she asked nervously.

'I'm warming up, getting some feeling back.' He rippled his fingers, beckoning her in. 'All working. How are you?'

She didn't answer, just stood there helplessly, as though she might cry.

'How are the kids?' he tried.

'Are you coming home?'

'Is that an invite?'

'You could have died, Colin!'

'Oh, it wasn't that bad.' He patted her awkwardly with his good hand. 'I'm still here.'

'But you do need looking after, and the kids miss you. When they phoned to say you were in here, I thought the worst.'

He noticed a faint tear in her eye.

'It doesn't make things any different but you do need somebody to look after you. Might as well be me! So just come back for now.'

'Just for now,' he said. Might as well, he thought; and they couldn't afford that shithole of a bedsit anyway. 'But I'm fine, really. Nothing wrong with me that won't be cured by a chip buttie and curry sauce.'

'Ever the gourmet.'

For the first time in months, Colin Anderson kissed his wife. Only on the cheek, but it was a start.

'*Twenty* of them,' Quinn said, appalled. 'Twenty young women whose lives have been ruined.'

'Well, maybe some good'll come of it,' said Batten. 'The urgent standardization of databases, for cold cases as well as ongoing investigations. Can't come too soon.'

'And this is the ultimate humiliation,' said Quinn, not listening to him. 'Look at these!' Each beautifully composed shot showed the face of a young woman, blindfolded and unsparingly lit.

'He caught them all at that moment of extreme terror,' Batten said. 'The moment when they really believed they were going to die. Look at their fear, their helplessness, the last emotion they thought they'd ever feel. Whatever Harry wanted, he got from those pictures. That was his fix. But what I still don't get is the brutality to the mouth. My first thought was pseudo-sex, but now I'm convinced it was something else. Question is – what?'

'What have they got over their eyes?' asked Lambie. 'It makes them look like bloody blinkered bluebottles.'

'It's what they use in sensory deprivation interrogation techniques,' explained Batten. 'It blocks out everything.'

'So they wouldn't see the flash,' said Quinn. 'Not one of them ever mentioned a flash. Because they never saw it.'

Some shots showed a hand, one or two a knee, holding the victim down. Each woman had something held against her head.

'That's not a gun,' said Lambie.

'No, it's a wheel brace for an E-type Jag,' Quinn said. 'Undoubtedly the one that we found skidded across the ice at Strathearn. There are traces of blood and DNA in the tool bag in the E-type, so if there's anything on the wheel brace that's not Costello's we have an evidential chain. They also recovered an old Nikon camera on the bank. I don't know if I want to see that film when it's developed.'

'Look – every one of these is dated.' Lambie pointed to

the small white figures in the lower corner of each photograph, and flipped one over cautiously with a gloved finger. 'And there's a location noted on the back. He's done our job for us.'

'You realize what else that means, don't you? Cross-referencing these attacks will keep the cold case teams occupied for a good long while. However, before we do anything else with these, I want a list of dates and locations, matched with any photos we have back at the station, sent to all relevant jurisdictions. These women have the right to know before anyone else that Harry Castiglia is dead. Lambie, you can be the one to tell the Corbetts. But . . .' she paused, frowning, '. . . why is there no photograph of Emily here?'

'Castiglia would have taken one, but he thought he'd killed her, so he didn't bother keeping it,' Batten explained. 'The attack on her was a botched job, less than perfect. He wouldn't want to be reminded.'

'I expect we'll find he'd already taken a photo of her — the one we have up on the board. I daresay Chamberlain's will still have a record of which photographer they used for Young Scot of the Year in 1999,' Lambie explained to Batten. 'We should be able to cross-reference those dates with Harry's jobs. We know he was based down south but his job allowed him to be all over the place. He could always find a reason to be wherever he needed to be.'

Quinn sighed wearily. 'Let's bag up this . . . vileness.'

Lambie held a plastic evidence sack open and she dropped in the box file full of photographs, with an expression of disgust.

'I wish we could spare all those poor women knowing about these. In fact, if they weren't the most heaven-sent evidence, I'd happily put a match to the whole lot.'

Diane Woodhall looked shaken. She had aged ten years in the last few hours, as if she had suddenly realized that her life was crumbling around her. The uniformed female constable handed her a mug of tea which Diane accepted distractedly.

'So before we charge you with perverting the course of justice, what do you have to say?' Mulholland asked.

Diane shook her head, saying nothing.

'Take me through the events of the evening. What time did Marita phone you?'

'About six.'

'And then?'

'I phoned the boys. I told Marita a bit later – maybe quarter or twenty past – that Itsy was not with Wee Tony and Bobby.'

'What happened then?'

'I don't know.' She held her hand up to her running nose.

Mulholland winced with distaste and handed her a handkerchief. 'I think you do. Just take your time and tell us what you can,' he said.

'Well, I phoned back to say that she wasn't there now but had left about half an hour earlier. I didn't see Marita again until the back of eight maybe.' Diane sipped her tea.

'And?' asked Mulholland.

'She'd been out to speak to Bobby, and they went out to look for Itsy.'

'Do you actually know that? Did you see them together? Or did she just tell you she was out with Bobby?'

Diane bit her lip, her loyalty torn.

Mulholland spoke gently. 'You'll feel better if you tell the truth, you know.'

Diane started talking again, her voice stronger now. 'Bobby and Marita met up later, once Marita came back. I don't know where she had been.'

'Maybe not then but you know now. Where had she been, Diane?'

'Out at the Moss,' she whimpered.

'OK, we'll come back to that. There's still a fair amount of time unaccounted for between Marita coming back at eight and DCI Quinn and DI Anderson getting there at one in the morning. What was going on then?'

'She was upset. We were . . . together.'

'Together?'

'In her bedroom. That's when she told me.'

'Told you what?'

'That she'd met Itsy outside, earlier . . . before seven, just after. I don't know. Itsy had been wandering about in the cold, looking for some bird with a broken wing. Marita said Itsy wouldn't stop going on and on about that bloody albatross. God knows, she didn't know when to stop.'

'Go on.'

'Well, she told Itsy to wait out at the van, and she came back for the set of keys we have in the kitchen. Then she drove Itsy out to the Moss.'

'Why did she take her out there? If Itsy was being so

annoying?' Mulholland asked, searching for any indication of premeditation.

'I suppose Marita's patience snapped. Also, she said she wanted to talk some sense into Itsy, somewhere away from the house where she couldn't run straight to Iain. That was Itsy's way . . . it was almost as though she thought Iain had provided the house for her, not for Marita.'

'Did Marita know at that stage that Itsy was pregnant?'

Diane shook her head. 'No, she'd no idea. I'd had my suspicions, with her being sick, but I didn't like to say anything. I mean, you can't, can you?'

Mulholland just nodded.

'Marita said Itsy simply told her, as though it was all some great joke, or some kind of treat. Then she started laughing, prancing around, teasing Marita, acting like a stupid wee girl. Itsy ran dancing off towards some trees, and Marita went after her. The ground was all rough there, she said. There was a bit of a struggle, and Itsy tripped and fell. She hit her head.' Diane shrugged her shoulders slightly.

'Her head?'

'Well, I mean, she fell sort of sideways and hurt her face. There was something . . .' Diane's hand flapped in an effort to explain.

'And . . .'

'She was just lying there.'

'There has to be something to explain all her injuries, Diane,' said Mulholland gently.

'Marita said she didn't know what came over her. She picked up the stone and . . .' Diane's hand demonstrated a slapping motion.

Mulholland said aloud so the tape could hear it. 'You mean Marita hit her sister with the stone?'

'Yes, on the head.'

'While she was on the ground?'

'Yes.'

Mulholland made a few notes, trying not to think how often Marita must have struck Itsy – and how hard? Hard enough to rattle her brain against her skull. He recalled the photographs – Itsy's boot half off – she had no chance to get away. Marita had brought her down like a lioness bringing down a gazelle. Suddenly he felt Diane's hand clamped on his forearm.

'But it wasn't Marita's fault. Really it wasn't. It was Itsy, she was fooling around, laughing, saying she was going to have a baby, and Marita couldn't stand it. She couldn't have kids, so it really upset her. She'd have had it terminated. Couldn't have children running around, not Marita.' Diane made it sound like the plague.

'And where does Bobby come into it?'

'We tried to give her some kind of alibi. Bobby is easy to confuse, and he does as he's told as long as you tell him with enough authority.' She sniffed. 'I was to say about Bobby and Itsy being close. Marita said the police would come and that's what I had to say, but it wouldn't be a lie. She wanted it to sound as if Bobby might be . . .'

'Dangerous?'

Diane gave him a shadow of her smile. 'She knew Bobby wouldn't be able to stand up to questioning. Tony had no sense of time anyway so we knew that wasn't going to be a problem, as long as you believed Bobby loved Itsy.'

'Well, you were half right. Bobby did love Itsy. So much that he hit Marita with a rock when he found out she'd killed her, the same way she hit Itsy.' Mulholland felt his stomach tighten. He was facing a disciplinary over that. But he had been so sure.

'Diane, how long have you and Marita known each other?'

Diane sat up, on surer ground now. The old smile was back in place. 'We were on the same beauty circuit in the nineties, and we chummed up. You know how it is. She had a forceful personality. Irresistible, really.' She pulled her cardigan around her, and looked down at the toe of her boot. 'I'll admit I hated Itsy. All that nonsense about making Marita feel guilty for making her the way she was.'

'What do you know about that? Marita was little more than a kid herself at the time.'

'Doesn't make it any easier to live with,' said Diane. 'It was a daft childhood thing. They were having a bath together. Marita pulled on Itsy's heels. Itsy's head went under and she . . . got damaged.' There was a dismissive gesture of the hands. 'That's all it was.'

Mulholland did a quick calculation. 'Yes, we knew about that. A five-year-old and a three-year-old, alone in a bath – we could accept that as a tragic accident. But Marita has lied about her age for years. We've seen her birth certificate. In fact, she was eight when it happened. Do you still think it was an accident?'

A shrug. 'Of course.'

'And Iain?'

'Iain was nothing to Marita, just a bank balance and the

chance of respectability. She didn't get it, of course. She didn't become Mrs Kennedy; he became Marita's husband.' She looked at Mulholland. 'I was there through it all, you know. I was always there, through all those men; I was the most important person to her, always there for her.'

'And you never got jealous of her?'

'Oh no. She loved me, you see. She didn't love any of those men.' Diane smiled. 'It was always me.'

Anderson heard another knock on the examination-room door and Gillian Browne came in, dressed in civvies. Her face looked worse than ever; the bruising had spread and was now chrysanthemum purple, and black under her eyes. But her hair had been washed, and there was something fresh-faced and youthful about her.

Anderson suddenly felt old. 'Have they let you out your room?' he asked. 'I'm still incarcerated.'

She grinned. 'I escaped.'

'Be careful you don't frighten your kids when you get home.'

'I know it looks awful, but it hurts a lot less. How are you?'

'I'm getting better, getting some feeling back.' He rippled his fingers again. 'All working.'

'Good, good. I've been signed off my work for a month. I really hurt the ligaments in my back when I broke the ice.' She rubbed her back to illustrate the point.

'What did you do exactly?'

'I just ran, jumped and landed on it as hard as I could.

It meant I could get Costello by the collar and hold her up.' She looked at her feet, and fiddled with a button on her jacket. 'But I owe you, because then I started to go under . . .'

'Well, I read somewhere that you should spread your body weight over the ice as much as possible. That didn't work either. It was all a bit scary.' He shook his head and smiled. 'I still haven't worked out who got who.'

'Well, Lambie and Mulholland heard the radio alarm, and they ran to the pond. At least they had the sense to get us out without them getting in. But at the end of the day, what does it matter? We got out. We're fine. And now you're going home.' Browne sounded quite resigned, and not bitter.

'Yes. We . . .'

'I know. Brenda's your wife.' Gillian opened the door to leave. 'Oh, there's one other thing . . .' She nodded to Nesbitt, who was tied to a chair leg in the corridor, snoozing, doing his usual trick of being quietly somewhere he was not allowed. 'I'd really like to take him home with me, but my daughter's allergic. I don't want him to be put down. He's such a nice wee dog. Could you not take him home to your kids?'

Anderson knew when he was outgunned and outmanoeuvred. One pair of pleading dark brown eyes he might have hardened his heart to, but not both.

'OK,' he agreed, with misgivings. God alone knew what Brenda would say. 'How are you getting home, Gillian?'

'Oh, I'm being taken home in a nice posh Audi.'

'Vik's driving you?'

'That's right. I may not do much for his image, but he'll do wonders for mine. Not many Audis in my part of Jordanhill,' she giggled. 'I might even invite him in for tea.'

17

Midday, Sunday 14 February 2010

Cautiously, Costello prodded the tender lump under the gauze dressing. A patch of her scalp had been shaved, and the unfamiliar skin felt rubbery under her fingers.

She inched her way to a sitting position – carefully, so as not to jar her head. She didn't need a mirror to tell her she looked a sight. If she squinted she could actually see her own nose, all bruised and swollen, and her jaw ached as though she'd gone several rounds with Mike Tyson.

The room was hot and stuffy, and heavy with the scent of flowers. She'd been so groggy with concussion the day before, she had no recollection of so many vases and bouquets being brought in. She moved her head a fraction to see a magnificent display of pure white roses by her bed, and reached for the card. *With grateful thanks, Donald Corbett.*

Happy Valentine's Day! – a big Snoopy card – *With love from Nesbitt! Best wishes from all at Partickhill CID*, said a raspberry-red azalea. Pink roses from Helena McAlpine – *Alan would be so proud of you.*

Costello felt nauseous suddenly, and couldn't cope with any more. Obviously something momentous had happened, but the last thing she could remember was setting off in the dark towards the lake at Strathearn with

Littlewood. Something or somebody must have dunted her on the head, but God knows what. She shut her eyes, hoping to doze off, when the door opened and a nurse came in, carrying an enormous arrangement of flowers so brightly coloured it hurt to look at them.

'Where would you like these?' she asked brightly.

Costello reached for the small white card. *With best wishes for your speedy recovery, Vik.*

'Somewhere I can't see them,' she mumbled.

As the nurse left the room, Quinn came in, followed by Anderson, Batten and O'Hare.

'Oh God, I'm either going to be sacked, arrested, or psychoanalysed. Or I'm already dead and this is a nightmare.'

'I presume you're feeling better,' said Quinn. 'Just in case you haven't got enough grapes and Lucozade, we've brought you some more.'

'And I've brought you a flask of black tea and some caramel logs,' added O'Hare.

'Food. Now there's an idea. Is somebody going to tell me why I have a sore head? I really can't remember a thing.'

'There's a lot to tell,' O'Hare said. 'But you'd best get it in easy stages. The main thing is that you look more damaged than you actually are. You're going to be fine. Were it otherwise, Costello my dear, we would have kept the flowers for the funeral.'

'Thanks, Prof. Didn't know you cared.'

'We all care, you daft cow,' growled Anderson. 'Good thing you've a thick skull and no brain to damage.'

Quinn drew up a chair. 'Do you remember anything – anything at all – about Friday night, Costello?' she asked.

'Going off to the pond at Strathearn, with John. He sat down for a smoke.'

'That's right. He sat down for his smoke. He had a mild heart attack and conked out. Held on to his fag, though.'

'Just like John. I did call to him, but he didn't answer. I should have gone back . . . How is he?'

'Better than you. Do you remember leaving him? Do you remember how you got out on to the ice?'

'Was I out on the ice?'

'Yes. How and why, we'll leave for another time. You weren't on the ice so much as in it, Costello. Browne jumped straight in and hung on to you, but couldn't swim back to shore because of the ice, so Anderson came out after you both.'

Costello blinked at Anderson. 'Did you?'

Anderson looked sheepish. 'I ended up in the water with the pair of you. But the cavalry arrived and got us all out.'

'Browne got all her life-saving medals at school, apparently,' Quinn said.

'And I was the one who thought she wouldn't be able to cope with stress when it hit her. Just shows you what people are made of.'

Batten said, 'Pity poor Colin. I mean, he was stretched out on the frozen bank with his head pillowed on the magnificent chest of the luscious DC Browne, and he can't remember a thing about it!'

O'Hare cleared his throat. Quinn took the hint, and stood up.

'Mick, you and I should get back to the station. Costello,

I'll leave you with Colin and the Prof.' She laid her hand on Costello's shoulder.

Vaguely Costello thought that it was the first time the DCI had ever touched her, apart from a formal handshake on first meeting.

'You're going to be fine, Costello,' Quinn assured her.

When she and Batten had gone, Costello said, 'I'm not so ill I don't know you have something to tell me. I'm not going to like it, am I?'

O'Hare drew his chair closer to Costello's bed. 'The Kennedys' gardener, Anthony Abbott, saw you being attacked on the ice . . .'

'Attacked . . .? But who . . . ?'

O'Hare lifted a silencing hand. 'We'll deal with that later. Abbott came out across the ice just as it was starting to break, hauled your attacker off you and clouted him. Then they both went through the ice.'

Costello lay back and looked at the ceiling. 'I saw a face . . . under the water. I thought it was me. Was that him? But why did he try and save me? I don't understand.'

O'Hare pulled the dog-eared Polaroid picture from his inside pocket. 'Remember this – the Costello family at the pond at Strathearn? You, your mum, and look – your dad.' He leaned forward and took her hand. 'Costello, did you never look at Anthony Abbott and see a resemblance?'

'Who to?'

'Well, did you ever hear him referred to as Wee Tony?'

'No.' Her eyes blinked. 'I'd have remembered. My dad was called that.'

O'Hare sat back in his chair.

It was Anderson who said, 'Costello, Wee Tony *was* your dad.'

By tacit consent, Batten and Quinn walked slowly across the Western Infirmary car park towards Quinn's Lexus. They needed more time to talk than the few minutes' drive back to the station.

Quinn buttoned the neck of her winter coat against the icy wind coming in off the Clyde. 'Those four photos, opposite his bed – Castiglia wanted them all back together again, didn't he?'

'The mum's wedding ring on a chain around his neck when he drowned seems to indicate that as well,' Batten agreed.

'The disturbing thing is that he also had Costello's door keys in his pocket.' Quinn shivered and wound her woollen scarf more tightly. 'I knew she'd left her rucksack out on the Moss – Mulholland handed it to Castiglia, who brought it to the hospital for her. I wouldn't be surprised if Castiglia let himself into her flat a few times, maybe found the wedding ring and helped himself. I don't feel like asking Costello about that just yet, though. It would really spook her – somebody in her house, going through her things. The DNA confirms it, though; Harry was her brother, Tony her father.'

'Christ, what a family.'

'Indeed. I'm not looking forward to telling her about Castiglia. Your long-lost dad dying to save you is bad enough, but your brother actually trying to kill you is something else. O'Hare says that Harry Castiglia's skull shows a massive cleft palate repair. So you can try getting your psychological head round that one – ramming wheel braces into young women's mouths just because your wee sister was pretty?'

'It's much more than that, Rebecca. It's the rejection and destruction of perfection. Harry, deformed and rejected; baby Costello, pretty and accepted – that's how he would have looked at it. It's what happens when a child feels rejected by a parent. Imagine, you're an only child, but different from the others, ugly, so people look away when they see you. Then a perfect second child comes along, and you mistake the constant attention a baby needs for the love and approval you're not getting. He'd have been desperate for his family's recognition, a sense of belonging.'

'But millions of people have younger siblings,' Quinn interrupted. 'And lots of people have birth defects . . .'

'But millions of people aren't born pathological narcissists, and that's the big issue. As she grew up, becoming brighter and more attractive, he receded to nothing. Narcissus became Echo.'

'Why do you suppose Abbott left, taking young Harry with him?'

Batten sighed. 'There's no one left to ask about that. Maybe the marriage simply came to grief. From what I understand, Costello's mother was a difficult woman; she withdrew emotionally from her daughter as well as her son.'

'To put it mildly,' Quinn interjected. 'And found consolation in a bottle.'

'Or maybe Abbott saw something in the child that

made him feel his son might be a danger to his little sister.'

'But why didn't he just tell her who he was? Castiglia, I mean.'

'And expose himself as a flawed and fallible human being? No, he'd want his full due of recognition, in his own time and on his own terms. In 1988, Harry Costello became Harry Castiglia. He made a decision to step outside the whole idea of his family, and then find his own way back in.'

'Why the exotic choice of name? He wasn't Italian,' Quinn asked.

'Does the name Frank Costello ring a bell? He was a notorious New York gangster, even more feared than Al Capone. But he was born Francesco Castiglia. Harry would have been a little kid at school when Castiglia died in 1973; who knows what sort of glamorous impression all the news coverage might have made on him? Then, later on, new face, new life. Who can blame him? He modelled himself on what he wanted to be.'

'Wee Tony changed his name too.'

'Yes, but he chose a name with benign associations. It's a fact that people who change their name tend to keep some sort of a handshake with the name they had. Bud Abbott was the straight man to –'

'Lou Costello,' Quinn said.

'America's answer to Laurel and Hardy,' Batten confirmed. 'And, though it has nothing to do with anything, by an ironic coincidence Lou Costello's little son drowned in the swimming pool at their home.'

18

'Have a seat, Jack. How are you?' said Kennedy.

'I'm fine,' said O'Hare. 'You?'

'Doing OK, I guess. Whisky?'

'Just a small one.' O'Hare settled into the comfortable leather chesterfield and contemplated a crystal tumbler of the Macallan. He cast a glance out the window in the direction of the gatehouse.

'We'll see her coming, don't worry.'

The two men sat in silence for a few minutes, the low growl of the fire warming them.

'Jack, do you think Marita would still be alive if that idiot detective hadn't told Bobby about Itsy? No, don't answer that.' Kennedy took another sip of whisky, letting it settle on his tongue. He went on thoughtfully, 'I think I might have killed her myself, if I'd been told she'd killed Itsy.' He leaned back and closed his eyes.

O'Hare wondered how much he'd had to drink before he had got there.

'But to do that, to Itsy! To strike her, in the heat of the moment, I could at least have understood. But to walk away and leave her! To my mind, Marita murdered her by doing that just as surely as she did by hitting her with that rock. And don't tell me Itsy would have died anyway

455

because I won't believe you.' He glanced out of the window in turn. 'How do you think she'll be – Costello? It's a huge thing to take on board – her father, her brother.'

'And in such circumstances.' O'Hare thought for a minute. 'Wee Tony put this family photograph up on your wall. Left it there for her to see. And she would have, sooner or later, with the force being featured in the exhibition too. I think he was trying to tell her, *If you want to find me, here's a way to start.*'

'Seems a strange way to communicate with your child.'

'How confident would you be about walking up to your sons and risking being rejected again? I certainly would rather my daughter came to find me, from wherever she is. I don't know that I could take her walking away if I went to find her,' O'Hare mused, gazing into the fire. 'You know, I think Wee Tony was watching, keeping an eye on Costello once he knew Harry was around. The squad remember seeing your white van. Indeed, I saw it myself, not far from my house. No wonder Browne and Costello thought they were being watched. They were.'

'Is she staying with you just now?'

'Just for a few nights. She couldn't go home alone after an injury like that.'

'That's decent of you.'

'I'm not there much. Anyway, it's a big flat,' said O'Hare dismissively. 'I screwed up my relationship with my own daughter, so I might as well look after somebody else's.'

'Will she be all right on her own, down there at the gatehouse?' Iain asked.

'I think she needs to be there on her own. And going

through her dad's stuff will answer a lot of her questions. Harry for one.' O'Hare shook his head. 'He couldn't have been a pretty child. Cleft palate, a bad one. I'm no expert but his cranium, post-mortem, bears witness to some major surgery, some of it after his second teeth were through. So he must have suffered severe facial deformity for most of his childhood.'

'Why do you think Tony took him away to London?'

'I'd imagine the wee sister was not safe around Harry. Pure supposition, but it's as good an explanation as any. Something may have happened, so Abbott realized what his son was growing into. The disfigurement, the arrival of a little sister, separation, painful hospitalization? Mrs Costello was a violent, unhappy woman – a drunk. Did she reject her son, as she later rejected her daughter? Something – all of it, maybe – set Harry on the path which ended up out there on the ice.'

'But why did Tony not make himself known to his daughter? Couldn't he have warned her about her brother?'

'He might have, in time. He may have suspected some of what Harry was up to. But he'd have no evidence. It's hard for a man to turn against his own son; would you turn one of your boys in to the police? But he did save her life. He didn't hesitate. The minute DC Browne mentioned that Costello was up here, he did a runner from the station. His wee Prudenza was in danger.'

'Was that what he called her? Not her real name, surely?'

O'Hare didn't answer.

Iain got up and reached for O'Hare's empty glass.

O'Hare shook his head reluctantly. 'I've to drive Costello home,' he explained.

'Jack, it's only a ten-minute walk.'

The amber liquid filled the glass, catching the echo of the flames from the fire.

Iain poured himself another slug of malt, and sat down again. 'She's very like her father,' he said thoughtfully. 'She has some of his qualities, his kindliness, his sense of rightness.'

'Grey eyes,' smiled O'Hare.

'I wasn't at all impressed by her when I first met her,' Iain admitted. 'How wrong I was.'

The gatehouse was warm and cosy. Iain Kennedy had put the heating on for her, O'Hare had said, and she was to take as long as she liked.

Costello stood in the front room and turned slowly in a full circle. It was almost like being in a doll's house. Scarcely anything was out of place. That tidiness certainly hadn't been passed on to her, but then she didn't have to share such a small space with another person. In the middle stood a small round table covered with a red cloth. The takeaway menu for Hazbeanz was neatly laid on top of a newspaper folded to show the television listings. A pair of felt slippers was pushed tidily under one armchair, and there was a pile of books on a wooden bench beside the other. It felt homely, companionable. A good place.

On the wall opposite the fireplace, Tony had put up a big piece of cork board. Pinned to it were dozens of drawings of birds. Costello went over to look at them more closely. Even without the immaculately neat captions, in the sort of writing no longer taught in schools, every one was immediately recognizable and vibrantly alive. There was a mallard, a robin, a pheasant, several sorts of gull, and other birds Costello had never heard of. And in the corners, again and again, in laborious capitals at odds with the fluency of the drawing, the name ITSY. Browne had been right – talented indeed.

Behind the front room Costello found a galley kitchen, a compact little bathroom, and two tiny little bedrooms, scarcely more than cubicles. One was clearly Bobby's – the floor was barely visible under flung-down clothes. She went into the other, and stood for a moment, trying to gain a sense of the man whose room it had been. Wee Tony. Her dad.

She hesitated before opening the drawers of the small chest of drawers. It was battered and old, but had been lovingly polished. Inside, everything was neatly folded – sweaters, shirts, socks, all carefully aligned. On top of the chest lay an old photograph album. She picked it up and sat down with it on the bed. The plastic cover cracked open. Inside, the brown-edged pages were pale lilac.

Every photo in it was of her. Her as a baby sitting in her pram, her playing in a paddling pool with nothing on, her in a frilly dress scowling into the sun. Each photograph was annotated in the same fine italic hand that had captioned Itsy's bird drawings. Her being held by her mum, smiling and pretty as Costello had never known her. And her with her head nestled into her dad's shoulder, baby arms clasping his neck and his lips pressed to her hair. Costello sat for a minute feeling as though a great tidal wave was poised over her head, waiting to crash down on her.

Then there was a gap where a photograph was missing. The caption read *A happy day at Strathearn.* This was where the Polaroid had been hiding all these years.

She turned over the pages, to read her whole life in pictures. A picture of her on the way to school, just walking past the camera, unaware. Her eyes narrowed; she remembered that school, that uniform, but she didn't remember her dad. Here she was in the three-legged race at the school sports day with some girl she couldn't stand. Under it was written *Prudenza, in the three-legged race, disqualified for punching her partner. It was a good punch. Boxing next year!* A cutting from the local paper of her doing a sponsored walk for Help the Aged. Her graduation from police college, all sparkling uniform and keen smile, ready to change the world. Cuttings about cases she had been involved in, and dozens of photographs of herself in the streets, hurrying across Byres Road at the lights, coming out of the supermarket, running up the station steps. And each one labelled *Prudenza,* and the date.

Weary, Costello closed the book and let herself slump sideways on the bed, her head on the pillow. She breathed in, trying to remember what the man who had held her in his arms had smelled like. The pillow held a human smell, of hair and breath and cigarette smoke.

She lay there for a long time, staring at the ceiling.

Costello carefully locked the gatehouse door and put the key in her pocket. At last the wind had blown the fog away and the night was sparklingly frosty and clear. For a moment she breathed in the sharp air, and carefully tilted her head back to look up at a sky full of stars. She didn't feel ready yet to join O'Hare and Iain Kennedy up at the Big House, so she fished in her bag for her torch and headed off in the direction of the pond. Memories of that night were flooding back now, and she would have to face up to it all sooner or later. Why not now?

At the top of the pond she sat down on the bench among the conifers, where John Littlewood had sat down for his smoke. She could remember how beautiful the ice had been then, sparkling through the fog.

Costello shivered, and steeled herself to walk along the path as she had that night. She reached the willow tree, and shone her torch again on to the globules of ice that hung like jewels from the whip-thin twigs. Just about here was where she'd been thrown down, had her head rammed hard into the ground, and where she'd heard the sinister *click*.

Just like Emily.

She had been lucky. She knew that.

The frosty lawn was still criss-crossed with the footprints of the paramedics, the crime scene police, the divers, photographers and everyone else who had swarmed all over the garden. Among them must be the footprints Wee Tony, her dad, had left as he hurried down the lawn and out on to the ice to save her. But she would never know which were his.

She shut her eyes for a moment. 'Thanks, Dad,' she whispered.

*

Rebecca Quinn walked into the empty investigation room, the click-click of her stiletto heels echoing against the bare walls. It was the dead of night, nobody around. A squad from Partick Central had been over the place like a plague of locusts, removing the evidence and all the paperwork for storage. Flat boxes ready for assembly, storage crates, vast piles of padded envelopes, lists and computer printouts cluttered the floor. There was paper everywhere.

The evidential chain was gradually joining together. They were ripping apart Harry's car after they'd found all kinds of DNA in the hollow of the wheel brace retrieved from the pond. They had found a phone at his flat with a number ending 666, which confirmed that he had been in touch with Donna McVeigh and Stephen Whyte's mother. The click of Quinn's heels echoed the faint tick of the clock. That was the sound of her career passing.

Strangely, she didn't feel alone in the deserted room. In her imagination she could hear them – talking on the phone, patting the dog, typing, gossiping, bickering. Her squad. Her team.

But no more. DCI Rebecca Quinn of Partickhill CID had been politely but officially told to bugger off. The big boys were going to play now. She was to work out her contract and, with annual leave, her last working day could be this Friday if she wanted.

At least, she'd been told that was what she wanted.

She looked up at the wall, like a general inspecting her troops. All those women could be taken down now, their cases laid to rest. A few more young men might have their deaths linked to Harry Castiglia, but that would be no more than a bonus now, a tying-up of loose ends.

Mulholland, still feeling fragile after twice being punched hard in the gut, and still living with the prospect of a disciplinary, had tried to redeem himself by repeating to Quinn his conversations with Bobby and with Marita.

Anderson and Browne's account of finding Bobby cradling the dead Marita in his arms raised similar questions. What had their relationship been? Quinn had duly repeated everything to Iain, and had asked what he could add.

'I always had my suspicions about Marita and Bobby. What you found on her scarf only confirmed them. Marita could easily have manipulated Bobby into sex. She only ever took lovers she could dominate, and poor Bobby was fairly easily controlled. Until . . .'

'Until he snapped.'

But when told that Bobby had said he and Itsy were 'lovers', Iain had been genuinely incredulous, and wanted to know exactly what questions had been asked. 'Bobby's a simple soul. Lover, to him, would mean someone who loves you, not a sexual partner. So asking, "Is Itsy your lover?" would be like asking, "Does Itsy love you?" Of course he'd say yes. Because she did. And he loved her. It was entirely innocent. Tony would have known if it wasn't.'

For a long time, Kennedy had not wanted to believe that his wife had murdered her own sister, the woman he loved. But a search of the white van had unearthed a pair of olive-green vicuna wool gloves, probably kicked under the driver's seat, which matched the fibres found on the bloodstained stone. They were Marita's and they were stiff with Itsy's blood. So Marita was now, beyond argument, linked to the attack on her sister. Quinn had surmised that Marita had left the house after talking to Mulholland, guessing they were going to re-examine the van. She had gone to Bobby and asked for his help in retrieving them. That decision had proved fatal.

Quinn had then explained carefully that the SOCO team had gone back to the Moss and found one sawn-off sapling stump, among the many, that had blood on it. After careful analysis of the crime scene photographs, a report had landed on her desk which suggested that Itsy had fallen hard on to the stump, damaging her face, dislodging her teeth, and injuring the palate of her mouth. But what the photographs couldn't tell them was what had then possessed Marita to hit Itsy. Hearing that her pitiable little sister was going to have a baby was only one of many possibilities, all of them painful.

'But in the end,' Quinn said gently, 'whatever made her lash out, Marita took off that beautiful scarf, folded it carefully, lifted Itsy's head, and placed it there as a pillow.'

She decided it would be neither kind nor constructive to point out that Marita must surely have known the scarf had Bobby's semen on it. Let Iain take some small comfort from believing his wife hadn't been a complete monster.

Epilogue

Costello made her way down to the lake on her own, and stopped at the little garden hidden among the shrubs. The snowdrops were out now, and soon little jonquils and daffodils would be nodding merrily in the spring sun. Mick and Colin were hovering tactfully fifty yards away, keeping their distance.

Near the bleak remains of the old boathouse, Bobby McGurk was standing handcuffed to a prison officer. Somebody had bought him a suit, tidied his hair, tried to smarten him up a bit for the funeral earlier that day. Tears streamed down his face as he set light to a little wooden boat, his boat, and pushed it out across the lake. The sails caught fire and flamed fiercely, and for a few minutes the blaze was reflected in the water, and a plume of white smoke swirled and danced around it. For a minute everybody watched in silence as the little boat went gallantly on, until it keeled over and sank. It was as if Bobby had given Itsy a Viking funeral, though her body lay in the cemetery in a coffin with a small brass plate that said simply 'Itsy'.

The black-suited prison officer standing behind Bobby patted him on the shoulder, telling him that it was time to go. Back to remand. Back to custody. Back to whatever fate had in store for him. Bobby wiped his nose with the back of his hand and took one last look at the pond, the willows, the koi, the smoke that rose and curled into the sky, and said a quiet goodbye to all of it, a quiet goodbye to his Itsy Bitsy.

As they left, Iain broke away from the knot of guests on the lawn and came over to clasp Bobby's shoulder and bid him farewell.

'That was nice,' Browne said to Anderson. 'That wee boat going on fire. She would have liked that.'

Anderson nodded absently. His mind was running along another track. 'You really should think again, you know, Gillian, about leaving the force.'

'I have to. That night, it made me realize, I can't do it – be a police officer, I mean. I just can't. I've Frank and Rhona to think of,' she said.

Anderson was casting an eye around the garden, wondering where his own children had got to. Suddenly Peter materialized at his elbow.

'Gillian, this is my son, Peter,' he said. 'Peter, this is DC Gillian Browne.'

'Are you the lady that smashed the ice with yer ar . . . bottom?' Peter demanded.

Browne managed to keep a straight face. 'Yes, I am.'

'Cool!'

'Actually, it was freezing!'

'And it was Gillian who sent me home with Nesbitt,' Anderson reminded his son.

Peter's open-mouthed adoration of Browne was total. But short-lived.

'Oh, look, there's Aunty Helena!' he shrieked and went pelting off to talk to her.

Helena was alone, Anderson was guiltily relieved to see – not with the man Gilfillan, the one Alan McAlpine used to refer to as 'the ponytailed prick'.

Iain Kennedy came over to join them. 'Thank you all for coming,' he said. 'You can't imagine how much better this is than the media razzmatazz there was for Marita.'

'It was good of you to have Bobby here today,' Anderson said. 'The authorities will go easy on him.'

'I hope so,' Iain said. 'I pulled what strings I could, got him a good defence counsel. It's hard for anyone to lose everybody they love, as he has.'

Well, you'd know, Anderson thought.

As Brenda sidled off to find Claire, Kennedy turned to Anderson and said, 'Oh, there's Sarah, talking to Jack O'Hare. Come and meet her.'

Anderson was introduced to Iain Kennedy's former wife, the one he had left Marita for, and liked her on sight. For a moment he wondered whether he was looking at the future chatelaine of Strathearn, then he realized he wasn't. This was a woman who had resolutely put the past behind her, and was here to support her ex-husband simply as a friend.

A few yards away, Anderson saw Costello being greeted by a pleasant-faced, smiling woman. For a moment he quite failed to recognize Jenny Corbett. She was holding hands with Lambie, who had lost the haunted look Anderson had come to know so well, and was shyly

467

holding out her left hand to show off her engagement ring.

Costello was being less than effusive.

'To some extent, I blame myself still, you know,' O'Hare said. 'If only I'd told you what I suspected.'

Quinn laid a comforting hand on his arm. 'You shouldn't blame yourself, Jack. If you'd come to me with a story about recognizing some old git because he had grey eyes and so does DS Costello, I'd have suggested a nice lie-down in a darkened room. I doubt I'd have believed you. Even you.'

'Thanks, Rebecca. But it will always haunt me.'

'Well, I suppose Mick Batten's going to get a bloody great book out of it, at least. He misses a narcissist right under his nose and gets a book deal. And what do I get? My pension!' Quinn knocked back the wine in her glass, and looked around for more. 'And Anderson's been told that a refurb for Partickhill Station will start in the summer.'

'So the old place will live again.'

Suddenly there was a shriek of shock, then a ripple of laughter as Nesbitt the Staffie burst from nowhere, galloping round the garden with the speed of a bullet, his tongue flying out the corner of his mouth. He darted up to his beloved Browne and jumped up at her, putting dirty paws all over her blue coat.

Guilty laughter bubbled round the crowd as Peter came running from the rhododendron bushes. Even Mulholland was smiling. And he kept smiling as Nesbitt jumped up at him, leaving muddy paw prints down the front of his cashmere coat.

'Sorry, Dad, I just wanted to show him to Aunty Helena. Nesbitt! Nesbitt, come here, you bad wee bugger!'

'I wonder where he learned language like that,' said Sarah Kennedy, failing to keep a straight face.

Nesbitt stopped, panted, looked at Peter, and charged towards him, veering round him at the last minute; dog and boy disappeared back into the shrubbery.

'Wee Nesbitt seems to have worked wonders,' Browne said cheerfully.

'Thanks to you, Gillian. As you can see, Peter never shuts up now.'

Alone amid a crowd of people, Quinn looked idly up at the sky. A single seagull was flying high overhead. She frowned. Not a seagull. Not that size.

Somehow Ally must have got himself up to a high enough part of the Moss in time to catch a strong gust of wind to get him off the ground. Then that massive wing-span would have lifted him, higher and higher, until he met a wind current that would carry him . . . somewhere else.

Somewhere safe, with plenty of fish.

She smiled. Everyone else was too busy chatting, pouring glasses of wine and accepting nibbles off silver trays, to notice him. She raised her glass to him in a silent toast.

'Safe home,' she whispered.

Acknowledgements

As usual, thanks to all at Penguin for their patience, especially Stefanie. And to all the girls at Gregory and Co., especially Stephanie. Big thanks to everybody at work for allowing me all the time off and to Annette in particular who, for some reason, still has faith that I will understand a spreadsheet one day. Thanks to 'fireman Simon' for his expertise on Google maps and all things mechanical, and for letting me borrow Liz, his wife, to be my long-suffering PA on 24-hour call.

And to all those who volunteered words of expertise: Eric Scott, Lynne Murney, Anthony Barton and Alex Gray. And a nod to Christine and Helen of Strathclyde Police Service. Huge gratitude to Robert J. P. Kerr for legal expertise and to Dr John Clark for letting me listen on a Thursday night.

Special thanks to David Lambie for being such a good sport, and for giving me free rein to use his name and raise money for charity.

And as usual to Mum and Dad, Emily and Pi.

Caro

He just wanted a decent book to read ...

Not too much to ask, is it? It was in 1935 when Allen Lane, Managing Director of Bodley Head Publishers, stood on a platform at Exeter railway station looking for something good to read on his journey back to London. His choice was limited to popular magazines and poor-quality paperbacks – the same choice faced every day by the vast majority of readers, few of whom could afford hardbacks. Lane's disappointment and subsequent anger at the range of books generally available led him to found a company – and change the world.

'We believed in the existence in this country of a vast reading public for intelligent books at a low price, and staked everything on it'
Sir Allen Lane, 1902–1970, founder of Penguin Books

The quality paperback had arrived – and not just in bookshops. Lane was adamant that his Penguins should appear in chain stores and tobacconists, and should cost no more than a packet of cigarettes.

Reading habits (and cigarette prices) have changed since 1935, but Penguin still believes in publishing the best books for everybody to enjoy. We still believe that good design costs no more than bad design, and we still believe that quality books published passionately and responsibly make the world a better place.

So wherever you see the little bird – whether it's on a piece of prize-winning literary fiction or a celebrity autobiography, political tour de force or historical masterpiece, a serial-killer thriller, reference book, world classic or a piece of pure escapism – you can bet that it represents the very best that the genre has to offer.

Whatever you like to read – trust Penguin.